The Loon Feather

IOLA FULLER

The Loon Feather

&

A HARVEST BOOK
HARCOURT BRACE & COMPANY
San Diego   New York   London

Requests for permission to make copies
of any part of the work should be mailed to:
Permissions Department,
Harcourt Brace & Company, 6277 Sea Harbor Drive,
Orlando, Florida 32887-6777.

Library of Congress Cataloging-in-Publication Data
Fuller, Iola.
The loon feather.
Reprint. Originally published: New York:
Harcourt, Brace & World, 1940.
1. Chippewa Indians – Fiction. 2. Indians of North
America – Michigan – Mackinac Island (Island) – Fiction.
3. Mackinac Island (Mich.: Island) – History – Fiction.
4. Michigan – History – To 1837 – Fiction. I. Title.
PS3511.U6592L6   1984   813'.52   84-19749
ISBN 0-15-653200-X (Harvest: pbk.)

Printed in the United States of America
I J K L

*To Roy W. Cowden
with gratitude for all
that he has taught me*

Part One

It was fur that made our lives what they were. Fur, and the people who lived by it. The earliest memories of my life are of soft deerskin clothing and warm fur robes that kept me as comfortable in winter as the bear in his cave. In these days a fine fur coat costs a great deal of money, but in that time it was the most natural garment to have.

One never forgets the luster of heaps and bales of furs. The golden fleece of the north, Pierre used to call it, for he had sometimes a bookish way of talking, and there was truth in that word golden. He had seen it, that sheen, like all of the French from the early day of the Sieur de la Salle, and his companion Tonty of the iron arm, down to the time of my story when large fur companies had thousands of voyageurs combing the forests. Others had followed the French, and were still coming in such numbers that instead of the narrow trails of single hunters, marked by a moccasin print or

3

a broken twig, it was almost as if a huge army had crashed through the woods.

Furs were the means of getting whatever the Indian and the white trapper wanted, for in those days they were the legal tender and there was little that prime beaver would not buy. Hunters and traders wintered in lonely outposts, and then came by hundreds in their bateaux and canoes to Mackinac in spring, to bring in their winter's catch and celebrate with enough zeal and abandon to drive away memories of the lonely months behind them. Dancing, drinking, fighting, gambling, spending in one month the earnings of the other eleven, they never rested. Nor did anyone else on the island while the traders' tents were there, and the beach was full of Indian lodges.

To this day the sight of a black feather brings it all back to me. A crow's feather in his hat was the badge of the leader of a brigade, and it was coveted by every man who hadn't it. It wasn't easily come by, but was rather like the laurel wreath of the olden days, as Pierre said. To win it a man must be a better man than the rest —he must be able to fight better, walk longer distances, and carry more than the usual hundred pounds over the portages, if need be.

The island of Mackinac, the turtle, rises high and rounding from the water. As I remember it, tall white stone cliffs rose abruptly in some places, and in others trees and bushes climbed a gentle slope. The high center was densely wooded, and ever quiet when the village in the half-moon harbor was wild and noisy. Groves of spruce, pine, and cedar, and the fragrant fir and balsam opened their green depths to make room for little, close-huddling maples, and birch and straight-limbed beeches. So close they were that even where a footpath passed among them, the trees closed overhead so it was like walking always in a bower, and a squirrel could go for miles without touching foot to ground. Everywhere the

4

fragrance of balsam lay like a cloud on the air, mixed at the proper seasons with the aroma of wild strawberries, the thorny roses, and the pink flowers called arbutus. In the darkest nooks was the damp delight of ferns and moss, and in the sunlight of a clearing I used to catch my breath at the great beds of daisies, the largest there ever were, spreading their solid masses of flat white and yellow blossoms.

And there was always the water, for Mackinac is where the lakes meet, in the straits flowing between Lakes Michigan, Huron, and Superior. Pierre read from a book once about "seas of sweet water," and that was what we had on every side and in every direction, pure, beautifully colored, yet transparent almost as the air itself. I spent many hours on the water, and gazing out over it, watching whitecaps fleeing from the east wind.

Striking deeper than thought, this memory sends me back to stand again on the western heights of the island, far above the lake, where my destiny spoke to me that night so long ago. The sun is going down, making the water red in its path. A quick twilight has come and is passing into darkness. Coasts of the mainland and of Point St. Ignace grow dim, letting Mackinac withdraw into itself. Like a star set in space it rides on the dark water. Untouched by the movements of the outside world, it is complete in itself, having a sufficiency of its own. Around me are huge boulders, dropped ages ago by the glaciers, inspiring the early red men first to marvel and then to worship. The wash of the waves on the pebbles is something that has always been and will always be. From the trees behind me comes a hymn to those ears that can hear it, as if the winds were playing a requiem for someone departed. Rather than fear, there comes a tremendous sense of personal security. It is right. It is the only way.

One

Somewhere south of the lakes, in the region we on Mackinac called "down below," I was born in the restless year of 1806. An uneasy year it was for us, for besides troubles with our enemies the Sioux to the west, there had been fighting where white settlers were taking our lands. Near the forts and trading posts the number of white men was growing, as they kept coming from some other part of the world. The first who came, the French traders and hunters, were our friends, but on their heels had come the redcoats, and then the Long Knives trying to drive them out.

Still, the efforts of one man or another to be the ruler had not upset for us the rule of Nature. It was before the real rush of settlers, before cities with their factories and railroads that make such noise and clatter. The compass and chain of the surveyor had scarcely entered these forests yet, and the streams had not been harnessed even so much as to turn the wheel of a mill. Back in the forests it was as wild and mysterious as it had been since the beginning of time. Plants and animals made our plans for us, even if they didn't know it. The seasons directed our wanderings by changing the location and condition of fur, and setting the time for the bees to make wild honey, and when the sap could be taken from the trees.

Pierre told me later that my mother had said I was born in maple sugar time, and that my first cradle was one of the sap troughs. But it was from Marthe that I learned most about my birth. Marthe was not her real name, but the one given her later on by French neighbors who could not pronounce the Ojibway word. She told me of my birth so often that my mind has made it one with my own memories, so that no matter how old I may come to be, and how faded some things may become, I shall never forget the happenings of that night. It seems as if, lying there beside my mother, I must have been concerned about her, as I was so often later on, and that I must have been watchful that no part of the ceremonies be left undone, as if I knew even then that a misstep in a dance, a mistake in a ceremony, would be sure to bring bad luck to the one who made the error. Birth ceremonies were impressive above most others, because one did not know whether the child would live to grow up. So few did. Any part of a ceremony omitted might give some evil spirit his chance to take the child. Traders and missionaries had tried to tell my people it was due to the rough life or climate, but it didn't make sense to their ears. They knew what they knew.

About thirty relatives had encamped with the chief of the loon-bird family of the Ojibways that night, on a river bank in a high cleared spot beside a barren thicket which lost itself in a swamp and rushes beyond. The woods behind were close and dark, except for the glow from fires burning under kettles of syrup at a distance from the half-circle of seven lodges, turned companionably toward one another and toward the stream. It was

8

the end of winter, the month when snowshoes may be broken, when the ice has just gone out of the lakes, and the bears have come forth from the hollows, thin from the winter. There was a chill in the air, and within our lodge a fire of cedar wood burned gaily in the center. Its light fell on the poles and bark seams of the roof and the dark faces of Marthe and Ajawin, both of them older women relatives of my mother—probably cousins, but we kept no such exact records of relationships even in our minds. Thin blue smoke curled up and out of the opening of the roof. On a bed of hemlock branches, laid over the carpet of twigs stretching from the fire to the encircling wall, my mother lay with her feet to the fire. At her head an extra blanket was hung against the wall to shield her from the wind. It was quiet within the lodge, for birth is easy for Indian women, and their training keeps them from crying out.

All day there had been no sounds but those of the forest until, just at night-fall, a French trader announced his coming by the notes of his boat song as his paddle dipped beneath the trees overhanging the stream, and his birch canoe had been seen, light as a mist-shape among the gray-green willows. Grandfather had gone down to the shore to make him welcome. "He is an honest trader," he told the rest. "He fills a measure of shot full, not with his thumb within the brim."

While Marthe squatted beside my mother, waiting, she heard their two voices above the general murmur of the camp.

"How many?"

"Three beavers."

"It is not a good blanket."

"*Sacré diable*, I know it ain't. You could stand ten feet off and throw peas through it. Now here's a better one, the kind a chief should buy."

There was a little silence, then my grandfather's voice came again, regretfully. "I cannot buy blankets at all.

9

We need food. The winter has been hard, with much deep snow. We could do little hunting, with all our braves away."

"Game gettin' scarce here?" asked the trader.

"No. The animals, like the rocks and water, will be in the land when the red men are no more. But aged ones cannot take them."

Another pause, and Marthe knew from the trader's next words that he was looking around the camp.

"I see. Only old men here? Where are the young ones?"

"Fighting near the beautiful-river, where we were driven out of our winter camp."

"*Oui.* Along the Ohio. It was a shame the way the settlers sicked the militia on you like that. My partner told me about it."

My grandfather did not seem willing to say more. When he spoke again, Marthe knew his words were more for the silent listeners around the fire than for the trader, for they were full of cheer. "The deep snow has gone now. We have traded the few skins we had for enough wild rice to last until we can trade our sugar for more food."

"That buffalo robe I saw one of your women carrying into your lodge—I could give you three of these blankets for it," insisted the trader.

"Buffalo robe is not to be traded. We have to keep that." Grandfather seemed then to be listening in the direction of the lodge-flap, and the next remark of the trader was not answered.

"I knew I couldn't get rid of these French blankets —told 'em so back at headquarters. You won't have 'em because they've got red stripes instead of white ones—"

His voice broke off as there came sounds of wild confusion from the edge of the woods and a scream from an old woman tending the boiling kettles.

Within our lodge, my birth kept Marthe from going

10

out to see what had happened. The noise outside died away into murmurs, as she put me into a sack of soft deerskin, heavily embroidered with beads and quills, and laced it up the front. She did not strap it to the cradleboard at once, but wrapped me in the great buffalo robe that lay ready to her hand. The naming ceremony must come first.

She pushed aside the smoke-colored blanket that served as a door. "It is a girl," she said.

No one paid any attention to her, though everyone in the camp had rushed to the great open space just in front of our lodge. Smooth and hard it was, the grass all worn off even in our short stay, for many had been the councils held there, and dancing to induce the friendly spirits to help in our trouble. Hunger had marked the circle of faces, some of them blackened in mourning. Food and clothing for thirty people cannot be supplied by the few squirrels old men can bring in. Shreds of blankets covered some figures, and parts of leggings. Calico worn and ragged from a long trip through the woods hung from the bent frames of the women.

When Marthe stepped out, they were looking down at an old woman on the ground, twisting and turning in silent pain. The circle stood helpless and waiting, trembling in restrained eagerness to do something for her. But any more help would only be in the way. Two other women were kneeling beside her, applying poultices of wet clay. And above the suffering woman, bending so that his wide-fringed sleeve swept her body, the white-haired medicine man began to sway, waving his rattles and chanting.

The woman's skin hung loose, great patches of it, and was bedaubed with syrup. Marthe raised her eyes to pierce the darkness about the row of fires, where one kettle dangled sidewise from a broken pole. A pool of syrup below it shone in the firelight.

The rattling and singing of the medicine man went

on. Fatally burned the poor creature was, and beyond his help, for even as Marthe looked back at her again she became limp. The women buried their heads in their blankets and wept.

As her spirit left her, the medicine man began the death chant. The tones echoed through the woods, rising and dying away again, until my grandfather raised his arm to point to the star-hung sky above the river. A quick intake of breaths broke off the chant, as all the others saw that one star had loosened in its place and fallen, and then another. The whole heavens brightened from the streaks of light that marked their fall.

Wondering, the circle looked, and silence fell upon the whole ragged, hungry band. They put their open hands before their mouths in amazement, awe mixed with searching thought. Even the children knew this was a sign. Was it in honor of the dead woman? Not likely, for she had been no one of importance. No one had heard her speak since the death of her husband, when, fleeing from the soldiers of the white settlers, we had run into a band of the Sioux. Fully eight new scalps had adorned the lodge-poles of our ancient enemies after that. This woman was only one of those left with no hunter in her lodge.

So the men puzzled, the women wondered, what meaning these falling stars carried. "Because of her death?" The question went around, denied in the very tones that uttered it.

But Marthe, standing with me in her arms before the door of the chief's lodge, knew. "It is for the birth of his child," she said to herself. "Perhaps even to let him know, where he lies wrapped in his war-blanket, that the child has come."

When the last brief gleam had gone, my grandfather stepped out of the circle and came to Marthe. He was an old man even then, with a fine head and large features.

His gray hair was drawn back and held with a single eagle feather. Chief not because of inheritance, but because he knew more than anyone else in his tribe, wiser on the warpath and in the hunt, knowing best about treaties and trading, he seemed taller than he was, for he held himself with the pride of an oak. No one but Marthe would have dared speak before he did.

"It is a girl," she said again.

The other women began to wrap the dead woman in her shabby blanket, making a sad gray mound of her.

"There should be a group of young men of another totem to try to take the child away, and a group of her father's to defend her. But we have no young men at all." Grandfather's face was streaked with vermilion, which gave him a fiery look when animated in talk, though his expression was usually mild.

Marthe waited. It was a serious matter not to do as should be done with a new-born child.

"We shall carry her around a fire, and name her." Grandfather turned back to the others with a sweep of the blanket thrown across his arm. "Instead of the usual struggle, we will all make great noise."

The women took the dead one by the head and feet, and carried her back to her lodge. They put out the fire in it, their hands reminding one another it must not be lighted until the lodge was moved, to show they knew the life in the body and the fire in the lodge were of the same origin and alike in nature.

Half a dozen children brought dry tamarack sticks and kindling to heap on the hardened ground where she had lain. A lighted bundle of twigs was carried from our lodge, and the heap blazed up, pushing back the borders of the darkness.

Marthe laid me, buffalo robe and all, in my grandfather's arms. Slowly he carried me about the circle. The children stared curiously, the women inspected me with real and childlike enthusiasm. The men each spoke

13

a word or two, and Marthe—for it was she who noted all these things down in her birchbark scrolls and told them to me later—remembered words that were different from the usual ones of welcome or good luck.

Grandfather himself said nothing, but put a necklace of beaver teeth around my neck that I might be industrious.

"Even braves will listen when her voice is heard," said an old man with a jagged scar across his face, the mark of a grizzly he had killed with his own hands.

"She will bring a warrior to the tribe." This was always said of a girl, for in our totem a woman stayed with her tribe and brought a man to it.

The old medicine man had been sulking because my arrival cut short his death chant in which he took much pride. Waiting until last for his inspection, he said nothing for a long moment while he wrapped about him his robe of skins and breasts of birds. Almost reluctantly he spoke, as if without his will something made him tell what he saw as he looked at me.

"She will bring to her tribe a husband greater than a warrior." No one understood his remark. It seemed to make no sense.

Wondering, the others forbore to look at him. But their eyes sought the shadows of the forests where spirits of trees and rocks were lurking. It seemed to Marthe almost as if in their welcome and joy over the birth, they questioned what manito had dared send a girl-child as the first-born of Tecumseh.

My grandfather walked solemnly four times around the fire, followed by the old men, then the men children, then by the women and the girl children in a moving, wailing circle, making as much noise as they could, so that the child would be brave, being used to fearful sounds from the beginning. Yet I have learned that it

14

is not the things that make most noise that hurt you, but those that come as silent as hunger.

Since my father was not there to speak, my grandfather stopped and raised his hand for an end of the wailing.

"She must have a star name," he said. "Shooting Star is one of her father's names, and even the heavens have spoken."

While the others were mumbling the syllables that would give me a star name—*Giwedanang*, star of the north, *Wabanang*, morning star—Marthe's eyes fell on the French trader where he had been sitting and watching. His face was thin and red from the sun and wind. He was small, but with something about him like the tight spring of a trap, full of energy not to be released until the proper time. He sat cross-legged on a low stump beside a blanket with trading goods spread upon it for inspection—a dozen scalping knives, several pieces of striped cotton like that the French used for shirts, a heap of small white beads, and a pile of brass-rimmed looking-glasses.

Suddenly, as Marthe watched him, he spoke. "I had a squaw once," he said, speaking broken Ojibway in a quiet voice like water riffling over lily pads. "She had some fancy name like that, but I called her Oneta— she was always saying something that sounded like that. It's a right pretty name, I think."

Silent mirth spread over the faces of those who heard him. The name he spoke could only be a shortening of our word for "yes"—Oneonta. She must have been an obliging squaw, their faces said.

Though the trader should not have intruded, my grandfather was tolerant. "She may have Oneta for one of her names," he said, for when a name is suggested, it must be used. "She may take that for her common name, until she is old enough to take a dream name for herself."

15

When my grandfather laid me back in Marthe's arms, Marthe spoke again, her words ringing among the trees as a reminder to all with ears to hear. "This little girl is different from others. It is not often that one has such a father." She sighed as she turned again to pass through the blanket flap into the lodge, and her shoulders drooped, as if they were bent less from burdens or age than from some long-ago disappointment, keen and tearing at first, but softened by time until it could be endured.

"Here, take this stump." The trader got up. My grandfather with a wave of his hand urged him to be seated again.

"The Indian likes to be close to the earth," he said. "It is like reposing on the bosom of his mother." He filled his pipe with savory red willow bark from a marten-skin pouch. One of the little boys came running to take it to the fire and lay a hot coal on top of the bowl. A small object fell from the folds of the pouch and rolled to the ground. My grandfather stooped, but the trader was quicker. He started to hand it back, but his attention was caught by a gleam from its surface. "Where do you find this dark red stuff?"

"It is only a lump of metal I carry for good luck," said my grandfather, replacing it in his pocket.

"It'd be good luck all right, if you had enough of it. Where did you say you got it?" My grandfather did not miss the tenseness under the casual tone of the trader.

"See here, I'd like a little good luck, too. I'll give you —let's see—" The Frenchman began gathering up items from the ground beside him. "Here—two yards of scarlet cloth, ten pairs of silver earrings, two white blankets, and five pounds of tobacco—I'll give you these if you'll tell me where you got it."

My grandfather smiled a little. He felt unspoken mirth in the circle behind him. It was very bad luck to give away the location of any place where one got metal from the earth. Certain death would come upon the one who told, and what good then are blankets or scarlet cloth?

The trader felt something in the atmosphere. He looked around at all the faces he could see, where huddled figures now toasted themselves before the fire, or strode about mingling their long shadows with the unmoving ones of rocks and trees. He slowly dropped the goods to the ground again, shrugging his shoulders as if dismissing the idea.

Marthe had taken me back and laid me beside my mother's couch in a clean birchbark trough filled with rotted cedar and fine moss. Exhausted, Mother lay with her face hidden against the blanket on the wall.

Stepping outside again, Marthe moved about the edge of the grove to gather firewood, tossing aside hemlock and pine that would crackle and sputter. Like all the women, her toes turned in slightly as she walked, as one used to being bent and heavily laden. Carrying an armful back to the fire now dying out on the hard ground, she squatted beside it, fanning the embers to keep it smoldering until my grandfather had finished his talk.

From the heap of trading goods the Frenchman picked up a comb and began absently to snap a calloused thumb over the points of its teeth. Grandfather sent a glance around the circle as permission for the others to come forward and deal with the trader if they would. Scarface pulled his ragged blanket about him, and drew near the stump. He fell on his knees and looked eagerly at blankets, knives, and baubles. He reached out a thin hand and seized a string of glass beads, whose brilliance was made almost dazzling by the firelight. From under his rags he brought out a silky beaver skin and held it up to the trader. The Frenchman nodded. Scarface laid the beaver down at the trader's feet, and took up che necklace. Still he hesitated, and his hand went to his mouth. Marthe knew he was thinking that if he had four beavers he could get a gallon of the drink that sat so deliciously on the tongue and stomach and gave one such queer feelings and filled the mind with images. Perhaps he could get a little of it, as well as the glass beads, for this one beaver. But when Scarface asked, the trader shook his head, opening his hands outward as a sign that he did not have what was wanted. Scarface, satisfied, withdrew to the outer circle, grinning and clutching the necklace, holding it up as if he would drink in its drops of light. He had made a good bargain, he thought, and laughed to himself that a white man would give a string of beads that must have taken much work to shape for a beaver skin that ran around almost anywhere for the taking.

"Never carry rum," the trader apologized.

Grandfather nodded approval, and, encouraged, the other went on. "*Il n'y a que* plenty of trouble whenever rum and an Indian get together. I never even carry it for myself. Don't know of any comforts in the wilderness but what a man carries inside him. You don't have to take something for courage. You don't have to cover up what you are out here—if you're afraid you can show it. There's nobody around to make fun of you. A man has got to learn to live with hisself out here."

"You are alone?" asked my grandfather. "Last year at wild-rice time you were with another man, one with brown and white hair on his face."

"*Oui*. Old Slim, my partner. Not around any more. I found his body one day in the woods, no hair on top of his head. Don't know who done it." The trader looked a little fearfully at the row of scalps dangling from the nearest lodge as if he dreaded to recognize one. He got up uneasily and began to walk back and forth, limping slightly.

"You have hurt your foot?" Grandfather asked.

"Yes, I've had some bad luck. Froze one of my feet this winter. I won't be in the tradin' business much longer."

A wave of the hand showed my grandfather's sympathy.

The trader looked sadly at a flame making itself a place to grow between two logs. He raised his eyes to where Marthe now sat beside our lodge, scraping a piece of deerskin to make it ready for shaping into moccasins. The trader's eyes fell on her only ornament, a sharpened piece of brown metal holding the rags of her shortdress together in the front.

"A man has to be a whole man to keep his scalp on his head out in the woods," he said. "After this trip I'm goin' to settle down on Mackinac and find something to do there, something easier. I'm lookin' for me a squaw, now."

There was a stir among the women clustered in the half darkness behind him. He turned around and looked at them, examining and rejecting. "I'm not struck with any of you." He whirled about with a deft movement of his lame foot. "There's only one I'd take home with me. There she sits."

And he pointed to Marthe, crouched above the deerskin. There was a faint gasp from the others. No one knew what Marthe would do. She was an unusual woman, and even the men respected her. Her love charms had never failed, and she was known to be able to cure the bite of a massasauga. She was a member of the highest order of the Ojibways, the medicine group of the Midé, in which she had reached the second highest of the four orders. Few of the secrets of herbs and long life were unknown to her. And it was no longer considered an honor for a woman to go to a white man's lodge. Too many had been turned out after a short time, to drift back and be a burden on their own people. Those who watched had an idea even that Marthe might call on one of her charms to kill the trader where he stood.

Marthe laid down the deerskin and the sharpened bone. She got up slowly and went across the open space to the trader's side. She looked him in the face, and he regarded her steadily, with eyes small from much narrowing in the sun and wind. Everyone was quiet, watching, and the shadows all were still. "I will go with you," she said.

There was a murmur of astonishment, as if the listeners thought the moon would sooner fall from its place.

"The only warrior I would have has long since chosen another. I will go with the white trader, if he wants me."

Unexpectedly, the trader pulled off his coonskin cap. "My name is Baptiste Lamont," he said. "I'm mighty glad you will go."

My grandfather spoke, his surprise carefully dropped out of his voice. "I am sorry. We need you, just now as this new baby has come."

"This baby is one that you should not ask me to take care of," said Marthe in a dull tone, leaving her reasons large in the air between the words.

Grandfather looked at her, and his tone when he next spoke, soft with sympathy, told her he was aware of her devotion to my father, which had never even been noticed by Tecumseh as he passed her over and chose the most comely one of the tribe to be his wife.

"I hope, then," said Grandfather, "you will be a good woman to this man you have chosen."

"Ajawin will do what is needed until your daughter is well." Marthe indicated the other woman who had been present at my birth. Squatting in the edge of the shadow, she nodded, showing her black teeth in an anxiety to please.

"Well, that's settled," said Baptiste. He handed Marthe a pair of silver armlets from the pile of goods, and measured off a strip of blue cloth, twice the length from his ear to the end of his arm, and hung it across her shoulder. "We might even get married," he added with an air of making a generous offer. "The first time the priest comes to the island."

Groups of women got up and turned away to the bubbling kettles, for the precious syrup must be watched. As Marthe went to her lodge, she heard them chattering about the many things that had happened so quickly— the death of one of them, and the plans for the ceremony of burying. The one Sioux scalp taken in the last raid they all agreed should be placed on her grave. Marthe's leaving was talked over, and occasionally one of them mentioned the birth of Tecumseh's first child.

The men gathered closer to the trader. "Now about finishin' up." Baptiste went back to his goods with a sigh of relief. Marthe, peering out of her lodge, saw him hitch up his trousers and pull down his capot with the relief of getting back into familiar business. She smiled a little and turned away to pack her clothing, her pots and pans, and her mystic rolls of birchbark.

Before she went away, she made a small bag of mink skin for me, and into it she put herbs and seeds which would keep me safe. She made a small bag for herself, from a square of buckskin into which she put a piece of snakeroot, for that was the herb to keep one safe on a long journey.

Two

⁖ The birds and squirrels that lighted on a branch where I swung lazily to and fro in my cradleboard had no fear, as if they knew from hundreds of babies they had seen before that my hands were bound inside and could not reach out to stroke them. All the forest folk I knew were intent on their own affairs, and I watched them when I tired of the spiderweb ornament that dangled from the hoop over my face. Herds of deer grazed in the open places and came down to the streams to drink. The clever and talented beaver drove his teeth repeatedly into the base of a sapling. A raccoon sat in the top of a pine while the otters below him played in shallow eddies. The black fox and marten did not disturb the badger sunning himself on his mound, keeping a wary eye on the thicket where berries were most plentiful and where could be heard the slow, heavy movements of the black bear.

Grandfather told me later that the first words I spoke were to these creatures. A blue jay settled near me, the very clown of birds, always in trouble or making it for someone else. A staid robin began to scold him, and exhort him to be good, but it was no use. Suddenly I began to talk, adding my scoldings to the red-breasted one's. But the jay paid no attention. Beneath the limb where I hung, Grandfather was teaching a little boy how to make a net to catch fish. "Watch the spider, and make your web like hers," he was saying, and then looked up when my voice was heard in reproof of the flighty blue-feathered one.

He laughed softly, and looked at me with head upraised so that the eagle feather above it tilted far back. "We will always have robins and jays. It has to be that way. Don't reprove him, but don't copy him either. Just laugh at his antics."

I learned early not to cry, for that might attract a wolf or panther, and the Sioux might come out of the woods, and they would be worse than the wild animals. Once out of the cradleboard, life seemed to become perfect. A girl-child was not expected to do woman's work until she was six. So in those early years I had nothing to do but explore with the other children for berries and sassafras, gathering hazel nuts and sweet acorns and wild anise roots.

22

My grandfather had little time for me. When he was not on the hunt, he spent his time in teaching the little boys of the camp. Being a girl-child, I had no need to learn what they did, but I used to stand quietly by without meeting reproof—since I was the child of Tecumseh and the grandchild of our chief—while some little boy learned to make a spear-point from the rib bone of a moose, or to chip a stone into an arrowhead. Grandfather knew everything. He taught the young ones to imitate the calls of the wild birds so their quavering notes would entice the wild turkey and partridge within reach of arrow or gun. He taught them to take fish from the clear water with nets made of the nettle and the inner bark of the cedar. Eagerly they listened, for they saw every day that life itself depended on learning the proper way to hunt, trap, and fish. This was not sport, acquired as boys learn how to play a game, but as they learn a trade that they may live without begging. It was work. The youths practiced the construction of traps and deadfalls, and nooses suspended above runways, to catch the beaver, the bear, and the moose, for our food, clothing and blankets. With forests and lakes abounding in fruit and game, with all the red man wanted in life, they made a paradise which only he, with his manner of living, was fitted to enjoy. Yet it is not without meaning that whenever one of our men spoke of the hereafter, he called it a land where one never had to hunt again, yet there would be food for all.

The earliest lesson I myself had to learn was not to be out in the woods after dark, because of the wolves. Even though they came close when the fire grew dim, they would not approach the fire-guarded lodges, and there was no use wasting an arrow or bullet on them—their flesh was not good for eating and their fur had little value. I even learned not to lie awake at night, imagining their eyes glistening in the dark. I learned not to hear them as you may have learned not to "hear" the whirr of one of these wonderful new sewing machines, even when it is right in the room with you, or the clatter of hooves on city streets.

I wish I could remember my father from the first time he came back from the border war after I was born. I wish I could remember more clearly those heavily arched brows above black, penetrating eyes that no one failed to notice, the face grave and noble, and full of courage, almost sad in its wisdom. I know that he came back so disturbed over the trouble with the settlers that he could not allow himself to stay in his lodge and be happy with his wife and child. He spent his time rather in council, telling of the danger he had been awakened to. For years afterward, while he was traveling from one tribe to another, telling them of his plan to save us all, I heard the words he had spoken to our own tribe repeated over and over in council until I know them as well as if as a tiny child I had stored them in memory.

"All the tribes should unite," he said. "The white men have driven the red men from the sea to the lakes— let us go no farther. They are coming into country promised by their own treaties forever to the red men, land that holds the graves of our fathers. They cut trees and make the land a barren waste, for when they come, the deer, the bear, and the buffalo, are gone.

"One tribe cannot stand against them alone, or trust the treaties made with them singly. They have made a union of their seventeen fires. Even now it is too late to regain what we have lost. The tribes must join their fires together to hold what they have left."

From that time my father went among the tribes, urging his plan. He traveled from north to south, to the east as far as the lake called Erie. He knew our movements with the seasons, and joined us for a few days whenever his path crossed ours.

It was not until I was five years old that I remember for myself the coming of my father, although as I saw

24

the preparations for his coming, I knew I had seen the same thing many times before. When I saw Mother put sweet pine on the fire and lean above it to perfume herself, I moved close to her. It was at that moment that I first remember noticing how beautiful my mother was. She was as tall as the chin of a man, and her voice was low and song-like. Her skin had the glow I later saw in dark amber, and her eyes were dark and full of expression. She embraced me, and I felt joy through her arms. I thought she must have had news, brought mysteriously through the forest, that my father was only a few hours away from us. Or, looking at the sweet calmness of her face, I knew that perhaps she had had a vision of his coming, just as a few days before Grandfather had dreamed of hoof marks of deer on snow, and the following day one of the men had brought in venison for the first time in weeks.

Returning to the river banks where the Wabash and the Tippecanoe met, we had settled in our winter camp. Uneasy we had been there, for while my father was gone, the near-by settlers had been raiding our corn cribs, and murdering any of our men that went out of camp alone. We did not understand it, but I know now that they were trying to provoke us to attack them, so the soldiers in blue coats would come and drive us out. We only knew that there was something in the air we didn't like.

A cold rain came up in the afternoon of that day, and still my father had not come. I stayed inside the lodge, playing with two of the camp dogs, and tending the fire while Mother put the last touches of quill embroidery on a coat she was getting ready for my father. She put on less quillwork than many an ordinary brave had, because Tecumseh would have it so.

At once above the tapping of the rain on our lodge roof came a loud shout outside, and I ran to the flap-covered opening, stumbling over the two dogs rushing out ahead of me. A cracking of rifle shots came so close together that I thought the thunder bird must have come right into camp, and I drew our flap aside expecting to see the yellow legs and green claws of the great bird, who flapped his huge black wings to make the thunder, and flashed sparks from his eyes to make the lightning dart. In the darkness all the camp was in confusion. Women screamed, dogs barked, and dripping shadowy figures ran to and fro in the rain.

Ajawin appeared, shouting in our doorway that the bluecoats were coming, and then we heard again the sound of their guns and a few shots close by, from guns of our own men. The women, as if they knew that our answering guns were only as campfires hissing back at a shower that would destroy them, began packing everything we could carry. Mother gave me our little packet of rice and sugar, while on her own arms she heaped all the clothing they would hold. Telling me to keep close to her, she ran out and to the farther side of the camp. I remember hanging on to her deerskin jacket, and plunging over rough ground to the river, where other women were gathering near the boats. I was not afraid, but felt a queer excitement above the discomfort of trying to keep up and having the rain soaking my clothes and making the ground slippery under my moccasins. I remember our piling into boats and crossing the river, where we cowered in the rain under a few sodden blankets, gazing with dull eyes toward the bright flames that were eating our camp. The air was full of the scent of burned corn. The old women sat with passive faces, as if this was only one more thing to be borne and gotten over that one might take up other sorrows.

When the sun came up it showed only flat earth covered with bits of unburned sticks and pieces of matting where our homes had been. Coming across the river

26

were two boats of wounded men. They staggered up the bank to us, my grandfather with them, and under his direction we began to move and by the end of the day we were as far as our overloaded canoes could be urged.

Removed from danger, the men set about making new birch canoes, and the women to piece together new mats for the lodges. From then on I remember always traveling long days, following the sun westward. At first we were on ground we had hunted over, and we came upon each hill, each turn of a stream, as an old friend. We noticed if the water was higher than the year before, and a big tree having blown down gave the place a look of strangeness to our eyes. If it had not been for the cause of our wandering, we would have enjoyed our life, for we had ever liked it when the circle of our horizon shifted from day to day.

We came where lush prairie grass invited the deer, the antelopes, and even a few buffalo, strayed from the great plains to the west. When Grandfather saw one of these shaggy beasts shot down by one of our men, he said that we were getting too close to the grounds of the Sioux.

The men who brought it in moved uneasily, and their leader spoke. "We have already seen them. We saw a band of Sioux just after we brought down this buffalo. They were painted red about the mouth."

"Out for blood," nodded my grandfather.

"They were more than we, so we hid in a thicket. And going back on their trail we found the dead body of Scarface, with the scalp gone."

Grandfather's sharp features set in regretful lines. Scarface had gone out to hunt that morning. "We must take this next branch of the river to the north," he said.

So constantly was I in a canoe that it became as much a part of me as my moccasins. I began to believe what

I had been told, that the world was so wide that a young wolf who tried to cross it died of old age before he finished the journey.

We went more cautiously through this strange land beyond the big lakes. My grandfather watched for signs of danger: a blade of grass pressed down, a leaf turned a way it could not have grown, a wild animal uneasy without cause.

The moon had grown to fullness and become hungry-thin again before my father found us and we learned what he had done when he came back from his journey and found the camp in ashes and not so much as a dog to greet him.

The day he came had been much the same as another, and yet I knew Mother expected him. She did not join the work of the other women when we camped. The instant we touched shore the others went into the woods with axes, cut small tamaracks and pines and set them up for lodge-poles, bending them and tying them with bast from the cedar tree. They spread our mats over them, cut cedar boughs and strewed them over the floor, carried boxes and kettles from the canoes, and finally hung up blankets for the door. Firewood was cut next, and the fires started in readiness to cook whatever might be brought in by the men who had plunged into the woods as soon as the canoes were drawn up on the shore. Mother had done none of this work, the other women willingly doing her share, and sending approving glances where she sat beneath a large beech tree by the shore, sewing and fringing the legs of two deerskins so placed together that they formed sleeves for a coat for my father. She had given up the other one to a warrior whose clothing was in shreds after the battle with the blue-coats. I sat beside her, handing the colored quills when she was ready to put in the last of the design she had been working on since the deerskins had been scraped and kneaded to softness three days before.

Darkness came, the men returned, and we had rabbit stew and rice, and the day's sounds were hushed as the camp settled to rest, and still my father had not come. I lay on my couch, wide-eyed, staring at the last embers of the lodge-fire my mother kept alive by putting on a stick now and then as she waited. Grandfather was in the near-by lodge of Ajawin's husband, Red Storm Cloud.

The blanket flap had been swaying a little in the breeze from the river, but at once it opened. A brief glimpse of the moonlit wood outside, and the doorway was darkened again. My father was there. He came in, and the manner of his coming startled my mother so she uttered a little scream. He was not in his deerskins, but in a coat of red, such splendor as my eyes had never seen before. Its collar stood up around his bronze throat, and a line of gold buttons marched down the front of it, and more gold shone at his squared shoulders.

After her first scream, my mother looked at him a moment in silence, and then went to the heap of kettles and began to warm some stew over the fire. Custom demanded that she ask no questions, that she act as if he had been away no longer than a day's hunt, and that she must wait until he was ready to speak. He turned as if in great fatigue and made ready to sit with his feet to the fire. There was such a bright flash as he moved that I thought he must have captured the lightning for his own, and then I saw it came from a great knife at his side.

He ate, and still he had spoken no word, only looked into the fire with serious eyes. Mother stood beside him, ready to hand him whatever he wanted before he should need to ask for it. As he handed the birch cup back to her at last, he smiled up at her, and she trembled for joy. She brought warmed moccasins and put them on his feet, and then he spoke.

"Little singing one," he said to me, for he had called

me that since I had been a baby in the cradleboard and had happened once to be crying when he came home. "Could you go tell your grandfather, the chief, that he must call the men together, at once, in front of our lodge?"

My heart almost bursting with pride at being asked to do even so trifling an errand for so great a one, I rolled off my couch and hurried out, feeling as light-footed as a spirit.

Mother's eyes were wet with happiness as she and I sat together just inside our lodge opening and looked out at the council in the open space in front.

When all the men had gathered, in breechcloths and blankets, their faces turned toward my father as if they were carved in wood, he rose and made ready to speak. Tall he loomed above them in the unfamiliar coat. His body was active and muscular, reminding me how they still told around the fire that he had been best in all the games in his youth.

With animated face and rapid gestures, with piercing eyes turned on one and then another of his listeners, he began to speak, and hearing him, a stirring came within me that was not from my knowing he was my father, or just from the words he said, but from something in his voice as he said them. Years later, when I heard men tell how Tecumseh's notes of eloquence stirred the blood, I knew what they meant, remembering that night.

I did not understand then all that he said, but when I grew older I was told that he began by explaining what had happened since our camp was destroyed. The blue-coats had feared the union of the tribes he was forming, and knowing its completion was near, had decided to strike Tecumseh's camp while he was away. These same bluecoats had just begun (the year was 1811) a war with the British redcoats.

30

"These Americans and the British will fight again," said my father. "Their wounds still smart from the last time they went on the warpath against each other. There has been trouble where they have met here in the woods and prairies, and trouble between their boats in distant harbors.

"The red men must join the British, and I will lead them," he told our braves that night, and the medal given him by the great chief of the redcoats rose and fell on his chest as he talked. "If the Americans are beaten, the union of the tribes can then draw a line on the ground and they will not dare go beyond it. It is the only hope now."

Their set faces admitted the truth of his words, memory furnishing enough cause for hatred of the bluecoats or Long Knives. One of the braves arose, and threw his tomahawk in the air, beginning at the same time the rapid steps of the war dance around the fire. One after another the young men joined him, and the thumping of their feet grew louder, until I thought it must be shaking the earth back to the sea from which the waves of white men had come. The fearsome war-whoop rang through the woods, and when the fullness of the dance was complete, each man looked to his arrows, his pouches of dried venison and corn, his flint-lock musket with bullets and powder-horn if he had them, and each one his medicine bag with the charms to give him victory. Those who had had favorable dreams the night before told of them loudly, and each one told a tale of past warpaths he had been on, pointing to the scalps on his lodge-pole as proof of what he said. One young man, known for his endurance as a runner, listened to soft words from my father, and put war-paint on his face and on the blade of his tomahawk and set off through the woods to spread the word.

Tecumseh had spoken. He wrapped himself in his blanket, and sat down before the fire. When the morning star first came in sight he would lead out all the braves, and many of them would never come back. And as he sat there with head lowered in thought, I stole out and put my cheek against his shoulder.

Three

❧ Since we were outside the path of the war, its sights did not meet our eyes, nor its sounds our ears. We had kept away as from a torrent that might overflow and destroy us. But within its circle, we heard the flames of war burned high as if mankind did nothing but heap fuel on them.

At first, word had come to us by runners that the Americans under a general called Hull had crossed the river at Detroit, thundering that the red men had no right to defend their land. General Brock of the redcoats made answer that the British would defend their subjects, red and white. Our hearts warmed to this Brock, for my father had sent word that he and Brock were friends, that Brock was a great warrior, that he stood erect in the bow of his canoe and led the way to battle.

Tecumseh, the word came again, had crossed the Detroit River and destroyed a detachment of Americans there. The general Hull had to retreat across the river to Fort Detroit. Brock and Tecumseh followed and attacked, and Hull surrendered Detroit to them.

Then we knew Brock had gone to the east, to Fort Niagara. Reports came of battles on land, and in big bateaux and gunboats on the lakes, scaring the wild fowl from the water. And then came the report that in the days of Indian summer, with the roaring Niagara below him, Brock had been killed on Queenstown Heights. Then, with the deep snow of winter, silence.

❧ ❧ ❧

Three times the seasons went around, maple sugar time followed hunting time, and went on into berrying and wild-rice time. Three times the sun weakened and grew lower in the sky until winter when he began to grow stronger and climb up again, and still we had no more word from my father. Having no home to go back to at harvest and planting time, our life was all wandering, and we kept to the west, as far as we could go and yet stay out of the path of the Sioux. I grew to the height of my mother's shoulder, and began to share her burdens. Though my age was never mentioned, for we paid no attention to such things, I know I must have been eight years old the winter when I first saw a black robe, as the priests were called.

We made camp that year in the freezing moon, November, and planned to stay there until the moon of flowers, in May, near a trading post and mission run by Frenchmen. One day over the snow came a black-robed figure with a small book in his hand and a gold cross at his breast. He went from one lodge to another, and everywhere he found something to do, whether it was stilling a crying baby, or mending pots or pans or fixing men's guns. As he worked, he talked, in the manner of missionaries before and since—even as he struggled with a broken flint lodged in a musket, or mended a broken bucket handle, his tongue spoke of the glory of God and the futility of material things.

As I make the long journey back over the years, I realize that the priest and the trader disturbed us little, and we were glad to see them come, not knowing they were signs of the coming end, that where they went the farmer followed, and where he settled the red men and the wild creatures could never return.

The coming of this particular priest was one of the events of my life that seemed to be nothing unusual at the time, and yet was to have effects far beyond what I knew. For when he had made the rounds, he gathered

33

the chief men together, and talked to them, asking that he be permitted to teach their children in his mission. He would send a dog team for them each day, and return them safely at night, he promised.

When the black robe had gone, there was much talk in the lodges. The black robe had promised new clothing and two meals of food each day for the children. It was decided that we were to go.

I am afraid I remember little about the school except the daily ride behind the dog team, scooting over the ground behind furry leaping creatures, up and down hill between snow-laden trees. The most important thing the school did for me was not intended for me at all, and I often think that may be true of teaching. For who knows what the mind of a child may take up?

I had heard of white men's cabins, where fire burned within and no smoke hurt the eyes, but I had never been in one before. The log-walled room we were in was bare, except for rows of benches for us to sit on, and the great fireplace in the end. I do remember the black robe standing in front of our benches talking and talking about something that seemed important to him. Though he spoke a rough Ojibway I understood nothing of what he said, for the ideas touched me not at all. I sat with the smaller children and thought my own thoughts, until the priest had finished, and a young woman with faded yellow hair—a trader's daughter—came in and started us younger ones on embroidery and weaving of simple mats. These were packed up once a month and sent away to be sold for money for the mission. While we worked at these tasks in the back of the room, she took a class of older children to a bench in front and gave them lessons in a new language. Wondering what tribe's tongue this was, I listened to her voice as I worked with my piles of colored beads, and began to understand what she was teaching, even though it was not meant for my ears.

Je suis, tu es, il est—over and over again in the front of the room. I found myself following that class, and practicing the new words on the squirrels and chipmunks when I was home again. Startled, I found they understood me in that tongue as well as in the familiar Ojibway.

Four

☙ The summer of 1814, that was to bring so many changes, began as any other summer, except for the mococks. When the women began making them in numbers—little boxes of birchbark that one could easily hold in the palm of the hand, covered with designs worked in colored quills, and meant to hold little cakes of maple sugar—I knew we were going to do something different. The women began gathering the bark for them the very day an Ottawa runner passed through the camp and stopped for a hurried word with my grandfather. From that day, too, I heard the word *turtle* spoken by them as they worked, and the way they said it I knew that no shelled animal was meant, nor anyone of the turtle totem. It seemed to be a place, and a wondrous one.

Our peltries were from then on kept in a stack in the corner of the lodge, instead of being traded to any Frenchman that came along, and a heap of other things grew around them—the mococks, dishes of fragrant clay, moccasins in all sizes, and little bags of doeskin covered with beading.

There were other new words in the air besides *turtle*. Gold was one of them, and mention of other tribes, Ottawas, Menominees, Pottawatomies, Hurons. Since these were friendly tribes, I knew it was no warpath we were setting out on. For by that time the talk had shown that

35

we were going somewhere, even if I had not known a
long journey was ahead from the amount of bear's
grease, pemmican, and corn that was being packed to
put into the canoes. I learned that at the end we would
be among other tribes, for the women talked of it with
happy tones in their voices as they made new robes and
dresses. They did not know how many tribes there
would be. There might even be Sioux, Pawnees, or even
Blackfeet, they said, and yet, once there, no trouble
would arise among them.

I touched Mother's arm to ask her about this. She
alone was making no mococks, but spent her days in
sewing on another hunting coat. After the skins had
soaked in ashes and water for several days, she had
stretched them on the ground between stakes, and
scraped them with a bone until dry and soft. While I
spoke to her she was smoking them over a hole in the
ground filled with burning rotten wood, so that when
wet thereafter they would ever dry soft, not stiff and
hard.

"Is it the red-pipe-stone place?" I asked, for I had
heard the story of how above a certain quarry at the
head of the father of waters, two tribes had fought and
their blood had run down and stained the rock a cherry-
red. The manitou had been displeased, and commanded
that this place must be free from fighting, and the rock
must be used by all for peace and council pipes.

Mother coughed and turned away before she spoke.
The rotten wood was sending up clouds of smoke with
little blaze.

"No. On the island shaped like a turtle it is not the
presence of the manitou that keeps peace—though he
once lived there, it is said—but the fort and agency."

Fort and agency—I wondered what they were. I
pictured them as strange gods like that of the thunder
and the wind, so powerful they must be if a Sioux and
an Ojibway met and tomahawks were not lifted.

36

We had wandered farther to the west than most of our people, and had seen no one but the trader, his fair-haired daughter, and the priest. They had paid little attention to what was happening between the redcoats and the Long Knives, but we had learned that the war had been over for many moons and that the Long Knives had won again. Of my father and the braves that went with him we heard never a word.

I often saw Mother look up at a drifting cloud as though it might know. And if she watched a bird passing over from the direction he had gone I wondered if she thought the feathered one might have seen him. She seemed to listen to the wind, expecting a message. But it passed her in silence, and her face took on a questioning sadness I have often seen in those who do not know whether they must grieve. As we began our journey, she worked almost stubbornly on the hunting coat in the night camps until it was too dark to see the colors of the quills. It was as if, by having the coat ready for him, she could bring him back.

We left the sugar camp along the Ouisconsin and began to follow the river northward. Crossing the portage to the Fox River, we came out at the settlement at Green Bay. We stood then where blue water seemed to stretch out to the end of the world. We paused only long enough for the medicine man to perform a ceremony, using a fragment from his medicine bag that he said was a piece of the horn of the prince of serpents, he who dwells in the Great Lakes. We knew that unless the serpent were given this respect, he would destroy us. Many had been the stories of how he broke ice and dragged travelers through to his hiding place, and in summer raised up tempests when they tried to cross above him.

We safely crossed the big lake of the Illinois to the straits of Mackinac, where rocky islands appeared, dressed in a few ragged firs and birches, like poor men who had not taken enough furs to get themselves blankets.

I had been so long used to the sight of new rivers and lakes, prairies and groves, and shores of small islands, that I paid little attention to where we were, though we knew the end of the journey was near. More and more often we had come upon the remains of campfires of many who had gone the same way. But when we approached the place that was to mean so much in my life, I was fast asleep with my head in my mother's lap.

When I awoke next morning on Mackinac beach and saw the unpacking of all our goods, the hundreds of other lodges crowded close about us with their birch canoes turned up against them, and saw how the island rose high from the water, I knew we had reached the *turtle*.

Troubled, I sat before our lodge, watching the beach where people in rags, buckskins, and bright calico were coming and going everywhere among the boats and canoes of all sizes scattered the length of the curving shore. The flap of our lodge moved softly in the morning breeze off the blue water. Inside, my mother lay weeping, for when we had reached the island the night before she had learned that my father had been killed in the war. The Ojibways around us, like the ones from Neepigan and Rainy Lake that my grandfather had already gone out to visit, had known it for many moons. I felt sad that he was gone, but there was no loneliness yet as of a hole torn in my life. He had never been a part of my regular days. I could not even get my mind on him entirely, when so much that was new was all around me.

The harbor had the shape of a new moon, with points reaching out into the water at the east and west. Following this crescent shape was a long curving road with only the pebbly beach between it and the water. On this were shops, low white buildings where I saw some of our women carrying heaps of mococks and coming back with cloth and finery they had traded them for. Because they followed the curve of the harbor, these stores were in a semicircle too. It made them look friendly like our lodges around a campfire, as if their fronts, turning to the water from which all news and excitement came, were also turned toward one another to share whatever it might be. Another road cut across the back of the crescent, where rows of low white-washed houses like those I had seen at trading posts nestled against the cliff that rose back of the village. Huge, box-like buildings, such as I had never seen before, puzzled me, since I did not know yet that they were the offices and warehouses of the great fur company. More beautiful to my eyes were the white fort buildings, the blockhouses and quarters high up on the cliff above the beach and the near-by houses. The tops of them gleamed white in the sun, where they rose above the stone wall and the cedar palisade around them. And highest of all was a great pole, where floated a cloth with stripes of red and white, and white stars on a square of blue. I studied this as it flapped in the breeze, feeling something triumphant in the very way it threw out its design against the blue sky and the white clouds beyond. "The white man's totem," I thought, and narrowed my eyes to see if any scalps dangled on the pole beneath it.

"*Qu'est-ce que tu vois là?*" asked a voice near me. I swung around to see who was speaking to me in French, and almost made answer.

A tall boy, a white boy, stood there. I sat back on my heels and looked at him in silence, pulling my eyes away from the friendly grin on his smudged face to see that he had on brown ribbed trousers and a shirt on which bright flowers had almost faded away. He wore moccasins, not as fine as mine, but still moccasins. I looked back at his friendly blue eyes and decided I would not run away.

He pointed one finger at himself and said "Michel." I did the same, and gave him only the name "Oneta," guarding as ever the secret of my real name.

"Tecumseh your father?" he asked in French.

I decided not to let him know I understood his language, but I thought it safe to nod and repeat the word Tecumseh.

"That's what they said. I wanted to get a look at you," he muttered to himself. "A little one," he sized me up, but his words were full of respect.

This Michel then lay down on the beach on his stomach and began drawing pictures on the smooth sand. By the French words he muttered as he tried to puzzle out how to tell me what he meant, I knew he was telling me about himself and his home.

"Around the point, in the fishing village," he said, extending his hand to the western point I had already noticed beyond the rows of lodges. In the sand he traced a crude picture of a low house, a boat, and a fishing net beside it.

"One brother, Jacques," he said, measuring a height just below his shoulder. "He's going to be a voyageur," pointing to men in buckskins and orange and red sashes, just crossing the beach.

As he pointed, a fat woman came toward us. She was so large Michel could no longer see the voyageurs beyond her. She was puffing like a she-bear on a trail, and clinging to her hand was a little girl about my size, with hair tightly braided. The little girl looked at Michel, who pulled off his cap as the fat lady spoke to him.

"Have you seen Big Charlie?" The ridges of her fat overflowed one another like waterfalls on a side hill. "He's due to go out tomorrow, and he owes me for a whole month's lodging. I've got to catch him before they have the final spree tonight for his brigade, or he won't have a cent."

"Big Charlie will pay," said Michel. "I've heard my father say Charlie is one of the best."

"Who's your father?" She peered at him, her chins doubling over one another as she looked down.

"Armand Benois. He plays with Baptiste for the dances."

"Oh, yes. You're from around the point, ain't you?" Her tone dropped him from notice.

"I don't feel good, Ma," whined the little girl. "And it's so dirty around here." She picked up her skirts, though they were already above her high shoe tops.

"You poor dear." The fat woman wet her handkerchief on her broad tongue, and wiped the little girl's face with it, looking more than ever like a she-bear with a cub.

The little girl had been staring at me, and I had stared back. Jerked by the hand of her mother, she turned away, and then, as if she had to, she looked back again.

"Come on, Currance, we can't stay here all day." Her mother caught hold tighter. "You mustn't ever come down here alone. Keep away from the Indians." She turned and looked back at me as if I were something that might claw or bite. "What piercing eyes that little girl has!" she said.

Currance, as if she couldn't help it, stuck out her tongue at me. And then they were gone beyond the next lodge.

" 'Around the point,' says she," Michel cried mockingly. "And the little brat sticks out her tongue at you."

Something about the incident seemed to have drawn us closer. I looked at Michel and smiled.

"Mrs. Ruggs may live in 'the village,' but she's not so much," he said. "I heard my folks talking about her. She runs a boarding house since her man left her and

41

ran off to some other woman on the mainland down below. That's her place over there." He pointed to a low building a little way from the wharf. Then he gave himself a little slap on the cheek. "But you don't understand a word of what I'm saying."

He threw himself to the beach again, and his forehead wrinkled with the problem of how to put it into pictures.

"What is a boarding house?" I asked in French.

Michel looked up, and a grin spread over his face, with amazement at its edges. "You know my language? Say, that's *magnifique*."

Just then the blanket flap of our lodge opened slowly and my mother came out, drawing a blue blanket over her head. Michel wiped out his pictures with one arm as he rose. He took a few steps backward, looking at my mother's tear-filled eyes. Then he touched his ragged cap, and started away toward the point.

I do not think Mother had seen him. With a gesture for me to come with her, she started down the beach to the west, in the same direction he had taken. I could see him ahead, wading in the shallow water.

We passed the Ottawa lodges, and those of the Menominees, the rice-eaters. Fronting the open stretch of beach beyond were gardens, their white picket fences covered with vines of climbing bean. They belonged to the low white houses, and women in sunbonnets were hoeing in them. They did not raise their heads as we passed. Beyond was a cluster of huts, leaning and sprawling instead of being neatly upright like the white houses. Beyond these, at the point, Mother spoke for the first time.

"We are going to see Marthe."

Five

So well had Mother described Marthe to me that I believe I should have known her anywhere, by the look of sad, tired wisdom on her face. She sat with shoulders bent, her feet far apart on the floor, spreading her knees to hold some work on her lap. Her dull black hair was drawn back so tightly from her wrinkled face that I thought it must be hurting her.

I had a feeling that she knew we were standing in her doorway long before she seemed to look up. It was as if she had been expecting us, and yet had to get something settled in her mind before she could speak.

"Naneda, and his little one," she said in a low tone. She put aside the pair of moccasins she was embroidering, and arose.

At the sound of her own name, Mother ran across the bare floor and put her arms around Marthe's neck.

"Did the word just come to you?" asked Marthe softly.

Mother nodded. "A warrior named Black Hawk, just now on his way home, came to the lodges last night. He was with Tecumseh when the white men killed him."

As if she could stand no more, Mother suddenly broke away from Marthe and ran out of the door. I hurried after her, but she was already far down the beach, not going back toward the village, but farther along the shore. Then she left the water and took a trail that led up the heights.

When I turned around, Marthe was looking steadily at me. She held out her hand, and I went to her. She sat down again and took up her work. I sank on the floor at her knees, feeling nothing strange about this woman,

43

or about the feel of her calico shortdress against my face, though I had never seen her before.

"You are the only child in your father's lodge?" she asked, as if only making sure of something she already knew.

"Yes."

She looked over my head, out the open door. I followed her glance, but there was nothing outside but a row of boats, and some nets drying between poles in the sun. Beyond was the blue water, and I felt that Marthe was looking at something even beyond that.

She put her hand then on my head, drawing me close to her knee, holding me with the gentle, almost reverent protection given to something very precious.

I must have fallen asleep there, for I awoke later on the bed in the corner and the room was filled with the purple shadow that is twilight on Mackinac. I was alone. I looked around at the rough log walls. It is easy now to tell what I saw, for the one-room cabin changed very little in all the years I knew it. Over the bed hung a crucifix, Baptiste's, and in the corner on a rough shelf were a heap of Midé scrolls. Strips of cured meat hung from rafters among drying herbs and ears of corn. Guns and fishing spears were resting on nails driven in one wall. Above the doors and windows were signs Marthe had made to keep evil spirits from entering. Two pelts stretched wrong side out on pointed boards to dry hung above pieces of an old net in one corner, and next to them hung some dresses and aprons of calico that would fit a girl a little smaller than I. Braided mats were on the floor near a bare board table, where three chairs were turned at the angles they had been left when three people got out of them. Flies hovered above a birchbark box of wild strawberries, and outside bees were talking above a window-box made of shells and holding a few scrawny blossoms.

Voices from outside had awakened me. I pushed aside a torn curtain. A pretty, dark-haired white woman was standing in front of the cabin, with her arm about the boy Michel.

"Rosanne was right here a moment ago, Marthe," she was saying. "She had been playing in the sand with the boys."

"Mother sent Jacques and me to the company store, and we thought Rosanne went home," said Michel.

"I wish I had watched her," said the pretty woman, troubled.

"It was not your fault, Louise," said Marthe. "It was just that something kept me from thinking about my own child for a while."

Louise—so the dark-haired white woman was called Louise. I repeated the syllables to myself, beginning with the difficult *l*. Ll-oo-ees—a strange name. I was puzzled at the new names I was hearing today. One can always take an Indian name apart and get a meaning, but these syllables—Louise, Michel, Jacques—meant nothing to me.

"Shall I go to the lodges and see if she is playing with the children there?" offered Michel.

"No. I shall go." Marthe opened the door and called to me. "Oneta, will you stay right where you are?"

"Right on the bed?" I always liked people to say exactly what they meant.

At her nod I settled back against the pillows. I heard a murmur of low talk as Marthe said something to Louise.

"I'll keep an eye on her," said Louise.

"No. She could never break a promise, that one."

"Is she as pretty as your Rosanne?"

"No. She has eyes and forehead like her father, but her mouth and small bones are like her mother's." Marthe's voice was fainter now, as if she had gone far down the beach.

The blankets on Marthe's bed were the cheapest kind I had seen in traders' packs. Three-point, they were called. But on the foot of the bed was a fine buffalo skin, its edges finished with beads and quills. I pulled it up and began to read the story in the embroidery. The pictures told that a little band of Ojibways of the loon totem stood once on a point of land and saw the island of Mackinac arise from the water like a giant turtle. It was complete with white cliffs and trees and curious rocks, but there were no people. It was to be the home of the manitou. The last picture showed the cone-shaped rock that was his wigwam, and canoes approaching with offerings.

That had been before the white people had come, then. I began to think over the ones I had seen that day. The men in buckskins and bright sashes that shouted to one another so merrily were like the traders I had known, and I gave them no more thought. There had been the fat woman, and others that were queer to my eyes. I had seen bowed and bandied legs, and a boy pushing a loaded two-wheeled cart from the wharf to the stores had a head twice too large for his body.

I wondered why these people had not stayed in the right shape. I tried to imagine a raccoon with a head too big, an otter as fat as Mrs. Ruggs. Bears were fat in the fall of the year. I wondered if that woman were storing up so she could go a whole winter without food. I have never seen fat people since then without measuring them in my mind against Mrs. Ruggs.

I had never seen so many white people before, only one or two at a time. Casting my mind back over them, I decided that, having seen a lot of them together, I didn't like them. As people have often done in judging a race in the mass, I admitted that I might like one or two among them. There was Michel, and the sweet-faced Louise.

I lay there until I heard a light sound of moccasins on stones. I looked out of the window. Marthe was coming back, and with her was Gray Wolf, the man most respected in our totem next to my grandfather. Beside him scampered his dog, a little spotted one I had often played with. Gray Wolf stalked silently ahead of Marthe, his white blanket clutched around his shoulders.

Louise called from her doorstep. "Had anyone seen her?"

"No. She has not been at the beach. But Gray Wolf says he can find her."

Louise bowed slightly, but Gray Wolf did not look at her. He began walking along the beach, looking at the mixed footprints in the little strip of sand. Where it ended and the deep pebbles began, he looked carefully at little dents in them.

"Woman's foot go this way," he muttered, pointing along the shore where my mother had gone. "Child go that way, too, before woman. Woman step on child's foot-mark here." Calling his dog, he set off without another word.

Marthe stepped into the cabin, and looked pleased to see me still on the bed. "You may get down now," she said.

"Where is my mother?" I asked as I slid to the floor and followed Marthe outside.

"She will come back soon, and her sorrow will grow less with every sunrise. Time has great medicine."

While I was considering this, Michel and a boy a little shorter than he, with black, curly hair, came running from the next cabin. "Pa's coming!" they called back to Louise. A boat was almost at the shore, and the younger man in it waved to the boys. The other waved at Marthe, his hand suspended in mid-air when he saw me, as if he had expected someone else.

47

"Baptiste thought you were Rosanne," said Marthe.

With a little swish their last stroke drove the boat up on the beach, and the two men got out and pulled the broad-bottomed craft still farther out of the waves. The boys grasped their father's sack of fish, and he followed them to his cabin. Sounds of happy laughter came from its windows.

Baptiste threw across his back in sack-fashion a net of shiny, restless fish. He limped up the path, and put them down in the grass by the cabin.

"Well, who's this?" He pulled off a shapeless cap and rubbed his bald spot with a red bandanna. I remembered the description I had heard of the trader Marthe had gone away with—the thin face, the energy, the good nature of the man.

Marthe told him who I was. "That so? Then you're the baby I helped name." He patted me on the head, and I didn't dislike it as I usually did when someone touched me.

"Rosanne has run away again." Marthe took an old pan that lay beside the cabin and bent to fill it with the fish.

Baptiste sighed. "Seems like, with only one to look after, you might keep track of her," he said mildly. "Which way shall I look?"

Marthe told him about Gray Wolf. Baptiste looked relieved. "That's real kind of him. Have him eat supper with us when he gets back." He looked at Marthe. She had taken the fish to a low bench and begun to scrape the scales from them. "You take it calm enough when that girl runs away. Sometime she'll get into trouble, doin' just what she pleases. You ought to make her mind better."

"When child is too young to understand, it is no use to correct. When child is old enough to understand, no one has the right."

Baptiste looked as if he had heard that before, and

48

knew there was no answer to it. "Now you take Louise. She makes those boys mind her, and a couple of good young'uns they are, too. She'd be frantic if one of them was gone and she didn't know where he was."

"There are times when feeling is too deep for one to get excited over a little thing." Marthe looked at me.

"I don't know as this time's any different from any other." Baptiste scratched thoughtfully at a large wen on his temple. "Well, let's get some of these in the frying pan. I'm starved."

Louise and her husband had come outside and were looking at his sacks of fish. "Why do you take so many? I get tired of burying spoiled fish. You can never sell all these in the village."

"You forget, the boats are in," laughed Armand. "Voyageurs can eat plenty, after living all winter on lard and lyed corn. I can get rid of a barrel or two towards my bill at the store. Mr. Stuart told me this morning to bring in some more. Five dollars a barrel we get, and you can have a new dress for the dances."

Louise gave him a playful push. "A new dress, with growing boys who haven't had new waists all summer? But I am going to earn some money, too. Washings I have now from five gentlemen from the fort. We will soon be rich."

"I'm rich now," laughed her husband. "Look at the wife I have."

We had just finished supper, and Baptiste had taken me on his lap to show me a little game he played with string, when we heard a scratching at the door. "Come," shouted Baptiste. The door swung slowly on its hinges, and the little dog scampered in. Gray Wolf tried to come in next, but a little girl in a torn calico dress, her bare legs covered with scratches, pushed past him and ran in. This must be Rosanne, I thought. Her face was narrow, like Baptiste's, and with a sulky expression on its fine

49

features at that moment. Her hair tumbled over her scowling forehead in a mass of curls. When she saw me on her father's lap, surprise took off her scowl, and she looked at me curiously.

"Where have you been?" asked Marthe.

"None of your business," Rosanne screamed, and as Marthe tried to talk to her, she screamed again, and suddenly threw herself on the floor, squirming so that Marthe could hardly pick her up. I had never seen a child behave that way before. I looked at her in dismay.

Baptiste paid no attention to her, but let me slip to my feet as he got up and went over to Gray Wolf, silent by the door.

"That was good work. Much obliged. Where did you find her?"

"In cave, the one they call Devil's Kitchen. She was talking to the cobbler."

"That's right. Old Mac moves his shop out there every summer when it gets too noisy for him in the village. I tell him he tries to make people wear out a pair of shoes on that mile of pebbles while they bring one to be fixed."

"My dog, he smelled her out."

At that, Rosanne wriggled out of Marthe's arms, and flew at the dog like a bunch of fury, lifting her foot to kick him. I threw myself in the way, and collided with her. She kicked me then, and began scratching with her nails.

Baptiste pulled her off. "See here, this Oneta is a nice little girl. You mustn't do that."

"Baby has bad spirit in her." Gray Wolf gave his opinion solemnly. "She kicked me when I dragged her from cave."

"Well, I sure appreciate your bringin' her back. Sit up and have something to eat."

"No. My woman waits at the lodge."

50

"But I'd like to do something to show you—"

Gray Wolf spoke to Marthe. "Medicine to make many animals come into traps, so I have big stacks to trade after winter snows have melted again."

Marthe nodded. "I will make charm tomorrow."

Gray Wolf, pleased, turned to go. The little dog sat up in front of me, waving his paws in the air. I was delighted. "Marthe, can't we feed him something?"

Marthe took half a fish from the plate on the table, and smeared it with bear's grease. This she offered to the dog with as much respect as to a chief. He took it gratefully, put one white foot on it, and began tearing the meat off a mouthful at a time.

"I'll bet you could sell him for a lot of money," said Baptiste.

"He not for sale," Gray Wolf said sullenly. "White men tell us much gold coming by boat for us, I have only to wait. I not need to sell dog."

"That's right—the government payments for your land. I heard they begin this year. You have to come here every summer for them."

Gray Wolf nodded agreement. "Every summer, we get much money."

By this time Rosanne's sobs and tears had gradually slowed, as water slows up from a gourd when it is nearly empty. No one was paying any attention to her, but she felt it in the air that she was unpopular. She had decided that I was liked by all those in the room, so she threw herself on me with a rush that startled me. I took several steps backward. But her arms were around my neck in an instant, and she was kissing me. That was worse than being scratched, I thought, and pushed her away.

Marthe picked Rosanne up and laid her on the bed. "You stay there until I get back. I must take Oneta home."

Gray Wolf slapped his hand on the side of his leg. His dog came running, and scampered out the door, waiting outside for him to follow.

"She could go back along with Gray Wolf, couldn't she?" asked Baptiste.

"I must listen at the edge of the council tonight. Black Hawk is going to speak to all the men," answered Marthe.

Before we were even out of the door, Rosanne had slipped down from the bed.

Following the path back to the lodges, I wondered why Marthe let me follow directly after Gray Wolf. Not being a man-child, I should have been behind her. We walked so quietly that I could hear the song of the waves, and a cowbell tinkling somewhere on the heights, and all the shouting and music that began to come from the village. Fireflies sparkled above the surface of the water, but it was too dark to see the blossoms of the scarlet bean vine on the picket fences.

After sobbing through the twilight hours on a couch of ferns and moss in a deep ravine, that night my mother mourned alone in our lodge, quiet in the dullness that had come upon her.

In all the length of the beach there was sorrow, since there could no longer be any doubt that Tecumseh was gone. Rumors of deaths had so often been made false by the return of the warrior thought to have been killed, and hope had grown that Tecumseh would after all appear—hope fed by the very vitality of their memories of him. But now Black Hawk sat in council, and he had seen him die.

From every side came the wails of women.

"Tecumseh is dead!" The lament rose from the Ojibways around us.

"Tecumseh!" sobbed all the Ottawas. The tents of the Menominees sent it back. "Tecumseh!"

"Tecumseh is gone!" It was as if the words moaned from one lodge to another, beating at the blanketed doors like messengers of bad tidings. In my mind it seemed that even the great echo of the islands took it up. "Tecumseh!" cried the trees on Bois Blanc. "Gone!" sounded from far Drummond's Island, borne on the winds from the great northern lake. "Dead!" sighed the pines on the mainland across the straits.

I put my eyes to the slit where the blanket did not quite cover the opening in our lodge, and looked out. I remember what I saw that night as if it happened yesterday.

A steady fire burned in front, with the youngest boy of our band, Ajawin's son Waubah, beside it to throw a stick on from time to time to keep it alive. Around it was a semicircle of the men of our tribe. Beyond them were small groups, standing, of men of other tribes gathered to hear the stranger speak. The firelight touched some part of the hundred or more, a bronzed cheek, a feather, a blanket's stripe; then in the flickering these were gone and I could see a hand folded across a chest, a feathered scalp-lock, an eye intent on the speaker. No face among them was turned in another direction now.

Black Hawk sat beside my grandfather. He was short, and his frame beneath his deerskin coat was spare. His head, shaved on each side in the manner of the Sauks and Foxes, was thrown back in quiet dignity. His full mouth, slightly open, and his piercing eyes brought expression to his pinched features. His forehead was high, and seemed higher because he had no eyebrows, no hair at all except his scalp-lock. His eyes were thoughtful and kindly as he talked in a low tone to my grandfather. He looked around then as a pipe was passed, first to him, and then to all the others, lesser and great, of the seated ones. Among the men in deerskins and blankets

53

sat others in calico shirts or mackinaw coats, new finery they had traded skins for at the company store.

Resuming a story he had been telling, Black Hawk said,

"And then Tecumseh stretched a roll of elm-bark on the ground. With his scalping-knife he drew upon it a picture, showing the rivers and woods and hills of the country we were marching into. A map, one of the white men called it.

"The general, Brock, was greatly pleased. He took off his own sash from about his waist and placed it around the waist of Tecumseh. But Tecumseh took it off and put it on Roundhead, Chief of the Wyandots, saying he would not wear such an honor in the presence of an older and better warrior."

There was a little murmur of approval around the fire.

"What of the end?" asked my grandfather. "Can Black Hawk tell us of the last fight of Tecumseh?"

Black Hawk rose and stood in silence before them, as if he knew this was a big moment for him. At last he spoke.

"The sun was an hour high at evening. Tecumseh, in plain deerskins, with no signs of his rank upon him, was hidden in bushes along a swamp. I was near-by with a party of Sauks. Many men on horseback came toward us. When we could see the flints in their guns, Tecumseh sprang up and gave the war-cry. At the first shots of the Long Knives, I saw him throw his arms in the air, and fall forward over a log. His rifle dropped at his feet. Then a great fear came over us all. If Tecumseh had fallen, the great spirit must have left us in anger. We fled."

There was a long silence about the fire, but the wails of the mourning women came rolling across from the lodges, setting up echoes that sought out every corner of the village and the fort behind.

"He fell with his face to the enemy," said my grandfather, in that way giving permission for others to speak. Black Hawk was seated again, his eyes on the fire in torment as if he were living over that dreadful hour.

"He knew he was to die that day," said Black Hawk.

A shiver passed over them all, and one or two cast their eyes up uneasily as if feeling a presence they could not see.

"He threw down the red and yellow garments of the British and put on his own deerskins again."

"It is well to die as one has lived, not in strange things put upon you by other men," said my grandfather.

"One of our greatest—" came a murmur from another of the circle. "A leader we can never replace—" said another. "When he spoke, the very rocks and trees were moved—"

"He was one who deserves that we remember him," said my grandfather when all other voices had finished. A sigh of agreement passed over the crowd. No greater tribute could be paid to a dead warrior, and behind the blanket flap I breathed deep in my pride.

Black Hawk rose again, in the manner of one ready to say his final word. His kindly expression was gone, and a hard look settled over his features that I was to remember in after years when I heard of the relentless, restless ambition he was to become known by.

"Sometime the Long Knives shall pay for this," he said, raising his hand like one taking a solemn vow. "I hate them for myself. They have torn up my roots over and over. And now I hate them for Tecumseh. Some day they will pay."

A few of the circle looked up uneasily to the heights. But darkness had swallowed up the fort, and the pole of the totem, and the cannon on the wall. Nearer at hand, more real, were the flaring council fire, the grim face of Black Hawk. When he had come to the end, his shoulders bowed in sorrow, but I could still see in him the boldness and pride that had sharpened his words. There was an omen in the way he stood and talked that night which I was only to remember when events gathered close about him.

"Some day they will pay." His words lingered on in our ears. And over all, came the mourning notes from all the lodges.

Sometimes on the straits, when the sun warms the air, and the water is clear and blue as the sky, a strange thing happens. There is no change of wind, nor any more wind. But suddenly a high wave forms in the center, and moves rapidly across to the island. It breaks there, high on the beach, almost putting out the first row of fires. Then it is gone. No cause is visible, yet it has formed and disappeared, leaving the water as smooth as before. Thus, among his people, was the life of my father.

Six

❧ Two days my mother lay fasting on her bed of hemlock boughs, her face painted with charcoal. I stayed inside the lodge with her, but I could not help raising the flap to look out whenever I knew from the words of eager respect that Black Hawk was passing, going to and fro among the tribes. At our door on the first morning he had left a bundle, and seemed to wait more for a reproof than for thanks.

"These should have been buried with him," said my mother as she opened it, and her eyes blazed when Black Hawk admitted that not he, nor anyone else, knew what became of my father's body. "But this," he went on quickly, drawing out a small bow and arrow, "Tecumseh sent in hope that there was a man-child in his lodge now."

It was Mother's turn to feel a reproof, though Black Hawk looked kindly at her.

There was something about the way the man carried himself that held the whole encampment under his influence while he stayed. At night, he looked on while ceremonial dances were performed by the tribes in turn. Fringes shook against deerskin-covered legs as the ground before our lodge was worn to hardness. A drum beat until late at night, sometimes so wildly that I saw the women scampering to the lodges, and knew they were hiding guns, knives, and everything I had been taught might hurt one. Many years later that wise habit of the women was to come into my life in a strange way.

Black Hawk must have known why we were there; that all the tribes had come in answer to a message from the victorious Long Knives that they wanted peace with us, that they would pay us for land taken, and make promises in council that they would never take any more. But while Black Hawk stayed, saying bitter words of hatred of the Americans, nothing was said about the coming treaties or the expected payments. When he went out to the ship again, and its white sails took him away, preparations began in every lodge for the talk with the government agent. Feathers and paint were put on, and every man's newest garments.

When Gray Wolf came for him, Grandfather stepped out of our lodge, carrying the pipe of peace, its long stem and bowl adorned with feathers, wampum, and drawings on the cherry-red stone.

"Aren't you going to paint?" I cried at sight of him.

"I need only the wrinkles age has drawn on my face," he said.

Seeing my frown, he laughed, and turned back into the lodge. When he came out again, he had three stripes of red from his eyes to the eagle feathers in his white hair.

"It's beautiful!" To admire him at a distance, I took a step backward, directly into a fire over which Ajawin had just hung a black kettle suspended on three sticks. As the kettle fell, Grandfather seized me by the shoulder, pulled me away and examined my clothing for flames and sparks. When he was sure I was unhurt, he looked over my head at Gray Wolf.

Gray Wolf returned his look, his eyes serious with memory. "Some day a fire will hold great danger for her. May the good spirits help when that times comes—"

A drum beat at the other side of the village. The men around the lodges started up.

"You stay here, chickadee," said Grandfather. "When I go for the payments, I will take you with me."

The other men followed him across the beach and up one of the village streets, but I could see him, he was so much taller than they. Even if he had not painted so much, he was the finest-looking of them all, his gray head erect above the fur across his shoulder.

"More land for the white man!"

"He can now hunt with us as far as the lake of the Illinois."

The belt of wampum was studied as it lay before them in the firelight. Blue shell-work, with figures in white, it told what they had agreed upon with the agent. The white man could come to the west of the Wabash, into the land later called Michigan and Illinois. The hunting range farther west, along the Mississippi, up the Missouri to the Little Sioux, was promised to us forever, safe from disturbance from white settlers. The rice district and sugar camps in the north were not to be molested, and everywhere our graveyards were to be untouched. The record ended with my grandfather's mark, a flying bird, and a picture showing that the agent had smoked the peace-pipe with our men. Great misfortune would follow the breaking of any agreement with that seal upon it.

The men studied it that they might never forget what it said. And as I think back to that day, and over the years that followed, I am proud that they were not the ones who broke it.

The payments began the following day, and progressed from tribe to tribe. When the turn of the loon totem of the Ojibways came, I hurried to dress in my best deerskin skirt and waist. Grandfather looked me over approvingly. The whole front of the waist was covered with bead embroidery in red and blue, and bands of the same otter-tail pattern ran along all the fringes at sides and bottom. I put on a pair of new moccasins, proud that their puckered fronts showed the tribe I belonged to.

"I think she should have had a dress of the calico at the store," said Ajawin, slipping new beaded strips over my braids.

"No," said Grandfather and I together.

Sad as I was because my mother lay with blackened face, I could not help being light-hearted as I took Grandfather's hand and started along the beach. I was proud to be with him at the head of a procession, for as we started up the village street, the men came from the other lodges and followed. The sutlers' shops and the saloons were filled with noisy Ottawas, who had already received their payments and were spending the shining pieces of gold.

A long house with a palisade around it had been built for the government agent almost directly below the fort. I did not notice then how easily the cannon from the heights could be turned upon it.

The porch and the steps up to it were narrow, so that only a single file could go up and into the room where the agent sat. My grandfather and I went in first, and the others were stopped at the door by a man in blue. Inside were other men dressed exactly like him, in straight blue clothes with gold upon them.

The agent, a short, heavy man with much dark hair on his chin, and only a little fringe of it around his head, sat at a table with quills and inkhorn, books and paper before him. At one end of the long table was an old man, with the totem of the bear tribe of the Ojibways pricked into his chest with vermilion. I learned later that he was hired as interpreter. An Ojibway was always chosen, for all the tribes understood that language, and most of them could speak it a little. It was the nearest there was to a common language. He nodded at Grandfather.

"Chief White Wing of the loon totem," he said.

The agent looked up and said something. "How many in your lodge?" the interpreter repeated.

"Two. My daughter and her child." He put his hand on my shoulder.

"All right." The agent motioned to one of the clerks, who turned over a new page in his book and made some entries. Another brought a double-handful of gold coins, flat pieces with the hue of corn, but with a harsh clatter instead of its gentle rustle. My grandfather stowed them away in his belt. A third clerk brought from another room a pack of goods, with an extra blanket laid on top of it.

The agent handed my grandfather the clerk's book, and a quill dipped in ink. My grandfather put his mark on the page. Through the interpreter, the agent asked my grandfather to sit at the opposite side of the table and identify the other members of our totem as they came in.

Casting a longing glance at the floor, Grandfather slowly seated himself on the low-backed chair. He drew me to stand close beside him.

The first man in line at the door was let in by the soldier. I watched him cross to the table, his face rigidly hiding his uneasiness. He had seemed a stalwart warrior on the beach, but somehow in this room he was only an embarrassed figure in sagging buckskins.

"Name?"

"Hole-in-the-Sky."

"How many in your lodge?"

"Two men-children, a squaw, one girl-child."

The agent looked at my grandfather. He nodded. The agent motioned to the clerk. Hole-in-the-Sky made his mark on the paper, took his gold coins, excitedly dropping them into a fur pouch at his side, seized his pack of goods and went out, slowly until he was past the uniformed man at the door, then breaking into a run back toward the beach. The next one in line came in.

"Name?"

"Little Pine."

"How many in your lodge?"

I soon got used to the questions and answers I heard over and over. I began to watch only unusual things, such as where each one put his gold. Some brought an old piece of blanket, put the coins in the center, and tied up the corners. Some of those in line were women, widows since the war. These were questioned sharply to be sure they were entitled to the payments, but my grandfather's word that there was no man in their lodges was enough.

No one ever thought of counting the money, and the procession moved rapidly. After a time, the clerk no longer bothered to have each one sign. Instead he held out the pen for them to touch, then wrote the name himself to save time. When even this got to be too slow, he reached out and hit each one over the knuckles with the pen instead of waiting for him to touch it.

When the sun was so high in the sky that its beams retreated from the center of the floor and barely reached over the sill, the agent stretched and yawned in the midday heat. "That's all of this I can stand until I get something to eat," he said as he rose. The interpreter asked my grandfather if he could come back in about the time it would take to smoke three pipes.

We went down the steps of the porch and out the front gate. Then I tugged at my grandfather's hand, and pulled him aside from the path, into the shade of a large tree. The agency building was east of the straggling line of stores, and a little above the level of the beach. I had never been up there before, and I wanted to look at the town spreading over the curve of the harbor.

But, once there, I watched only the noisy crowd that packed the village and the beach. A few white men in drab colors and soldiers in blue uniforms were hurrying along. But it was the red men among them I could not take my eyes from. Most of them were in the bright blues and reds of the gift clothing, so that at first glance I could not always tell them from the gaily dressed voyageurs. The sight disturbed me, but I did not know why, only that my people had become something strange. I was almost frightened as my eyes went from one to another in the queer garments. I sighed, and my grandfather looked down at me.

A thoughtful look came into his eyes. "I have seen Tecumseh sigh over the same thing," he said. It was many years before I understood what he meant.

"We shall go down now," said Grandfather, but I still held him back. A sudden lull came into all the noise below, for no reason—one of those unexplainable silences in the midst of commotion, when we often say, "A spirit is passing over the lodge." In the second's stillness, I heard the grating of a boat being pushed off the beach into the water. A group of boats was going out, voyageurs leaving for the distant winter camps.

In one boat I counted eight men among their packs.

Caps of fur sat above clean-shaved faces that now would be allowed to grow bearded again. Fringes of buckskin dangled from powerful arms, and fringes traveled down the sides of their buckskin trousers, ending above embroidered moccasins that had not yet seen the mud of their first portage. The kerchiefs around their necks made a moving rainbow of color as they swayed at their oars.

These voyageurs looked just like those we had seen on the Wabash, on the Mississippi, on the many little rivers we had followed in our canoes. We might meet these very ones in the approaching winter. The winter—that thought held me curiously. Except for a vague looking ahead to the next visit of my father, no thought of any time beyond the day just dawned had ever before taken hold of my mind. Past years crowded up to me, and I tried to set the next one against them. I began to wonder what would take the place in my mother's life of the hope of seeing the tall figure of my father come into our camp.

"Grandfather, will we go to the west again when we leave?"

He looked at me oddly, recognizing the unusual question.

"No, first to the east. We have another island to visit. At the Manitoolins the agent of the redcoats is waiting to make payment to the tribes that fought with your father on their side. Then we go to the wild-rice country —do you remember it?"

I did, and a picture came to my mind of women pushing their canoes among the tall stalks and pulling great armfuls of them over, and beating the rice off with the paddle to be caught in the bottom of the canoe. I remembered the rice broth, and the tender meat of wild ducks, taken where they came in large flocks to feed upon the rice. I frowned with the newness of casting my mind forward into the winter life.

With restless thoughts, I turned back to the rowers. They had paused, and were waving back at the shore.

"Good-by, Charlie," shouted someone at the wharf.

"*Bon voyage*—a good winter," called others.

The fringed arms took up the paddles, and the heavily loaded canoe sped away, light as a locust-seed on the waves. The boat song began and was joined in by the people on the shore.

> *"Par derrièr' chez mon père,*
> *Vole, mon cœur, vole—"*

The earliest music I had known, aside from the bird songs and running water, had been these same boat songs. It was to be many years before I knew how foreign to these streams they were, how they had come far through time and space, from the slopes of Normandy, two hundred years old, and now forgotten there. As I stood on that hillside at the age of eight, I thought the men made the songs up as they went along, so well did the rhythm fit the dip and rise of the paddle, slow for leisurely work, faster with short quick phrases for spurts. And of course many of them had been made up that way, as the voyageurs dipped paddles or tugged on oars, or ate their lyed corn and tallow around the campfire, recalling and weaving into their song an incident of the day, a joke on one of their number. In the open air, coming across the water, enhanced by the grace of the canoe flying before the wind, one could ask for nothing finer.

These men had visited Mackinac many times, and were not changed by it. Perhaps the Ojibways strutting about in their new finery, once away in the wild-rice country, would be just the same as they had been before. I was comforted by the thought, and smiled gratefully at the voyageurs. What I did not see was that their change had come long before, was completed now, while a new way of life was just unrolling across the

64

land of the Ojibways and I was seeing the edge of it creep upon them.

The boat song grew fainter with distance, until it was drowned out by the noise of the village. As the canoe went out of sight around the eastern point, Grandfather took a firm hold of my hand, grasped his bundle of goods, and we started down, making our way through the crowd before the narrow shops. We reached the mat-covered lodges, and Grandfather set his goods down before our own.

Ajawin motioned to us that she had cooked enough in her kettle for us to eat with her family. Red Storm Cloud had been the last one to receive his payments for the morning. Squatting before his own door, he was just loosening the knot of the white blanket and spilling its contents out. Bundles of cloth for leggings and breech-cloths, thread, needles, knives, combs, calico shirts, and tobacco fell in a confused mixture on the sand.

"*Ai-ee!*" he shouted. "For four years I have not had even a blanket for my children. Look!" He pulled a packet from his belt, and a handful of gold coins joined the heap on the beach. Ajawin's mouth fell open, and, dropping her wooden spoon, she fell to her knees to look at the coins closer, holding her hands carefully away.

"Here!" Red Storm Cloud swaggered. "They will not bite you." He forced one of them into her hand. When she found they neither stung nor burned, she made to take up another, and then two more.

Red Storm Cloud struck her hand with his fist. "Enough!" he shouted. "The rest I will take to the stores. Here, woman—this is your bundle."

She seized it and ran into the lodge. When she came out, her rags were gone, and she was strange in a dress of bright printed cotton, with ornaments in her ears, and green glass-set bracelets pulled over hands rough and calloused with toil. I frowned, but was comforted as I thought of the winter. In the woods the ornaments would be lost, the glass would break, the dress would be torn. Ajawin would soon be in her deerskins again. Everything would be all right when we were away from the island.

My grandfather waited in silence for the bringing of the soup kettle now simmering over a fire, untended, while Ajawin admired herself, and compared what she had on with the other garments she saw all along the colorful beach.

"I have to go back to the agent's lodge," said Grandfather after we had eaten. "You stay with your mother this time."

I nodded, and went into our lodge. Mother was up, and had put on her oldest clothing, a torn calico short-dress she had worn for picking berries. Her pretty blue blanket and silver armlets had been put away out of sight as not suitable for mourning.

"Come," she said. "Your grandfather has said that we are to leave the island tomorrow. We must go to see Marthe once more."

My mother looked strange, her face black and her old clothes standing out against all the bright finery of the beach. But everyone stood aside in respect as we passed.

The cottages around the point were sleeping in the sun as we came up to them. Low and bark-covered, they were almost like boats come to rest after a storm. A few nets were strung up to dry, and far down the row one boat was turned over on its side, and Michel was fitting in a new strip of wood. He waved at me, then turned back, whistling softly to himself as he worked.

Beside the second cottage, whitefish were laid to dry on a rack over a slow fire, and Marthe was turning them. She saw us as we came along, so we sat down on her steps and waited. Coming to join us, she picked up a roll of birchbark from the ground and began to peel off a

66

thin layer, quite as if she were alone. Then she doubled it four times, put it between her teeth, and began to bite it carefully. In the silence I watched Michel for a time, and the white gulls circling out over the water. The straits were blue with streaks of gray and green, and the distant passage into Lake Michigan stretched to meet the sky.

Just beyond Michel, Rosanne was playing by herself at the water's edge, picking little blue flowers. She put each one into her curls, and ran to admire herself in a pool of quiet water.

Marthe took the birchbark from her mouth at last, unfolded it, and held it to the light. A whole row of little girls appeared on it in pictures she had made by biting dents into the bark. As she handed them to me, her sleeve pulled up from her hand. I saw a fresh cut on her right arm, above the wrist. I put my finger on it before she had a chance to hide it again. "To let the sorrow out," she said. There was another cut on her left arm.

My mother held up her own wrists. "Please, Marthe."

Marthe rose and went into the cabin, but as one who didn't want to share something. She came back with a scalping knife, and pressed the sharp point into my mother's wrist. Mother's face showed no pain, but her arm jerked back a little as blood came, and a drop fell on my new deerskin dress. Then she was calm again, and held out her other arm. But Marthe shook her head, and laid the knife behind her on the bare wooden floor of the cabin. "You are weak," she said.

My mother watched the blood run slowly down her arm. "There is much grief to come out."

"Grief to come from all of us," said Marthe. Her voice was low and beautiful in contrast to the plainness of her looks. Her tones were almost plaintive, though she was unconscious of it, I am sure. It was the first time I had heard the mournful overtones that seem to hover

67

about the speech of those who have given up their natural mode of life, and are not quite at home in the one they have chosen.

"No fire was kindled on his grave. How can he be lighted on his road to the land of the dead?"

Marthe did not answer directly. "Did you hear Black Hawk say that Tecumseh knew it?"

"Knew—"

"That it was his last fight. Before he went into it he tore off the red-coated uniform of the white man and put on his own fighting clothes."

Mother began to rock back and forth slightly, looking at the wound on her arm. Marthe peeled another strip of bark.

Just then Jacques, Michel's dark-haired brother, came to the door of the next cabin. He was only ten, but he acted as if he were twice as old as I. When he saw me, he swaggered out like a voyageur, and motioned to me. I ran to see what he wanted. Behind him came a sturdy little boy of the moose totem of our tribe. His calico shirt, evidently a cast-off of some larger man, hung to his knees. He was muscular from the waist downward, and looked to have unbelievable strength in his legs.

"I call him Chase—*le chasseur*, you know," Jacques said, and I nodded. I was used to names that came from something unusual about one's body.

"Come on, Rosanne," Jacques called, his face brightening as he saw her. "We're going to play Chase's game."

Rosanne shook her head. When Michel was asked, he waved a hammer as a sign that he was too busy.

Chase drew out of his pocket a set of three red beans and one white one. He and Jacques took off their moccasins and Chase lined up all four on the beach, upside down. Jacques and I looked away while Chase put one bean under each moccasin. In turn then we guessed under which one the white bean lay, and Chase counted our correct guesses by scratches in the sand. As we played, I listened to what Mother and Marthe were saying.

"He was always away from me," my mother mourned.

"It had to be so," answered Marthe. "It was a great plan, to form a union of the tribes as the white men have done." She jerked her head backward in the direction of the village. "That piece of cloth on the fort is the totem of all the white men that drove away the redcoats, Baptiste says."

A few minutes later, I remember hearing Marthe say, "The tribes could keep their own totems, but Tecumseh wanted them to stop fighting among themselves and stand together against the wave of the white men. I heard him make a talk once. He asked the red man to give up whiskey, for it was a white man's drink. They should give up blankets and wear fur robes again. They should keep the fire burning in their lodges, and if it went out, make new fire with bow and firestick, not with flint and steel. They should not lose their own ways."

"He did make wonderful talk," agreed Mother.

"The Shawnees are a nation of much talk," said Marthe, "but none so strong as he. When Tecumseh spoke and cast his gaze on them, all others were silent. The tribes will now be like reeds lacking the touch of a weaver. They will not be firm like a well-woven mat, but will fall loosely apart. I wonder if anyone else will ever try to join them again?"

"And I could not even take from him the lock of hair —how shall I know him in the next world?" Mother went on in her own sorrow.

It was time for my last chance at guessing the right moccasin. I struck the first one sharply with my stick.

"I've won!" shrieked Jacques, when Chase lifted the moccasin to show one of the red beans.

The loser had to give up whatever he had on that the

other demanded. I drew my knees up on the sand and waited, willing to give up my beads, my bracelet, anything Jacques wanted. My grandfather would give me new ones.

"That little gold cross you wear under your dress," said Jacques. "I saw it once when you bent over."

I was startled. I had no idea he knew about that. The black robe in the forest mission had given it to me. But I had lost the game, so I pulled the slender chain from my throat, and over my head, untangling it when it caught on my braids. Jacques seized it in excitement. "Look, Rosanne!"

Mother saw the cross dangling from his fingers, and came running to us. "That's Oneta's!"

Jacques stood before her defiantly. "It is mine now."

Marthe was approaching slowly. "It is a white man's charm," she said scornfully. "But let Oneta keep it. There is no harm in being sure no evil spirit is waiting to pounce on the child when the charm is gone."

Jacques stiffened his lips and scowled.

"Here, I will give you something," said Mother. She drew out a small gold piece from her pocket. Jacques's eyes grew wide. He had never had so much money for himself. He dropped the cross willingly into her hand, took the gold piece, and started on a run to the village.

Mother put the chain back around my neck and held me close for a moment. "There is no harm in being sure," she echoed Marthe's words.

"What will you do now?" We were all sitting on Marthe's steps again, when she asked the question.

Mother twisted the fringes on the shoulder of my jacket. "I can live in my father's lodge."

"Your father is old. He may not live beyond this winter."

"He is well and strong."

"You know what must be done," Marthe accused.

"Now that it is known your husband is dead, you will have to choose another within a year."

"No," said Mother tearfully.

"It has to be that way," said Marthe. "Is there one you could look upon with favor?"

"No." Mother's hand was still on my shoulder, and I could feel a shudder go through her fingers. "Not after Tecumseh. No one can take his place."

Marthe's face filled with pain wrinkles. "How well I know that." Her usual calm voice broke.

Mother got up quickly and took me by the hand. Then she staggered, and almost fell. I tried to hold her up. "It is nothing," she said. "It is only from the fasting. I am not strong enough, not strong enough for anything."

Marthe looked at her, and then at me. Finally, as if to put off the moment of farewell, she said, "I will come and help you with the loading tomorrow."

As we went back along the shore to the lodge, the west wind came up and bent the little trees, and the lake was dark green with little specks in it.

Seven

❧ I have always been one to awaken early, when the day's sounds first begin, and I like to be out before the dew is gone, to see what changes the night has brought. Even at the age of eight it was hard for me to lie still in those wide-awake moments before the daylight spread through the openings in our roof. Openings were there in plenty, for mats were loosely spread on in summer, when chinks and crevices did not matter, and there was the large hole left in the top for the smoke to escape when a fire was built inside. In the early morning I could watch the stars fade and give way to a slice of sky, first gray, then blue with little clouds drifting across.

Since I was not allowed to get up until my grandfather woke, I used to slip quietly from my couch to my mother's and lie close to her in a silent companionship until the first rays of sun struck my grandfather's eyes. Those minutes with her gradually became the most precious of the day. Snuggled close and warm like a cub with its mother, I felt a delicious contentment. My mother's skin was as soft as milkweed down, but I felt something more than pleasure in its smoothness. I came close to the essence of her spirit. The only way of teaching she knew was to make herself what she wanted me to be. Lying close to her there, I knew she could restrain herself from moving for an entire day, if need be. If she were cold or hungry, she would be patient; if she were suffering, she would not cry out. I felt a strengthening in which I believe something of her character passed into mine. Many and many a time through the years I have awakened in those few minutes before daylight, and felt deeply, hopelessly, the need of a silent morning visit with my mother.

I like to think my father knew that spirit, too, and that the need of her pulled against that other need that drove him on from council to council, persuading, organizing. There must have been moments when he knew the peculiar loneliness of a leader, when the memory of her grace, her calm, her pretty little ways, must have made him homesick, when he wanted to give it all up, and live at ease in his lodge.

On the morning we were to leave the island, I slipped in beside her, to become instantly aware that something was wrong. Only her quick clasp of my hand kept me from speaking My mother's skin, usually so cool and soft, was fiery to the touch. Uneasily I settled down and lay there until my grandfather should stir beneath his buffalo skin. Without knowing my mother lay under

72

the bearskins in pain and great fever, he finally awoke and tossed off his covering. Beneath him was hard ground, for he could not risk losing his suppleness and hard strength by lying on soft branches.

Only when he had brushed his deerskin coat and leggings and arranged the eagle feathers in his hair, and stepped out of the lodge, did Mother release me from silence. I hurried out behind him. He had gone directly to the edge of the wide blue water, where he always went first in the morning to splash its coolness over his face. Early as it was, Marthe had already come and was sitting near-by on our overturned canoe. Her hands folded in her lap, she regarded each lodge-flap as it moved and someone came out, and it seemed that all the women in their gay calico were subdued by the eyes of that silent figure in a shabby dress. One or two spoke to her hesitantly. She answered only a word, and they scrambled back to their kettles. Everyone stood a little in awe of Marthe.

All along the beach there was a stir as the lodges awoke. The fresh breeze off the straits mixed with the smell of fish broth and baking corn cakes. Even while the women tended their kettles they began to take down the lodges, rolling up the mats, hampered by children running about and getting in the way in the excitement of departure. Marthe got up when my grandfather appeared, as if she would speak with him, but before she had a chance, I ran and tugged at his sleeve.

"Mother—her skin is burning!" I said.

A look of something very near contempt came over Marthe's face. Illness was weakness, to her, and showed a failure to live as one should. I had believed this before. My only sickness had come when I had eaten too much corn cake and maple sugar. But I was sure this was something different.

Marthe's fame as a healer had spread through our

73

whole tribe, and I began to feel easier when she plunged head-foremost into our lodge. My grandfather waited, anxious.

Marthe came back almost at once, smoothing down the folds of her calico shortdress, a gesture that was a sign of concern with her. "The Evil Spirit has his claws in her," she said softly. When one is near the water where they dwell one must speak cautiously of spirits, unless the water is frozen over so they cannot hear. "You will not be able to go for many days."

My grandfather looked down at the sand in thought. "My foot is on the path, and I must go. It is late; our canoes have been already too long out of water. We must go at once to the Manitoolin Islands."

"She cannot go," said Marthe.

My grandfather looked out over the water, as if he would summon an answer from the shimmering waves.

"You must leave her here."

Grandfather took this statement of Marthe's and turned all sides of it about in his mind. "We go to the Islands," he said thoughtfully, "and then to the wild-rice country along the river Ouisconsin. When the harvest is over, we go south along the great lake of the Illinois."

"Then come back for her on the way south," said Marthe.

"Before then we have five hundred miles, many portages, and we need time to gather the harvest." He considered the problem. "Still, I think we can be back in a month."

"Then in the moon of falling leaves you can return for her—and Oneta?"

"Oneta must stay here, too?" He frowned. "Yes, I'm afraid she must."

"The cabin next to mine is empty, since old Louis died two moons ago," said Marthe. "Your daughter and the child could live there."

"I can take care of Mother," I said. My grandfather smiled and laid his hand on my shoulder. "You and Marthe together could make her well," he agreed. "And we will be back before the winter's snow."

Grandfather seemed to think it was all settled, for in the woods a deserted lodge could be taken by anyone who wanted it. But Marthe knew that was not the white man's way. She waved her hand toward the saloon where Ajawin's husband had spent his gold coins. "The man in there owns the cabin. I have heard Baptiste say that old Louis had to pay money to him."

Grandfather took a packet from his belt, and spilled about half of his coins into Marthe's hands. "Will this be enough until I come back?"

She nodded.

"My daughter will also have money from the British —a 'pension,' Black Hawk called it when he told me. I am to arrange it when I meet the agent of the Great White Father at the Manitoolins. For that reason, too, I must not fail to go."

"They pay her for her husband as the Long Knives pay us for our land," said Marthe bitterly.

My grandfather was silent. Marthe turned abruptly and set out for home, with long, toed-in strides.

Ajawin beckoned for us to come to her fire for breakfast, but we shook our heads, and sat close together outside our lodge, waiting, miserable.

I looked across at Round Island where a heavy covering of pines and white birch rose in a perfect half-circle from the shores to the high place in the center. Smoke from the campfires of the lodges was rising in little clouds above the trees. A departing canoe pushed away from the shaggy bank. It was piled high with household goods, yet turned and moved as easily as a chip upon the foam-covered waves as it swerved to miss the long reef of sand and rock that stretched out from the edge of the island.

When Marthe came back, Baptiste was with her. "He will see about the cabin," she said.

"Too bad the poor girl's sick," said Baptiste, his narrow blue eyes full of sympathy. "My woman can make her well if anybody can, so don't you worry none." He looked closely at my grandfather. "Goin' north again, eh? Maybe, er—to that place where you get the brown metal?" Grandfather shook his head.

Baptiste wiped his red face on a bandanna. "Some day I'll get it out of her," he went on, jerking his head toward Marthe. "She could lead a man right to the stuff, *toute de suite.* Then we'd all be rich. But she's the stubbornest one. No use beating her to find out, either. I don't even try. But some day maybe I'll bring her around to it. Well, I'll go on and see about the cabin." He limped across the beach to the saloon, his feet crunching unevenly on the stones.

Ajawin came to help Marthe take down our lodge, for her own canoe was loaded and ready, her husband loafing beside it, waiting. She put her baby in its wooden frame beside me. Its black eyes peered out between the good luck images dangling from the arch over its head. I brushed away a fly that annoyed it.

The two women worked silently, rolling the mats on sticks, as in this day you may have seen housewives arrange their best starched lace doilies around a rolled-up newspaper. The lodge-poles they stored in the bottom of the canoe, forming a backbone for the light birch-bark craft. Kettles and blankets and rolls of mats were piled in next, with a space left in the end for my grandfather.

The beach was gradually becoming empty, except for scattered leavings of bark and scraps of food, discarded rags, broken ornaments, gaudy and soiled bits of cloth, all trodden into the sand and pebbles. The row of canoes stood ready to go, a long line of them down the beach.

"It's all right," Baptiste shouted above the noise of

excited children and barking dogs as he came back. "She can move right in."

Ajawin had taken down the lodge from over my mother, leaving her on the couch. The breeze stirred in the fur robe and blew her hair back from her burning cheeks. Baptiste took charge. "Here, bring back a couple of those poles. We can take this here bearskin and make a litter to carry her on."

Marthe brought the poles, and Baptiste fastened the bearskin to them with cord from his pocket. When my mother had been laid upon it, Ajawin finished the packing and swung her baby up on her back. All the others now sat in canoes, waiting for the chief to go first. Above the bright new clothing their simple brown faces showed no regret that their holiday was over, that they must go back to a harder life. I knew that most of the gold coins they had received had stayed right here on the island, where the shopkeepers had them in return for a little pork, a little clothing, a little rum. Being people who scarcely planned beyond the next sunset, accustomed to subsist on whatever the surroundings offered —they had done the same on Mackinac.

Grandfather drew me to stand beside my mother. She lay quietly on the bearskin, her face reddened under the black streaks of mourning, her hair in disorder.

"Have courage, daughter. Marthe will make you well before we start our long journey." His words brought no answer from my mother, only a gasp as if her breath was cut off as she tried to speak.

Grandfather turned to me. He smoothed down my hair on each side of the part. His hands were so large they almost encircled my head like a ball. "Keep your hair this way, shining like a raven's wing," he said. I put my cheek against his sun-hardened arm, clinging to him until he had to go.

As I record this it comes to me that none of the important things I had been taught were mentioned be-

77

tween us. The ideals that had been my first lessons—
courage, truth, hospitality, bravely to suffer, bravely
die—these ideals he knew I had taken into myself from
his code as the corn draws nourishment where its roots
lie, and he said nothing about them.

I held back tears in my eyes as he climbed alone into
our canoe. Ajawin waved at me from the next one, her
blackened teeth grimacing in a way she meant to be en-
couraging. She sat crowded among boxes and odd-shaped
packs, her two boys and three girls, a dog and its two
puppies. As her husband pushed the canoe away and
leaped in, the gunwale almost dipped beneath the water.

My grandfather gave the signal, and the loaded canoes
shot live-winged away from the shore, as if eager themselves to reach the Manitoolins. The most comfortable
seat on top of the heap of household goods in Gray
Wolf's canoe was given to the little spotted dog that
had helped find Rosanne. When he saw me, his one stiff
ear twitched, and his tail wagged. As the canoes straightened into a line and turned to the east, a tear at last es-
caped and ran down my cheek.

Part Two

One

❖ Our cabin was the first one on the western shore around the point. It was perhaps thirty feet from Marthe's, and hers stood the same distance from Louise's on beyond.

Seeing the wild grape vine climbing over the low, bark-covered cabin, holding it to the earth, I remember thinking it was the first home I had known that had stayed in one place long enough for a vine to grow on it. On the inside, mortar had been smeared between the logs, and dried moss stuffed in where the mortar had fallen out. Cobwebs draped the slanting roof timbers, and dust lay heavy everywhere. A piece of ragged carpet sprawled over the bare, stained boards in front of the dark stone fireplace. A few tin pans, cups, and plates were scattered over narrow shelves and the rough pine table. A box marked INDIAN GOODS sat on end to hold a washbowl and a gourd of soft soap, dried and shrunken around the edges.

Baptiste and Marthe laid my mother on the corn-husk

mattress of the low bed built into one corner, and put the bearskin over her. I rubbed clean a spot on one of the small window panes and watched them go out to the space between our cabin and their own. Baptiste had cleared some leaves from a little hole in the ground, and Marthe brought a kettle of water that fitted into it, its top level with the ground. She brought out an armful of blankets, and some minutes later a hot stone from her fireplace, throwing it into the water, which hissed as it received it and began to send up steam.

Returning to our cabin, Marthe quickly took off my mother's clothing and rubbed her chest with bear's grease, and wrapped her in a large gray blanket. She lifted Mother in her arms and carried her out. Baptiste held a small stool at the edge of the sunken kettle, and Marthe put Mother on it above the rising steam. Then they wrapped blankets, tent-like, around her except for her head, layer after layer of them, so the steam was kept inside.

After a time Baptiste reached into the kettle, pulled out the stone and took it into their cabin for reheating, bringing out another. Shadows had shrunk with the coming of midday before they finished. I stayed without question at the window, for Marthe had told me I must not go outside. If they did drive the evil spirit out, she didn't want it to see me.

Finally she said, "Enough." Wrapping Mother in all the blankets, she carried her back to the bed, covering her closely, with the bearskin over all. Mother was breathing a little easier, but her face was more flushed than ever. From her own cabin, Marthe brought something for my mother to swallow. It must have been bitter, for her mouth twisted as she drank it.

"That will sicken the spirit if it is still in you," said Marthe. She sat on a broken-backed chair and waited. From time to time she offered a cup of the brew to Mother, who drank it obediently.

82

In the evening Mother took a little of the soup Marthe brought. "Do you think it is all right for me to break my fast so soon?" she whispered feebly.

"You must eat. You are weak," said Marthe.

The next day, Mother was stronger, and sat up for a little while. A week later, she was almost as well as ever, and began to look forward to Grandfather's coming for us. Baptiste brought fish every day, and with her coins Mother bought corn and fat and potatoes from the village stores. We carried dead branches from the wooded heights, and at night we piled them high in our fireplace for love of the color of the blaze, marveling that no smoke came out in the room. By daylight, the fire shrank to little flames, busy below our kettle.

The moon of falling leaves came, a mellow autumn with the soft mist of Indian summer. Smoke from the pipes of long-gone warriors, Marthe said it was. The freezing moon came, and Mother began to worry. "The ice will come," she said, "and then it will be too late to make the journey to the shores of the big river."

Baptiste came to tell us it was time to pay for the cabin again, and went away thoughtful when he heard Mother's coins were all gone. The idea of money that must be paid every moon for a place to live was new to us, and it began to haunt my mother.

"Marthe, how can I get more gold pieces?" she asked one day, with puzzlement in her voice that one should need such a thing.

We were in front of our cabin, and Marthe was at the edge of the water, washing a pair of trousers covered with fish scales and seaweed, and the tar Baptiste used on his oarlocks. She lifted the trousers, heavy with water, and dropped them in a heap on the beach. "Baptiste and I will share with you."

"You have no more than enough for yourselves," said Mother.

83

Marthe's deep-set eyes looked out over the straits, as if she were hoping my grandfather would appear at that moment.

"Some of the women from the Ottawa village who are well-favored in looks work at the fort, where the ladies pay them to cook and sweep their rooms," she said at last. "But I would wait until ice fills the straits and your father cannot come."

Mother laid her hands on the waist of her torn calico. "Do you think I might wear something else when I go to see those ladies?"

"Are you so ready to give up your mourning?" asked Marthe bitterly.

Mother's dark eyes were not far from tears, but her face was determined.

Marthe softened. "Put on your deerskins again, and do not blacken your face. Whenever we have dealings with the white ones, we have to give up something." She sighed. "But you need not go yet. Baptiste and I can share with you until the ice comes."

Marthe spread the trousers on a flat rock, and padded across the stony beach to her cabin. Then she turned and told me she was going to the woods, and when she came back we would go in the canoe to gather rushes for mats.

As soon as Marthe was out of sight, Mother washed her face, put on her best deerskins, and combed and braided her hair. Taking Jacques with her, she started along the beach road, casting fearful glances ahead and up to the fort on the heights. Jacques could help her talk to the strange ladies. He had already learned our language. He knew he would need it when he became a voyageur.

With nothing to do but wait for Marthe, I sat down on the steps of her cabin. I had been taught that it was good for one just to sit and wait—one learned patience that way. I knew Marthe had gone after herbs and roots, which she found in her own secret places. After hours spent in the interior of the island, trudging over the knolls and digging in the woods, she would bring back a basket filled with pokeroot, balm and wintergreen, and the bark of the ironwood and the red willow.

The view across the straits was not the same as from the village beach, for there the trees of Round Island and Bois Blanc, and the gray line of the mainland stopped any far-looking. Here one's gaze could slip through the channel between the mainland and Point St. Ignace and see the endless water in which the sun went down at night. When my grandfather came, we would go out through that channel, for beyond was the great lake of the Illinois. And beyond that were many things—there was the great river I remembered, flowing wide and deep, the old and wise father of all the rivers. Farther west than that I had not been, but when members of other tribes had sat around our fire, I had heard that on beyond were wide prairies and the mountains of the gods with strangely glistening tops that the white men said were only snow. But our people knew better, and worshiped as they should.

I watched the lithe birch canoes and the heavy mackinaw sailboats crossing from Point St. Ignace opposite, and the gulls wheeling above the deserted beach. The straits lay before me in bars of blue and gray and transparent green, with each wave golden where it met the sun. A ridge of pines on St. Ignace made a green fringe between the water and the deep blue of the sky. High above sounded the call of wild geese on their way to the south, and in a tree in the waste stretch of beach beyond Louise's cabin a belated land-bird made scornful answer. I turned to see what kind he was.

It was then I saw the strange man. He had not come by the beach path, but straight across from the village, over the meadow, a way we never used. It looked like any meadow with a hill rising at its back, but we knew it was an old burying ground. Under its sod lay countless men of the early tribes, their heads to the rising sun. Only a white man would walk across and disturb them.

This one was young, tall, and very pale, as if his skin had never felt the touch of the sun. His clothes were of fine blue cloth, broadcloth I suppose it was, and there was lace at his throat and cuffs. His legs were in black silk stockings, his feet in black leather shoes, and there was not a wrinkle to be seen. From head to foot his clothes lay as smooth on him as the skin on a deer.

He came down the little slope into the space between Marthe's cabin and the next, and paused for a minute, looking out over the water. He took off his beaver hat, but the breeze did not move the brown hair that lay in even waves from his forehead to the back of his neck where it was cut as straight across as its curliness would allow. I had never seen such sleekness of wavy hair. His skin was almost as transparent as the Mackinac waters, and yet there was no kinship between him and this island. He looked like one just alighted from a boat, one who would soon go back into another world, a world I had never been told about.

He did not see me there on Marthe's steps, so I went on staring at him. Indeed, I could not help it. There was something more to this man than his finery, and something familiar in the way he carried himself. As he turned his back to me and started for Louise's cabin, I knew what it was. My grandfather walked like that, showing his intense self-respect, his pride of rank and family. That was it—pride holding his head erect, his lean body straight.

Before he reached the steps, Louise came running out, her hands fluttering up to straighten her white frilled cap.

"Oh, M'sieu Pierre," she said. "Come in while I get your washing. It is not yet in the basket."

"I shall wait here," he answered courteously in French, as she had spoken to him. His voice was low and clear, like the tones of Armand's violin.

"Then please sit down," Louise drew up a bench, and dusted it hastily with her apron.

"No. I prefer to stand."

"Oh, then I'll hurry." Louise went in, ruffled and fussing in her movements. Almost at once she was back with a round basket in her hands. The young man bowed as he took it.

"I am so sorry, but your shirts were hanging up to get the dampness out after the ironing. I had to fold them—"

The man she had called Pierre made a polite gesture to stop her apology. "It was nothing. You were really very quick," he said.

"I hope you will like the way I have ironed them. I have never done any with so many pleats and ruffles before—"

"I am sure they will be all right. And how much is it this time?"

"Always the same. I charge two dollars a week for a single man, and four for a married couple."

He handed out two bits of green paper from his pocket, and I saw that his hands were long and slender. The hands puzzled me, and I kept my eyes on them as he took up his basket ready to go.

"I trust your husband is well," he said politely, and made as if to put on his hat and turn away.

"Oh, thank you, M'sieu. He is always well. Did you not see him at the ball last night?"

Pierre looked as if he were trying to remember.

"He is one of the fiddlers," she reminded him. "But then, I saw you with the charming Josette on your arm. I do not blame you for seeing no one else. Such a beautiful girl. I saw her get off the boat when she and her mother came up from the trading post at Grand Haven three weeks ago."

Pierre tried to leave again, but Louise beamed on him so he could not find a chance to get away.

"Yes, indeed. Her mother seems an unusual woman."

"Oh, yes, M'sieu. All up and down the lakes they talk about how she took over the trading post after her husband was knifed by that rum-crazed Winnebago. May his soul rest—" she murmured and made the sign of the cross.

Pierre took a firm grasp on the basket again, as if leave this time he must. "Yes, yes—" he said, taking a few steps backward. I saw then what it was that puzzled me about his hands. No large knuckles or calloused spots marked their whiteness, no marks were laid on them by work. How had he handled fish-line or hunting knife or followed a brambled trail or lifted packs or paddled canoes with no little cuts or bruises, scratches or hardened spots? I drew my knees up under my chin in thought. I had never known anyone who did nothing with his hands.

Louise was not to be stopped, or drawn away from the subject. "She's an ambitious woman, that Madame La Framboise. And she has brought up her daughter Josette to be such a charming girl. She is lucky to have such a fine gentleman as you to pay her attention, if you don't mind my saying—"

"Mademoiselle Josette is ambitious, too. She has decided to marry Major Pierce, the commandant of the fort," Pierre said coldly, slipping his basket over his arm again and turning away so that his gray eyes passed over me, but without seeing me at all.

Louise clapped her palms to her mouth, speechless. But she didn't need to say anything. With his last words, the young man strode away over the same path he had come.

Two

&c. "I'm going to stay with Louise," said Rosanne as Marthe and I, paddles in hand, were getting into the canoe. "I hate gathering rushes." A beam of sunlight flashed across her dark curls as she lowered her chin ready to resist if Marthe should oppose her.

Marthe nodded. "When the shadow of that big rock reaches the little one," she pointed with her paddle at two stones near the water's edge, "you will put the kettle on."

Rosanne laughed. "Mother, *other* people don't tell time that way. Why don't you have Father buy us a clock?"

"The sun and the seasons have always been good timekeepers," said Marthe.

"Well, I'm not going to run and watch shadows. Louise is teaching me to hemstitch."

We were so far from shore then that Marthe could not make reply without shouting. She paddled in silence, taking short strokes that matched mine. She was strong, and if she had been paddling alone, each of her strokes would have driven the bow of the canoe entirely out of the water.

Except for one mackinaw boat, the straits were deserted. All along the shore and up the slopes to the high center of the island the autumn brightness of color blended and shifted with hidden shadows. Vines came down from above as if they would clothe the naked rock. Fallen leaves, caught in the long grass, stood on end and danced, trying to shake themselves free to run away before the wind. The old Irish cobbler stuck his beard out of his cave and snorted in disgust when he saw we were moccasin-wearing people. Paddling stead-

89

ily on, we came to a high bare rock standing far above the lake. Marthe sang a song about an Ojibway girl who had jumped from it to her death.

Stopping there to pull rushes, Marthe handed them to me to arrange in a neat pile in the bottom of the canoe. As we drifted on, I laid the rushes flat, straightening the curves in them where the tops had bent toward the water. They would be glad to be kept from the winter's ice, I thought, and be made into things of beauty and live with Marthe in the warm cabin.

I remembered a story Marthe had been telling me the day before, which hadn't had a satisfactory end. Her stories seldom did. They were like the run of notes on a flute, throbbing, then quickly silent, the melody resolved into nothing.

"You were telling me about my birth, and the falling stars. And then what happened?"

But Marthe could not be led back to a story she had left off telling. I would have to wait until she came back to it of herself, when she would begin anywhere in the events that struck her and end in the same fashion. I had to put the fragments together to get the whole of it.

So when she spoke, she did not answer my question. "They have all gone back to their hunting, their corn-planting, their fighting with other tribes, forgetting the great plan of Tecumseh." Suddenly she turned and looked at me. "You are all there is left of Tecumseh on this earth." Sadness tore at the words, pulling them from her heart.

But I was thinking of something else. "Marthe, is there a world where people do not use their hands?" I asked.

"No. There is always work for hands," she said. "But some people do not use them for our kind of work. The officers at the fort, and their women—"

M'sieu Pierre was not from the fort. His clothing

was not like the uniforms I had seen coming down the incline to the village. I must remember to ask Louise about him.

My brief thought of the fort reminded me that my mother had gone there, and I worried a little about her.

"Marthe, is money something important?"

"It is becoming so, even to our people," she said. "It was not so in the early days. Then people lived from what they could grow or catch or make themselves. Or they traded with their neighbors to get something different from their own."

"Talk to me, Marthe. Talk about the early days."

So Marthe told me of the old times, the days when only the French had come. And the days when there were no white men at all were like an age that one could hardly believe ever existed, it was so splendid a time. Ever since that day whenever I have handled rushes I have heard some quality of Marthe's voice in them.

I thought no more about the white man called Pierre until that evening when Baptiste and Armand came in with their fish. I looked at their baggy brown trousers, calico shirts faded from sweating, and noticed their sleeves rolled up and their trousers legs turned up to keep them out of the water in the boat. They jumped to the shore in bare feet.

"Hello, there," Armand called to me. "What are you staring at?"

I could not tell him it was their clothes, and that I was thinking of others I had seen that day. I turned and went back in the cabin. That evening I got out one of my rolls of birchbark and made a picture of a man, putting a hat on him to show he was a white man. I stored it on the lower shelf of the cupboard beside the one showing Gray Wolf and his dog.

Three

❧ That night Mother came back happy. "I am going to work for one of the fort ladies," she said. "And, Oneta, you never saw such a house as the one I've been in. Under foot was a carpet so soft it was like walking on grass in the spring, but it was dark red, and long strips of cloth to match it hung on each side of the windows, and—" Mother stopped for breath.

"Have you been there all day?" I asked.

"Oh, yes." Mother almost sang. "This morning Jacques and I went to the door of that house, and a tall thin woman opened it. The surgeon's wife, Jacques said. He told her what I wanted, and she looked at me for a moment, and then asked me to come in. 'I'm glad you came,' she said. 'We need an extra woman right now. You may begin at once.'

"There is to be a big wedding feast," Mother chattered on, "and I am to help get ready for it, and if I do well, I am to work after that in the bride's home, the home of the girl who is marrying the chief."

"Mademoiselle Josette," I said.

Mother looked at me curiously. "Where did you hear the name?"

I told her about the young white man and his talk with Louise. But Mother didn't pay much attention.

"I will get money from this lady," she said contentedly.

Neither one of us thought of wondering how much. We could give it to Baptiste to pay the man at the saloon and we could stay in the cabin. That was all we thought about.

Mother came and went every day after that, bringing home talk of the doings at the fort. As I look back,

I know she didn't understand what she had seen any better than I could picture it from her words, as she tried to describe the knitting and crocheting, the card-playing and gossiping such ladies filled their time with, while the men who weren't on sentry duty hunted and fished or had card games of their own. There were festivities in the evening we knew, for sometimes two or three soldiers, arm in arm and singing a song about "Benny Havens, O," came around the point to ask Armand and Baptiste to bring their fiddles and play for the dancing.

Autumn was passing on the heights of the island. The nearest maple began to turn yellow and scarlet, and as if the box of paints were passed from one to another, colors deepened and spread back across the heights, picking out the hardwoods from the evergreens for a brief time of glory. Each day they grew more brilliant, and then all the color was fading on the ground, and the branches were bare above, while the pine, the cedar and balsam stood unchanged in their cool dark green. They had kept what they had, and knew it was good.

Cold winds foretelling the coming blizzards had hurried all the boats away to reach the snugness of winter quarters. Then the ice formed and was broken again by the current into great cakes which piled up against one another and the shore, freezing that way into blue mountains of ice, sparkling in the sun.

Mother, caught up in the excitement of her new work at the fort, seemed not to be worried because Grandfather had not come. "The harvest may have taken so long there was not time to come back this way," she said one evening. "He will return in the moon of flowers, or the strawberry moon. We can tell him that we have not had to eat from Marthe's kettle the whole time."

I stayed with Marthe most of the time while Mother

was gone. I remember that Baptiste, like many of the villagers, hired a sledge and four dogs from someone on the mainland and spent most of his time hauling wood over the ice from Bois Blanc. Looking out of the window of Marthe's cabin, I saw the strange white man again six times that winter when he came to Louise's cabin for his shirts. He must have arranged it himself, this coming for his basket, or Jacques and Michel would have taken it to his house on their sled. Knowing Pierre as I did later, I often wondered why, and could only think that he was lonesome, having cut himself off from the circle of the fort and the fur company when the new wife of the commandant became its center. And Louise and Armand had a home people liked to be in. They were lively and good-natured, and Armand was an artist on the violin that hung in every Frenchman's cabin.

Louise told us his story one evening when Mother and I went with Marthe to get Rosanne at bedtime, as she had to do nearly every night. I didn't understand all of the story then, but pieced something of it together from what I heard that night and later. I had known that many Frenchmen came from the north and east of us, in the land called Canada. Louise and Armand themselves had come from there. But Louise said there was a country, far across the wide water toward the rising sun, where French was spoken even before it was in Canada, and Pierre had come from that far land. He had lived in a great city hundreds of times as big as Mackinac village, where the houses were big and fine, and even the shops stood tall and beautiful in stone and bricks.

Pierre's father had been a great man. He rode in a coach with gilt upon it, and servants rode behind. I kept asking about this coach, and as Louise told of it I saw in my mind a cabin on wheels, drawn by deer or buffalo.

In this fine city not everyone rode in coaches. Many poor people were there, too, and they got angry at the people who did. They started on the warpath, and Pierre's father had to run from the city or he would have had his head cut off.

I did not understand that either. So Louise explained about the guillotine, its tall heavy frame, the big knife that cut off one's head. As she talked I tried to imagine what this weapon was like, comparing it with the slender scalping knife. I remember thinking it must have been hard to carry such a big thing when they chased their enemies. When I said something about it, Louise laughed. They didn't carry it, she said, It stayed in one place, and they had to catch their enemies and take them to it.

That seemed so awkward a way to do that I wasn't surprised when she said they didn't catch Pierre's father. He hid in a boat until it sailed, he and his wife and the baby, Pierre. They came to Quebec in Canada, and the father worked there, writing letters for a rich man and taking care of his books.

There Pierre had grown up, and his father had died. When Mr. Stuart of the fur company was in Quebec signing up new voyageurs, he looked about for a book-keeper, to go to Mackinac with a boat-load of goods and stay and work for him. He wanted someone who could speak French, who could buy from the French traders at Detroit and Mackinac. He had met Pierre and offered the place to him.

Pierre's mother had stayed in Quebec and he had not seen her now for over a year. The young aristocrat had been very popular with the best people on the island, Louise sighed, until his pride had made him stay away from them since Mademoiselle Josette had become Madame Pierce.

The winter passed quickly. In Marthe's cabin I learned mat-weaving, beadwork, and embroidery, and more of the art of picture-writing. Marthe made deerskin moccasins while she helped me, telling me stories while her fingers worked. She could sell all the moccasins she made, but she spent so much time on each pair, curing the leather, choosing the embroidery pattern, sorting beads and dyeing the porcupine quills, and finishing the whole with such exactness that she never had many pairs to sell.

It seemed but a little time until the warm winds came, and the ice broke up and was swept out of the channel by the current. Then one day Marthe and I saw a robin on the beach. Marthe stopped and listened intently to its song. Then she smiled. "That means a happy summer," she said.

"Why?" I asked.

"When the robin's song is a laughing one, there will be peace and enough to eat. When it is harsh, there will be war and trouble. The robin is a young girl of our tribe who died from too long fasting. She asked that her spirit might go into a bird, and that she might come back to her people every spring and tell them what the year would hold. She painted her breast red as a promise that she would always come, and that we may know her."

When Baptiste took the dog team back to the mainland, he came back with two doe skins. Rosanne, grown tall and long of legs, met him and exclaimed over them. "They are beautiful! So white! For me, *mon père?* They *must* be for me."

Baptiste let them slip out of his hands, and she held them up against the front of her green striped calico dress. "A coat for me!" she said eagerly. "I shall be lovely in it."

"Well, now, I'm sorry, *bébé*. Not for you."

They had approached the steps where Mother and I sat with Marthe.

"They're for Oneta. That little Chase boy that plays with Jacques when his folks come over to sell their potatoes—he sent 'em to her, when he heard she was still here. 'I give skins for Tecumseh's papoose a coat,' he told me."

Mother's eyes grew soft, and she put her arm around me. "You are a lucky girl," she said. "All your life people have been kind to the child of Tecumseh."

Marthe rose to turn the meat drying on a rack nearby.

"They should be used for a new jacket," she said. "That old one is too small for you. You have begun to grow." As if I were corn that had stopped for a time, and then with rain and sunshine had begun to lengthen again.

Rosanne was still holding the skins. Suddenly she threw them down on the sand by my feet. "Take the old skins. I won't wear anything but wool coats any more. Louise is going to help me make a coat of gray wool like the village girls wear."

She turned away indifferently, and then ran and disappeared into Louise's cabin.

Baptiste picked up the two skins. "Here, Oneta, stand up and let's measure 'em on you."

I stood up and let him hold the skins against me

" 'Pears to me they'll just make you a nice jacket." He stood looking at me. "You're gettin' tall. 'Most as big as your mother, though that ain't as big as it might be. You'll soon be as much of a size as a pair of moccasins."

I did all the embroidery on the new jacket myself. All the edges of the fine white skins were finished with fringe, and a border of red and white beadwork ran down the sleeves and both sides of the open front. The night I put it on was the warmest one of that spring, and everyone in the fishing row was out on the front steps of the cabins. Mother and I went over to Marthe's to show my work.

97

"Say, I like that. All them colored bands on the white. I like lots of red," said Baptiste.

I pulled back the front to show how on the inside I had worked in black thread the totem of Mother's tribe, the long-necked bird with the collar about his throat.

"That's nice, too," said Baptiste. He reached over and seemed about to swing me up on his knee as he had always done, and then changed his mind, and just drew me close to him. "You look too much like a young lady in that," he explained. "But about that loon—you know, he's a funny bird. He's a lonesome, a melancholy bird, but he's got a lot of sense. We can learn something from him. The way he's made, he can't walk much, so he don't get out on land—you never seen one on land, did you?—He don't get out of the water unless he has to. A lesson to some of us to stay where we're meant to be."

I scarcely listened to what Baptiste was saying, for just beyond on Louise's steps, I had seen Pierre. He was visiting with Louise while Armand tuned his violin inside. As soon as I could get away from Baptiste, I went over and settled down in front of the cabin to play with the two boys and Rosanne. Pierre was wearing the same clothes as before, except that his white shirt had little folds down the front instead of the ruffles. He sat on the steps, not sprawling as everyone else did, but erect, like a chief in council. He looked more than ever like one who would not be staying long. Though he talked and laughed with Louise, and with Armand through the door, he seemed to hold himself away from them a little.

Jacques pulled the red and white beans out of his pocket for his favorite game, but I shook my head, feeling the cross against my skin as a warning. "Let's make houses," I said.

Jacques agreed. He liked that next best. I began making a set of round houses with curved tops like the eggs Mother sometimes brought from the store. I dug a little

98

pool in front of them, making myself a little lake of my own, cut away from the great body of the straits, its size right for my lodges. That must have been the way the great spirit had made the big lakes, then dragged his finger across between them to make the straits so he could go from one to another to tend his beaver traps, as Marthe had told me.

From bits of driftwood stacked like logs, Jacques was building a set of square houses he called a trader's winter camp. He made a river past it, and a path in front of it crossing the river. "I will sell to the Indians when they cross here," he said.

I looked at his work. "They would not cross there," I told him, "because here"—I pointed to another place— "the river is narrower."

"Oh, *sacré diable*," he shouted, and did not heed the gentle reproof that came from Louise. "They'll cross where I tell 'em. I can't move my camp. Here, I'll dig the river wider all along so this *is* the narrow place."

When Louise spoke to her son, Pierre had looked at us. I watched without seeming to, to see if he had noticed me. I felt that I had to make him see me, so long had I watched him without seeing his eyes light on me. And they were on me now.

"Who is that child in the white coat? I didn't know the Indians had come in yet."

I heard Louise explain about Mother and me. He turned away indifferently, and began to talk to Armand again. With a sinking feeling I saw that the name of Tecumseh meant nothing at all to him.

Violin notes began to come from both cabins now, for Baptiste had gone inside and was tuning his fiddle too. The very first boats had come in, and there was to be a dance in the village. Baptiste was humming as he played as if he couldn't get all he felt into the notes, and perhaps he couldn't, for he was always complaining that his fingers were getting stiffer than they used to be. Louise talked along in her usual lively way, and the white man sat contented, dreamily listening to her and to the violin notes. Scraps of tunes from one cabin were taken up by the fiddle in the other, and then turned into another tune, as if to say, "Yes, we'll play that, and how about this one?"

Whenever a tune grew long enough, Jacques kept jumping up from play and going into a little dance on the beach, shaking his heels about as I had seen the voyageurs do the first time they heard a fiddle when they landed from the boats.

Rosanne sat contented, doing nothing at all. "You are to live in my house when it is done," Jacques had told her, and she sat with toes curled under her, watching and telling him what to do—to make it bigger, or not quite so near the river.

"I wish I weren't going, but Mr. Stuart has no one else to send just now," I heard Pierre say.

"Marthe," called Louise. "I'll bet you can help this gentleman. He has to make a long canoe trip—up to St. Mary's and over the long portage around the rapids and then on to a post on the Ontanagon. The fur company has bought out a trader there."

"Squeezed him out, most likely," came a growl from Armand within. "They're makin' it hot for the free traders—"

Louise ignored him. "M'sieu Pierre is to see that the man turns over all property and attaches himself to the company," she went on. "He is looking for some good canoe-men. All the regular ones are working. You know all the Indians on the beach—couldn't you get someone for him? The company will pay well—"

Marthe came over slowly to answer Louise. "I will go tomorrow and see who has come in."

"See, M'sieu," said Louise. "It's all fixed. You just go ahead and get your provisions ready."

"Really, I know nothing at all of that. I suppose Mr. Stuart will see that whatever I need is put up."

Mother had followed Marthe so quietly that Louise hadn't seen her before, small as she was behind Marthe's greater bulk. "Oh, hello there. M'sieu, this is the young woman I was telling you about—the mother of the child in the white jacket."

Pierre stood up and bowed. He stared at my mother for the time it takes a leaf to fall from a tree to the ground, and then offered her a place on the step, but she moved away to sit on the beach at a polite distance, as Marthe had already done. Her pretty brown face had its own color now, and her hair was neat, with little red bands upon it that matched the sprigs of flowers in the calico dress she wore to work at the commandant's. In the last days she had been too tired to change back into the rags of mourning at night.

"That was the first time I ever saw your mother," Pierre said to me years later, "and I couldn't tell you what she wore. She was adorned by her goodness. Kindness and modesty stood around her like a silken cloak," he said. There was always something about her that he couldn't grasp, and I know he felt it over and over again. And yet she was not mysterious. I understood all of her, animals understood her, and even the trees and corn were near to her. Whenever she built a fire its crackling was like a sweet song of her own. Perhaps that was it—perhaps Pierre had never known anyone simple and unmixed before, anyone who always did what her instinct told her.

Louise had been looking at Pierre's shoes, polished to a bright shininess, marred only by traces of dust from the meadow. "You should have moccasins on a trip like that," she said. "Marthe, don't you have some that would fit him?"

"Oh, no, I couldn't wear moccasins," he said.

Watching, I knew more than ever that the difference in this man was not all in his clothes. His speech and manner set him apart. His voice was soft, but it was not the warm softness of Indian voices. It was cold and rather high. Something about it reminded me of frost that looks beautiful and invites you to touch it, and then freezes you when you do.

"Oh, but you'll have to wear moccasins on a canoe trip—we all do," insisted Louise. "Marthe—"

Marthe looked at Pierre's feet. "Long and very narrow," she murmured. "But I have one pair, made long ago—I'll bring."

Though Pierre began to protest again, Marthe was already on the way to her cabin and did not stop. Baptiste passed her, coming out with his fiddle under his arm, wrapped in a square of gray wool. He whistled. Armand called out, *"Oui, toute de suite,"* and came out with his own fiddle.

"It's time we were going," said Baptiste. "They'll be down here after us, the whole crazy lot of 'em."

"Coming along, Louise?" Armand strolled down the steps, lazily smiling down at her. She looked up at his lean figure, his dark hair as unruly as Jacques's. *"Mais, oui!"* she laughed happily, her voice feeling already the good time she would have. "I would not miss a dance—but I'm going to talk to M'sieu Pierre."

Pierre got up. "No, no. Go right along with them. I must go back, anyway."

Baptiste stopped and looked at Pierre good-naturedly. He had seen Pierre staring at my mother. "Haven't seen you at the dances lately, M'sieu Debans. Not since I used to see you with the beautiful Mademoiselle Josette on your arm—hmm." He stopped short. "Sorry."

Pierre's face had reddened a little.

"If I was you," began Baptiste. "Well, why not console yourself? Copper's a good color—sometimes it wears better than pink and white."

Baptiste turned, chuckling, and went away with Armand along the beach path. Louise ran after them, waving to us.

Pierre rose abruptly and picked up his basket to go. Mother, who had understood nothing of what had been said, except that Marthe had murmured to her that this man was going on a long trip, spoke softly.

"May your canoe touch no snags or sand-bars, no drifting logs or sharp-toothed rocks."

Jacques came out of the cabin in time to hear. "That's a nice thought," he said, and repeated it in French to Pierre. "Hope it keeps you out of trouble." He laughed, and ran after Louise and the men.

Reddening again, Pierre swung about and looked at my mother. She was looking at the pebbles beyond her spreading calico skirt. "Thank you. You are very kind." He drew a little away toward the path to the village, but stopped as if he were not anxious to set foot upon it. He seemed a lonesome figure as he stood there. He looked back, and seemed not sure in his own mind about going. But by the time Marthe appeared in the door of her cabin with the moccasins, he was striding away across the meadow.

Four

✠ It was so early—only the strawberry moon—that no one but a few Ottawas and near-by Pottawatomies had come in to camp on the beach. More than a week passed before Marthe found a man among them willing to go on a long canoe trip. "We want to wait for the payments," they protested to Marthe, and closed their ears to her reminder that they could go and return before payment time.

Baptiste laughed and said, "With all that government

money comin' so soon and so easy, you'll never find one of 'em willin' to paddle eighteen hours a day to earn some. When a man once gits the idea the government is goin' to take care of him, it just takes the stiffenin' right out of his backbone."

Marthe went visiting at the lodges every night. Mother never went with her, but I knew that on her way home from the fort she walked through the encampment, asking for news of our own band.

Though I must have been nine years old that summer, I was not allowed to go to the village at all after the boats came in, and I knew nothing of the exciting summer life except as it overflowed the edges and came close to our cabins. I heard it in Baptiste's talk, for he seemed to know everything that went on among the traders. He liked to talk to Pierre, and always went limping over when he saw him at Armand's.

"The war put quite a crimp in the fur business, didn't it?" I heard him say once.

"Yes," said Pierre. "But it is picking up again, to judge by the figures in my books."

"Figures?" snorted Baptiste. "I'd tell it more by the heaps of fur in the warehouses, and the number of traders swarmin' in the yard these days."

"I'm afraid I don't pay much attention to those things. I have nothing to do with it all but keep accounts."

"That may be the job for you, but I'd want to be right out among 'em." Baptiste's eyes sparkled. "I'd like to stand right out there by one of them tables and sort the furs as they come. My eyes and fingers know the grades of fur as well as ever, and whether the worms have been at it," he said wistfully.

A little smile flickered over Pierre's lips. "Why don't you ask Mr. Stuart—?"

Baptiste waved away the idea. "*Non.* I was an independent, and fought the company to the last ditch.

I'll never get any favors there. The company won't forget. They would have drove me out in time. The lameness was only an accident that helped them. Wherever I went, the last few winters, I found the company man had been ahead of me, offerin' a better trade, tellin' the Indians I had been cheatin' 'em, anything to turn 'em against me. I could fight another trader, but all the money of the fur company, *non*."

Pierre coughed gently. "I don't know anything about that," he said vaguely.

"Oh, I don't bear no grudge. Hear they've bought up all the Southwest Company, too."

Their talk went on, and I paid little attention, wishing only to watch Pierre, the movement of his thin lips as he spoke, the way he moved his slender hands in their lace cuffs, hearing in the talk only the same things I saw from a distance every day. The company barracks were packed like fish in a barrel, and more men were arriving in the endless daily procession of boats. All the traders were drinking hard and playing hard as usual, spending all their money and parading in their finery. They boasted of their conquests of the hearts of the village girls, they fought over anything and over nothing; they got up when they were knocked down and wiped the blood from their faces, had a drink, and forgot what they had quarreled about.

"Have you heard about the new law?" I heard Pierre ask.

"No, I ain't."

"Mr. Stuart just had news—in a letter from Mr. Astor—that the American congress has passed a law that no one but American citizens may trade with the Indians."

"So-o." Baptiste whistled through his teeth. "I'll bet Monsieur Astor had a finger in *makin'* that law. He'll git it all his own way now. With the Northwest Fur Company out and all the other Britishers—yes, sir, Monsieur

Astor's ridin' high from now on. You hang on and git your share."

"I intend to," said Pierre.

The new jacket was so beautiful I took thought to see if there was any way I could keep from growing out of it. There were times when I thought I could, and then came signs that my frame was being slowy added to in spite of me. I put it on whenever the rough work of the day was over, though at that time I had never heard of the habit of fine ladies to dress up in the afternoon.

I had it on the evening I was all alone when Pierre came down to the cabins. I was sitting in our doorway, birchbark scrolls of pictures in my lap. The sound of his shoes on the pebbles announced him, but I had known of his coming before that. I had heard the meadow grass sigh when he passed over it.

He came up to me, making signs toward Marthe's cabin, to ask me where she was. I waved my hand toward the beach lodges. Thinking he must have come for his moccasins, I got up and ran into Marthe's cabin. Coming back, I held them up to him, saying nothing. I had been taught that actions need no explaining in words.

A look of distaste came to his face. I lowered my hands in surprise. Nothing about those moccasins should cause a look like that. They were of fine deerskin, tanned to a golden brown, with more embroidery than even a chief's usually had. I examined the otter-tail pattern running from the puckered seam in front all the way to the plain seam in the back. No part of it was missing. The cuffs were neatly fringed below a wide band of porcupine quills in red and blue. I must have looked hurt and puzzled, for suddenly Pierre took the moccasins from me, and sat down on the step, carefully as one not wishing to soil his clothing. I sat at the other end, pleased to be with this man who dressed every day as for a feast.

His blue coat and trousers were spotless, his lace cuffs as fine as the white garments of the priest, as I had heard Louise say so often.

He set the moccasins on the ground, and from the way his fingers left them I knew he didn't intend to pick them up again. Suddenly I knew he didn't intend to wear moccasins at all. I began to worry about how he could take such a trip without them. His own shoes were stiff and heavy, with hard edges on the soles. Canoes are made for soft things, for bales of fur, and moccasins; their sides are tough but thin. When he must walk, it would be still worse. On the portages there would be steep hills with rough and sliding stones, there would be swamps and marshes where heavy soles would sink in. His shoes would not dry from wetting as quickly as moccasins would.

While all these thoughts were going through my mind, Pierre silently looked out over the water and toward the sky. Night was marching across the island, driving the day retreating before him to the west. The sun slid like a plate edgewise into the water, sending up his last light in gold that filled all the air, making the panes of Marthe's windows full of flame, the smoke a purple thread. Soon it would fade into green and violet and then the dark blue for the stars to come out in.

He must wear moccasins, I thought. I would ask Baptiste to talk to him about it. I took up my picture writing again, drawing with a sharpened stone on a piece of birchbark, my vermilion handy in a little box ready to fill in the lines. Pierre looked with interest at my work. "What are you drawing?" he said at last, and then, thinking I didn't understand his language, he pointed at the drawing and tried to make a question with his eyebrows.

I pointed to one of the figures, then up to one of the island birds just coming home for the night. Pierre smiled a little, and nodded. He leaned over to study the pictures, and I caught the clean fragrance of his clothes, the smell of store soap on his cleanly shaven face. He put a long slender finger on another of my drawings, then gracefully turned the finger inward toward himself.

I nodded, yes, a man.

Pierre smiled then, and pointed to the place where the head should be, but I had forgotten to put one on the figure. In turn I pointed to the heart I had put in the center of the drawing, a large heart for a man of courage.

"You're a queer one," Pierre said to himself, for he thought I couldn't understand. "I wonder, is the heart really more important than the head?" He lowered his eyes and sat thinking. I finished that drawing and began another.

"You're a solemn little mite," he said after a time. "I wonder what you think about, here alone." Then he tried to ask me in signs, pointing to the inside of our cabin, then up the fort hill as if to ask me how long my mother was gone.

I pointed my finger to the sky in the east and drew it slowly along until I was pointing to the horizon in the west. "All day," I said in French.

He jumped as if he had sat on a thorn-bush. "What? You speak French!" He looked at me as if one animal had changed into another before his eyes.

"Only a little."

"But how is that?" He was still dazed, as if he had to remake all his thoughts about me.

I told him about the school and the black-robed man.

He laughed a little, and looked as if he had been made ridiculous, and he didn't like it. When he saw I wasn't laughing at him, he settled a little closer to me on the step. "Now, for punishment, you may tell me about your pictures. What are you doing now?"

"This is a story," I said.

"Then tell it to me."

I spread out the roll flat, and pointed to each picture as I told how it came into the story.

"A gentle little rabbit was going one day along a path, when she met a fierce panther. She ran quickly into a hole, and stopped to get her breath. The panther saw the end of her white tail, just far enough inside so he couldn't reach her.

" 'Come out,' he said in his softest growl.

" 'No,' said the little rabbit. 'My mother told me to keep away from big animals like you.'

" 'Oh, no, you must be mistaken,' he said in tones as soft as fur. 'I am a cousin of yours. I only want to send a message to your mother. Do come out where I can talk to you.' He waved his tail and smiled at her.—And what do you think happened?" I looked up at Pierre, covering up the last of my pictures.

"I know," he said solemnly. "The little rabbit was foolish. She forgot what her mother had told her and came out. Then the panther seized her and ate her up."

"How did you know that?" I felt a new respect for him.

"My mother told me a story something like that once," he said.

"Is your mother as pretty as mine?"

Pierre laughed, and I saw shining, even teeth. He was a handsome man, I thought, when one got used to white man's looks.

"Not now," he answered. "She was a beauty once, when she was young in France. She is old and wrinkled now. She is small, not much larger than you," he went on, his words flowing as if he had wanted to talk about her for a long time. "She is as lively as a child, and her eyes sparkle just as they always have." He sighed then, and looked down at his hands, folding and unfolding them on his knee. I hoped he would go on. I liked the slow way he spoke as if he thought a great deal more than he said. There was less of the frost in his words now, though a hint of it remained in their precise delicacy of pattern. Softly he talked, as if he were not used to great expanses like the broad blue water in front of us. Later on I came to think of his voice as one suited to rooms where there were velvet hangings, being improved by them as fine crystal graces the wine it holds.

He straightened up, as if thoughts were closing in that he wanted to shake off. Darkness had come on. The song-birds were hushed, only the night-hawks and the gulls adding their voices to the human ones in the village. "By the way, isn't this late for your mother to leave you alone? Where is she?"

"The major's wife made her stay to help her dress for the big ball the fur company gives this evening. The major is sick and cannot go, so Mother must go to the ball with her, too. She didn't want to."

Pierre looked white and cold. What had I said to make him angry?

"A foil for her blondness," he said under his breath. Strange words, I thought. I didn't understand what they meant, but saved them up carefully in my mind to ask Louise later on. I thought somehow that Mother or Marthe wouldn't know any more about it than I did.

"Her husband is sick, but she must go to the ball, with a companion to make her look respectable while she flirts with some good-looking *homme du nord*. And then she will let your mother come home late at night, through crowds of drunken men—"

He got up and looked down at me. "Will you be all right here alone?"

"Yes," I said, "but I wish you weren't going."

He smiled then more than I had ever seen him. "I'm glad you like my company. I have had a better time than I have had since—well, for a long time. But I think I'll go to that ball myself."

Five

❀ Mother was excited about something when she came home late that night. In quick movements that sometimes abruptly changed to long pauses in motionless thought, she took off her moccasins and her dress—the new calico would not stand being slept in as our deerskins would—and slipped quietly into bed with me. Even when sleep came to her, she kept muttering to herself, turning over on the lumpy corn-husk mattress and waking me all through the night.

The next morning I got up first and laid the fire, starting it with a pile of dried moss. I filled the kettle and hung it over the first crackling flames, then hurried to open the door wide and see what the world was like. The island had changed back again from a mass of purple shadow to green and white. The sky was clear. I remember always this clearness and the breezes even on the warmest day. I wanted to run up to the heights and through the woods, to tread on spicy wintergreen and feel ferns brushing off their dew against my knees. But I turned back to the fire, now sending long flames pointing up the chimney. Into the boiling kettle I threw a handful of corn, parched and finely ground, and when it had softened I poured it into two bowls, steaming hot. Into another bowl went wild strawberries, small but red and juicy. The fire burned itself to coals, and I warmed some corn cake on our little grate.

Mother seemed tired when she got up, but when we had seated ourselves cross-legged near the hearth, our bowls on the floor before us, she praised the breakfast, dipping the strawberries into maple sugar and taking them between her teeth in pleased appreciation of each one. When she tasted her corn soup, it was as if the warmth loosened her tongue. She began to tell about the ball.

"It was in the big wigwam where furs are stored, but the furs were moved out and a great open space left for dancing. You know, the white people's dances are not ceremonies."

I nodded. "Like smoking for them," I said, for the use of a pipe was always part of a ceremony for our men.

"They mean nothing," she went on, "no appeal to any spirits or thanks for good harvests. They are only for pleasure, as their firewater lies more pleasant on their tongues than pure water from a spring. Last night all the soldiers and ladies from the fort, voyageurs and village girls danced together, and so much laughing I have never heard. They ate and drank, too, standing by a long table filled with plates of meats and cakes."

Mother nibbled at the edge of a corn cake. "The room was full of the music of violins and the noise of feet, and girls' laughter rising above the deeper voices of the men. When the violins were still, all the company drifted away to the walls, where groups of candles burned to light the room. But when the music began no one sat still but one man who froze his heels in a blizzard last winter.

"And so many pretty dresses—" Mother paused to lift her soup bowl and drink, in little sips as dainty as a humming bird at a blossom. "The major's wife wore light blue silk, and shoes with high slender heels. Around her hair was a black ribbon with a rose at the side of it. She was so popular for the dancing, all the evening long. She was so gay, except once—" Mother's face colored lightly and she stopped.

"Go on," I urged.

"You see, whenever she wasn't dancing for a few minutes, she came and sat in a corner with me, waiting for some man to come and ask her. Once a new figure began without her, and she was restless. All at once she saw a man coming, and she got up, so glad she was to see him. The whole room could see how pleased she was. She held out her hands, and was all ready to be led into the dance. The music was playing, and her face glowed. 'I haven't seen you for so long—why have you stayed away from me like this?' she said to him.

"The man didn't lead her away into the dance." Mother's cheeks were flushed as she told it. "He took one of her outstretched hands gracefully and bent and touched his lips to it. 'How are you, Josette?' he said, then dropped her hand again. He walked right past her, and bowed—in front of me!"

"Oh, Mother, I know who it was!"

Mother went on over my words. "He said something I couldn't understand, and took up one of my hands. I looked at Madame Pierce, puzzled about what I should do. And she looked so strange. She had gone all red and then so white. She told me the gentleman wanted to dance with me.

" 'Oh, no, tell him I can't,' I said to her. But the man —it was your M'sieu Pierre, Oneta—kept tight hold of my hand and would not let me go.

" 'It seems you will have to. M'sieu Debans is a very good dancer,' the major's wife said.

"I tried to draw back into the shadows, but the white man pulled me gently out on the floor, where six others made a little circle with us." Mother was silent for a moment, as if passing over some confused time in her thoughts. "It wasn't so hard," she sighed at last. "I had seen that dance over and over. It was one of the easier ones, and the voyageurs had kept the fiddlers playing it all evening. And the white man was so graceful and kind—he led me through the dance, and it was easy, somehow, with him. All the white people in the same figure helped me when I made a mistake. They seemed so amused by something, but I don't know what it was. They kept looking at the major's wife and at M'sieu Pierre and smiling at him. We danced another, and another. I liked it, Oneta!

"But one queer thing—" Mother looked worried as she remembered—"the major's wife didn't dance again at all. She sat with Mrs. Stuart and afterward she left without a word to me."

"Did you come home then?"

"Yes, and the white man walked all the way down here with me," said Mother, wondering at the memory. Such courtesies were new to her. "I said I could walk with Baptiste and Armand, but he didn't understand. That was a queer walk. He held my fingers around his arm, and would not let them go. He is very tall, have you noticed it?" Mother went into another moment of silent memory. "We couldn't say a word to each other, but it was nice."

Two days later, Pierre came once again, near midday when my mother was not there. Marthe had found canoe-men for him and he was all ready to leave. I gave him a little bark cup of bear's grease to clean himself with, protect his body from mosquitoes, and keep him from getting a cough. He took it between two fingers, and hesitated as if he were looking for a place to put it down. Then, seeing my eyes upon him, he bowed. "*Merci,* the thought is a kind one. Good-by, and be a good little rabbit." That last seemed to amuse him, for he said it twice.

I saw his canoe leave the shore. Four canoe-men he had, and he sat in the stern alone. Around him were stacked bales of goods holding dry supplies, and kegs I knew held powder and shot and the rum the men would never start without. Pierre waved to me, and I watched as long as I could see him, until the last wave disturbed by the paddles had resumed its even movement.

I wondered about him as Marthe and I gathered wild berries to dry for winter use. I held the birch basket up to Marthe, wishing it was to him I showed it. "See, Marthe, the bottom is covered," I would say, or, "See, half full again." Marthe always spoke some word of praise that urged me on to even greater effort. As we worked she told me stories, and if she did not begin at once, I would coax, "Tell me another legend, Marthe."

She sometimes excused herself, "There are so many, I would not know which one to tell."

"Tell me the oldest one you know," I would say.

Marthe's way of telling a story was her own. The life was all in the story itself, not in any animation of the speaker. Slowly, evenly, it came out, like the movement of a stream, or rustling far back in the forest.

One day, thinking of Pierre again, I asked, "Why are some men white instead of red?"

"I have heard that the great spirit tried three times to make a man as he wanted him," said Marthe. "With clay he formed one in his hands and put him by the fire to bake. Too anxious, he pulled him out too soon. The man was not well baked; he was too pale. That is the white man.

"The great spirit made another, and left him in the fire too long; he was burned. Thus there are black men on the earth. The great spirit had learned. The third time he tried, the man came out just right—the red man."

I thought about this, and saw no reason why it was not true.

One night, about half a moon later, Mother came home weeping. She threw herself on the bed, and when she had sobbed herself quiet again, she told me she could not work at the major's house any more. Since the ball, the major's wife had found fault with everything she did. That day, she had spoken sharply just as Mother handed a cup of tea to an officer's wife, and Mother had dropped the cup, and the tea had gone on the lady's dress and the rug. The major's wife had shrieked at Mother for being stupid, and had told her to go home and not come back.

It was after that we began to play our little game. Mother sat upright in our one good chair, imitating the way the major's wife would receive her servant.

"Madame," I asked, "what shall we have to eat to-day?"

Mother pretended to think carefully. "I liked that fish soup we had yesterday. Shall we have some more of that?"

"With or without maple sugar on the top?"

"Without, I think. I am a little tired of sugar."

Our supply of sugar had been gone for many days. Baptiste brought us the fish that were to be had for the catching—trout, whitefish, and the proud sturgeon, the king of all the fish. But sugar, corn-meal, and vegetables for our soup-pot we could not get without money.

We did not let Marthe know how little we had. The beach was crowded with lodges, and Marthe visited there, or searched the woods for herbs and roots to prepare all the charms and cures she was asked to make. She did not notice what we were eating. Fish and the wild fruits of the island kept us alive. We tried not to think what would happen when the time came to pay more money for the cabin.

The strawberry moon passed, and the raspberry moon, and it was the moon of the whortleberry. Payment time came, and still no news of my grandfather.

The meadow grass had grown long, and lay flattened in little cushions for the feet by the time I saw Pierre coming across it again. I started to meet him, and then stopped and waited for him to come up to me, looking

116

at him in wonder that the journey had made no change in him. His blue suit covered his slender arms and legs without a wrinkle, and his brown hair lay in untouched waves. His pale face was a little browner, so I could see a difference between it and the white shirt-collar whose points came high on his cheeks.

"Why, here's the rabbit-girl. You've grown since I was away." His smile came to his lips slowly as if it started a long way inside and was not anxious to come out where the world could see it.

But the smile, when it did come, brought a whole stream of words to my tongue. All the things came out that Mother and I had kept silent about the whole summer. I told him about Mother not working any more, and how we had nothing to eat but fish and berries, and that no one had seen my grandfather since he left the wild-rice country.

Pierre thought about this, and brought his gray eyes suddenly back to me. "Your mother doesn't work any more? Why?"

I told him about the major's wife. He looked cold and angry in an instant. "Took out her spite against me on your mother, did she?" Pierre took my hand, and walked slowly along the path toward Louise's cabin. Before he got there, he turned and started toward ours. "See here, I've an idea, but I must think it out. It is an idea that followed me all through my journey."

I stood at the edge of the meadow, my hand still in Pierre's, and saw him look at our cabin almost as if he were seeing it in a new way. I knew that his thoughts were flying out and away from me, coming back in endless circling like the flight of the island birds over our heads, sailing out over the water and back. The restless straits spread before us, in little waves with golden surfaces where they rose to meet the sun. Gulls made deep spots of white in a world of gold and blue. The wind came from the south and west. It is the home-wind, I thought, and lifted my face to it. It raised the grasses of the smooth meadow, leveled by the years over the graves that had once been there. The water had been rushing past the island, I thought, in just the same way when those men whose bones were now under the meadow grass had ridden the waves in their canoes.

The whole fishing colony was below us—our cabin, Baptiste's, and Armand's. Clustered together on the beach they were, so close to the waves that if the straits should ever rise they would be swept away, if indeed they did not ride the waves as they looked as if they might.

"Why not? Why not?" Pierre began to say, over and over, as if he couldn't quite believe his thoughts.

Then he took hold of my hand more firmly, and we went down the little slope and around to the front of our cabin. And those steps took him forever into a different world.

"Sit down," he said. "No—there, right in the middle of the step."

I sat where he pointed.

"Now ask your mother if she will please come out."

I called to her, and she came shyly to the door.

"Ask her to sit down beside you, there on the other side," he said.

Mother sat down, wondering. "Now," said Pierre, sitting beside me so that we three were in a line, there before the water.

"Now," said Pierre, "we can talk."

But for a few minutes the calm, yet unquiet voice of the straits had the air to itself. I looked along the shore toward the cobbler's cave. Evergreen trees huddled together now in their hollows, and here and there the naked rock broke through. Even the clear bright green of the leaf-bearing trees and bushes could not hide the rock of which the island was made. No brooks or streams cut into it; there were only springs that scored their way down its cliffs and spilled their silvery drops to be whirled away into the great movement of the straits. Unchanging the rock was, as Pierre was unchanged by his journey. As he looked at my mother, something within him that is the same in all men showed on his face, breaking out as naked rock from the fine foliage of his dress and manner.

His lips partly opened twice, but the right words were not ready to come. Then,

"I—how do you say *I* in your language?"

"I—what?" I asked.

"Just *I*, to begin with."

"You can't say that alone."

He was bothered by this, as if it made him come out with more than he wanted to. He ran his fingers through his hair, then settled them quietly in his lap. A few hairs were left out of line, the first time I had seen them that way.

"Well, *I love you*, then—tell me how to say that."

I gave him the Ojibway word, all one word it is in our language. "You say it all by the way you say *love*, I told him. The *I* doesn't stand by itself. It's part of the *love*."

"Say the word again," he answered. When I told him, he leaned over and repeated it solemnly to my mother, speaking across my lap. Mother had been puzzled by all this talk in French, understanding only the Ojibway word I had given him.

"What is he saying that to me for?" she asked, startled.

I didn't know why, either. That was an expression we used as mother to child, or child to pet animals. No man ever said it to a woman.

"We don't know what you are talking about," I told him.

There was a queer look on his face. "I think that's plain enough," he said almost stiffly, but with a curious sense of being let down from a height of getting the thing said. "Well, it's this way," he said quickly. "I want to ask your mother to be my wife—do you understand that?"

I clapped my open hand over my mouth in amazement. This man who dressed in blue cloth and lace, who was so admired by all the people I knew—he wanted to marry my mother!

"Like Baptiste and Marthe?" I asked, astonished, and almost trembling with a confusion of thoughts. He swung around toward the other cabin, as if something had struck his mind he didn't like.

"Yes, I suppose," he murmured, "like Baptiste and Marthe, as far as you can understand."

It was against my training to let my surprise show as I had. No matter how astonishing the idea thrust upon me, I knew I should begin at once to plan how it could be done. Steadying my mind with that thought, I asked,

"Why didn't you bring some meat to our door and see if my mother would take it in and cook it?"

It was his turn to be confused. "Meat—cook?" he stammered.

"That is our custom," I said. "If Mother hadn't had a husband before, if she was living with her father, you would bring him presents. But my mother has had one husband. So you should bring some meat to her door. If she takes it in, you can come in to stay."

"That is not my way," he said. "Please tell her the way I told you. I have to do it, at least," he added, "like a white man."

I was silent for a moment, and then I saw a quivering come to the corner of his mouth, as if in spite of himself he wanted to burst out into laughter.

"Explain to me how a white man does," I said. Then I remembered stories of things that happened before I could remember. "I know—like Baptiste," I exclaimed.

"You want her to get in a canoe and go away with you."

He twisted his hands in his lap, and the quivering set up around his lips again. "This is getting worse and worse," he murmured. "No—see if you can understand this—I do not want her to go away in a canoe with me. I have to stay right here, where the fur company is. And you—you are an important part of it. You see how it is—I can't even talk to her without you."

That comforted me. I was intensely excited about it, though now I let no part of it show in my face. I turned to my poor puzzled mother, and began to tell her about it, syllables tumbling over one another, all the long words it took to tell it all running at each other's heels like a pack of sled-dogs. As I talked I held my hand out to Pierre, palm up in a sign of friendship and agreement. Pierre took my hand, with no knowledge of the meaning of the sign. But my mother understood. If it had not been for that, she would have run inside like a frightened animal, so strange were the words she heard from me.

Once Pierre stopped me. "Now, mind, be sure to tell her the white man's way. First I say 'I love you,' and then I ask her to go to the priest with me—"

"No," said my mother in a hushed voice. I repeated it to him.

The red crept up into his face. "Are you sure she understands? Tell her I want to take care of you both, and she will never again need to work for women like the major's wife."

I repeated this. "No," said Mother softly.

Pierre lowered his head and stared at the pebbles under his smooth black boots. He must have had many a talk with himself before coming to this decision. And when he had brought himself to the asking, it was something he hadn't counted on hearing, when my mother said "No." As I saw him there, silent and ill at ease, I felt closer to him than ever before. Mother offered no further word to help him. I can see now how she sat with her calico dress spread neatly about her, modestly pulled down to her moccasin-tops. I remember thinking that she had learned that from white women, that she wore this long full dress now as naturally as she had her short deerskin skirt and leggings when we first came to the island. Her two braids hung down upon the dress, the loosened ends making a splash of glossy black against the red pattern of the calico.

It was quiet there, except for the breaking waves, though in the distance the noisy village life came in upon us in bursts of laughter, scraps of songs, shouts. Mother was listening to something else. From the beach lodges now came the occasional beat of a drum. I knew from its rhythm that the corn dance was not far away, that preparations were even then being made. That meant that the payments were over, that the boats would be leaving, that the ice would soon shut us off again.

I laid my hand on Pierre's, marveling again at its whiteness. He sat tensely, as if he wished to go, but something stubborn in him made him stay.

"Come back tomorrow," I said. "Maybe she will talk to Marthe about it."

"Tell her again," he said, "about going to the priest, and then that I will pay for the cabin and you will have all the food you want from the company store." Drops of water broke out on his high forehead, in his effort to put it in a way I would understand. "When your mother needs a new dress, I will buy that," he explained. "When you need something, I will buy it for you. You see, I will be your father from now on."

At this I held up my hand. "I will tell her the rest," I said gently, "but not that. That cannot be true. I am the daughter of Tecumseh."

Six

�֍ That night Mother and I lay awake, with arms close
about each other, and talked in fragments. "Tecumseh,
what would he think?" asked Mother. "The widow of
Tecumseh to be the squaw of a white man? No, I cannot do it."

"Not squaw," I answered. "He said he would marry
with a priest. That makes a difference with white men,
Louise says."

"You like this white man, Oneta. I see it whenever
you are with him. Tell me why you like him."

"Words cannot tell it," I said. "It is something in his
clothes, the way he walks, the slow-coming smile, the
way Baptiste and Armand want his approval, though
they can do many things he cannot do." I could not tell
her then all of why I liked Pierre, nor can I tell it now.

"If my father were here," said Mother, "he would
know what I should say if the white man comes again."

"If we go with Grandfather, what then?" I asked.
"Would we always stay with him?"

"Yes, of course—" began Mother. "No, Marthe says
I would have to choose another husband within a year."

The wind came through the cabin walls, a soft
whisper. "Let's ask Marthe," I said. "That will be almost
like asking Grandfather."

The morning sun drove long shadows from the
cabins into the very edge of the shining water. Early as
it was Marthe had already tramped the heights to find a
five-pronged root to heal a cut on Rosanne's hand and
returning, had gathered an armful of rushes, dried ones
she had put out on the beach overnight in the dew to
take away their brittleness. As we went in and sat on

the floor beside her, she took up a partly finished mat and began to weave, setting the pattern as we talked, to lose no precious time while the rushes were soft.

"Oneta's white friend came back yesterday," began Mother.

"More than a moon he has been gone," said Marthe. "What did he say of his journey?" She raised her eyes briefly to my face.

"He wants to live in our cabin," said Mother.

"He wants to marry Mother," I said at the same time, my high voice sounding like an overtone to Mother's soft one.

No change came to Marthe's face. Since there were no strangers there, it was not that she was hiding her feelings. Surprised, I realized that she looked as though she had thought it all over long ago.

"What did you tell him?" She bent low over the mat, so that we could see only the tightly drawn hair, the bend of her wrinkled brown neck above her sun-faded calico waist.

"I told him I would not, but Oneta thinks he will come back. Oneta wanted to ask you about it."

Marthe raised a pleased face that went suddenly stern. "It is not I you must ask. Have you forgotten that you must fast for a guiding dream?"

Mother kept her eyes away from Marthe's gaze, ashamed that she had not thought of this herself. It was the only way to decide a thing rightly. Mother had told me of other times she had fasted and waited for a dream, beginning with the first one when she was just entering womanhood. That was the most important dream. She sought it that she might be shown some object whose spirit would be her particular guide all through life. Her dream had shown her a pine tree, broken by the spirit of the storms. When we first came to the island, she had been pleased to find just such a tree on the heights beyond the fishing village. In our trouble she had already laid offerings at its feet, a little portion of our food, burned on the hearth and its ashes gathered up and laid at the foot of the great pine. We knew the manitou was the essence of all life, in control of all living beings, but he was too far above and too busy to pay attention to the wants of everyone. It must be a lesser spirit who would have time to help in particular problems. And if this spirit had help to give, it would be offered in a dream.

"Where can I go?" Mother asked softly.

"Back into the center of the island, where no paths lead."

"I know a place," said Mother. "I found it when—" She stopped, but we knew she meant when the news came about my father. "No—I cannot go there."

"Give up the thoughts that distress you, until you have had guidance," said Marthe gently. "Up on the heights toward the north star from the rock of the sorrowing maiden, is a place where I often get herbs. Trees bend close to the earth all around. You can take your blanket there and fast, and no one will come."

The second day after this, Mother came back tired and so weak she lay on the bed for a long time without speaking. Marthe came then, and put a kettle of water on the fire. When the steam arose, she dropped into the kettle a pinch of herbs from the pouch at her belt, and carried Mother a cup of this warm, sweet-smelling tea.

When Mother had taken it all, she lay back against the head of the bed. Marthe drew near and Mother looked up at her. In the silence I felt the two of them drawing together in an intimacy I had no part in. They had forgotten all about me. I went out and closed the door of the cabin.

Baptiste was just drawing his boat up on the beach. "Hello, there. I looked around for you when I went out. Thought you might like to go along. Rosanne went."

He jerked one elbow toward the boat, then suddenly looked beyond me and touched his ragged cap. *"Bon jour."* Pierre was coming down the slope from the meadow.

Rosanne lay among the fishes, asleep. The light slid off her glossy black curls and turned scales and fins to silver. It was a pretty thing, I thought, and lifted my eyes to share the pleasure with Pierre.

His eyes were on the same thing I had seen. "Dreadful," he said, with a shiver of distaste. "A child among those slimy things."

Baptiste began to pick up the fish around Rosanne, and she awoke. She stretched out an arm, felt the strange bed she was on, and sat bolt upright.

"Look at my dress—all mussed up and wet," she screamed.

"Now, see here, young lady," her father said calmly, "you went to sleep there yourself. I didn't have no other place to put my catch. They didn't hurt you none."

"Oh!" she wailed, and struck her father in the chest as he bent over. About to go on into a storm of rage, she suddenly noticed Pierre. She lowered her head and jumped out of the boat. Her wet dress flapped about her bare legs as she ran to the cabin, and she began to peel it off as soon as she got through the door.

"Pretty child," said Pierre.

"Yes," Baptiste agreed, his hand wandering to the shirtfront where she had struck him. "But sometimes I don't know—I guess Indian blood and white makes kind of a devilish mixture." He lifted with both hands a large sturgeon and carried it up to the cabin. On the way back he said, "Speakin' of devilish—did you hear what became of old Jim Mack?"

"No. I don't know who he is—or was."

Baptiste bit off a generous piece from a twist of

tobacco he sorted out from a fishline, a jackknife, a box of hooks in his pocket. "One of the best-known traders in these parts. Used to be in the northern brigade. *Il semble* he met up with some stray Iroquois pushed this far from their own territory. They took his goods and skins, and when he raised hell with 'em about it—torture. He wasn't pretty to look at when they got through, *je ne pense*. Before they quite finished him, he managed to rub a stick on the black bottom of a kettle and write a message on the inside of one of his beaver skins. When that skin came in, someone at the yard read it.

"Them savages come here for tradin', and act as meek as all get out," Baptiste went on. "But scratch one of them lazy-lookin' ones and the savage is right there. Any time, they might rise up and kill us all. You heard about that massacre, *n'est-ce pas*, when the fort was over on the mainland. Got in the fort by a trick—lettin' their ball go over a fence in the midst of a game, and askin' as polite as could be if they could go in and get it. Then they pulled out their scalping knives and tomahawks and went to work. One man lived to tell about it, because some Indian girl was soft on him and hid him over here in Skull Cave—"

Our cabin door opened, and Mother stood there. She had taken off her deerskins and put on the sprigged calico again. Her hair was smooth, her face flushed and a little shy. Pierre left Baptiste and took a step toward her, and then hesitated and looked around, almost as if he wanted to run back across the meadow. Then my mother lifted one small brown hand, and he tossed his head as if shaking away some unwelcome thought and went toward her.

"The dream was favorable," she said. He didn't understand the words, but her tone and deep flush told him she was accepting him. He started to take her by

127

the hand, and then stopped as he caught sight of Marthe behind her.

"Will you come to our cabin today?" I asked him.

"No," said Marthe, speaking across' the two of them to me. "The white man will do it his own way. He will wait until the black robe comes in his canoe."

Marthe towered, almost menacing, there beside them. I felt she had seen Pierre's hesitation and stood there as a force that would not let him go.

Under her steady gaze, he dropped Mother's hand and bowed. "I shall come to see you this evening." He waited for me to repeat it, and took out a large gold watch. "It is two o'clock—time for me to be back at the company office."

Baptiste squinted upward, confirming the time by the position of the sun. "*Oui,* just about two."

When Pierre had gone, I began to chatter happily. "This cabin is much larger than the lodge where three of us lived easily. We have plenty of room for him."

Mother smiled faintly. "Oneta likes him. He pleases me, too," she confessed.

"Men are the same, of whatever color," said Marthe, her tone growing more bitter as she went on. "When you are beautiful, they want you; they will fight and cheat, lie and steal to get you. When you are ugly, they do not see you, or they sneer and turn away. If they cannot have the beautiful one, they will take the ugly, considering it kindness to let her do their work and bear their children. Do you think this white man would have looked at you if your face was not pretty? Even the most successful hunter, the finest warrior, the wisest in council—yes, even he who was all of these in one—saw only a pretty face when he chose his wife."

"Father saw more than a pretty face when he saw my mother," I said. Marthe was startled when I spoke so abruptly, and was silent until her bitter thoughts had gone. She laid her hand then gently on my mother's.

Baptiste went on unloading fish, caring not at all that Marthe had been talking about the great disappointment of her life.

Seven

✻ Though Pierre did not come at once to live in our cabin, there were signs that a change was taking place. At one side of the room hung the new dress he had sent from the store. Mother was to wear it for the marriage when the priest came. It was of stiff, light green silk, with darker, balsam green stripes running down the full skirt. Mother sometimes put it on when we were alone, and practiced walking about in it and the slippers with high heels Pierre sent a little later. They were green silk, too, and just like those Mother had seen at the dance. She had great trouble to stand in them at first, but kept wearing them until she walked in them almost as well as in her moccasins. As I recall that dress, I realize that Pierre wanted his wife to be as well-dressed as the ladies at the fort. Mother understood what his bringing it meant, and from that day on I never saw her in deerskins again. She looked beautiful in the green silk, and learned to handle the long, full skirt with grace, catching it up with one hand as she walked. The color was right for her dark skin and black hair. And when she added her silver armlets, I thought no one could look finer.

An armchair came to the cabin next, and three straight chairs, and Mother and I knew our meals must be eaten from the pine table after Pierre came. But we decided not to give up the coziness of sitting crosslegged at the hearth until the very last day. Baptiste came with boards and nails, and put up shelves where Pierre wanted them for his books. The shelves filled all of one corner near the fireplace. On the other side, Baptiste put together and set up the cot Pierre had sent from the store. Mother explained that I must sleep there now, instead of in the large bed with her.

"Your mother is lucky, gettin' such a fine man," said Baptiste. He was impressed by the number of shelves Pierre needed. "I don't believe the government agent himself has more books than M'sieu Debans, and they say he has a sight of 'em."

"Pierre is a fine man," I told him seriously. "But you must remember, that's what she is used to. She was married first to the greatest man in all the world."

"Does you credit to feel like that," said Baptiste. "But I don't know how this is goin' to work out. He just don't seem to be the kind." Baptiste scratched his head briefly. "Well, it's none of my business. All I got to do is put up these shelves."

The days that followed were as unruffled as the sky itself, then in its good-natured summer mood, and when I think of them now, I can no more see what lay behind their peace than if I were trying to look through that same very solid blue that was spread above the island.

Pierre came often to our cabin, and we three sat and talked. He seemed glad to be there. He had been rooming at Mrs. Ruggs's boarding house, he told us, and the noise of the summer visitors and the traders that filled her other rooms kept him from resting or reading. He now felt he had somewhere to go, a refuge where nothing annoyed him. What he felt with us was as simple as the coziness of being under a roof when it is raining.

He was at our cabin one Sunday afternoon when Baptiste called over from the steps of his own to say that the priest's canoe was crossing from St. Ignace. Pierre turned to Mother.

"Do you want to go to the shore with me? I must see him, I suppose."

I remember everything he ever said to her, since I was more than a child listening. Every word of one to the other had to pass through me. I could not help putting something of myself into it, like one taking up the raw cloth of speech and turning it into a garment another could wear.

Listening while I repeated Pierre's question, Mother shook her head shyly, and did not move. Pierre held out his hand to me. "Then you'll go with me?" I waited only for Mother's nod of permission.

We walked slowly over the pebbled beach, for there was plenty of time. Beyond waves crinkling in the sun, we could see the canoe following along toward the harbor, a black-robed figure seated quietly in one end, in the other a canoe-man. There was something impressive about their coming. It was different from the frantic rush of most canoes approaching the island as if they could not wait to get to the land. This one moved rather as if there were no hurry, as if time meant little in its work. I learned later that this slow approach gave enough time for the news to spread in the village, and a crowd to form on the shore. Already a cluster was at the wharf.

At that time I felt only something of the dignity of this approach, and felt it to be connected with the dark seated figure, with the upright way he held his back, his face uplifted a little, pale under the black hat he wore. Just as we reached the edge of the crowd, the bow of the canoe touched the pebbled beach, and the figure rose, his long black cassock falling to his feet. I remembered the black robe of the mission school in the west, and looked at the face of this one to see if it might be the same. It was not. This man's face had not yet been touched by the wind and sun. From its pinkness showed suddenly unexpected blue eyes. He stepped on shore with eyes uplifted. Men took off their hats and held them in their hands, as Pierre did, or put ragged caps under their arms. Women hushed the children around their knees. All faces were lowered before the black robe as he raised his hands, uttering strange words in a clear voice. I tugged at Pierre's coat to ask him what the black robe was saying. "A blessing," said Pierre softly, in a tone that urged me to say no more just then.

The black robe moved slowly through the crowd, and then it surged together and followed him toward the village.

"He goes to Mrs. Ruggs's to hold services, since there is no chapel here," said Pierre as we followed. A few hangers-on of the crowd looked at Pierre and me curiously. I wondered if he noticed it, but he only took hold of my hand the tighter, and let his face show no response to their staring. I was glad I had on my white coat, and that I needed to have no shame of the embroidery on it. I wanted to look nice beside Pierre.

Men in blanket coats and women in shawls made up most of the crowd, but there were a few men in clothes more like Pierre's, and a few women in black dresses and smooth, tight-fitting black coats. I saw them walk as close to the black robe as they could, yet respectfully leave him room to walk on the best part of the path. I watched the expression on their faces. Bearded or smooth, dark or pale, dirty or washed, they all turned to the black robe as if they wanted something, yet they did not hold out their hands. And indeed he carried nothing but a small book, and even his canoe-man carried only some pieces of wood that I later learned made a portable altar. The faces were rather those of people expecting words that give good news. Some looked almost as if they already had what they wanted, or were so close to it that a deep contentment had begun to settle within them.

I looked up, and found the same expression on Pierre's face. He began talking softly then, for we were a little back from the rest. "They all expect something good to come to them now. They will lose troubled feelings and uneasy memories and they will gain strength. It's like showers to thirsty plants, this visit of the priest. He's keeping alive seed sown many years ago on this soil by the first Jesuits. This priest is a new one, they tell me, and yet he does not look unhappy at his change from a life full of good things to the hardships of traveling from one trading post to another. The church makes up for everything."

At the door of Mrs. Ruggs's long, low white house, the black robe stopped and turned to the crowd again, standing a little above them on the step. A little group separated from the others and stood at one side. It was to these he turned.

"They are the ones who have something special to ask him about," said Pierre. "They want him to say the office of the dead over graves made since the last visit, or to baptize children newly born, or to perform marriage ceremonies. All these things he will do tomorrow. Today he will hear confessions and impose penances, and say mass and vespers."

I understood nothing of this last, but one word had stayed in my mind. "Then you should be with that group?" I said, half inquiring. Pierre started, and looked down at me. "Yes, yes, that's right," he said in a surprised way, as if he had forgotten entirely what we came for.

Years later I found out that Pierre also joined the group waiting to make confession that night. I knew then only that he came to get my mother the next day with a happier face, with the doubt gone from it that had hovered in its shadows since he had first asked her to marry him. I can only suspect what the black robe said to him, from knowing that the priests ever encouraged the marrying of Indians and white people, believing that to be one of the best ways to get the Indian tribes to stop roving, live in villages and plant fields, and be amenable to the dictates of the church. In this they were ever opposed by the traders, to whose advantage it was to keep the tribes on the move and in want, to gather furs for them. Knowing nothing of those forces then, I saw only the change in Pierre, remarking that the glow upon his face was like that upon my mother's when she had come back from her fasting alone for a dream.

Mother dressed in her new clothes, and went with one hand on Pierre's arm, the other holding her dress off the beach. Watching to see if Pierre noticed how easily she walked in the new shoes, and seeing that he took it for granted, I kept my eyes on them until the curve of the path took them around the point and out of my sight.

When the postmaster's helper appeared with Pierre's things in the two-wheeled cart, it really seemed that the cabin changed over completely, its only reason for existence being to house Pierre. The helper was the boy I had seen whose head was too large for his body. Besides bringing the mail from the boats, he used his cart to do odd jobs for people in the village. His forehead was low above bushy eyebrows, his hair always matted and dirty. Saying nothing, he unloaded the boxes from the cart and carried them inside. He took the coins Pierre laid in his hands, with only a brief ducking of his head for thanks.

The strangeness of having a bed of my own gradually left my thoughts as the days went on. Pierre bought a new table to hold our washbasin and soap-cup, and I took for my own the box marked INDIAN GOODS. I put into it my scrolls and the bow and arrow my father had sent, closed the cover, and set it under the narrow window near my cot, where I could draw up a smaller box to it when I wanted to do my picture-writing. That side of the fireplace then became a little world of my own. I sat there often in the evening when Pierre was in the new armchair beside his bookshelves on the other side of the hearth.

Those evenings are the times I remember best. For me the delight of seeing Pierre across the hearth with his pipe and book was always new and fresh. Mother sat near-by, her brown eyes quietly content at the sight of us both. Though she was always tired from carrying wood and buckets of water, or gathering berries, she must always fill her hands with work of an evening, as if idleness would bring reproach. But Pierre would not have cared. I had already discovered that he was not one for noticing things, as long as he was comfortable.

In the evening when he had trimmed the candle to tease out its best light, he was lost in a book—English books first for duty, for he was not perfect in the language he must use in his work at the fur company, and then when the fire burned low and Mother and I put on our night-clothes beside the hearth, Pierre would take up an old French book with singing words and his brow would relax in happiness.

He wrote once to his mother, and took the letter to an eastward sailing ship. "I am telling her that I have married the most beautiful woman on the island," he said to me, as one who had long thought how the news might best be told.

And then sometimes he would sit and look at the fire as if he had forgotten us and the cabin and even the fur company, as if he were thinking of those days when he lived in a house he had told me about. Bigger than any on the island he said it was, with fine carved tables and chairs and silk and down covers for his bed. He talked of the people who came there in silk clothing and powdered wigs and talked and danced and had good things to eat brought on silver trays. He told me how a young man lived in the house just to teach him to read and find out about all things that happened before he was born, and in other parts of the world, even in early ages, for it was all set down in books. I turned this over in my thoughts many times, wishing I might find some birch-bark scrolls someone else had made long before I was born, imagining to myself the excitement of reading what the other had set down. And then I watched Pierre after his thoughts had stretched far back, and seeing his smooth face, his eyes half-closed, a great feeling went out to him. I wanted to do things for him, and wanted him to smile approval when I did them.

Eight

❧Autumn came, with the ripe beauty of completion, of harvest, of falling seed that assures a renewal of life in the spring.

But before that, we had many days not entirely peace-ful. The second day Pierre was with us, he brought home a pound of Hyson tea, and asked us to have that at sup-per every night instead of the maple sugar in water we had given him. The following evening, its fragrance stole out from the kettle and through the room, giving the little cabin the feeling of a new spirit in it.

"I am glad I learned how to make it while I was at the fort house," said Mother, doubtfully peering into the rising steam. "I think it is strong enough now," she said just as Pierre came in the door.

"No time for you to read before supper," I said to him, as he laid his beaver hat on the bed. "The soup is almost hot enough."

"Good." The tones were distant. "Is that the way you always leave a bed all day?" he asked suddenly.

I nodded.

"With the covers all rumpled like that?" he persisted.

I nodded again. There was nothing different about the

136

bed since he had gotten out of it himself. I wondered what was wrong with him.

"Come to supper," said Mother, and I repeated it. I took all the cups to the fire and dipped them into the kettle one by one, carrying them back to the table brimming full. Drawing up my chair noisily, I felt again the strangeness of sitting at a table. Strange, too, it was for us to eat at the same time with a man. The first night we had begun to serve him, planning to eat afterward, but he had made us sit with him.

Mother and I had taken great pains with the supper. Yet Pierre pushed the fish soup away, and took on his plate only a little venison and one of the little ears of corn we had baked in a hot ash pit all afternoon. "Do you always have corn bread?" he asked, taking up a slice.

I waited to see what he meant.

"There are other kinds of bread, you know," he said. I did not repeat this to Mother.

"Yes, we will bake another kind tomorrow," I said. He must be thinking of the little cakes made of grass seeds ground and made into a paste. It would take a great deal of time, but that didn't matter if he wanted them. Things like this he was to mention over and over, and we never came close to the white bread, the puddings, or the pastry he had in mind.

When his cup was empty, I took my own and filled it in the kettle and poured it into his. Surprised, I saw him frown. That was the way to do honor to a guest, my grandfather had taught me.

Pierre looked around the room, and then sighed. I saw him making plans in his mind, as he finished the venison and went to his chair by the fireplace and took out his pipe. Dismayed, Mother and I looked at our lovely supper. He had eaten hardly any of it, and he had not touched his second cup of tea.

The next day he came bringing a china teapot. I remember it because I saw so many scenes like this one when Pierre brought something strange into the cabin. I remember his face. There was a strain in it that appeared more and more as he came to know the distress it caused us. He knew and we knew it was more than the bringing of presents. It was a criticism of what we had already, an attempt to strike killing blows at our old way of life. It had begun with the new chairs, and china dishes in place of the ones we had worked to make fine for him before he came—new wooden plates we had colored orange by rubbing them with the fresh root of the bloodroot, and bowls dyed red from being boiled with red-osier, dogwood, and alder.

I remember the way the teapot looked when he set it in the middle of the rough board table. White it was, with red roses about the fat body of it. He called me, and explained how it should be used. I explained it to Mother, and Pierre listened, in good humor. "Are there any parts of speech in that language?" he asked, after the long flow of Ojibway syllables was over. "Every sentence sounds like one long word."

Mother stood looking down at the teapot, silently. She stretched out a hand toward it, and then drew back. She was always afraid to handle china—it broke when one treated it like tin or wooden dishes. She wanted to tell Pierre that she knew what it was for, because the major's wife had one. But we had already learned that mention of the major's wife made Pierre frown, and it was a hard frown to take away.

"We know how to use it." I took it up carefully and started for the kettle of tea.

"Oh, wash it first!"

I was amazed. There was nothing in it. How could it be dirty?

"Workmen's hands have touched it, and it was packed in straw to come by boat," said Pierre.

Looking at the whiteness of the inside, I wondered how anyone could be so particular.

"Little by little we progress," said Pierre when I began obediently to rub soft soap inside it, and rinse it carefully, feeling as if I were going through a silly performance.

"Perhaps it is a ceremony," Mother said to me in Ojibway.

Of course! That must be it, and I worked more willingly. Mother and I from our first acquaintance with soap thought it something particularly suitable for a medicine ceremony.

Pierre avoided looking at the bed, and went to his chair by the fire. We came to feel most secure when he was sitting in his own place, for his brow always cleared over a book, and he asked no puzzling questions about cobwebs across corners, windows that one could not see through, or little rolls of gray fluff drifting across the floor. We learned that he could not abide stepping on spilled maple syrup that stuck to his shoes, and the grinding of sugar under his feet made him squirm. We took counsel with Marthe about it, and she told us we might have to sweep every day with the ash broom across the paths he might follow in the room.

There was no end to the new ways. Mother and I learned to wash our hands just before eating—another ceremony, we decided. We used the washbasin where Pierre always washed his white hands, with sleeves rolled up, before he sat at table, even though they seemed spotless before he began.

Seeing Pierre in the early morning in his dressing-gown, a full purple silk coat he always wore until after he had shaved, seeing him brush his hair before the mirror he had bought for the wall above the washbasin, we felt that something new had come into the cabin. The teapot, the armchair, the shelves of books, were part of a new presence even when Pierre was away. Mother and I worked together, never any longer planning what we would like to do, but always in terms of what would please Pierre. Our reward came in the evenings, when over one of his books, his frown cleared, and he looked with affection at Mother when she drew near and began to rub his head with skillful fingers, and we saw that less often his glance went toward the bed, the kettles wiped out with dried moss and scoured with sand and ashes.

Winter passed, and the soft winds of spring came again. Mother began to plan for the coming season.

"Now that we are going to stay here, we must plant corn," she said one day. "When the moon is right, we shall plant it."

Marthe was away from home most of the time in her own garden. Baptiste had bargained for the use of a small open space at the northern end of the island, belonging to the farm there. Marthe had been going around the western shore to it in her canoe, preparing the ground for corn and potatoes.

When Mother asked me to tell Pierre about the corn, he refused to hear of it. "No. We do not need to raise corn. We can buy what we need."

I told Pierre that Mother did not want a field, or even a garden such as Marthe had, but only a few rows behind our cabin. "Let her do it," I said. "It will make her feel better. We have always planted corn when we intended to stay long in one place. We left beautiful fields of it behind when the soldiers drove us away from our home on the Wabash."

"I cannot work in corn," said Pierre.

"Oh, no. A man must never touch it," I agreed, not knowing I was taking his words another way from what he meant. "Only a woman has the power to give life and can teach it to the corn."

At last Pierre agreed. "Only a few rows, like some of

the other women of the village put among their sun-flowers and turnips."

So Mother and I began to dig where the sand and pebbles of the beach left off, on a ledge of earth just below the ridge of the meadow. We cleared out the weeds and nettles and dug the earth to softness and waited for the right time of the moon. When the time came, Marthe gave Mother an ear of red seed corn, and Mother and I dropped the kernels into the hills, arms-length apart, adding a fish and a few ashes in each hole.

Every day we watched the ledge, and when the first green blades came through, we knelt beside them in wonder at the new life we had brought. We caressed the earth about each tender leaf, and murmured our thanks to the corn spirit.

It grew tall and straight at first, with a plume at the top turning purple, forming little ears with pale green tassels. But then no grain came within the husks to make them plump and round. "The evil spirit has been here," said Marthe when we told her about it. It was always the evil spirit that kept corn from growing or chased away game to make bad hunting. We knew this so well that we paid no attention to Baptiste's comments that, so near the beach, the soil was not good enough to raise anything but sand-burrs.

Added to Mother's worries about pleasing Pierre—for it seemed we no sooner made one change when he wanted another, was this worry about the corn. She felt it was some weakness in herself.

One night after we had snuffed out our candles and gone to bed, I heard a noise in my sleep. I sat up and looked out of the narrow window. I could see nothing, though the moon shone bright. Again that noise came, of footsteps on the pebbles. I saw then that Mother was not in the big bed. "Pierre," I called.

He groaned in response, and turned over. I ran to his side and touched his shoulder. He threw off the blankets then, and sat up. "What is it? Where is your mother?"

Then Mother stepped into the doorway from the outside. The moonlight threw silver fire all around the brownness of her, for she had nothing on.

"Naneda! What have you been doing?" Pierre's voice shook.

Mother moved out of the door-frame into the darkness and snatched up a blanket to wrap around her. "Mother!" I called.

"It was to make the corn grow," she said to me, but in the way she spoke when she wanted me to say it to Pierre. "To make the corn grow," I repeated.

Pierre was on the edge of the bed now, drawing his purple dressing-gown about him. "Naneda, are you ill?" He walked across the room, groping for her where she stood in the corner against the bookshelves. He put his arm about her, his hand to her forehead. "She doesn't seem to have a fever," he said in a puzzled voice.

"Why don't you tell him, Oneta?" asked Mother, in one of the moments she was almost impatient that Pierre could not understand if she told him herself.

"It is a medicine rite," I told him. "A woman must run naked through the corn, to keep insects and worms from working there, and give the spirit of the corn a chance to make it grow."

Pierre moved across a window in the darkness, and I saw that he was drawing away from Mother. She still cowered where he had found her.

"It doesn't make sense," he said impatiently. "Are you sure she isn't ill?"

I assured him again that it was a custom. He walked slowly back to the bed, and sat looking out of the window into the path of the moonlight. "We go along for days and I am content," he murmured. "And then something like this happens—" His voice trailed away as though swallowed by the dark, and he went back under the blanket in silence.

The next morning as he started for the fur company, we heard of it again. Baptiste had stopped him to ask about the number of packs brought in, and how it compared with other years. "Looks like a big season for Monsieur Astor." He always said that name as if it fascinated him, as if he had made much conversation only to be able to say it. "My woman tells me she seen yours out in the corn in the middle of the night," he said suddenly, as Pierre was about to go on across the meadow.

Pierre hesitated. "Did you ever hear of any such thing?"

"Oh, sure, it's one of their ideas. It's something about woman being the symbol of fertility, or some other notion. Funny about corn, they are. They'll never let a man set foot in the field if they can help it."

Pierre looked back at our cabin, and I lowered my head from the window. I could hear little of what he said, but it was in a disturbed voice. "I hope she gets over such ideas. As my wife—"

"If you'll excuse me," said Baptiste, "for giving advice to my betters, I'd say—well, you'll be happier if you don't try to make her over much. The young one, now—but not Naneda. She's a good woman, let her have a few notions, I'd say. But of course it's none of my business—" Baptiste's voice came fainter now, as if he had gone down to his boat. "I wouldn't worry none about the corn. Probably some man started that in the first place. It's as good an excuse as any to get the women to do all the planting and weeding."

In the fall, Mother began to stay quietly indoors. She never went to the village any more, but sat by the fire embroidering the edges of the buffalo robe Pierre had bought from a northern hunter in a moment of thoughtfulness about what she would like. It was the first thing she had ever asked him for. Soft as a cashmere shawl it was when she had scraped the hide to softness and

143

brushed and cleaned the fur. "Beadwork around the edges it must have, like the one you were laid in when you were born," she said. "It will have the same beads. I saved them from the other robe when it was worn out."

She took so much pleasure in it, and such a different pleasure from any I had seen before in her face and voice that I asked her at last, "What is the new robe to be used for?"

"There will be a new child here before the ice goes out of the lakes. It is for the new child."

Ice captured the waves of the straits and held them motionless, and the snow came down. Baptiste fixed our cabin for the winter, banking the snow all about it, and piling balsam boughs on the side next the wind. The wind blew hard along that shore, intent on whirling away every flake of the light dry snow that fell with it. It stripped the forest of leaves, but there was still the beauty of evergreens and flecked white birches.

It was in the first moon of 1817 that my brother was born. When the time had come, Marthe sent Pierre and me to her cabin, while she waited alone with Mother.

That day, after several weeks of clear, frosty weather, a sudden thaw had come. When we stepped out of the cabin, all around us was a dense haze, black and disagreeable. The late afternoon heavens were full of dull gray clouds, almost blue at the horizon. Our feet slipped into a wet mass of softened snow at every step. "This is the weather a hunter dreads," I said to Pierre. "It makes the snow cling to his snowshoes until he can't walk any more."

Pierre did not answer. He was looking with disgust at the wet leather on his feet. Moisture from the roof dripped on our heads as we entered Marthe's cabin.

Baptiste, alone, made us welcome. "Rosanne, she's

144

over to Louise's, I guess. Want to go over there, or sit here with your—er, pa—and me?"

"I'll stay here," I said, and when the men were drawn up to the fire, Baptiste warning Pierre not to dry his shoes too close to the flames, I sat at the window, looking out at the haze. It was one of those moments when Mackinac seemed a world of its own; and when people left it they went out into nothingness and only lived again when they came back. When days were clear, the mainland asserted itself with a fringe of pines on the skyline, but only a slight mist was enough to shut it off and make us completely alone. Later I remembered this, and wondered if thus were the men on Mackinac deceived, believing the island's fate was its own, and its future could be as big as the men on it could vision and plan.

As evening came on, the dripping stopped, and a cold breeze came through the chinks of the cabin. "Goin' to freeze right up again," said Baptiste, stooping to put more wood on the fire. "Be nice and slippery in the morning, with all this water freezin' up solid."

Pierre had fallen silent, as if he were listening for sounds from the next cabin.

"You won't hear nothin' until the kid himself lets out a yell," said Baptiste, taking up his fiddle and tucking it under his chin. "And that won't be for some time yet. Your woman won't let out a sound. They have a funny notion about that. If the mother can't endure the pain without cryin' out, the baby won't have the courage they think so much of. And she wouldn't expect you to be decent to her if she didn't give the child that to start out with."

Baptiste's good foot tapped on the bare floor, where a spot was beginning to show wear from many years of his beating time. He began to play softly, gentle tunes that let one slide down them into memory, or vague, endless yearnings. I had not thought of the new child as a person yet, but more as one of the new things that had come to our life along with Pierre. Admiring Pierre as I did, and fond of him, too, still there was sadness in my thoughts as I went over in my mind the difference in our life. It was as if the old ways had died, for every change meant death to what it touched. I felt within me that the coming of this child meant we could never turn our faces backward. This tied our lives to Pierre's. As I sat there, half drowsy under the soft melodies Baptiste's fingers wove and spun into threads to build on, I wondered about the future. Still, in all my thoughts, I had no idea of what this new child was going to mean to me, his sister, or to Pierre, his father. The family relationships I had known were simple ones, where a son looked up to his father as perfection he should attain, and the father took pains to teach the child what he should know. But I was to learn it was not always that way.

Because he could not sit still, Pierre took up one of the candles in his hand, and walked up and down, holding it over the book he had carried along in his pocket. He read aloud the gentle French poetry as if the words would push away the reality of what was happening in the next cabin. Untroubled, since the future hid from him behind its own gray mist, he awaited the birth of his son.

The words he read seemed in my dreaminess to be woven from my own thoughts and the music as the fiddle went gliding from one tune to another without pause.

> *Ce qui fut, se refait; tout coule comme une eau,*
> *Et rien dessous le ciel ne se voit de nouveau;*
> *Mais la forme se change en une autre nouvelle,*
> *Et ce changement-là, vivre au monde s'appelle,*
> *Et mourir quand la forme en une autre s'en va.*

Once Pierre stopped by the window. "These are cold shores," he said. "Cold and hard. I wonder sometimes what the early explorers thought if they came this way in winter. La Salle came at that dreary season, expecting every day to find balmy weather, the trees and fruit and spices of the Orient. He must have despaired when he found nothing but icy winds and barren shores."

"I'd just as soon be inside tonight myself," said Baptiste, lifting his bow from the strings. "I ain't got enough top hair for a cold night. But don't be bluffed by these winds. The cold of a clear day when the sun shines and no air stirs will fool you worse than the driving wind of a blizzard. It was a day like that I froze this foot of mine."

When the music and Pierre's reading began again, I was soothed by the soft words and tones, and the heat from the fire. I fell asleep at last, my head against the side of the chair Baptiste had made from a barrel.

When I awoke, dawn had come, and Pierre was no longer in the cabin. Baptiste had been outside and came in just as I awoke. "Better hurry over to your house and see what's come," he said, as I straightened the cramp from my back and wiped the sleep from my eyes.

I stood above the new baby in wonder, for new life has a beauty not found in anything that has been long upon the earth. It makes no difference whether it be a green blade just pushing up through the earth, or the look in the eyes of a new-born child.

Nine

❧ The ice went out of the straits, and the island prepared itself for the moon of flowers. Bright warm days came, the days when ferns begin to curl upward from the ground, and the bear gets tired of his cave. On such a day, when the sun hung low in the sky and a long twilight of northern spring was about to begin, I watched Mother putting on her dress with the stripes of light and balsam green. We could hear Pierre coming home, whistling *Au Clair de la Lune* as he often did to let us know he was on his way across the meadow. He came through the door, laid his cloak across a chair, and bent above the baby, lying on my cot in a long white gown. Through the open door, I could see Baptiste beside his canoe, waiting to take Pierre and Mother over to St. Ignace to have the baby christened. Pierre did not want to take his place with the other villagers and parents from Shantytown in the group christenings that would be held when the priest came to Mackinac. He had not thought about the matter at all until I had asked about a naming ceremony like the one at my own birth.

"His name is Paul de Ronsard Debans," Pierre had said. "But we must take him to the priest."

I saw Baptiste look toward the cabin, as if expecting them to come out. He laid down the paddle he had been mending, and took from his pocket a handful of the sweet mast-nuts of the beech, chewing on them as he waited.

Mother tied her best bonnet above her neat braids, and took up her shawl, but Pierre stood silent above the child. Little Paul was looking toward the rafters, waving his arms in short, jerky movements. I was kneeling at the hearth, washing grains of ripe corn that had been boiled with wood ashes, slipping from them the loosened skins. Swelled grains we would have for supper when they came back. Feeling that Pierre stood unusually long beside the baby, I turned and saw that he was looking at its head and the fuzz of hair black as the fur of a sable, grown so long that we could comb it down over the little forehead. I make no pretense of always knowing what was in Pierre's mind, but there was certain signs that told me much when they appeared. A deep line, not quite a frown, came between his eyes when he was puzzled or displeased. It was there when he bent above Paul.

"Can you see any sign of a curl in it? All the Debanses have curly hair."

"No. It seems as straight as mine," I said. Pierre drew back from the baby.

Baptiste was in the doorway. "Give him a chance to grow. I've seen hair change a lot. The two first leaves of a weed is the same as those of a seedling flower. Not until they shed them two false ones and come out with their own do you know what they're goin' to be."

"The baby won't have all those wrinkles when he gets fatter, and his face will not be red," I said, smoothing the soft down above the little face. The baby caught my thumb with his hand and held on tight. I was going to say that the sun and wind would give him a nice brown skin when he could be out of doors more, but Pierre interrupted, saying,

"Of course his skin will be whiter when he is older." I let the words stand, and wrapped Paul in a blanket for the journey.

"Got away a little early, didn't you?" Baptiste turned to squint at the disappearing sun.

"Yes, Mr. Stuart was kind enough—" The rest of the words were lost as I soothed Paul, who had begun to cry at being disturbed. Rocking him on my knee, I thought of the figure brought to mind by the name Stuart. I knew what sort of man was this head agent of the awesome, far-away Mr. Astor. A few nights before, Pierre had had a visitor. I had come in from Marthe's and found him sitting in the chair Mother usually had, while she had withdrawn into the shadows with baby Paul on her lap. I had slid on to the edge of my cot. Round-eyed, I had looked the stranger over, knowing by the way Pierre treated him who he must be. I had heard of him, of his great feat of crossing the west through dangers on all sides to found a trading post near the mouth of the distant Columbia, calling it Astoria in honor of his chief. Pierre had spoken of him so often in terms of respect for his position on the island that he had been to me like a figure in one of Marthe's legends —someone with great influence on what we did, yet really no more visible than the spirits of the water.

It had been a shock to see that stocky figure in my mother's chair, his sharp, deep-set eyes taking in every detail of the room and ourselves, his scrutiny softened by the way his lips were ready with a smile of good-nature at it all. His stubby, active hands had tapped thoughtfully the tall beaver hat in his lap, yet there was no restlessness in the man. His feet in their black-buttoned shoes were squarely on the floor before him, and I watched his white stock under the black coat lapels move leisurely up and down with his breathing. Here was a man who could do things, or could be quiet when there was nothing that needed doing. The tails of his coat hung between the chair seat and its back, making him look a little like a plump sparrow. When he spoke, I could not understand, and Pierre answered in a language I knew must be English. Pierre, so straight and proud, had been anxious to please that little man.

"Bring the little tike and come on," suggested Baptiste, breaking into my memories of Mr. Stuart. He sauntered on ahead to his canoe, while Pierre arranged his blue cloak about his shoulders and waited for Mother to take the baby up in her arms. She smiled as she cuddled the child against a breast as round and soft as a robin's.

Outside, we could hear Baptiste singing.

"*Là-bas derrière ma tante,*
Il y a un coq qui chante,
Des pommes, des poires, des raves, des choux,
Des figues nouvelles, des raisins doux—"

"This ceremony," I asked, "is it as good as the real one? Will it put him under the protection of the right spirits?"

"It makes him part of a great church, and puts him under the protection of the saints," said Pierre.

Having no knowledge of saints, I wondered. I said no more, but when Pierre had helped Mother into the canoe, into which she could have gotten easier by herself, and Baptiste's singing grew more faint and blended with the sound of the waves, I hurried to put the swelled grains in a kettle over the fire and add water and a few pieces of dried venison to them. Then I went over to ask Marthe if something could be done to make sure that the baby would also have the protection of the spirits of the breathing wind, the water, and the sky, the rocks and the forest, since man must live close to all of these.

That summer, I took almost all the care of the baby upon myself, as Mother and Marthe began their long season of gathering berries, preserving and drying them, drying fish and corn and making pemmican when meat was plentiful. Paul had a little bed of his own, so low it could be pushed under the big one in the daytime to get it out of the way in the crowded cabin. During the day I kept him on my cot, waving flies away from his round little face as I worked on a bit of embroidery, or carried him outside and for walks along the shore, letting him sleep sometimes on a blanket in the sun.

Marthe thought such a life was too idle for a girl eleven years old. It was not long before she spoke to Mother about it. "What is Oneta making now?" she began one day, looking closely at the strip of birchbark I had sewed into a round shape to slip over Pierre's tobacco can. I held it up to show the binding on the edges, the pattern in red and blue quills around the top and bottom. But Marthe gave no praise as she usually did for the work of my hands. Instead, she turned to Mother, impatiently.

"Oneta should be working with us, learning the things we do. The baby should have a cradleboard. Then you could carry him on your back, or hang him up while we work, freeing Oneta to work with us."

Mother did not answer. Since it was the father's duty to make the wooden frame, Mother, through me, had asked Pierre about a cradleboard when Paul was born. Pierre had had the little bed sent up from the store, and we had not had courage to tell him that was not what we meant.

"We have no more soap, I see," I answered, to appease Marthe. "This afternoon while the baby sleeps I shall make soap."

"See," she turned to Mother, "she is growing up ignorant. At her age she should know that soap made before the full of the moon will shrink away."

Marthe uttered her reproof in different ways from time to time, as she and Mother carried the work into the moon of fading leaves again, and dried corn in its husks under a leaf-smothered fire, later to be boiled up with deer or bear meat, when all its retained sweetness would come out and flavor the meat. Still later she repeated it on the day when Armand and two men from the village went to the mainland on a bear-hunt, to try to get one just before he crawled into his cave for the winter, when his fat-sac would be full, his meat juicy and tender. Returning, Armand skinned his bear, cut up the meat and divided it among the three cabins. "See," said Marthe, "this preparing of bear meat is something Oneta should be learning. She will be a hunter's wife some day, and it will bring shame upon her family if she cannot take care of meat."

Then Mother gave in. She got Baptiste to help her make the cradle, saying she would make a fine one that would be a surprise to Pierre.

Baptiste didn't seem eager to work on it, but Mother didn't notice. I remember how she held up a little sack she had made of the last of her mourning clothes. "See all these beads for the swathing band," she said, joy rising in her voice. "All the beads from the old deerskin clothing I don't wear any more. They will make the band very fine."

Baptiste hefted the bag. "Most a pound of them, must be." Looking at the pleasure on her face, he hadn't the heart to object any longer, and went to work with her.

From pliable linden wood he carved the board that would support the baby's back, the footboard, and the arch that would protect his head. Mother fastened these parts together with deer sinews Marthe brought from the endless store of such things in her cabin. Working in secret, hiding her efforts under the bed when it was time for Pierre to come home, she made the swathing band from a length of fine white cloth Mr. Stuart had given Pierre when the baby was born. Intertwined with the broad pattern of beading was a ribbon Baptiste brought from the store as his gift. Even I had a chance to help, for Mother let me go up on the heights and gather moss to line the cradle.

The night it was finished is one time that stands out with every moment clear and sharp in memory. Mother wrapped Paul in a blanket, and settled him into the cradle, arranging his legs carefully with moss between so they would not grow crooked. Then around the whole cradleboard was wrapped the swathing band with its rows and rows of beadwork.

"Isn't it fine?" she beamed, her eyes soft, melting, as she caressed the serious-faced baby with her small berry-stained hands. "It is nicer than the one you had, Oneta. We had so little then. I had never seen such fine white cloth as this in that time."

It did look showy, almost dazzling when the sun rested on all the wealth of beads. Across the arch in front of Paul's eyes, Mother hung a bell-shaped rattle Pierre had bought him, and a good-luck charm Marthe had woven in the shape of a spider web. At once I wanted to give him something, and ran in to get the red stone from the arrow my father had sent.

"Oh, do you want to give that away?" asked Mother, but with no reproach.

"Yes. This is a man-child such as my father hoped would be in his lodge. He should have the arrowhead." Pleased, Mother fastened it beside the charm.

So encased, nothing could harm the baby, and he was comfortable and content. It was late in the afternoon when we finished, and Mother hung him up on a nail on the outside of the cabin, and we sat on the steps to await Pierre's surprise at our work.

Paul began a soft little cooing as he swayed in the new cradle.

"See, Mother, he is watching the white gulls," I said.

Before she could answer, we heard, on the breeze bearing the smell of cut sweet-grass from the meadow,

"*Au clair de la lune,*
Mon ami Pierrot—"

Mother trembled a little in anticipation, and then sat still in quiet joy.

Pierre came around the corner, swinging his walking stick. He did not at first see Paul.

"Resting a little before supper?" he asked, and whistled another bar of the song.

"*Prêtez-moi ta plume—*"

Mother cast her eyes down, waiting. I pointed behind her back at the suspended cradle.

Pierre stopped whistling, and before my astonished eyes his face tightened in a new expression, almost one of horror. "What have you done?" he shouted.

Mother jumped up and shrank back against the cabin. He had never used that tone before.

"No son of mine can hang up in a thing like that!" he shouted again. Dropping his walking stick, he seized the cradle, jerked it down, tore off the ornaments and threw them to the ground. I watched in stunned amazement as he tore the beautiful swathing, ripping across the embroidery Mother had spent so many hours in perfecting. Paul whimpered with fright as Pierre pulled him out of the cradle and threw it to the ground. Then, his face white and cold, he strode into the cabin with Paul and laid him on the bed.

Paul began to cry loudly. I started to go to him, but stopped when I saw Mother still shrinking against the wall. I caught her by the hand, and urged her with gentle pressure to sit on the step with me again. "What did he say?" she whispered in puzzled fright.

I told her, and her head fell forward, her happiness crushed. Inside, Paul wailed on. When I thought I must leave Mother and go to him, I heard Pierre go to the bed again, take up the baby and begin soothing him, the tension going out of his voice as he did so. Somehow, hearing his voice become natural again, I knew it was all over. At least he would say nothing more. Now that it is all past, I can count on one hand the times I saw him angry, but each time brought a change to his life, and the last, a tragic one. As I look back, I see that he was never completely happy in the cabin again. It was as if this cradleboard was a symbol of all the ways he did not like.

The shock of what had happened left a scar on my mother's heart that never healed entirely. I sat there for a long time with her, stroking her hand, not knowing what to say. I was as puzzled as she about the cause of Pierre's temper. "Never mind, never mind," I whispered to her. She was silent, as if her feelings rushed from her heart but hesitated on her tongue.

I slipped my hand from hers, and walked slowly out to where the arrowhead had fallen among the stones. I took it up, holding it lovingly cupped in my palm, turning it over and caressing it in apology for the roughness with which it had been treated, and I brought it back to Mother. Then her tears came, falling on my hands with a soft blessing as of rain.

"Why is it not good for his son?" she asked. "In a cradle like that the great Pontiac was once wrapped, and Tecumseh!" She put her head down on my lap, her sobs almost choking her as she tried to keep Pierre from hearing.

Ten

ॐ "Cute little *chicot*," said Michel one late fall day, when he and I were tending large flakes of sturgeon drying on Marthe's rack, and Paul was playing in the gravel beside the cabin steps. Smiling at the wordless chatter of his seven months, as he tried to tell Mother what he was doing with the colored autumn leaves and scraps of birchbark in his hands, and hearing through the open door the sound of Mother's voice as she approved, I did not at first realize what Michel had said.

When I did ask about it, he told me *chicot* was the name he had always heard for those who were half one race and half another, that in the *pays d'en haut*, Canada, where his parents had come from, it was the name for the half-burned stumps in the cleared forest. It was just a new word to me. I felt no disparagement in it, and my serenity was untouched as I looked around at the sun-baked shore. Summer was already announcing her farewell in the colored leaves on the heights. The meadow grass was long, and had waves in it when the wind blew up off the water, making it look as if the water and the island were all of a piece and the fishing cabins were on a raft in the midst of the waves, a raft on which Michel and I stood and turned the drying fish.

Mother came to the door and took Paul up, smiling at us over his dark little head. Michel touched his forehead in respect.

"Quiet around here," he said when she had gone back in the cabin. "Where is Rosanne?"

"She went to the village with Jacques."

"Did he have Mother's market basket?"

I nodded. "Then you won't have to go, will you?"

"Not to the store, but I have a washing to take back to the village later on." He gathered up the smoke-dried flakes and tied them in a little bundle that could be hung from cabin rafters. As I spread fresh ones on the rack, I thought briefly about Rosanne. It had already become a natural thing for her to be with Jacques wherever he was. She had grown beautiful, with the same dark curly hair, the dark skin touched with rose and creaminess she had had as a child. The same temper she had, too, but she never showed it with Jacques and everyone marveled how he could so well manage her. Though he was only thirteen, he had already announced that when he had become a voyageur and then a brigade leader, with a comfortable home of his own in the winter camp —one of the important posts of the fur company it must be—he would marry Rosanne.

Little clouds, round and fluffy as a rabbit's tail, moved slowly through the sky above, and closer about our heads, gulls no less white than the clouds, circled out over the water and back again. The dull smoke rose in the still air. We heard throaty shouts and songs in French *patois* as canoes of traders went past. These were such accustomed sounds that for all the attention we gave, there might as well have been silence, until at once we heard a strange noise on the beach near the point. I dropped my turning-fork and ran out near the water, Michel following, until we could see what it was.

Coming down the beach was the postmaster's helper, this time leading a pony hitched to his high-wheeled cart, for it was full of bags and boxes, as many as the shallow cart could hold without tumbling them out. He came on down the beach so close that we could see his bushy eyebrows and his vacant eyes, before we saw that someone was walking behind the cart.

An old lady was coming down the beach, small and dressed like the village women, but with a difference. Her gray skirt had a black band as soft as fur around the hem. I later learned it was velvet. She was most careful to hold it up off the pebbles with one hand, while the other held a small bag of red woven goods. The dress had a high collar that seemed to be pushing her head in the air. On her head was a little cap of white, its ruffle standing up stiffly around her wrinkled face.

Many people were seen on our beach in summer that were never seen again, for the island had already become a stopping place for schooners, a place to rest overnight for travelers bound for Green Bay or the Chicago settlement at Fort Dearborn far down the lake of the Illinois. Many of these travelers strolled around our point on their way to see the mountainous bluffs beyond, the cobbler's cave, the spring, and Lover's Leap, as they had named the rock of the maiden. These always walked slowly, in groups of two or three, exclaiming and uttering admiring remarks. "Like a beautiful park set in blue water," they would say. "Such a quaint village." And, "We must all go to see the arched rock before we leave."

But no visitors had come alone, with a cartful of boxes. I looked at this old lady more closely. Her eyes were bright, and kept moving about, taking in the cabins, the rack of fish, and Michel and me. Her steps were quick and lively, so that her gray hair and wrinkles were her only sign of age. She was like a cedar that has long fought wind, snow, and hail, but at last begins dying in the top branches. She walked along as if she knew where she was going, yet by the way she looked at things I was sure she had never been on this beach before.

As we watched, one of the boxes slipped from the overloaded cart and fell to the ground. Instantly she raised the red bag and tapped the boy on the head with it as he bent to lift the box. "Don't you dare drop that!" she exclaimed in French. "That has my best spoons and china in it. *Vite, vite,* get on past these huts and to where my son lives."

The boy replaced the box and stood up, resting his hands on his hips. "He lives there," he said sulkily, twitching one shoulder toward our cabin.

"What? I believe it not!" shouted the old lady. She walked with short quick steps to where Michel and I were standing, her little silver shoe buckles catching the sun in quick flashes. She gave me only a curious look, and turned her back on me, speaking to Michel. "You tell me, lad, if you can, where does Monsieur Pierre Debans live?"

But Pierre had heard her voice and came running out of the cabin before Michel could answer. "Mother! Mother! What in the world—what are you doing here?"

She dropped her package and threw her arms around him. He gave her frail body a joyous hug, swinging her completely off the ground. Seeing them there, her wrinkled cheek against his pale white one, I saw how like they were. It was in the straightness of the nose, the height of forehead, the curl in the hair, though hers was almost as white as the cap that sat upon it. It was in the frailness of their bodies. Most of all it was in the way they held their heads up to face all the world, their backs in a straight line, and in their calmness with fun and fire beneath.

"How in the world did you get here?" Pierre asked again.

She put a wrinkled hand up to his face, fine lace falling away from her wrist as she did so. "*Mais, mon Dieu,* I got lonesome for you. And when I got your letter about your marriage, I understood you were not coming back to Quebec. So, *tout à fait,* I knew I must live here with you. Did you not get my letter about selling our house, and my plans to come?"

"No. I have had no letter from you in the whole winter."

"Maybe it was lost," Michel offered in explanation. "Do you remember, M'sieu, that one of the couriers drowned? Her letter may have been in his pack."

"It matters not about the letter," said the old lady. "I am here now. Let's have a look at you." She held her head on one side like a saucy wren and looked into Pierre's face. Then she threw her arms about him again, swinging around so her back was toward me. She had a row of curls all around under the cap so that from the back she looked like a little girl with her grandmother's clothes on. At once I was not shy of her, and stepped to her side.

"*Bon jour,* Madame," I said. "I have heard Pierre speak of you."

"Mercy on us!" she exclaimed. "Does this little native then speak like civilized people?"

Repulsed at her tone, I backed away, but I went on staring at her until she took her eyes away, turning back to her son. "She calls you Pierre—do you then know some of the natives so well?" Before he could answer, she came back to the first thing that had puzzled her. "But how is it that you live in such a—" She pointed to our cabin. And then a strange look came over her face. I followed the direction of her eyes. My mother had been attracted by the voices and stood looking out of the doorway. "Pierre—*Pierre*, that is a servant?" The old lady said it weakly, as if she already knew the truth.

"No, Mother, that is my wife." Pierre spoke with an effort, as if he were dragging a weight, as when one travels on snowshoes loaded with rain-softened snow. It was not as if he were ashamed, but as if he had to say something he could not make her understand.

A silence fell between them. The old lady looked as if she were suddenly ill. "Why didn't you tell me you had taken an Indian squaw?"

Embarrassed, Michel and I turned away. I was angry at her tone, but kept silence, remembering an admonition of Marthe's, "Say nothing that is unworthy of you."

The boy, standing impatiently by his cart, called out, "Want the boxes dumped here?"

"No," said the old lady. "Take them right back to the village. I'll find some place to stay there until the next boat."

"They ain't goin' to be any more boats," the boy said in his high voice. "I heard the captain of this'un tell the postmaster there wouldn't be any more mail in by boat —there won't be another one through. It's too near time for the ice to come."

"I will find you a place in the village until we can talk this over," said Pierre. "Mrs. Ruggs keeps a very good boarding house."

His mother looked like a trapped animal at the words that there wouldn't be any way to go back to Quebec.

Pierre went on. "But of course you will live here with us. We'll arrange it somehow—we'll build you a room of your own."

"A woman who has bowed at the court of France, to live with an Indian squaw for a daughter-in-law?" she asked with spirit. "Have I then made this long journey, risking my life for that? Never!"

161

Pierre bowed his head. "She is good and kind, and she has made me very comfortable. And it is not unusual here—"

"Say not another word!" she said angrily. "And I suppose you've got a flock of papooses you haven't written me about, too," she stormed.

Pierre straightened up then, and turned to me, laying his hand gently on my shoulder. "This is her daughter, whom I have adopted. And we have now a son."

"A half-breed! Bringing half-breeds into the world!"

I knew suddenly that half-breed meant *chicot*, but her tone had put something shameful in it that had not been in Michel's word.

While I was thinking about it, she was still talking angrily. "I'm glad your father didn't live to see it. Could you do nothing better with your education, with one of the proudest names of France?"

She turned back to the boy, and motioned to him, commanding. He hastened to turn the pony around. Michel picked up her red package and handed it to her. "*Merci,*" she said sadly. "*Sainte Vierge, ne m'abandonnez pas,*" she sobbed as she turned away. Pierre hesitated, then took her parcel, and side by side they followed the cart around the point.

Eleven

℣ Madame Debans was not contented at Mrs. Ruggs's for long. Within two days she was demanding that Pierre find her a house where she could move in with the contents of the boxes she had brought from Quebec. We heard Pierre asking Baptiste one evening if he knew of a house to be had.

"Ye might get Mr. Denby's," said Baptiste, after some head-scratching. "He's been driven out for good, they say. Too stuck on the Britishers, he was. Followed 'em to Drummond's Island when it got too hot for him here some years back. His family hung on here for a while, but they finally flew the coop day before yesterday."

"Where is his house?"

"Right on the street where the fur company is. Just a piece this side of it. When you come this way from the big yard, it's Mrs. Ruggs's first and then some empty land and then this house. You know it. Biggest one in the village."

"Mother would like that." Pierre smiled tenderly, as if he could already see her moving in, taking it as her right. "Whom do I see about getting it?"

"Might ask the postmaster. I believe Denby left him in charge. Probably you can buy it, or rent it, either one, and cheap—"

As I listened, I was glad my mother knew no French. She knelt at the hearth, over a little basin in which she was boiling wild rice in syrup made from the sap of the woodbine. She was disturbed enough already. She had understood that Pierre's mother had come, and refused to stay because of her, his wife. Pierre did not know that she had taken in the meaning of the scene, and told her that his mother didn't want to crowd us, and would stay with Mrs. Ruggs in the village during her visit. Mother tried to take that as a reason, asking me, "Why then does she never come to our cabin for a visit? Why must he always go to see her at Mrs. Ruggs's, alone?" Her face had grown sadder every evening when he made some excuse to go out. She was easily hurt by those she loved; her affections were all the stronger for being given to so few of us.

"Does she not want to see her grandson?" she asked Pierre on the day Paul took his first uncertain steps across the cabin floor. When he made no answer, her eyes filled with tears.

I remember most of that winter by the tears of my

163

mother. Pierre seldom sat by the hearth with his book any more, but took it in his hand and set off for the village as soon as supper was over. Large gaps appeared among the books on the shelves, for he never brought one back. As I thought of it later, it was as if he were removing himself piecemeal from us. After a time it became more than usual for him not to come home for supper at all. "Mother is lonesome here," he said to me once. "I must keep her company as much as I can while she is here. No doubt she will go back to Quebec in the spring." His last words were unsure.

He was kind and thoughtful otherwise. When new goods came in, he bought things he thought we might like, even more than he had before, sending even special orders for new clothing and furniture for the cabin to be brought when the boats came back in the spring, sending the letters by mail now carried by runners on snowshoes.

The ice froze smoothly that year, and there was fine skating on the straits. Jacques and Michel got new skates for Noël gifts, and really enjoyed being given errands to do in the village. A broad stretch of their tracks marked the ice past our cabin and around the point. Baptiste bought skates for Rosanne, and a bright red wool cap to wear over her curls. She was taller than I, almost grown up that winter, and striking in appearance. Louise helped her make pretty dresses from the lengths of calico Baptiste brought from the store whenever he sold a barrel of fish. Louise brushed and combed her curls, and showed her how the ladies wore their hair for the dances.

Grown-up though she was becoming, she still enjoyed the times when the four of us went sliding on a sled Baptiste made from three boards, carving two of them into runners and nailing the third one above. We slid down the fort hill and across the meadow, climbing up again, laughing at stumps covered with

164

white like ermine caps, shaking evergreen branches loaded with white flakes that scattered in a shower. Returning home with snow melting on our warm clothing, we stopped in at Louise's and had cookies before the fire. Or, when the heaped-up snow and the winter storm kept hunters from going out, and the fishermen away from their nets, we went in Marthe's cabin for some of her cakes and Baptiste's stories of the days when he was a trader. He told us hearsay tales of the land of the powerful and fierce Blackfeet, among whom no trader would go unless he was ready for death. Baptiste liked the Great Lakes tribes, but he had a horror of those farther west. Sometimes he grew dramatic. "Paddlin' down one of them streams, and suddenly—a hiss, an arrow, and before you can pull it out of your skin, you know you are all through and you never know why." Michel and Rosanne would shudder, but Jacques's eyes would dance in excitement. He always stopped his frolicking and settled down on the floor, his eyes fastened on Baptiste, eager not to miss a word. He took in the stories as a hungry one takes meat. "That's what I'm going to be. Oh, I wish I were old enough to sign up with a brigade!" he always exclaimed when the tales were finished.

One early spring day, Mother asked, "When is Madame going?"

"I don't know," I said.

Two ships had come and gone back to the east, and still Madame lived on in the big house. Pierre came home so irregularly in those days that we could not depend on him always to bring food we needed, so I had gone to the village more often. I had seen the little old lady in her white cap going in and out of stores, or on the way home with a basket on her arm.

Before Mother could say more, the light of our doorway was cut off, and we both turned to see who had come. It was a black robe, still facing outward, his hand

165

raised in blessing above Louise and her boys, with whom he had walked from mass. When they went on, he faced us, smiling.

"I hope the blessing of health abides in this home," he said in a gentle voice.

"Yes," I said uncertainly.

He spoke to my mother in French, and then seeing she did not understand, in broken Ojibway. "I am just learning your tongue," he said. "You will excuse my mistakes. In time, in due time, I hope to know it well."

His tone was so kind that my mother smiled happily. He held out his hands to Paul, and the baby walked across the floor to him, eyes wide with interest in the long chains dangling at the black robe's side, the big shiny cross on his breast. The priest murmured some words neither Ojibway nor French, which I know now must have been a Latin blessing. "I am glad to find you all in good health." He sat down, holding Paul on his lap. "A man died at the boarding house this morning, with a fever, though the fort surgeon gave him emetics and bled him repeatedly. I came just in time to give him final absolution." The black robe made some gestures across his chest and murmured some more of the strange words. "A very sudden thing. In the midst of life—"

He was interrupted. Marthe came through the door, in her dress of coarse brown linsey, with the green leggings and dark brown moccasins she wore only for a journey. Her hair was glistening with bear's fat, and she wore a gray blanket tied about her waist, the upper part covering her shoulders loosely so her arms were left free.

"Oh, Marthe, where are you going?" I asked.

"To the Midé gathering, beyond the lakes." She sent the black robe a look of defiance, and stared at him as if waiting for him to go. In a few moments he rose to his feet and gave Paul back to my mother's arms.

"Since you have company"—he bowed to the unyielding figure of Marthe—"I shall come back another time. I want to talk to you about having your daughter taught by a good Catholic woman in the village, with the rest of the children from these cabins." He bent to me a smiling face, with blue eyes keen in it. "She should have a chance to learn to read. Her eyes show she is bright, and she speaks excellent French. I am sure she would do well."

When he had gone, I ran excitedly to Mother. "Did you understand what he said about having me learn to read? Did he mean I could read in books like Pierre? Oh, Mother, did he mean that?"

In the midst of my joyous excitement, I had forgotten Marthe. She looked up, scowling. "The wisdom in the world does not come from such things," she said. "It comes from seeing, and knowing what you see. Watching the movements of birds, the ways of animals, and knowing what the spirits tell you in dreams, those are the ways. As soon as you have passed into womanhood, I shall myself begin to teach you the secrets of the Midé. You will learn to read an omen in the flight of a bird, to call upon powers that only wait to serve you. That I have planned for you. That is what your father would want. I will have no black robe changing my plans. Such as he, and the firewater-bringing traders who ever follow, have left our race in worse condition wherever they have been."

"He seemed kind," murmured Mother. "He held Paul so gently. Paul seemed more content with him than with his own father." Over and over she and I had wondered if Paul's fear of his father's hands came from the episode of the cradleboard. But Paul was so little then.

"The black robe means to be kind," said Marthe grudgingly. "He does not know that we were better off in our own ways."

"Michel told me that the black robe has a book that

167

speaks to him and tells him what he must do and the things he must not do," I said.

"Tecumseh once said he thought it would be well if some of our young ones learned to read," said my mother suddenly. "Perhaps then we could use the source of the white man's wisdom as a tomahawk against him, he said."

Marthe frowned. She would have liked to deny that Tecumseh had ever approved of reading, any more than he wanted his people to use the white man's gun, or his flint and steel instead of two sticks rubbed together. But she was not sure he hadn't said it.

"It would do Oneta no good," she insisted. "It would lead her to want more things not of her own making, things beyond the reach of any one of us, even as the trader's store has led our people into more and more wants. Let me hear no more of it."

"Tell me where you are going, Marthe," I said, to drive the scowl from her face, and because travels always interested me. "Tell me what the journey will be like."

"This time I will have a canoe-boy to paddle with me, for I must go quickly. A boy from the mainland will go, the boy you used to play with, he of the heavy legs."

"Oh—Chase!" I had not thought of him since the day we children had played on the beach so long ago. "Where does Chase live now, Marthe?"

"His family has gone to the Porcupine Hills, near the bay they call Little Traverse," said Marthe. "For a love-charm I will make for him he will take the long journey with me. We go through the straits to the west, into Green Bay and past the mouth of the Menominee River. Up the Fox River, too, we go, and across Lake Winnebago to an Ottawa village on its farther banks. All the Midé from all the lake tribes will be there."

Mother helped Marthe carry out her bundles and pile them on the beach in readiness. Chase was trading some furs in the village. Marthe's eyes kept looking up and down the beach for Rosanne, but there was no sign of her quick-moving figure, no sound of her voice always alive with excitement. Wherever she had gone, she evidently didn't intend to come back to say good-by to her mother. Marthe's face took on a sad look as she realized it.

I walked up and down the shore with the baby, thinking less of Marthe's journey than of the child toddling close to me, his face in wrinkles of contentment as he watched the pebbles slide from under his little moccasins. I remember thinking of his name, that the de Ronsard must have a meaning hidden in its parts. Pierre had said it had none, being only the name of a poet, but I understood he might not want to tell what it was. My own people were secret with names, knowing it gave others a certain power over you to possess your name and its meaning. Names were solemn and important, for they lasted longer than the body; they survived even death.

Among canoes passing, I saw one whose upturned front was embroidered with a six-pointed star. Turning with a graceful curve toward our beach, it rose lightly again and again over the waves, mocking them as they tried to beat against it. When it scraped the pebbles where Marthe stood waiting, I looked curiously at the brown-skinned man in it. Chase had grown tall and straight, with a thin face that showed the high bones in his cheeks. He wore a bright red shirt that still bore the folds in which it had lain on the fur company's shelf. The warmth of the day or pride in his totem made him leave it open wide at the neck to show the figure of a moose pricked into his chest with gunpowder and vermilion.

His first words called attention to his shirt as an event

169

of importance. "White man tried to sell me two shirts. I told him, of what use two shirts?" He laughed, as one never encumbered with extras of any kind. "I got gun fixed, got powder and shot, and twists of tobacco."

Marthe asked him something about how many skins he had.

"Many beavers," he said, raising outstretched fingers several times in quick succession. "One pack of silver fox, and one of the best otters." He said the last with pride, for not everyone could trap otters.

"You grow much since we play on beach," he appraised me as he stretched full length on the beach, one arm across his eyes to keep the sun away, while Marthe and Mother loaded into the canoe the bags of pemmican and corn, and the Midé scrolls carefully tied in a blanket.

I remember that Mother said something about the long journey.

"Not far." He dismissed the hundreds of miles. "For a love-charm, a good one, I would paddle—from the Seminole country to the Blackfeet land." He spoke as if that was the greatest distance he had ever heard of.

Mother laughed softly. "She must have a hold on your heart."

Chase nodded, a little embarrassed. "I have sat around the meat-kettle and forgotten to dip my fingers in when it was my turn. I have sat in the woods and let a deer pass without lifting my rifle." He looked up at Marthe. "Is it made?"

She nodded. "Did you bring your part of it?"

He smiled broadly as he sat up and took from his tobacco pouch a bit of soiled green calico. Unwrapping it, he held up a long black hair. "One of her sisters pulled this from her head."

Marthe took from a pouch at her side two figures about an inch high, carved from wood, one representing a man and the other a woman. Next she took out a tiny

170

packet of seeds which she added to the figures, tying all together with the hair Chase gave her. Then she handed the little bundle to him. "Wear this night and day," she said, "and the girl you have chosen will soon be able to think of no man but you."

He took the figures with great respect, wrapped them in the piece of calico and put them in the pocket of his shirt. A smile of satisfaction began to spread over his face, until at last he laughed aloud in great joy, his teeth gleaming white against the brown skin. Suddenly he was serious again. "Even at a distance will it work?" His face clouded in worry. "It may be that she will choose another before I return."

"Distance makes no difference in the charm," said Marthe. "You will see, when you return your chosen one will be on the shore, or trembling in her father's lodge, waiting for you."

Chase laughed again, as if his desire were already attained. Marthe had taken her place in the canoe, and he glided into it, pushing away from the shore with a paddle. He picked up a twist of tobacco and threw it overboard for the spirits of the water, and then lifted a hand in gay farewell, and we raised ours, happy with him. Watching them shoot with long strokes out into the great waterway, we raised our hands again in farewell.

Twelve

☘ Three dawns later, baby Paul was sick, with blotches on his skin. I remember that Pierre wanted to get a doctor, but Mother feared the strange ways she had heard were used by white men to cure disease. And yet she didn't dare suggest a medicine man. "If only Marthe were here!" she said over and over, until it was in my dreams like a chant, such as I had heard in our ceremonies to invoke good spirits. I began to see forms in my dreams, all with leaf-brown faces, hair strained back from the forehead—Marthe's face multiplied many times.

She tried to remember the song Marthe sang when someone was ill. "Through my power you will walk in health," was all she could recall of it. She sang it, but with no faith, for she knew she had not the secrets of the Midé that must accompany the song. She longed to put up a medicine pole before our cabin as her ancestors had done before the lodge of the sick, but she was afraid of Pierre's anger, and prepared a table full of flowers instead, to appease the evil spirit.

And then on the sixth day of Paul's illness, Mother became ill herself, with the same hotness of skin, the same blotches. "I can no longer sit up, Oneta," she moaned, and staggered across to the big bed. I loosened her clothing and got her between blankets. Holding the baby, I sat beside her until I heard Pierre's whistle. Then I laid Paul beside Mother and ran out on the meadow to wait.

Even in my anxiety I remember thinking of that other time I had waited for him, before he came to live in our cabin. How I had admired him then—and as I saw him approach in almost the same clothes he wore before, and saw the grace of his walk, the slow-coming smile that had been touched with worry since his mother had come, I knew I still admired him as much as ever. I remember the long grass I stood in watching him approach, and the sound of frightened wings as a bird rose when he stepped close to her nest. "The evil spirit has touched Mother," I called to him. "She has the same sickness as baby Paul."

Pierre stopped, his face becoming serious as he looked down at the path, thinking. "We must get help at once."

"If only Marthe were here," I said. "She could make them both well. The last time Mother was sick—"

Pierre shook his head impatiently. "I will get someone with more power than Marthe." He walked rapidly back across the meadow.

It seemed a long waiting in our cabin, though I kept my hands busy, getting Pierre's supper. To keep the baby from crying, I moved from table to hearth carrying him across my shoulder, his face in the curve of my neck. Even thin as he was from illness, he was almost too much for me to carry.

Pierre came back with a man I remember only as being short, with a white beard almost covering his shrunken face. "This is the fort doctor," said Pierre. "He has come to help you, Naneda."

Mother did not answer, but tossed in burning fever. When I think back over the years, it is hard for me to record how frightened I was of that man. I had heard strange tales of white doctors, how they worked with knives that sometimes failed to let out the evil spirit and let out life itself. Strong medicines they used that made the stomach give up all the food that it held, or caused a painful sickness in the bowels. I watched in silent fright while the doctor laid down his walking stick and took off his hat, uncovering a shock of white hair. He set down a little black bag he carried and stepped toward my mother.

Terrified, I stepped between him and the bed. "No! No!"

"Why, Oneta, what is the matter with you?" Pierre took me gently by the arm. I stood where I was, defiantly looking at the white-haired doctor. He paused and smiled at me. "Why, now, I wouldn't hurt anybody. I may not be anything else, but I'm harmless." He chuckled at his little joke, and waited to see if I were more at ease. "You're about the age of my little girl. She and her mother have gone on a trip now, down to

173

Detroit, and left me to eat in the company mess-hall. Sometimes I try to get myself a little something when I get tired of soldiers' rations, but I'm not as handy at it as I might be." He sniffed the air, then looked toward our hearth. "I'll have to get the receipt for whatever you've got in that kettle. It smells like ambrosia for the gods—get Pierre to tell you what that is, sometime."

His gentle tone, while he made no further effort to go past me to my mother, gradually lowered the fluttering in my breast. His reference to our food reminded me of the duty of hospitality, of sharing food with anyone who came in at mealtime, that had been instilled in me from my earliest days in the lodge. I smiled uncertainly at the little man, and moved away to the hearth to fill a bowl with the stew, a venison broth thickened and flavored with dried corn hair. I watched a little uneasily as he stepped to my mother's side. He put his hand on her head, bent low to examine the blotches on her skin, and held her wrist between his fingers for a long time. I could see her eyes fluttering like the heart of a tiny bird when you catch and hold it between your two hands. In spite of his kind way, he might be putting a curse on her, I thought. And what evil spirits rode in that black bag?

At last the doctor looked up at Pierre. "I'm afraid it's scarlet fever. You say the baby is ill, too?" He took Paul in his arms and sat down in Pierre's big chair. "I'm afraid there's no doubt of it. Scarlet fever." He laid Paul back on the bed, opened his bag and laid out on the table round tablets of different colors, white and pink and brown. "I shall write down when each of these is to be given," he said. "The child should have only the white ones, half a tablet every three hours."

"Will they cure—" began Pierre, sitting on the edge of a straight chair drawn up at the table.

The doctor took the steaming bowl I handed him, and thanked me. "I hope so," he answered Pierre. "I have two cases in the village—both caught from that man that died at Mrs. Ruggs's. They seem to be improving with this treatment. But there are so many things we do not know. The search goes on—"

"Like the endless search for the philosopher's stone, to turn everything to gold," said Pierre.

"Yes. Yes. But a greater search to my mind is the search for the universal panacea, to cure all disease. If they ever find that— It seems that wealth and long life are the two great desires of men." He sipped appreciatively from his spoon. "This *is* good stew. When I have time, will you tell me how you made it?" He looked at me.

I nodded. There seemed to be no evil in the presence of this man. He finished his stew almost as eagerly as a child. I took the bowl to get him more.

"No, thank you. Mustn't encourage me, or I'll sit here an hour. I've got other patients." He took out a slip of paper. "Let's see now, the brown ones once a day, just before she goes to sleep." He looked up at a sudden thought.

"Who will take care of her?" He looked at me appraisingly.

Pierre saw his thoughts. "Oneta is very dependable. You may trust her to do anything you tell her. That's right, isn't it, Oneta?"

I nodded rather doubtfully. Though losing my fear of the man, I still had little faith in him.

"Now here," the doctor laid out another packet, and a small bottle. "Drop some of the contents of the packet in boiling water. That makes a febrifuge tea, which she should drink—one cupful every three hours. At least twice a day rub some of the fever liniment from the bottle on her head and then apply a folded muslin cloth dipped in cold water and wrung out. Wring it out of the cold water again when her forehead has warmed it through."

175

He rose and nodded cheerfully to Pierre. "The baby will not be sick much longer—a very light case. He is almost over it now. Your wife—I can't tell." Struck by another thought, he added, "Maybe you'd better stay somewhere else if you can, if the girl can handle everything. She's probably exposed already, but you being away so much, may not be. That's just a guess. We don't know how these things work."

"I think I should stay and help," protested Pierre, but I saw in his eyes that it would be a relief to have an excuse to stay with his mother. And I knew how little help he would be.

"You must go," I said. "I can manage alone, and if you will bring food to the doorstep I will take it in." Queerly I thought back to the time I had told him he should have left meat on the threshold.

"You are brave," said the doctor, closing his bag and taking up his cane. "Are you not afraid of taking the disease?"

"I am afraid of nothing," I answered quietly. "My father was never afraid, nor his father before him, and back to the earliest of his tribe. I shall not take the disease."

The doctor looked at me in wonder. "You know," he said, "I don't believe you will."

Thirteen

⚠ In those days Michel often came and tapped on our window to ask if we needed anything. "You ought to see how happy that old lady is," he said once. "She hops like a bird all over the village, trying to buy all the fine foods her son likes, and bullying the storekeepers because they don't have everything that enters her mind. She tells everyone all about Pierre from the time he was a baby. Well, I'll stop around in the morning. Just call out in the night if you want any help."

I noticed, too, as Pierre came to the cabin to bring food and ask about Paul and Mother, how happy he looked.

Paul got better at once, making it easier for me to take care of Mother. She lingered in the same state, weak and ill, her eyelids always partly closed as if they were heavy. The doctor came again several times, and left more of his colored tablets. Every day I watched all the canoes gliding down the current from the north and west, hoping that by some chance Marthe would return. I had seen how other Ojibways and many Ottawas came to ask for her herb tea when they did not feel well, or had taken too much strange food or drink, and how they were as well as ever in a few hours. I knew some of the roots she used, sassafras, pokeroot, and wild turnip, and herbs like pennyroyal, lobelia, balm, and wintergreen, but I did not know which of them would help Mother now. And the Midé conference was far away, and always lasted fully half a moon.

Time went on without change until the raspberry moon was beginning, when the thing happened suddenly that changed all the rest of my life. I awoke before dawn one morning, feeling that a strange wind had passed over my face. I sat up, and as soon as my thoughts were cleared, I ran across the room to my mother's bed. She lay with her eyes open, but they did not turn toward me when I spoke to her. I touched her hand, lying outside the blanket. The burning was gone. I touched her lips, and they were cold. Suddenly I knew they were too cold, that her little brown hands were stiff. I pulled my leather jacket over my nightdress and ran over to Marthe's cabin. "Baptiste! Baptiste!" I called.

Rosanne came running to the door. "What is it, Oneta?" she asked sleepily.

"Baptiste!" I called again.

By this time he had heard me. He pulled on his hunting shirt as he came to the door with his leggings only half strapped on. When he saw my face, he limped as fast as he could over to our cabin.

He touched my mother's hand, and stood silent for a long moment. Then he did a strange thing. He stooped and closed her eyes gently, and immediately afterward made the same signs across his chest I had seen the priest make. He came back and put his hand on my shoulder, and I saw his eyes were full of pity. "Your mother has died, Oneta. Her spirit has begun its long journey."

I seized his hand and held it tight, not believing, scarcely understanding. My mother could not have left me. She had been no worse the night before, and had even smiled a little when I put out the candle and said good night to her. I stood there trying to tell Baptiste that it could not be, but the words would not come.

"Will you stay here while I go and get Pierre?" asked Baptiste at last.

"I will stay with her," said Rosanne, standing in the doorway.

"*You* will—?" Baptiste looked up, surprised at her willingness.

"Why not?" snapped Rosanne.

In the numbness that came over me, I accepted her staying as nothing to be wondered at. I do not remember the next hours, and even the next days appear in memory only in scattered pictures, fragments of things that were said. A great weight pressed on me from which I could not get free. Rosanne and I sat on the bed when Baptiste had gone, and she put her arms about me, and even tried to repeat some of the things she had heard Marthe say about death. "Her friends will be all about her. She will have flowers that will never fade, and she will be always beautiful; she will never grow old and wrinkled there. On beautiful vines will hang ripe fruit, and she will never need to work any more."

I held tight to her, grateful for her nearness. Then the numbness broke for a time, and before Baptiste and Pierre came, I began to weep. Letting my head fall in Rosanne's lap, I sobbed dully, careful not to wake baby Paul. First I cried for grief that my mother's spirit was gone from my side. And then came the terrifying thought—what will we do now, Paul and I? What will become of us?

Fourteen

❧ Before sunset of that same day, Marthe came back. Told of the story of sickness and death, she began to mutter. "The black robe. He made her sick, your mother and the baby too. He brought sickness to the child when he said those strange words over him. I knew his powers were evil ones."

The carpenter in the village made the plain coffins used for burial in those days, keeping two or three ahead of need, stacking them in the back of his shop, awaiting the deaths of those who would be laid in them.

Pierre had one of them brought to the cabin on the postmaster's cart. He reported that the priest had gone on his round of visits to the north, even beyond the settlement at the rapids of St. Mary's, and could not return in time for the burial. I saw a look of quiet satisfaction in Marthe's eyes. Pierre said there would be no ceremony now, except for a prayer Mr. Stuart would offer at the grave. The priest would be asked to perform the offices of the dead for her when he did return.

Marthe put the green striped silk dress on Mother because Pierre insisted on it, though she muttered all the while that it would have been better to put on her deerskins. She refused to put the green silk shoes on

Mother's feet. "She cannot walk on those heels," she said, "in the long journey she must make."

"The new shoes would hurt her feet," I agreed.

"Do as you like," said Pierre sadly. "Her feet will not show in the coffin."

Many people came to our cabin the day Mother was buried, women I had never seen before, dressed in silk petticoats, shawls and buttoned shoes. The sweet perfume from their clothing mingled with the odor of burning nutmeg they said would drive out the disease that might linger in the cabin. These must be the fort ladies, I thought, seeing they liked Pierre and were sorry for him. Pierre accepted gratefully the food and bunches of flowers the ladies brought, but said little to any of them. He merely bowed and murmured words of thanks to each one. The major's wife came, followed by a sad-eyed Negro woman carrying a large cake. "Thank you, Josette," said Pierre.

She moved in a rustle of purple silk to join Marthe and Pierre beside the coffin. "So sorry," she said to Pierre. "So sorry for everything." She looked at Mother, and I wondered what she was thinking. Then, as if she couldn't get away without saying something more, she asked, "Could you not fix her hair to look better? In a soft roll at the neck like mine?" She turned to show the back of her blond head.

"No," said Pierre to Marthe. "No, leave it braided. I loved her hair." He himself laid the braids gently down, arranging them on the front of her dress. "She was so good she had to be beautiful," he said. My own eyes full to the brim, I knew he shared a little of my numb loneliness. I forgave him then for all my mother's tears.

I did not go to my mother's burial, for when they were all ready to leave, baby Paul began crying, and would not be comforted by anyone but me. I tried sev-

eral times to leave him with one of the women who offered to stay in our cabin until we returned, but each
time his loud wails brought me back. Since he could not
walk so far, and I could not carry him the long distance
to the village and up the fort hill and on to the burying-
ground beyond, I stayed at home with him. Holding him
by the open door I saw them start out, first the two-
wheeled cart with the flower-covered coffin upon it,
then Pierre and his mother who had come at the very
last. Marthe, Baptiste, and Rosanne followed with Armand, Louise, and the two boys, all dressed in their best
and wearing a stiff, solemn manner which subdued even
Jacques's dark stormy face. I watched them go around
the point and out of sight, as I had so often watched my
mother go when she worked at the fort. This time, I
realized with a swelling of pain within me, she would
not return to eat the supper I would prepare when the
sun went down.

Late that same evening, after I had put the baby to
sleep and Pierre had settled down to forget his sadness
in a book, I got out my deerskin dress. I drew it on,
though it was now so small I could hardly get into it.
Clinging smoothly to my skin, it was like the touch of
my mother's hands. I could not believe she was gone.
Something of her hand must still be in the embroidery on
my moccasins, the beaded strips I wound about my
braids.

I slipped out of the cabin door and went over to see
Marthe. There was no light inside. I pushed open the
door and called softly. No answer came.

I knew that Baptiste might have gone to the village
as he so often did in the evening, but where was
Marthe? Not at the beach lodges, for I would have seen
her start out. I had sat long at our own window with
the baby, looking away to the west. As I think of it now,
I wonder whether it was then that I began to look with

a particular affection toward the west. It might have been earlier, in the days I watched for my grandfather to return from that direction, or was it really in these times when I looked upon it as holding the place to which my mother must be journeying, where my father must be waiting to take her into his lodge again? Perhaps I am wrong, perhaps even farther back that feeling went, into the sun-worship in my blood, from the people whose eyes had ever watched the setting sun with thanks in their hearts for the day he had given and a humble prayer that he would return. Whatever it was, this feeling stayed with me.

When I could not find Marthe, I was more than ever lonely, and thought of the only place I might go for comfort. I knew where the burying-ground was from having seen it when Marthe and I gathered roots and herbs in the woods. I knew, too, how to get there without going by way of the village and the fort.

I set out along the shore to the north, and took the path up the heights. Up the steep side of the cliff I climbed, over wooded slopes hung with roots like monster spiders, into which the dusk had already settled itself for the oncoming night. A flock of wild ducks had gathered on the grassy edge of the water below, and I took care that my moccasins should disturb no stones to roll down and frighten them. I could not have borne it, so miserable I was myself, to have harmed or frightened any living thing. I stopped and looked down at them as they rested there, getting ready for their long flight.

The full round moon, the night-sun, came out before I moved again. By its light I found my way at last up to the pine at the top, my mother's manito. Ragged and torn it was, and twisted limbs and long streamers of bark hung from it, but its trunk still stood defiant. My mother's latest offerings had been put there when Paul first became ill, and they still lay at the foot of the pine

—bits of burned food, a handful of corn, and a few beaded strips of cloth. The strips were wide and neatly made, and since they were still there, I knew no white man had passed this way. No Indian would take them.

As I turned away from the pine, a cloud came over the moon and took away its light. I ran down a hillside. Here there was no trail, but I knew my way by the trees. I came to a thicket and pushed my way through. My deerskin clothing had no fear of its briars. A rabbit peered out from his sheltering bush, but did not run from me. A tall birch stood in my way, offering his bark, but I was too heartbroken to think of scrolls now.

I had no fear; I had lived in the forest too long for that. But the farther I went, the more my thoughts filled with sadness and misery, as if the darkness pushed them in upon me. They gave me no peace; I wanted to cry out, Mother! Mother! The laugh of a loon came to my ears, as I pushed through the last of the bushes and stood on the edge of the graveyard.

Someone was there ahead of me!

Beside the only fresh grave there was a dark presence. I might have been frightened, but I stood still and told myself that none of my ancestors had ever known fear. "Courage is part of my flesh and bones, I cannot be afraid." These words came to me from my grandfather's teaching of long ago, and I said them over again. "I cannot be afraid. My fathers fought in many battles, and their scars were all in front."

I stood there a long time, trying to see through the darkness. When I could not bear it any more, the moon had pity. Shining full and bright again, he showed me that the figure was Marthe. She was bent above the grave, leaning far over, really leaning into it, it seemed! Rosanne sat watching her at a little distance. I began to run, and came to Marthe's side, calling, urging an answer. "What are you doing?"

Then I saw she was digging up the earth with a

clumsy bit of iron. She had already gone so deep that the coffin was half uncovered. I sank down in the grass on my knees beside Rosanne, my heart beating strongly. Was my mother coming out again? I wondered, for Marthe had begun to pry out the nails in the lid!

I watched her pull out the nails, one by one, but she did not open the coffin. Instead, she began to cover it with earth again. She filled in all the dirt, scraping it with a large clam-shell. "They would not listen," she said, "when I told them they must not nail the box tight. Now the soul can get out." On top of the grave Marthe began to build with sticks a little shelter with a hole at one end. That, too, must be for the soul, I thought. Under the little roof she placed a bowl of broth, some dried fish and a kettle to cook it in. At one end she put a heap of dry bark and struck with her flint a spark to light it. The little flame began slowly, blazed up, and then settled quietly to its business of lighting the soul on the way.

The wood paths were sweet with the incense of flowers to the good spirits when Marthe took Rosanne by the hand and went down. I followed so close behind that the blades of grass had no time to spring up when her moccasins left them before mine had pressed them down again.

When we came to the twisted pine, Marthe stopped and took me by the other hand, and we three stood side by side for a long time, looking down at the offerings. Then Marthe began to speak. Answering the silent bursting thoughts within me she said,

"You are beginning young to suffer. But you must never question it. It is the way of life. Too much happiness would make you too fond of this life. We must have troubles here that the life after may be sweet. War axes must grow bloody, hearts must be torn by loss—"

Her voice died out, but a sudden wind across the

rocky heights seemed to take up her words and carry them again to my ears, low and sadly at first, then with a loud and threatening gust, "war axes . . . torn hearts . . . suffering."

When the wind had gone, Marthe went on sadly. "There is one more thing you have to bear. At the Midé gathering I met a medicine man who had seen Ajawin. She and Gray Wolf are the last of our family yet alive, and they have been too ill to make the summer journey to Mackinac."

"Grandfather?" I asked.

"He has gone along the path of souls with all the others. Smallpox—" She needed to say no more. She had named the disease most dreaded by all the tribes of that region, the disease that had wiped out whole bands and had thinned the tribes to a small part of what they had once been. I had heard of the terror and despair of it, when, unwilling to last through the slow, painful death, men threw themselves from cliffs or plunged into the waters of a stream and drowned. So dreaded it was that a white man at one of the posts had only to show a bottle which he said contained the disease and threaten to let it loose, and he could control the actions of any red man.

In all my life that was one of the most cruel moments. My mother was dead, and now my grandfather would never return for me. What had I left?

For a long time, Marthe did not speak again, and then not of my mother or grandfather as I expected.

"Here is where Pontiac once stood," she said, "and the story is that when the soft airs of spring return he comes back here to stand again. My eyes have never seen him, but maybe some day the sight will be granted to one of you."

Rosanne and I were silent at the thought.

"Remember, Oneta, that your father was the greatest of his race since Pontiac, and many say even greater than he. Remember in your trouble now that he was always

185

alone, even as you feel alone now. Honored as he was by so many, your father was even more alone than you. And yet—he was not alone."

I looked up at her, trying to understand.

"Once," Marthe began again at last, "I sat on the edge of a council with the general they called Harrison, and heard Tecumseh say these words,

It is true that I am a Shawnee. My forefathers were warriors. Their son is a warrior. From them I take only my existence; from my tribe I take nothing. I am the maker of my own fortune. I have a voice within me, communing with past ages.

Marthe waited for her words to die away. "At another time he said,

The sun is my father, the earth is my mother.

"Remember those words, Oneta. Your father spoke in the softest tones of the breeze, and he thundered in the voice of the wildest storm. From his words you may see from whence he drew his strength. When your own need is greatest, your strength will come to you from all these things."

The next day I went back to the grave again. The bark cup was empty, the fish was gone. Marthe and I knew my mother had not had to start her journey empty-handed.

Fifteen

☙ One evening, a week after my mother had gone, Pierre pushed his chair back from the supper table and pulled out a fine white handkerchief to wipe his forehead. The day had been warm, but it was a nervous hand that held the cambric square. As if he were disturbed by something other than the heat, his fingers trembled slightly, like poplar leaves before a storm.

"Let's go over to Marthe's a little while before you wash the dishes," he said.

Remembering as we went that Pierre had been in Marthe's cabin only once before, on the night Paul was born, I tried to think out the meaning of this visit. The only expression on Pierre's face was one of aversion as he walked carefully around the fish heads thrown on the beach for dogs and birds and odorous in the August heat.

Split trout lay drying on the rack outside Marthe's door, and finished strips lay in heaps on the beach, covered with squares of birchbark held in place by stones. Baptiste, still at the table, saw us through the open door. "Well, hello! come in." I helped Paul up the steps and, letting go of his hand, watched until he had settled himself on the floor. Pierre, closing the door behind us, took with a nod of thanks a chair hastily drawn up by Baptiste. I sat in the barrel chair, watching Paul turning and examining something he had found just under the edge of the bed—a painted wooden minnow such as Baptiste used for fishing through the ice in the winter.

"Have a cup of tea?" Baptiste offered heartily. "This here's some of Marthe's best herb tea"—and then he added in a loud whisper, "It's got a drop of whiskey in it for seasoning."

"Thank you, no." Pierre sat as erect as though the chair had no back to lean against.

Marthe, putting away the supper dishes, had not spoken, but her eyes had been searching Pierre's face. He did not state his errand, so Baptiste began talking about the company work—the one interest they had in common. Pierre did not know the difference between a sturgeon and a pike, or between a dragnet and a seine, nor did he know the uses of a mackinaw boat against those of a canoe, and he knew nothing of traveling with a trader's pack on his back.

Pierre fell into the subject readily enough, saying that the latest letter from Mr. Astor told of a falling off in prices and demand for furs in London.

"Queer, *n'est-ce pas,*" said Baptiste, "how the notions of a bunch of women over there can cut down the amount of whiskey a trapper here in Michigan Territory can buy with his winter's work."

I heard all this talk as part of waiting for something being held back. Marthe put the left-over food on a shelf, threw the table scraps out of the open window, and took up an awl and a pair of unfinished moccasins. She sat down near the fireplace, her face as expressionless as its rough stones. Baptiste took his pipe and a twist of tobacco and sat on a home-made bench against the wall. Above him two ragged caps hung on the antlers of a stag he had killed the winter before.

Pierre leaned a little forward, and coughed gently. But before he could say anything, a loud knocking sounded on the door, as if someone were hitting it with a stone or piece of wood. Startled, Baptiste jumped up. "What in the name of the saints is that?"

He limped to the door, opened it, then stood back, jerking off his cap, and waiting uncertainly. Leaning forward, I saw Madame Debans on the step, clutching a small cane with which she had been striking the door.

"Well, have you lost your tongue? Am I welcome to come in, or am I not?"

Baptiste bowed gracefully from the hips, a gesture he performed as well as Pierre when he wanted to. "Of a certainty, Madame. Come in."

Madame stepped in with a flutter of white cap ribbons and a swish of many muslin skirts. She looked around with black eyes not missing any detail of the cabin or the people in it. She saw the barrel chair, the battered kettles, a fish net draped in one corner, nails scattered about the walls holding Marthe's plain dresses, Rosanne's aprons and extra petticoats, and Baptiste's oilskins. She frowned at the piles of furs and skins in the corner of the room where they had lain since they were no longer needed on the walls to keep out the cold. A heap of soiled clothes lay near the door. Even as I watched Madame, one corner of my mind thought, Marthe is going to wash. I must gather up the baby's things and wash them at the same time. The sun was going down red. It would be pleasant the next morning to be out of doors swishing the clothes to whiteness at the water's edge, I thought.

Madame's eyes traveled on, taking in the stone hearth where Marthe never bothered to clean up the cooking stains, the bed where the covers were never straightened, the seats of boards nailed together or cut from barrels and logs. Then she took her place on the bench Baptiste had left, sitting straight and a little forward like Pierre.

At the sight of his mother, Pierre had started to speak, but stopped as if waiting for her to say something first. Madame's eyes finally came to rest on Paul, now singing to himself in contentment over a lump of maple sugar Marthe had given him to suck.

"I decided to come myself and hear what was being said." She looked at Pierre.

"Yes, Mother."

"Well, go on. What have you told them, and what did they say about it? How does the Indian girl feel about it?"

"I haven't mentioned it yet."

"*C'est bien.* I can then hear it all. Well, begin." She smoothed down her skirts with hands in tight black gloves.

Pierre folded his hands across his knees, and his fingers went white with the tenseness of his clasp. He must be going to say something he didn't want to.

"It is of course not practical for Oneta and the child

189

and me to live on in the cabin alone. Oneta is too young for the responsibility—"

"According to our ways, she is not young." Marthe lifted a calm face. "Our girls begin woman's work when they are small. Oneta has for years been trained by her mother and me."

Madame looked around scornfully, as if she would say that no good training could have come from a place like that. "How old is the girl, exactly?"

Marthe did not answer. Not one to think in terms of years, I am sure she did not know just how old I was. The number came from Pierre.

"From what her mother said about her birth, she is twelve."

Madame broke in almost before he could finish. "Well, let's get on with this business. You'll never get it out, *ma foi*, the way you're going about it. I'll tell them." She settled herself as if ready for any opposition. "I want my son and his child to come and live with me."

"His child? There are two in his cabin," said Marthe.

"That is the only reason we are talking with you about it," snapped Madame. "It seems to me the girl has no claim upon him. She should go back to her mother's people. We are asking you to help find them." Her words were nipped off short, like frost-touched stems.

I heard those words and I heard no contradiction from Pierre. He did not meet my eyes.

"Her mother's people—" said Marthe. "No, she cannot return to them, ever. Her grandfather is dead."

Pierre looked up in surprise, and I realized I had not told him. I sat looking straight before me in the silence that followed. So Pierre and Paul were going to leave me. In the pain of that my training could bring me no help except a reminder not to let this strange woman see my feelings. I kept my face composed, so much that Pierre told me later I had even deceived him, and he thought

I did not care what was decided. Not so Marthe. She knew I was wondering what would become of me.

"Oneta must stay with me," she said.

Baby Paul had been toddling about on the floor, coming at last to rest beside me. He pounded his little fist against my knee and chattered something happily about the minnow he still clutched. Pierre looked at the child and up at me, and caught me showing my feelings.

"No, Mother," he said firmly. "Oneta must go with us. That is what I have insisted from the first. I gave in to your idea that we should give her a chance to go back to her grandfather if she should prefer it. Since he is gone, she must stay with us."

Madame's lips were in a tight line, her black eyes angry. She was about to explode with a whole mouthful of words, when Pierre spoke again quickly. "That is the way it must be. I shall not separate Oneta from her little brother. Either she goes with us, or I shall go on living in the cabin with her and the baby. We can hire a woman to do some of the work." Whenever Pierre spoke like that, one knew he meant it. When he once made up his mind, he would not touch it again.

Madame brought out the thought that had been in her mind all the time. "We can take the baby and bring him up so he will be like us in all his ways. A girl as old as Oneta, that is different. And she is all—"

All Indian, she was going to say. But Baptiste stopped her. "A nice willing girl like Oneta would be a help to Madame. Marthe and me would be glad to have her, but you see how this baby hangs on her, and she's been with him every minute since he was born. It'd be cruel to separate the two of 'em. And Oneta would do anything she was told. You can't expect more than that of anyone."

"Oneta must choose," said Pierre kindly. "Shall we go on in the cabin awhile longer, until you make up your mind?"

191

"It is ridiculous for you to live here and for me to be all alone in that big house," said Madame impatiently. Then she gave up, and did it as gracefully as she could. "I shall give Oneta a home if she cares to come. We shall try it, and if it does not work out, we shall try something else."

I had no idea what she meant, that she was holding something back. Unlike the bee, she had more than one arrow in her quiver.

Pierre looked as if some pressure had been removed from his mind. He smiled. "Then you will come with me and the baby, Oneta?"

I could feel Marthe's thoughts pushing against me. I knew she wanted me to stay with her. She had kept me close to her all the time since I had first come to the island, and spent more time in teaching me than she spent with her own Rosanne. But Paul's little fists were buried in my skirts as he stood unsteadily on his tiny feet. His earlier attempt at walking had been broken off by the long fever, and he was just beginning again. Reaching down for the shining minnow he had dropped, taking two or three steps in too great a hurry, he fell forward on his face on the bare floor. He began to howl. I picked him up quickly, and wiped his face with the edge of my skirt, repeating in Ojibway, "A great warrior never cries. You must be a brave warrior."

"What is she saying to the child?" asked Madame suspiciously. No one answered her. Paul clung to me, sobbing until his eyes were taken by a necklace of dried red berries I was wearing. He began to tug at them. Feeling his little body against me, I knew I could not be separated from him, letting that strange woman be the only one he could turn to when he was bumped. And, more important, there would be no one to teach him what he should know.

"Yes, I will go with you," I said.

192

Pierre smiled, and I knew whatever might be the feelings of his mother, he was really glad to have me. I had never felt more dread of anything in my life than I felt at the thought of living in the same house with Madame. I looked at her, sitting there with her black-gloved hands folded in her lap, her face a puzzle beneath the stiff white cap, as if she too was wondering how it would all turn out. I ought to hate her, I thought, for my mother and myself. And yet, seeing her puzzled face in that moment, I knew it was not easy for her. I could see how she felt at having to take two she didn't want, Paul and me, in order to get Pierre back again. Seeing the shining cleanness of her, the liveliness of her eyes, the love of fun she could not hide under a precise manner and severe speech, I knew living with her might be an even greater adventure than any I had had before. Certainly I didn't hate her. Even after all these years I cannot write of it without marveling at that. Truly, I had come a long way with Pierre.

Sixteen

"When are we going to move to Madame's house?" I asked Pierre the next morning at breakfast, feeling a desire to put it off, as one waits for auspicious weather before attempting a *grande traverse*, as we used to call a crossing that took our canoes far from land.

"Oh, the end of the month, I guess," he said. "There's no hurry."

"No hurry about what?" came in a high voice from the doorway. I turned around quickly. Madame herself stood there and behind her was the postmaster's helper, holding his pony by the bridle. "No hurry about what?" she repeated, coming in and putting down her cane. I remember her dress that morning was of blue calico, with black cuffs and a full black apron with a green edging.

Pierre got up and kissed her on the cheek. "Good morning, Mother. No hurry about moving. We'll pack up in a few days—"

"Nonsense. You're moving today," she said with decision. "Now which of these things are to go? Your books, of course. What else? What about this blanket?" She picked up the white one on the bed. "Hurry up, girl, and get the baby's things packed."

"See here, Mother," began Pierre.

"Silence!" she ordered. "Don't talk. Do something."

"But, Mother, I must go to work. We'll have to move some evening."

"*Ma foi*, will you get to work on those books? I stopped at the office on the way and told Mr. Stuart you wouldn't be there for a while."

"You did?" Pierre was astonished. "What did he say?"

"Oh, he was cross at first. He said he couldn't spare you. He was up to his ears and beyond with work. But I talked him out of it. Before I got two dozen sentences out, he laughed and said, 'By gum, Mrs. Debans, I guess I don't need him after all. Just send him here whenever you get through with him, will you?' And bowed me out of his office as nice as any Frenchman."

Pierre shook his head in wonder. "So you're giving orders to Mr. Stuart now, are you? But, Mother, I must have boxes for these books. They can't just be dumped in a cart—"

Madame turned to the boy gaping on the threshold. "Haven't you brought those boxes in yet? Get a move on!"

In a few seconds wooden boxes were being tossed through the door to drop with a clatter on the bare floor, for Madame had already piled up the mats. "Mr.

Stuart gave me all the boxes I wanted from the store. Now get busy."

"It seems we are moving today, Oneta." Pierre was annoyed and amused at the same time. I began to gather up the baby's clothes. Madame moved about the cabin with the speed of a whirlwind. She pushed Pierre over to the corner. "Pack up your precious books. I know you don't want anybody else to touch them. Hurry up—" Pierre began to empty the shelves.

"This little bed goes." Madame pulled it from under the big one. "Now just lay some of the baby's clothes on it, and we'll put a blanket on them and tie them down. Here, boy, load this on your cart, and take whatever Pierre has ready for you—and get along. You hurry back here as fast as you can for the next load."

It was all I could do to keep up with her. We sorted cooking pots and bedding, and took down the curtains, and soon everything was in as much confusion as if a bear had been trapped in the cabin and scattered dishes, chairs, and blankets in trying to get out. We put the tea-pot and the new dishes in one box, and packed around them the pieces of bleached sacking I had used for towels. I looked up from stuffing in the last one to see Madame peering into my box in the corner, the one that held my scrolls. "Here," she called, "we can dump this stuff out and use this box for your clothes."

"No! No!" I said so anxiously that even Pierre looked up. He had not gotten far with his packing, for he could not put a book into a box without taking a look into it, and then he was likely to forget what he was doing.

"No!" I said again, pleading this time.

Madame looked around. "Why, it's just some old scraps of bark and some other stuff—" She pulled out the bundles of my father's things, to which I had added some of Mother's, tying all together with the buckskin thong that had once held Tecumseh's scalping knife.

"What's all this—in Heaven's name, feathers and sticks!" She pulled out the bow and arrow and threw them in the pile of things to be burned when we were through. Hastily I sprang up and began to gather up my treasures.

Pierre came over to see what was happening. "I don't know what all these things are, Mother, but Oneta thinks a great deal of them. We must take them along. We can take the box just as it is."

Madame faced him, her hands on her hips, a frown appearing between her eyes. "Now, see here, Pierre. I thought it all over last night. If this girl comes into my house, she becomes from then on a French girl, or as near one as I can make her. She will want none of these filthy trappings. Feathers, indeed. And dirty skins, and scraps of bark. And what are these cheap bracelets?" She held out my mother's silver armlets.

Pierre's face grew hard, and I expected an angry reply. Gradually he softened, looking at Madame. She was so little and frail, and everything about her reminded him that she was in a strange place, that she had come a long way from all her friends for his sake.

"I must keep these things," I began to explain to her.

Pierre put his arm around Madame before she could say any more. "They will do no harm in your house, *ma mère*. Let Oneta have them."

She protested no more, and I carefully packed everything back in the box marked INDIAN GOODS.

Louise and the two boys came over to say good-by. "So the little cabin becomes again a *maison condamné*. But you will come back and see us often?" asked Louise.

"Oh, yes."

Madame came up behind me then as if to challenge that statement. Jacques, gently prodded by his mother, bowed to Madame. Then he looked at me. "Sorry you've got to go away," he said almost gruffly.

Louise laughed, and her laughter was like the ringing rock at L'Arbre Croche. "Now, Jacques dear, you talk as if Oneta were going a long ways away. We'll see her often."

I walked slowly over to where Marthe stood in her doorway. "I'll come down every day," I promised her. She laid her hand on my head, without words. Then she turned suddenly and disappeared inside. I was about to follow her when Baptiste appeared in the doorway and took me by the arm, walking back toward our cabin with me. "Marthe'll be all right. She thinks she's lost you, but when she sees you running down here whenever you get a chance, she'll be all right. She sat up all night makin' up charms of all kinds for you, but I persuaded her not to give 'em to you this morning. It would just have riled the old lady." Baptiste fumbled in his pocket. "Here, take this for the little tike." He drew out the minnow Paul had played with the night before. "I'll have plenty of time to carve and paint me another." He patted my shoulder, stopping and turning as if to go back to his cabin. "You'll get along all right." His words seemed flung in the teeth of something that threatened. "But there ain't much *give* to them people." With a last glance toward Pierre and Madame, he limped away.

The half-witted boy chirped to his pony, and our last load started on its way. Madame nodded to Louise and turned to walk behind it. "You, Pierre, do you have that list of things I told you to get at the store? Why don't you go around that way now?"

"All right, Mother," said Pierre. He bowed to Louise and turned to where I stood letting Paul play in the pebbles at my feet. "Are you ready?"

I swung Paul up in my arms. "He's getting too heavy for you," said Pierre. "Let me take him."

As Pierre took him from me, Paul began to cry.

"Now, young man, Oneta cannot carry you so far. Let's have it quiet."

I wondered if Pierre realized he had never carried Paul since the day he was christened, or if he remembered that Paul had cried the few times he had tried to take him up in the cabin. Pierre was not the kind to hold a baby on his lap very much.

Paul cried until we were around the point, then settled to an occasional whimpering. A seagull, like a piece of white foam, moved along at the edge of the blue water. Reddened vines trailed from the trees like the gay robes of autumn. Almost as if he were beside me, I could hear the remark Baptiste made every fall. "Them leaves is gettin' kind of tarnished, ain't they?" Already a lonesomeness for the cabin life almost choked me. It was as if I knew this was more than just moving "around the point."

Then almost at once we were in the midst of the lodges. Kettles were boiling above open fires, women and children and dogs were moving in and out of the blanket doors. Men lay on the graveled beach, casting admiring glances at their new finery and waiting idly for the meal to be cooked. Suddenly I tugged at Pierre's sleeve. We had reached the lodges of the Ojibways, and I wanted to stop for a moment at a familiar place before taking a path into the unknown.

An old woman was sitting on a blanket, watching a baby playing between her outstretched feet. A young woman carried another child peering from the folds of the blue blanket behind her back. Two young men stood talking together, naked except for white blankets and pieces of blue cloth about their loins, and bands of cotton tied about their heads. Four older men were sitting cross-legged on the beach, quietly playing a game of cards, with twists of tobacco in front of them to use as stakes. I knew none of them and expected them to pay no attention to me. But one of the young men said something to the other, and their eyes turned on me, alight with interest, though by nature their dignity would never let them notice the presence of a woman. The old grandmother looked at me, patting the head of the baby she was tending, as if she wanted me to admire him. A short, gaily dressed youth I knew as Four Legs strolled up from the Ottawa lodges. Remembering Marthe's words about him, I looked at him curiously, at his face painted red on one side and black on the other, at the raccoon tails tied at his knees and flopping as he walked, giving him his name. He stuffs fur into his moccasins to make himself appear taller, Marthe had said of this vain one, and she had told me how he added length to his hair by splicing on extra pieces with red earth glue covered by a band of beadwork.

The young woman came up with a timid smile and fingered the cloth of my calico dress—one of Mother's it was—admiring it in murmurs like the plaintive tones of a dove. The two young men crowded close behind her, the players got up from their card game, and other men came from a near-by lodge, until I was surrounded by a murky cloud of faces. I heard my father's name, and my grandfather's. In all their eyes was respect. Closer they pressed, until Pierre was pushed away from me.

Even as I turned to see what had become of him, one of the young men went up to him, saying, "Brother." Pierre's face was puzzled and apprehensive, and he took a step backward. Knowing he had not understood, I said, "He calls you brother." And, since the young man had gone on speaking, I told the rest. "We welcome you, and call you one of us. You married our cousin and she has been taken from you. Brother, we join in your sorrow."

The young man held out his hand. Pierre's cheeks flushed and then the color was gone. He looked at the young brave almost in horror. When others came up with extended hands, he backed away. In his slender form I saw a tightening as annoyance and disgust flowed together in a sudden flood and became anger. Worrying about what he might do, I tried to push my way out of the press about me, as Pierre answered, his words snapping over their heads like whip-lashes.

"Stop! I will not have every filthy, drunken Indian on the beach calling me brother. I am nothing to you and you are less than nothing to me. Never dare to speak to me again, any of you."

I did not need translate his words even if I would have. His wrath flared in them and went through the little crowd as a great blaze through a forest grove. They were astonished, being men that respected themselves and assumed they would be respected by others. Eyes that had been on Pierre in friendly appeal grew puzzled and then hostile. The Ojibways around me fell back in a little circle and looked at him with unsmiling faces. Freed, I rushed to Pierre's side.

"Come, I am ready to go now," I urged quietly. Pierre hesitated, then turned abruptly away. As we went, I heard low growls of anger behind us, and words of resentment Pierre could not understand, making me anxious—not for myself, but for Pierre, since the man-meaning in them told me that the words, flying after us like sharpened arrows, were for him. I must go back as soon as I could, I thought, and make excuses for Pierre. Else, they would never forget.

With set face, Pierre marched past the little shops and up to the company store at the corner of Fort and Market streets. A little cluster of traders loafed around the door. Pierre handed me the baby and disappeared inside, reading now in a voice almost even, from the list Madame had given him, "Plain white thread, fine, and a box of spermaceti candles—"

If my mind had not been so full of what had just happened, I would have enjoyed seeing the short back street of the village, as we turned on to its limestone path when Pierre came out. All the houses were larger than the cabins of the fishing village, and all of them were whitewashed and surrounded by green lawns and shrubs and enclosed with white picket fences. We came close to the enormous buildings of the fur company, and passed near the yard where shouts of laughter and excited talk came from the men sorting furs around the tables. Next was the long white house Michel had long ago pointed out to me as the boarding house. Beyond it, in an open space, two spotted cows moved slowly from one piece of grass to another, while black and white chickens kept out of the way of their feet. Beyond their yard was a space full of tents, and voyageurs strolled among them. The tightening was gone from Pierre, and his usual air of remoteness, of following some inner rhythm, had settled back upon him.

It was not his anger my mind dwelt on, but the superior look in his eyes—just as the fat Mrs. Ruggs and her little girl had once looked at the lodge people.

Passing the last of the voyageurs' tents, Pierre slowed his steps before the next house. "This is your new home, Oneta."

The cart was gone, and we could hear Madame singing in a high-pitched voice inside. I leaned against the picket fence, and looked at the large house with smooth clapboard walls and gleaming new whitewash covering up all traces of its age. On rising ground, it stood almost under the brow of the low cliff, and rocks clothed with bushes rose like a wall behind the square of ground it stood on. As one searches the face of a stranger he is going to have to live with, I searched the front of that house, hoping to find something I could understand. My eyes ran over its centered door, the two heavily curtained windows on each side, and the long roof sloping down to the front with two dormer windows peering out of it as if they were examining me in their turn, and leaving me in doubt whether I was welcome. But I took comfort when I noticed that, since it was on a rise, from any of its windows one could look out over the village houses, past little gardens and white fences and see the straits, flowing past like an old friend. Its waves were calm between the two horns of the crescent harbor, but I could see the familiar large waves farther out.

"One thing before we go in," said Pierre. "You will of course want to go back sometimes to see Rosanne and the others, but I must ask you never to go to the beach lodges."

Never. How could that be, I thought, when summer after summer they would be there, right along my way to the beach cabins, unless I took the path across the meadow.

"I'm afraid," said Pierre firmly, "that I must insist on it."

"But I should go there as soon as I can, to explain—"

"No. You must not go there at all." It was the first time Pierre had ever spoken to me with that tone of authority. Paul began to cry again, and I took him from his father's arms, wondering even as I soothed him what answer to make to Pierre. There was no appeal from his words, or his tone. It said that if I lived in his house, I must do as he said in this matter. I might yet turn back but there was the baby in my arms. I could not leave Paul for the sake of those others I did not even know.

After all, all ties I had with the beach lodges were now far down the starry path of the souls. Closer to me now was Pierre, and the approval I had wanted from him from the first day I had seen him. All I had now were the cabin folks and Pierre, and the little boy in my arms.

"Unless the time comes when for some reason I must, I will not go to the beach lodges," I said.

Pierre smiled, and laid his hand on mine where I held

baby Paul across my shoulder. The three of us went through the gate and started up the narrow board walk to the front steps. After my promise, the house itself seemed to have mellowed in its look. The broad stone chimney was sending up smoke into the still air. Evergreens with pale fringed tips sparkled beside the path, lazy in the sun. And then, as a figure not tolerating laziness even in little trees, Madame opened the door and stood in the frame.

"*Mon Dieu,* give me that child. His poor head is all uncovered." She came down the board walk, smiling in good humor. She looked up at Pierre, and I saw the cause of her happiness. Her son was going to live under her roof again. So happy it made her that she even smiled at me. No matter how much trouble Paul and I might be, it was better for her than not having her son at all.

Seventeen

&⊗ Once inside Madame's house I stopped just over the threshold, until I remembered to show no surprise at the crowded, rich-looking, yet precise room. Feeling the deep red carpet soft under my moccasins, I looked at dark polished furniture, hangings and ornaments, without seeing any one of them distinctly. I breathed heavily of a new odor, a fragrance as of flowers, but those of a land I had never seen, where airs were warmer and scents heavier upon them, as they were sometimes in the north country after a rain. They would be flowers of rich heavy petals, so enticing that the very bees would be drunk with their fragrance. I was to learn that one of Madame's extravagances was this perfume she got all the way from Paris.

Madame sank into a rocking chair with great tassels

on its arms, and began to unwrap Paul, who was surprisingly content in her hands. Pierre hesitated, looking at the confusion of boxes on the carpet. "I should unpack these and get them out of the way for you."

"Nonsense," said Madame. "You run along to work I promised Mr. Stuart. And anyway, I'll have these boxes out and a nice dinner ready for you before noon. *Vite,* get along now." The sharpness of her tone told nothing of the joy in her eyes.

As soon as his steps were hurrying down the board walk, Madame looked at me, and, as if there were so many things to be said between us there was no use to begin, she asked simply, "*Eh bien,* about feeding times for the child. What has he been having?"

"Milk," I said, "and a little soup. We fed him whenever he was hungry."

"Sensible enough." Her tone was business-like, neither friendly nor unfriendly. "Now if he will play by himself, we might as well unpack at once." She put Paul on the floor, and he began to creep toward a metal figure holding open a door into the next room.

"You may play with that old iron cat if you want to. Pierre used to like it when he was little."

I watched her as she looked at the baby. Relieved, I saw tenderness in her wrinkled face. Suddenly she shook herself and rose, and went quickly out into a little back room, as if she did not want me to see her face any longer. "After all, it's my own grandchild," I heard her murmur to herself in a voice that broke on the last word.

I began on the boxes then, and noted as I worked what kind of room this was. It seemed to be in the center of the house, with doors leading to other rooms on all sides but the front. It had more cloth than I had ever seen before in a house. The windows, one on each side of the front door, were heavily covered with lace curtains. A beam of light traced their pattern on the dark red carpet that covered the floor to the base of the gaily papered walls. A table at one side had a large red and white cloth over it. The two rocking chairs had cushions in them, and bits of lace on the backs where one's head would rest. The couch was covered, too, with a heavy gray blanket that fell down to the floor at sides and ends. On it were two cushions of brocaded silk, which Pierre told me later were the remains of a court costume from the days Madame had lived in Paris.

Wherever there was space around the wall, a straight chair was set squarely against it. The fireplace was an enormous one, with a huge crane that would hold four or five kettles at once. Over its mantel was a dark wooden clock, tall, and with a sharp pointed top. On each side of its face were gilded wooden columns with points at their tops carved to look like pine cones. Before I had time to notice more, Madame appeared again. Her tones were even now. "Out there is a little kitchen where I wash and prepare food. Now off here"—she pointed to the east—"is my bedroom and back of it is the one where you and the baby will sleep. On this side" —she pointed to the west—"are two more rooms. One is Pierre's bedroom and study. Back of that is a small bedroom we won't need. I store things in it and keep my loom in it when I am not weaving." Her voice rose with pride as she reflected on such a wealth of rooms in a village where one or two was the rule. "But *ma foi*, why do I stand here explaining? You'll soon see everything for yourself."

With an armful of my clothes from one of the boxes, I went over to the door Madame had said opened into my room. It was beautiful and fresh-looking, I admitted, though I was still homesick for the cabin. Then a rush of pleasure came over me at sight of the window, where the late morning sun was coming in to flood the room. Madame had transplanted wild cucumber and eglantine to the side of the house, so the window had a natural drapery of vines tracing their shadows on the white curtains and in the sun's path on the floor. Before the window sat a low brown chest. Over the single bed was a woven coverlet of blue and white squares. A long strip of rag carpeting covered the wide boards of the floor in front of a low dresser, over which hung a looking-glass with a dark brown frame. I stood on tiptoe and looked, moving back and forth to see how much of myself showed in it, seeming a stranger to myself, seeing a puzzled, serious face with big dark eyes above the yellow flowered dress with its short puff sleeves. I was about to stand on a chair to see my feet, desiring to add my familiar moccasins to that unnatural picture, when I heard Madame calling me from the other room. I hurried out.

The first day, I ate scarcely anything at all. When the sunset gun boomed out from the fort, seeming so much louder there, and the following bugle call more clear, we were at supper, and Madame was looking at the food I had left on my plate. "What is wrong with it?"

I wondered whether I should tell her, and then, as if my natural self were smothered in all the cloth, the close-packed ornaments of the room, and choked between the two stiff presences about the table, I said, "Nothing. It is only that I do not feel—"

Pierre interrupted kindly. "She's upset, Mother, at such a change. She has had the shock of her mother's death, and the news about her grandfather, and now coming here to a strange house—"

"That is true." Madame looked at me thoughtfully. "You needn't stay at table then. Take the baby in and get him ready for bed. By tomorrow you will be all right."

Pierre nodded. He was eating more heartily than ever before in the time I had known him. Madame's little cakes had been as white as snow when they went into the oven at the side of the great fireplace, to come out again browned over the top. Pierre had eaten at least six of them, spread with melting butter. Tea and white-fish and fried potatoes had gone down with them, and when I got up he was just starting a large slice of apple pie.

As I undressed Paul in my room, I heard fragments of their talk. Pierre was telling of boxes received at the fur company, wet, dirty, and broken, and with many articles missing. Complaint had been made to the captain of the boat, who said they were that way when he got them on this side of the Niagara portage. "I must write letters to see if we can find out where it happened." A strange contentment was in his voice for one discussing trouble.

I wondered how soon they would find out that I could not eat food cooked in that house. Madame had used the salt shaker with a free hand, and I had never before eaten salted food. It tasted dreadful to me. Everything we had cooked, even whitefish, had always been seasoned with maple sugar, or sometimes the spice-bush, sweet flag, or wintergreen.

When Paul had fallen asleep in his little bed, I lay down on top of the blue and white coverlet on my own. Besides the strangeness of bed and mirror and dresser, I felt something else I did not understand at first. Then I knew I missed the wind through the chinks in the cabin wall, its soft muted whisper.

The door was partly open, and the fire in the other room joined its light to the candle's to throw a reddish glow on the wall above the red-checked tablecloth. In a large frame in the center of the glow was a picture of a man in uniform like those of the soldiers at the fort, but much gayer, all gilt and red and white. His hand rested on a long knife, and his face was serious. On a little shelf below was a small vase of flowers beside candlesticks of ancient silver that was like birch in moonlight, like a trickling stream, like my mother's armlets.

Madame crossed the room, and little points of light danced on her glasses, her knitting needles, and the silver buckles on her slippers. I heard the creaking of the rocker as she sat down.

"How did—everything go today?" came Pierre's voice, somewhat hesitant. By moving along my bed a little, I could see him at ease in his big armchair, his long legs stretched out in front of him, on his face the peace of one who has come home. As tiny puffs of smoke arose from his pipe, his eyes roamed about as if greeting familiar friends on every side, and he looked at pictures and cushions and the row of old silver as one who has wandered away but is beside his own council-fire again.

"We got along very well," said his mother, with an edge of surprise on her voice as if she had just realized it. "That girl works so quietly. Why, she's as noiseless as—as a shadow. We must get those heathenish moccasins off her at once."

"Oh, I don't know, Mother. She has never worn anything else—"

"Now, Pierre," she said, raising her voice so I heard distinctly. "With no liking for the task of bringing up a baby and training an Indian girl, I take it up. You must remember that and let me do things my own way. This girl must behave just like one of us. That is the only way I can endure having her here. They say Mr. Stuart's first wife was an Indian, and quite charming. That gave me hope that we can do as well with this girl, and make her fit to marry—"

Pierre laughed. "Now, *ma mère*, that is going too fast. Oneta is only a child."

"It is never too soon for a girl to make herself fit to make a decent marriage."

Pierre let that go. He seemed intent on the smoke from his pipe. "I know you will try to be patient if she doesn't learn rapidly at first."

"I feel more encouraged after today," Madame admitted. "She did everything I told her to, and that's all she ever needs to do."

"She has a great deal of character, and an unusual mind. Quite a bit of charm, too." Pierre's words did not seem addressed to anyone, but rather into the fire before him.

"She is good-looking, in a sober way," said Madame. "Something queer about her looks." She was silent for a minute. "I guess it's her eyes. Those heavy, arched brows are unusual for a girl."

"And her eyes are so black and penetrating," agreed Pierre. "They're unforgettable."

I paid little attention, for I was used to talk about my eyes. Strangers to our lodge-fire had spoken of "Tecumseh's eyes," when they saw me, even before they knew I was his daughter.

Madame knitted and rocked for a little. "Keeping her in good surroundings may make quite a change," she admitted. "When I think how these Indians live—they don't stay in one place long enough. A woman can't learn how to make a decent home if she has to follow hunters around all the time. You couldn't expect a flower to grow if you kept transplanting it every day, could you?"

"By the way, Mother—I got her to promise not to go down to the beach lodges any more—"

Madame interrupted. "*Ma foi,* you didn't need to bother to get a promise. I wouldn't have let her go."

Pierre did not answer. The only sounds I heard for a long time were the crackling of the fire, the squeak of the rocking chair.

"How much money do you make, Pierre?"

"Twelve hundred dollars a year. I hope it will be more sometime."

"But that is a fortune, here. We shall live like the best ones of the village."

"It is not as much as you think. Food is more expensive here than in Quebec. Nearly everything comes by boat from a distance. This island is almost completely barren rock."

"But I have a garden, and an apple tree. I have whole strings of dried apples in the garret now. And I have pumpkins as large as your fist already on the vines, and onions—"

Outside my window, Mackinac lay in shadow, and dew gathered upon it. As one becoming drowsy by the sound of running water, I felt the talk in the other room flowing past me, and in troubled sadness I fell asleep.

When Madame made her decision that I should be sent away, I do not know. The first I heard of it was one night about a week later, as I lay in bed again and heard the talk beyond my door. Listening to the crackling of the logs, I had been thinking that Pierre had bought the wrong kind of wood for an indoor fire. He should have insisted on cedar or basswood that would burn gently. I remember thinking I would tell him to let Baptiste get his wood.

I had not been to see Marthe even once. Madame had kept me occupied taking care of Paul and helping her with her never-ending round of cooking and cleaning the house. Floors, windows, dishes, ornaments—everything had its turn at being scrubbed and polished, and when all were done, she began at the beginning again. For the first time, I saw how easy-going the cabin life had been. I felt like a keg that had drifted down a peaceful river, at once to be caught in a whirlpool and sent around in its basin for weeks, sometimes descending to rise again and make the same dizzy circuit. Madame had scolded when I made mistakes, but when I got used to her ways, her chiding hurt no more than the nibble of little fishes when one stands with bare legs in the water. She tried to be kind, but she was impatient. It was quite as if she had acquired a new chair, perhaps serviceable, but that did not quite fit in with the delicate French furniture that had followed her from Quebec. But, having it, she expected it to take its place and do its work with no foolish demands of its own for more space or a different treatment.

"I think the girl should have some schooling," said Madame suddenly in the other room.

Pierre said nothing. I could imagine how he was sitting, looking into the distance as he thought over her words.

"I could teach her to read and write," he suggested at last.

"No, someone else should do it. You haven't the time."

"I think some of the children go to one of the French women at the end of the village for lessons. Shall I find out?"

"No. I want to send her away to a good school. The child has character, as much trouble as it has been to teach her. If she stays here, she'll drift into being the squaw of some Indian that comes out of the woods one of these summers. Having her on our hands as we do, let's try to do something for her."

"Away?" I heard a queer edge on Pierre's tone. I knew he was thinking the same as I. She wanted to get rid of me. She had had it in mind all the time. In the silence that fell between the two, I could sense a wordless conflict, as if Pierre were thinking all the things he might say, and she were getting answers ready. The smoke drifted out from Pierre's pipe, and the knitting needles clicked firmly through to victory.

"Perhaps you are right, Mother. Where would you suggest?"

"The convent of the Ursulines at Quebec."

"Quebec! So far away as that?"

"The distance doesn't matter. If she's going at all, she can't come back until she has finished."

"It seems hard to send her into strange surroundings again, when she has hardly had time to get used to the changes we have already made."

Madame pounced on that. "A good reason to make another right away."

The wood had sobbed its heart out in noisy sap and lay quiet. Pierre sighed. "I see you have made up your mind. Well, write a letter and see if they will take her, and how much it will cost. I'll try to take her there myself. Mr. Stuart has to send someone to Quebec to sign up voyageurs for next season. I'll ask him to send me."

As a river finding a passage through mountainous rocks, every way I had turned since coming to that house, I had come up against some strange whim of Madame's. Troubled as I was over that latest one, the manitou sent sleep over me at last. In my dreams the fire turned to brilliant stars, and the voices to a cool wind in the pines.

Madame did not wait for an answer to the letter she sent out on the next boat, but began at once to work on new clothes for me. I sewed with her on the strange garments of brown and gray wool, the little white collars of linen, trying to think what those coming years at Quebec would be like. My boxes were packed and repacked, as Madame happened to think of something that might be added or changed for the better. She forbade me to take anything I had brought from the cabin. Saying nothing, I managed to pack in two things—the red stone arrowhead and one of my mother's bracelets. I, too, wished to have some familiar faces about me.

And so she had her way. I was separated from Pierre and my baby brother, for the time at least, as if I had gone away with my grandfather as Madame had planned at first. I was cut off from them still more than if I had chosen to stay with Marthe.

Part Three

One

❧ Early one morning, in a birch canoe swiftly paddled by four Hurons that knew the St. Lawrence like the inside of their own medicine bags, Pierre and I passed the last of the close-set fences of the ribbon farms stretching back from the river toward the Laurentian hills, and approached Quebec. From many leagues down the river we had seen glistening roofs high on a towering rock— the reflections of bright sunshine on the spires and towers of the upper town. Down to our ears had come the sounds of many bells as the city was called to prayers. I paid no attention to the cluster of buildings along the river below, for I knew I was to go up there among the spires. We came to the wharf among other canoes with paddles, rafts, and heavy-oared craft, and a few boats with flying sails. Still looking up, I saw that around the edge of the rocky height, enclosing those gleaming towers, was a solid wall of stone and wood, with breaks in it only where black cannons poked their

215

muzzles through, or a heavy gate was set in it below a tower.

Pierre and I left the wharf and made our way through a winding street between the irregular old tenements of the lower town and started the ascent of the hill, climbing a narrow pathway broken now and then by steep stairs where the rise was especially abrupt. Mountain Street, Pierre called it, and he followed its zigzag course to the top with the sureness of one whose foot had been often upon it.

At the top, we stood for a moment on the parapet before the arched gate. Wondering whether, once inside that fortress town, I could see flowing water, I leaned over in silent farewell to the sparkling curve of the St. Lawrence, stretching out far below like a sky-tinted highway. I knew it was the outlet for all the great lakes and connecting rivers over which we had traveled eastward from the berry moon to the beginning of the moon of falling leaves, and I thought some of that very water might once have caressed the far-away pebbled shore of Mackinac before our cabin and Marthe's. "Long ago," said Pierre softly, just behind me, "someone called it 'beautiful as the Seine, rapid as the Rhone, and deep as the sea.' " The words meant nothing to me, but somehow in that moment of gazing on the blue water together, I felt closer to Pierre than I had since my mother's death, the approach that ever comes to two souls gazing on the same object with affection.

And then the feeling was gone, and confusion came, as Pierre drew me through the broad gate into one of the narrow, irregular streets of the upper town. It rambled here and there like the trail of an aimlessly browsing deer, but it had been a long time, I thought, since any deer had found a path for his foot on this uneven summit. The close-set houses of gray stone or wood, with their tall, steep roofs and tiny dormer windows, had a look of great age about them, and the narrow shops were fronted with crumbling pillars of brick around their doors of time-stained wood. The sidewalks bordering the dirt roadway were of boards laid end to end, with grass growing through where they had rotted away. Tall posts with lamps on top seemed to have grown through the walk in the same fashion.

The spires I had seen from below were on high stone buildings scattered everywhere among the broad roofs of the houses. Pierre pointed them out reverently one after the other, his voice rich with the joy of recognizing old acquaintances—the château, the cathedral, the Jesuit college, churches, schools and convents. Twice, as we neared the wall again, he pointed out the rutted dirt roads of St. Louis and St. John passing out through city gates toward near-by, straggling towns.

The bells were still ringing as we walked, and the sounds of chants poured from convent windows—two sounds I hear in memory whenever I think of Quebec. I noticed that Pierre had not pointed out the convent where I was to be left, but I asked no questions, tremulously glad to put off the moment of parting. Each winding street seemed much like the others to me, but each brought new pleasure to Pierre's face with every turn. He pointed out the house where he had lived, the shops of the cobbler who had made his shoes and the tailor who had made his suits, and the great house of the rich man his father had worked for. Once we came out on an open square filled with little tables roofed from the sun and heaped up with vegetables and fruits. Saturday was market day, Pierre told me. Among the tables were French *habitants* like those I had seen at Detroit, with lively eyes and sunburned skin, long coats of dark gray with hoods to be pulled over their heads when it rained, and drawn in at the waist by a worsted sash of red, orange, or green, and heavily trimmed with beads.

Since the day was fair, the hood hung down the back, and on each head a *bonnet rouge* sat above a long queue of black hair.

As some of the chants came to an end, black-robed men and women began to fill the street, bringing the odor of incense as they passed us. A clamor arose in the market-place as little crowds gathered around the tables to examine the produce. Pierre looked at his big gold watch.

"Come." He turned away from the market-place and set out purposefully on a street marked "St. Anne's" that led toward the end of town far back on the heights, where we turned on Des Jardins Street. In silence Pierre walked along past the houses until he came to a high picket fence enclosing a stretch of rising ground at the top of which I saw, high-perched, a long, plain building of brick and stone.

"This is the convent of the Ursuline nuns," said Pierre. He opened a little gate and we went through and ascended the path to the low arched doorway. The heavy door grated on its hinges, and an old man with a short beard, whom I came to know later as the porter, faced us in the opening.

"I am Pierre Debans. I should like to speak to the Superior."

The porter nodded, and motioned for us to follow him. Pierre took off his high beaver hat and we went inside. The old man led us through a dim corridor into a small room with walls and ceiling darkened by smoke. He pointed to a bench where we could sit and wait.

Trying to hide the choked feeling those plain walls gave me, avoiding the pity and something like regret I saw rising in Pierre's eyes, I stared at the floor sparsely covered by braided rugs of black and gray. On the largest one, just across the room from me, sat a chair before a grille in the wall separating the little parlor from another enclosure beyond. As I looked, a woman in billow-

ing black robes and a white coif about her face entered
that enclosure. Pierre rose, and as the nun seated herself
close to the grille-work, he took the chair on our side of
it, and they began to talk through the opening. I
watched the sunlight from a high window play on the
blue cloth of Pierre's shoulders, the smooth brown waves
of his hair, and throw shadows of the grille on the nun's
white coif and tranquil face framed in the fullness of
her black dress and veil. I heard their voices dully, while
I tried to repress the panic, the desire to run out of this
place where there was so little light, to force my way
out of all the doors between me and the air, to find a
place where there were no walls, no corridors and heavy
doors, where only a swaying blanket hung between me
and the friendly woods.

I heard the nun tell Pierre that he need not pay for
my necessities, since it was for the teaching of Indian
girls that Mère Marie had long ago brought her band of
nuns to begin the convent in the new world. I heard
Pierre's voice saying that this was a special case, that he
was responsible for me and would pay whatever the
parents of the French girls did. After that, I understood
dimly that Pierre was trying to reassure himself that he
was doing right to leave me there.

"I hope she will not be unhappy here. My mother
thought it was the best place to have her taught."

"*Madame votre mère* was right. All the efforts of the
Ursuline order are devoted to the teaching of young girls
in Christian doctrine and the conduct suited to their
sex. We care for their bodies and nurture their souls,
like true and loving mothers." The nun sounded as if she
were reciting.

"I do not doubt that," said Pierre. "It is well known
how the Ursulines have given their whole soul and effort
to the work here for nearly two hundred years. But you
may need much patience at first with Oneta. She has
never known anything about regularity and formal

training." He sent a worried look to where I sat motionless on the bench.

The nun smiled, but the change brought no softness to a face firm of character and clear of purpose. "Put your mind at ease, sir. She will soon be contented here. We teach by the value of good example, and our discipline is mild. Now," she went on, business-like, "we require that girls be at least six years old and know their alphabets when we take them. This girl is well above the age—"

"I am sorry to say that she can neither write nor read French," said Pierre, "but she speaks it well, and she is very quick. She has a truthful, dependable character."

The nun looked at me thoughtfully. "I think we can admit her. It will not be long before she makes up the lack. Our instruction will fit her case very well, for it is all individual or in very small groups. She can progress as fast as she wants to. I shall ask Sister Celeste to devote all her time to your ward until she can take her place with the others."

She rose and looked at me. Mildly severe, as one at all times intent on the duty of the moment, she spoke. "Come, Oneta." She pointed toward a little door in the corner of the room.

Pierre crossed the room and took my hand, and I stood up.

"You will like it here when you are used to it." A question hovered about his words.

I could find nothing to say. The nun, complacent and heavy, had opened the door. She stood waiting beyond it, and Pierre let my hand slip from his, as if I had already been removed beyond his control.

I do not remember that I said good-by, or turned to watch him go. I went through the door and the nun closed it. The lock snapped into place behind me with a sound of finality. I followed those gently swaying black skirts into a long hallway, cold, bare, excessively

220

clean, but full of the odor of stale incense. Around a turn, we met a procession of nuns, chanting and walking two by two. Seemingly all alike in their full black robes, they looked like an army against me. I pressed close to the wall as they passed. I know now that their chants were in Latin, but then the sounds only alarmed me as one more unfamiliar thing, and I believe there is nothing that makes one feel more alone than hearing words from human lips fall strange upon the ear. I felt like one lost in a bewildering land with no blazed trail to guide him.

The nun I had been following did not pause or turn around, even though she must have known that I had stopped and had to run to catch up. Up a flight of stairs we went, and then another, and down a hollow-sounding corridor. Around a dark corner at the end, the nun opened a door, and we were in a large room with two long rows of beds stretching across toward high windows at the far end.

"This is the dormitory. The other girls are at breakfast," said the nun gently. "I shall let you rest here alone for a time. In a half-hour, a tray of food will be brought up to you. A little later, Sister Celeste will come, and give you a short reading lesson, and begin your instruction in prayers. Tomorrow you will begin with the regular order of the day."

I was obedient because there was nothing else to be. When she had gone, I lay on the white spread of the iron cot, looking at the walls so determinedly closing me in, and thought of how far I had come from the lodge-days. I felt like a plant uprooted and thrown to lie on strange ground, withering and feeling its roots parched by wind and sun, not knowing whether there is strength enough in them to reach down into cool earth again. Pierre had seemed dismayed at the bareness, but it was not that which depressed me. It was the lack of color. I thought how strangely uniform were the black and white of the nuns' garb, the gray of the stone and the braided rugs. Strange to my eyes, used to the hues of green trees and blue water, of purple and yellow and red flowers on hillsides and river banks, bright palpitating colors repeated in the bright wool coats and sashes of the voyageur, and the embroidery on the garments of braves and women, animated and vivid to match the life that went with them.

The nun had left the door open, and I could hear matin-chants faintly from a chapel. The words came softly through the resonant halls, ". . . from anger and hatred and every evil will, O Lord, deliver us . . . lift our minds . . . we beseech Thee . . . deliver our souls . . . grant eternal rest. . . ." The sound echoed on, down the corridor as if it would leave no space unfilled, and then all was still, as if all life had ceased. But at least I had no fear of silence. It was natural to my people, who knew better than others what wondrous things took place in it. No shouts or beat of drums announced the opening of a bud to full bloom, a blade of grass pushing through the earth, or the morning return of the sun. A little flicker of light passed over the window nearest me, as some branch outside moved in the wind. The sun is in his place, I thought, and tried to hold fast to the tiny comfort. The sun will come up tomorrow. At last I closed my eyes and slept like a tired voyageur.

Beginning the order of the day the nun had spoken of, I was amazed that every moment from rising at 5:30 to bed at 8:00 was parceled out for a definite purpose. There is no chance that I will ever forget that order, forced gently but relentlessly upon me for twelve years. Toilette and morning prayers were followed by mass and then breakfast. At the sound of a bell, we marched two by two in silence to class, curtseying to the nuns who opened the doors. In the classroom, gray and bare except for a religious picture in front, and benches and tables scattered about the uneven floor, we curtseyed again to the class mistress, and took our places, kneeling at our benches for morning prayer, with one of the older girls leading. Then we rose, curtseyed to the mistress and sat upon the bench. Every morning we had reading lessons, and I had mine alone with the aged, thin Sister Celeste, while most of the others recited together. Now and again a nun would appear in the doorway, and a small group of girls would rise, curtsey, and go out two by two after her to another room for writing lessons, to return an hour later and resume reading, while another group went out.

After dinner, we were allowed to walk in the grounds, or play battledore and shuttlecock or bowls, but if the weather was bad we stayed indoors and played chess. When time was up, we went to our places, knelt and recited the Litany of the Blessed Virgin. Catechism came next, followed by our second lesson in reading, with groups leaving for arithmetic as they had for writing in the morning. At the end of the day we had a quarter hour for examen of conscience, and another nun instructed us in the catechism. Then supper, recreation, prayers and bed.

All was senseless and confused at first. To me a prayer meant a dance of invocation, of petition for rain, for game, or for a good crop of corn. I could see that here I was asked to substitute other symbols for the ones I knew, and, guided by the gentle teachings and repressions of Sister Celeste, I put up with the inconvenience in the same way I accepted shoes instead of moccasins. The fussing about the right way to make the sign of the cross, the insistence on exact wordage in catechism answers, seemed to me childish, but any idea of revolting was repressed—not from fear, but with a dread of the special attention the unruly girls received. I wanted to be let alone as much as I could be, to wait out my time.

I do not believe the nuns felt I was a very difficult girl to teach. In childhood I had been taught that inattention to a speaker was unpardonable, and they took my politeness for interest.

Slowly I made friends with the other girls, mostly French with a few Iroquois and Hurons among them, and here and there a French girl who had borrowed something from a half-Iroquois grandmother—a special straightness of the hair, a way of keeping her feelings to herself, a way of not looking straight at you to offend. Since they were not of my tribe, I felt little more akin to the other Indian girls there than to the French, but they had at least prepared the way so no special curiosity was directed at me.

When I began to learn English, I started writing in a composition book the unusual happenings of each day. If the dullness and coldness around me failed to give me words to put down, I tried reviving memories of my childhood, and set down here and there a legend. Only once did I tell one of these stories to the others. It happened when I was eighteen, after I had been at the convent six years. Whenever our morning and afternoon lessons were done, we always took up some handwork and sat quietly over it at our benches. That particular day was so fair that the nun took us out of doors and we sat under a tree in the convent court, our hands variously busy with knitting, mending, embroidery on muslin or silk, or making of flowers in cloth and wire. As we worked the nun read aloud an instructive story, but in the midst of it, another nun came and called her away inside, and we were left with one of the older girls in charge. It chanced to be Annette, special friend of mine, a solid girl with copper lights in her hair.

"We shall tell stories," she said. "It is your turn, Oneta."

Instead of repeating some story that had been read to us, as we usually did, I began one of Marthe's.

"Long ago a woman of my tribe fell in love with the morning star. She sat in adoration whenever he shone in the sky. All her people told her how foolish she was, for the star was distant and could never be approached. But in secret she went on loving him.

"One day when she went to the river for water, she saw a handsome young man on its banks. 'I am the morning star,' he told her. 'I have come to take you to my home in the sky.' She trembled, for she knew this must be a god, but he took her by the hand, and they rose to the sky-country, to his great and shining lodge, and they dwelt there in content and happiness."

I paused to break off a thread in my sewing, and Annette leaned forward. "Is that all? Did she never want to go home?"

"Yes. She became at last sad and homesick, and returned to earth like a falling star."

"Was she happy then?" asked another of the girls.

"No. Happiness never came back again. As much as she might stretch her arms to the eastern sky, morning star could not take her back. She was forever shut out of the sky-country."

Tears came to my eyes, and I wiped them away, ashamed because I did not know why they were there, and I bent low over my sewing. The others fell to talking of the legend, and then of men—the men they would like to marry. They chattered like a tree-full of birds making plans for a long flight, as they variously praised a good *habitant* farmer, a trader, a government official.

"You have not told us what kind of man you would like to marry, Oneta," said Annette at last.

Strangely stirred, I lifted my eyes and told of the prophecy at my birth.

"A chief or a medicine man it must be," said one of the Iroquois girls when I had finished. "Only such men are greater than a warrior."

225

The girls smiled, and Annette put her arms around me. "You are going back to your people, then, Oneta?"

Feeling her touch, I shook myself as one coming out of a dream, and said lightly to cover up the seriousness beneath, "No. I must go back to Pierre and my little brother. I shall never marry anyone." I believe that was the first time I thought of what I would do when I went back.

Another girl began telling of her hopes and dreams, and I never spoke of my future again. But from then on, I began to think and plan. I had a natural duty to Paul, but no greater than that to Pierre. He, and Madame, too—whatever her motive—had done much for me in giving me these years at the convent. They were sending money regularly, and clothing handmade by Madame. I remembered one of the earliest teachings of my grandfather: any favor must always be repaid in full and complete measure. I could not escape that and live at peace with myself.

Before I thought of anything else, I must find a way to repay them. As time went on, the words of the medicine man sank back in memory as only a story told by someone else, lost along a winding trail.

I could tell of other days. But it does not matter now what happened in those years, except for what they gave me. I shall let the events themselves settle, as tea leaves lie at the bottom of the kettle, taking into my cup only the essence from them.

Coming out of a life in which the chief teachings of the nuns—self-control, consideration for others, discretion and modesty—had already been imbued in me from my earliest days, I feel now that little change in my character was made, except for the addition of a sense of order. In accomplishments, my gain was greater. One of the nuns noticed my voice when I sang with the others, and gave me special lessons from then on, saying my voice was good and I should know how to use it.

Twelve years of speaking French made it as my own tongue, and I added Latin and English. I learned to paint in water-colors, and worked David playing his harp in neat stitches of chenille and gold thread. An old, very elegant Frenchman with a white wig, black silk stockings and buckled shoes, came once a week to the convent to give us dancing lessons. From him, too, I learned the little forms French people took so much pride in—the proper thing to say when I went to call or when people came to call upon me.

Best of all, I learned what made reading so interesting to Pierre. The quiet-voiced Sister Celeste had a way of effacing herself and bringing the material of books into my mind with no flavor of her teaching. I drank deep of the lessons about strange folk and their ways, of the joy of reading singing words. I took to books as Jacques had taken to Baptiste's stories.

One study among the others—geography—came to me more easily than to the girls from city homes. A river was more than a crooked black line on a map. I knew rivers broad and deep like the great father of waters, and rivers so shallow that a canoe might easily damage its frail sides on the rocks along its bed. I knew smooth murmuring rivers, and rivers where foaming, swirling rapids raged and threatened. Points and bays, too, I knew in my home country, and I did not need to learn by rote that an island was entirely surrounded by water. I had only to close my eyes and see Mackinac with the straits on all sides, making it a world of its own.

There were times when I wanted to run away, brief moments, yet painful ones, for in one minute a fire can consume, an avalanche can bury, or a life's decision can be made. Ever coming between my eyes and the pages of my books were sounds and pictures that left me with a vague emptiness that I know now was homesickness. Sounds of paddle blades, frightened birds rising from deep meadow grass, moccasined feet on limestone paths, a sound of low-rolling thunder as a partridge took to his wings in flight, the sight of low white buildings with a white fort on the bluff above them, fish nets drying in the sun, heaps of shiny fish on a pebbled beach, a distant shore line holding a narrow fringe of juniper trees against deep blue sky.

How surprised the nuns would have been, I have often thought, if they had known how little the religious life had touched me. For those twelve years it was only another form into which I had to fit the movements of the surface of life. It was easy to conform to what was expected, and avoid the extra burden of penalties. I sang the hymns, I told my beads, I went to confession, but the ideas behind the words I learned to say did not seem to be anything that applied to me. They were no more mine than the history lessons about court life and wars in France, not even coming so close as those, for the history of France had already touched me in Pierre's stories. I sat still or knelt with others in the chapel, but if a bird came to the high windowsill, I let my mind soar away with him when he went, or I watched a soft white cloud briefly framed by that narrow opening, or the gently moving fingers of a pine-branch shadow on the dark stained glass. I was less skeptical than untouched. I looked at the dark pictures and the statues without interest, but I often thought of the grave beneath the chapel flooring, where lay the body of the Marquis de Montcalm, that leader of the lost French cause, who had died in defeat, knowing that with him the hopes of his people were lost, even as my father must have felt when he put on his deerskins to go into his last battle.

On the days when flowers appeared between the massive silver candlesticks on the altar, I kept my eyes on them throughout the service. They fed a hunger ever with me in that place. Dimly I understood why they were there, for I had early been taught by my mother that fragrance was acceptable to spirits, whether it is of flowers or the fragrance of a life. Saints were ever less real to me than the many spirits of trees and rocks and streams. When the priest spoke of eternity as going on forever, the picture of the endlessly rolling, tumbling waters of the straits went through my mind. The music of the choirs, the chanting of the mass, only made more vivid the sound of the waters in the straits, the quietly dripping springs, the wind and rain of autumn storms. Borne by the monotonous chanting, like a canoe on a quietly moving stream my thoughts went out and away. Among the organ notes deep and high came disturbing notes of other music—thin notes of a wooden flute, the beating of hands on a skin drawn tight over a piece of hollow log set in earth, boat songs, and even the endless scraping of fiddle strings. It was as if I were using these things as a barrier to something trying to crush me, as though if I ceased to be myself I should not live.

The other girls went out sometimes for a day or a week at home, but I never passed beyond the high iron fence. Pierre wrote to me every two months, and with each new season came money for new clothes and the little necessities of the schoolroom. The Mother Superior wrote him little notes about my progress, and at last, at the end of twelve years, she wrote him that I had completed all the convent studies, and that I had shown no vocation to become a religious. After a long wait came a letter from Pierre. He would come at once to take me back to Mackinac.

I met Pierre again in the same room where he had left me years before. When I opened the door, he was sitting on that same low wooden bench. I was so glad I could not speak beyond a murmur of joy. He looked tired— Pierre never liked long journeys—and older, though until he turned his head and I saw the gray among the smooth waves of his brown hair, I was not sure it wasn't a trick of the dim light.

He rose and came to take my outstretched hands.

"Oneta?" he asked in wonder. His gray eyes came to a kindly focus on my face in the way I knew so well.

I could do nothing but smile faintly and try to keep the tears back. It was so good to see him again, his long thin face so kind above the same immaculate white frills at his throat. He was richly dressed in dark blue, in a wide-lapelled coat and trousers of the new long style coming down to shoes of black shiny leather, with gray cloth, buttoned tops. Over his arm was a heavy cloak of the deep blue of midnight water. Beneath the wonder as he looked at me lay peace, as if the years had been so kind he had not felt their passing.

"You don't look much like the little rabbit-girl now," he said. "Why, you're grown up. The Superior wrote that you behave as if you had been born and brought up in Paris, but I couldn't picture how you looked. With the right clothes, you'll be lovely."

"Thank you, sir," I said in my best convent manner, but holding tightly to his hands as if I were still the child of long ago. A long-carried burden seemed to slip from my shoulders. He was really glad to see me. His marriage to my mother had been so brief I had wondered if when he came at last it would be only to take on a responsibility he could not evade any longer.

By his next words I knew his memories of my mother were kind ones.

"Your voice is like hers. Remember how she used to laugh when something pleased her?"

"Yes—low and like the sound of little waves," I said softly, as if words about my mother were strange between these cold, plain walls.

"You laughed that way when you opened the door just now," said Pierre. "But you are a little taller than she, and your eyes aren't like hers. You've always had such dark, penetrating eyes." He said the last so thoughtfully that I knew his mind had gone back through the years. At last he took a long breath, and stirred, shaking off the soft clasp of memories. "Are you glad to be going home?"

"Oh, yes!" I could not help letting out my tense happiness, my longing for this time so long deferred.

Though I had not intended it to be so, my joy brought a sense of guilt to Pierre. "I should have come for you sooner."

"Oh, I've been happy here," I said quickly. I did not want him to feel, in this moment of reunion, that he had been unkind. "I've learned a great many things— to read French, and Latin, and I can speak English, too —and do mathematics and all kinds of sewing—" I stopped, breathless with the attempt to put the gains of twelve years into words.

Pierre's slow smile came up again. "They have been kind to you here, then?"

"Oh, yes. The nuns have always been kind and patient. I am very fond of them." Still, my hands closed tighter in Pierre's, and I looked up into his eyes. "But when shall we go home?"

"I have a canoe waiting below." Pierre took up his cloak from the bench. "We shall leave as soon as we buy some clothes."

Much later, when farewells had been made, and my belongings, already lying packed in boxes for many days, had been sent down to the wharf and we were making the rounds of shops to find a dress, coat, and bonnet fashionable enough to please Pierre's taste, I asked him about Paul.

"He's quite a big boy now," was Pierre's vague answer. Never in his letters had he told me what I wanted to know about Paul as he grew—how he looked, or what he liked to do. It was almost as if Pierre did not know.

"He's thirteen now," I said. All through the years

the sense of the age of my brother had been closer to me than the addition to my own. "He has not been a troublesome boy?"

"No—that is, not until the last few months. He seems to lack the ambition of a Debans—"

I waited, but Pierre said no more, and the frown line had appeared between his eyes. I decided to leave all questions unasked. I would soon be home and could see for myself.

I remembered then to ask politely in my best manner, "And Madame? I trust she is well?"

"Just the same. You'll see, she's not a bit different. Doesn't seem to feel her years at all. You know," he mused, "she's never had the slightest doubt that sending you away was for your own good. I'm anxious to see her face when she sees how successful the plan was."

But Pierre was not to see my first meeting with Madame. At Montreal where we stopped while he engaged twenty new voyageurs for the fur company, and bought goods for the company and wines for his own cellar, a letter from Mr. Stuart reached him. Before returning to Mackinac, Pierre was to go to New York to see Mr. Astor.

Pierre read the letter twice.

"What can he want to see me about?" he asked, and the wonder of it hovered about his face as he made ready to go, and arranged at the same time for canoe-men to take me on up the St. Lawrence, across Lake Ontario and around the falls of Niagara to Buffalo where I could get passage on a steamboat for Detroit.

Two

✿ Detroit in 1830, seen from the water, was a little settlement clustering about a fort high on the river bank, with pigs wandering about its unpaved streets among people on foot and in wagons and carriages. Above the noise of a general bustle came the shouts of chimney-sweeps and itinerant locksmiths calling their trades, and the bells of ragmen's carts. Back from the shore above the town stretched the ribbon farms of the French *habitants*, their houses, backed by sweet-flowering orchards, standing sociably close along a street of their own.

The *North Star* fired a small cannon to give notice of its arrival. Ropes made it fast at the busy wharf, and the gangplank was put down. As over a bridge to an unknown world, settlers' families began to flow across it, huddling together, the mothers carrying the smallest children and moving on toward a new life with a courage that could not quite cover the dread in their eyes. Leaving them, I made my way through the piles of freight already being unloaded, picking my footing around barrels and bags, plows, pigs, and crates of chickens. Waving aside the drivers of horse-drawn cabs, who, booted and whip in hand, stood at the wharf urging passengers to ride to the Marion House or the Steamboat Hotel, I hurried along the dock. There was a schooner at anchor, and passengers were going aboard. I wondered if by any chance it were sailing north. Inquiring, I was told by a deck hand that I was just in luck. The *Andrew Jackson* was loading for Mackinac.

Within an hour all passengers were aboard and we had left the wharf. Once beyond the town, the captain used all his skill to keep us off the St. Clair flats that often

233

caught and held vessels for days before they could be pulled loose. Across the smooth, broad basin of Lake St. Clair we sailed, and through the swift water above, until the lake of the Hurons came from the farthest horizon to meet us. As one clings to the shelter of a wall instead of venturing alone into great space, the schooner sailed up the lake close to the forest rising from the western shore. No storms came to delay us, and at last, on the fourth night, the captain told us that the next morning would find us close to Mackinac.

Perhaps sitting on deck so late that last night, peering ahead and hoping for the sight of familiar land, made me sleep later in the morning than usual. The sun was well up when I awoke, and the other women sharing the cabin had dressed and gone out. By the time I had on my white cotton stockings and my shoes, I knew something was wrong with the ship. Its motion had stopped, as if we were resting like a canoe on glassy water. And yet we were not in a harbor, for there was no noise of embarking, no sound of feet, of the captain shouting orders and the crew springing to obey. I put on my gray dress and my bonnet and went out on deck.

Passengers and crew stood at the rail, looking off, but not as if they were seeing anything in particular. The captain stood at the bow. His usual energetic motion suspended, he leaned against a rope, one foot curled behind him. With him stood a young man I had noticed since the first day out of Detroit. Well-dressed in gray, with a tall gray hat, he had an immaculate look, while most of the men had grown careless in the many days on board. He was a little taller than the captain as they stood there, and he had an arrow-like straightness I had always taken for granted as a child, but had not often seen among white men. With it he had no stiffness like the dignity of Pierre. This young man was lithe and active.

His hair was brown, like Pierre's, but with reddish

234

lights in it in the sun. I had decided that he was handsome, but it was not so much in perfection of features as in a sort of aliveness in his face. He had not shown the bored, idle curiosity of the rest of the passengers at the sights along the way. Whenever something new had appeared on the shore line—a group of lodges, a tree being felled, a brush row burning, a canoe being launched for night fishing with a pine torch in the bow —this young man had hung over the rail with eager interest.

I had wondered a little about him, because he did not seem to belong in any of the regular classes of passengers. He showed only a slight interest in the talk about western lands. Though it was plain that he was well-educated, he was not a priest, not a teacher. None of the passengers had been able to find out much about him. I had heard him turn aside their prying questions, seeming to find an amusement in doing it that I was sure covered the same reluctance I felt about satisfying the merely curious.

I hesitated a moment as I saw him there, and then went on to speak to the captain. "What is wrong, please?" My low voice seemed to shake the silence like the beat of a drum.

The captain paused in the act of pulling out his pipe from the side pocket of his blue pea-jacket. "A calm, just a calm," he said mildly, but he sent an impatient glance aloft and began jamming tobacco vengefully into his pipe.

"Can't something be done?"

The captain turned a gray-whiskered face to me. "Nothing but wait, Miss. The sailor hasn't been discovered yet that can do anything about a calm but wait."

I looked out over the water. "Oh—! That's Bois Blanc! Then Mackinac is not far—"

"Nope, not far. But might just as well be a hundred miles unless we get some wind."

"We are *degraded*, then," I said.

"That's voyageur talk. You from up here?"

"Yes. Mackinac is my home. I haven't been there for twelve years."

"Well, it's too bad you have to wait like this, right on its doorstep. There's something tricky about the winds here between these big lakes. I've been held up as much as a day and a half without a speck of wind. If it wasn't for that mist you could almost see your island."

Something I hadn't thought about for years came into my mind. "Have you offered tobacco to the spirits of the water?"

Some of the near-by passengers laughed, and the captain heard them and scowled. "Have I what?" he asked kindly.

Quite a knot of passengers, having nothing else to do, gathered around. The captain looked up at them from under the greasy rim of his cap.

"It's one of the beliefs I was brought up on," I said simply.

"The French have a belief like that, too," said the young man. His words were eager and yet so polite that they did not seem an intrusion, but he at once bowed and said, "I beg your pardon. Captain, may I have the honor—?"

The captain, caressing his pipe in his hand, introduced us. "Miss, er—Debans, isn't it?—Mr. Martin Reynolds."

The young man bowed again, and beneath his small brown mustache a quick smile came to his lips. "Miss Debans," he said. "Please excuse my joining your conversation so abruptly. I heard about the French custom when I was at Detroit. I had to wait there three days. I wasn't as lucky as you."

So he had noticed me leaving the steamboat and coming on board the schooner.

"I spent a lot of time along Jefferson Street and the docks," he went on. "Picked up some fascinating things there. One of them was that precaution of the French voyageurs—throwing offerings in the water for *la vieille* —the old woman of the water, who could let them go safely, or turn up all sorts of danger."

"Well, now, I tell ye, I never pass up any chance," said the captain, taking in the attentive passengers out of one corner of his eye. "Might as well be on the safe side." He pulled a huge twist of tobacco from his pocket and tossed it over the rail. The young man smiled at me, as if we shared something the others couldn't understand.

The three of us fell silent. I looked at the heavily wooded Bois Blanc, with no sign of life upon its shaggy shores. Since it had always been full of marshy land and was heavily infested with mosquitoes, no one lived there, and it was not the season for woodchoppers. It was too late for Mackinac people who did their cutting during the winter when wood could be hauled on the ice, and it was not yet time for choppers to be getting wood to make the lyed corn for voyageur rations. As early as this, it was possible not a single boat had returned from the winter's trading. Everything was still, even the clouds hanging motionless above silent dark forests that looked like a double fringe along the rim of the smooth water, reaching as far down into it as they reached toward the sky.

From the shore a single crow arose into the still air and flew toward Round Island beyond. The young man ended our silence.

"A calm doesn't keep him from going where he wants to," he said lightly, his eyes following the deliberation of the bird's flight.

"No," I said. "Did you know that the crow was once as white as snow?"

"No, really?" The young man smiled. "What happened to him?"

"He was caught in a hollow tree with a fire beneath and smoked until he was black."

"Why?"

"Punishment for mischief," I said.

As I spoke I was watching a large birch canoe, one of the thirty-five-foot *canots du nord*, pushing away from the beach at Bois Blanc where voyageurs from the north often stopped and scraped off their whiskers and put on their best clothes before going on to Mackinac. The men, taking in our situation, looked toward the ship and waved.

"Get out your paddles!" one of them shouted derisively.

"You know what they're sayin'?" asked the captain.

I repeated it in English. The captain grinned, half amused, half annoyed.

More laughing and scornful shouts came toward us, from men glorying in pushing their craft along by the strength of their arms, glad to see a new-fangled usurper of their waters lying helpless. The better to taunt, they swerved from their straight course and came closer to the ship.

How glad I was to see buckskin-fringed arms dipping paddle blades in those waters again! I could count nine men in bright headbands or caps of red wool, gay neckerchiefs, fringes on their arms, and a breadth of striped shirt where their buckskin jackets hung open in front. They were just like men of their occupation had always been, broad in shoulder, stronger in arms than in legs, light in weight, thinner now than they would be after a summer on Mackinac, and with long hair they had let grow as a protection against mosquitoes.

The captain waved a nonchalant salute to them, and I raised my arm in greeting. They were coming nearer, so I could hear them talking among themselves.

"Wonder who the girl is? She looks ver-ree happy," said one of them.

And then in the center of the canoe a voyageur got up so suddenly that the rest let loose a flow of curses. "*Sacré diable!* Want to spill the whole winter's catch in the water?"

The one who had jumped up paid no attention.

"Oneta! It's Oneta!"

I looked at the gold rings in his ears, and his buckskin coat heavy with beading.

"Don't you know me?" He pulled off the red handkerchief knotted about his head and waved it at me.

"Don't you remember me?" A shock of black curls fell over his forehead.

"Jacques!" I cried.

"Yes, it is Jacques." He laughed, and his white teeth shone in the sunlight. "Coming in from my fifth year in the woods." He said it proudly, paying no attention to the burst of laughter from the other men.

"Oh, Jacques, I'm so glad to see you. I'm so anxious to get to the island—"

He snapped his fingers with sudden thought, and turned to the steersman, a tall, heavy-built man with a crow's feather gleaming black against his red cap—the brigade leader. I could hear Jacques talking to him in a low voice. "Her mother married M'sieu Debans of the fur company, you remember."

The leader finally nodded, and Jacques turned back to me. "Want to ride in with us?"

"Oh, Jacques, could I?"

"Of a certainty. One moment."

Some of the others grumbled a bit. Before getting out at Bois Blanc, they had sat motionless for hours to avoid breaking the bark seams of the canoe. And now here was Jacques leaping up, and then inviting a passenger to jump in from above.

"Never mind," said the steersman. "We are so close

239

we can bail if we crack now." He seemed to be looking for something near his feet.

"You won't need the big sponge," said Jacques. "She was brought up in a canoe." The others looked more closely at my face under the round brim of my bonnet. "An Indian!" I heard them say in wonder.

They lifted their paddles and shot the canoe to the side of the schooner.

"Sure," said the captain. "You go along, Miss. You'll be puttin' your feet under a good dinner-table on Mackinac while we huddle here and wait. I'll bring in your baggage safe and sound when the wind blows up."

Swiftly he uncoiled a rope ladder and lowered it to the canoe. Jacques seized the end, and while the other voyageurs steadied the canoe, I swung down easily, hand over hand—that being easier than using the rungs of the ladder, with my hampering long skirt.

"Well," drawled the captain. "That's darned good, for a girl. Where did you learn to go down a rope like that?"

Jacques answered for me. "On grapevines in the woods."

Then I remembered Mr. Reynolds and realized what he must be thinking. Young gentlemen didn't approve of undignified actions in young ladies. I knew how distressed Pierre would have been if he had seen me. For years at the convent I had been drilled in ladylike behavior. This sudden leap into a boatful of voyageurs was anything but that. Almost against my will I raised my head to see the young man's face.

I found myself looking full into his blue eyes as he leaned over the rail, and what I saw in them was pure admiration and a spirit of fun, as if he were taking part with me in a fascinating adventure.

Jacques had noticed his interest. "Very sorry we can't take any more of you," he said.

The young man laughed. "I'll see you later. I'm going to Mackinac, too. I'm to be the new surgeon at the fort."

The men, occupied in balancing the canoe, sent quick glances upward. They would have plenty to do with the fort doctor before the summer was over, what with one fight and another they were sure to get into.

"*Eh bien,* glad you're going to be on Mackinac," said Jacques. "It's a great place."

"I can see it is," the young man laughed, looking down at the canoe.

We were pulling away from the schooner's side, and, mindful of not disturbing the balance, I crouched down among the bearskin-covered packs of fur in the center. The steersman took his place in the stern, grasping a paddle longer than the others. Jacques was back in his place, and all the fringed arms were dipping and rising together.

I settled myself among the bundles. A corner of the bearskin over one pack of beaver had slipped away, and I stroked the fur, soft, brown, and with the silky sheen I remembered. My fingertips lingered on its smoothness in sheer delight in its beauty and in being back where such things were a part of life.

I turned to Jacques, as I heard his voice joining in the boat song the men immediately struck up. It was one they used for rapid paddling, for they were near their destination.

> "*Derrier' chez nous, y a-t-un etang*
>   *En roulant ma boule*
> *Trois beaux canards s'en vont baignant*
>   *En roulant ma boule.*
>   *Rouli, roulant, ma boule roulant,*
>   *En roulant ma boule roulant*
>   *En roulant ma boule,*"

they sang and Jacques's voice was as deep as the rest. Even yet I found it hard to believe that he was one of these men. He was still short and stocky, with a face full of expression. At that moment it was of joy, like the faces of all the other men as they swayed, dipping and lifting their paddles—anticipation of the summer they would have on Mackinac, the joy of being at the end of their winter's work, the thought of having money in their pockets, and being where it would buy pleasure. Long-bladed hunting knives shone at their hips, catching reflections of the sun faster and faster as the boat song grew livelier, and the paddles kept up with the rhythm. Gently swaying in the lift of the canoe with each stroke of the paddles, I felt I was in a fur-lined cradle.

"How far have you come today?" I asked Jacques in the first pause of the song.

"*Trois pipes,*" he said. "A short journey."

Three pipes—that was about twelve miles, I remembered. It had been a long time since I had heard distance measured by the intervals of stopping for a five-minute smoke.

"Where did you spend the winter, Jacques? What outfit is this?"

"Tahquamenon River."

"Now, Jacques, your song," said one of the men, and they all laughed. I didn't know why, for it was usual for each man to have his special song in which he led, giving the verse alone, to be repeated in chorus.

"*J'aimerai toujours,*" Jacques began with a full voice, and the men laughed again. "Suppose she's still there?" one of them asked. Jacques went on with the song without answering, and the rest joined in.

"Jacques is in good voice today," jested one when they had finished.

"Yes," agreed another, "he drives everyone else off key."

Jacques paid no attention, as one who knows such aspersions are untrue.

"We wouldn't put up with him at all," commented

another, "except for the way he can spot a honey-tree or a turtle to flavor our lyed corn and tallow."

"And who is it that can pull fish from a stream where none of the rest of you can find even a minnow?" demanded Jacques. They laughed.

They pulled up even with Round Island, and passed it. Suddenly the leader called out, "There, *messieurs*, is ze gem of ze lakes."

I sat up, eager for my first glimpse of Mackinac. A little breeze had come up, and was lifting the fog that lay over the island, showing it rising steeply from the water to a height greater even than I remembered. The dense and fleecy mist drifted away, and I saw the white cliffs and green foliage. Other canoes were close around us, the rest of the brigade coming up, but I had no eyes for them. At the same time, near the western point we heard the sound of a musket, and after a pause for reloading, it was fired again.

"Baptiste!" I said.

"Yes, he's seen us," laughed Jacques. "He's announced the first boats that way ever since he's lived on the island."

The men dipped their paddles still faster. I kept my eyes on the village, looking for changes.

"Oh, Jacques—a church, *two* churches!" I exclaimed at the sight of two white spires pointing upward against the heights, with nearly the width of the village between them, contending with each other and with the flagpole at the fort for one's attention; but all three of them were as nothing as we drew nearer and the huge fur warehouse rose higher and higher before us, casting its shadow over half the settlement.

"A chapel of St. Anne's was put up soon after you left." Jacques turned his head. Even as they paddled, the voyageurs nodded their satisfaction that Mackinac's chapel was named for their patron saint.

"We have a new priest—a young Dominican from Italy," said Jacques. "He has to travel through all of Michigan Territory, but he tries to spend most of the summer on Mackinac."

"But what about the other church?" I asked, looking at the one on the point of Robertson's Folly. "There seems to be a group of buildings around it."

"That's a Presbyterian mission and school. Some man and his wife came up here and started it about six years ago."

"A school for village children?" I asked. It seemed too large for that. The main building was really two upright houses connected by a low narrow one.

"Mostly a boarding school for Indian children," said Jacques. "Lots of the traders leave their little ones there for the winter, too."

We were getting closer, turning into the familiar crescent-shaped harbor. There were only a half-dozen lodges on the beach. Ottawas, probably, I thought, seeing their pointed tops, but not able to make out any other signs at that distance. Why weren't there more, I wondered, and a queer dread came up in me, a feeling of aloneness as of one left behind on a strange shore. And then I remembered it was too early for most tribes to be there. It was strange what a feeling of lightness, of something averted, that thought gave me.

The row of shops along the road from point to point was just the same. Their peaked tops pushed against one another like the folds of a partly opened fan. The village houses still sat among snow-white picket fences. I looked at the fort, high on the rocky cliff. The flag of stars and stripes looked strange to me, for I had seen the British flag more often in those last years. But there it was—the white man's totem, I remembered thinking it was when I was a child. I had come to understand something of how many totems were united under it. In that one village had been put aside the fleur-de-lis, the union

244

jack, and a half-dozen or more tribal totems, all to live together under that one with its patch of stars like the night that covers all.

The flag hung in limp folds that suddenly were lifted by the first strong breeze of the day and flung against the blue sky, asserting that it had won its place above these rocky shores. "There's the breeze," I thought. "The schooner can come in now."

At the sound of Baptiste's musket, the usual crowd had rushed to the shore, shouting greetings, beating tin pans, and waving. The first brigade was for them like the coming of the whippoorwill, a sign that winter was really past. Their welcome was not only for the men in those boats, but for liveliness and excitement, for dancing and hearing tall stories, for money passing from hand to hand—for summer itself.

But nowhere did I see any of the people in my thoughts. I was about to ask Jacques about them, when I realized he had no more recent news than Pierre. He had been gone nine or ten months.

A few moments more of rapid paddling, and the canoe was brought to a stop just off the shore, for the heavily laden craft would be damaged if driven up on the beach. In an instant every man was in the water, seizing a pack of furs, swinging a hundred pounds on his back as easily as a mother lifts a child in his cradleboard and puts him across her shoulder.

"I'll get mine in a minute," called Jacques. Squatting before me, he presented his broad back. "Mustn't let Oneta come home with wet feet."

There was nothing else to do. Hesitating only a second, hoping Madame was not in sight, I put my arms around Jacques's neck and rode pickaback to the shore.

The crowd saw nothing unusual in that procedure. A few stared curiously when they saw that a woman, and a well-dressed one, had come in the canoe.

The canoe-men scanned the straits as they let down

245

their packs on the shore. Their pleasure would not really begin until their friends in other brigades were there.

"Jacques, boy! I tole 'em it was you! Yer ma and pa is back there tryin' to get through—" It was Baptiste, with his worn cap askew. He held his musket in one hand and pounded Jacques on the back with the other.

"I like to be the first one in just to hear that old musket of yours," said Jacques. "But say—do you know who this is?" He pulled me forward.

Baptiste jerked off his cap. "I beg your pardon, Miss —why, say! It ain't—"

But I had thrown myself on him, and was almost choking him with my arms. And, my cheek close to his, I felt a tear between them and did not know from which of us it came. By the time Baptiste took my arms gently from about his neck a little group of curious men had gathered to look at this well-dressed young lady throwing herself in the arms of a fisherman in dirty corduroys and ragged mackinaw coat.

"Well, you look like a real French mademoiselle, now," he said, looking at me from my fashionable black bonnet to neat buttoned shoes. "But you'll come down to see me and Marthe—"

"Oh, yes, Baptiste. Right away."

"Well, maybe you'd better go home first," he said. "Just to keep everything peaceful. And you want to see Paul."

At a little distance, Armand and Louise, older, but with the same liveliness, now tearful with joy, were both trying to embrace Jacques at the same time. They had no eyes for anyone but their son.

"I'll be home, Mother, as soon as I take care of my pack," he was saying, hugging them in turn. "I hope you've got a whitefish in the kettle."

"The biggest one in the straits," laughed Armand. Louise caught her husband by the hand. "Come—we'll run and get a breakfast that will surprise this great boy—" They were away down the beach road like two children. Jacques looked after them with a smile, and then came back to me.

"Well, Baptiste, I'll see you later on, too. Oneta, want to walk along with me? I'll be going past your house, soon as I leave my furs at the warehouse."

"Yes, I'd like to."

Baptiste was already surrounded by voyageurs from the rest of the boats in the brigade, asking him loudly if his fiddle arm was still good, slapping him on the back in affection until he fairly danced from one to the other, his lameness making him hop like a bird.

Remembering my manners, I turned to the brigade leader. He was adjusting his cap before taking up his pack again, putting the black feather in the very front of it. Here on Mackinac that made him a superior man, and he must be sure it was in plain sight of any voyageur—and any girl—he might meet.

"Thank you," I said. "I cannot tell you how much I enjoyed the ride. I am so excited at being home again."

He turned slowly to me. Bigger than any of the others, older than most, all his movements were so deliberate I wondered if he were going to move at all. There would have been something terrifying about it in a man of his size if he had not had such a gentle face.

"Very glad to have had your company," he said, with the easy grace of all these men. "Shall I see you tonight at ze dance, no?"

Suddenly I knew who he was. Even in my childhood he had been called Big Charlie. He had indeed been long in the company service.

Since my name had meant nothing to him, I did not tell him I knew his. "Dance—oh, no," I said. "This is my first night at home. I shall not want to go out." I murmured my thanks again, and hurried to join Jacques.

On our way to the warehouse, a few children tumbled

247

along the street in front of us, in the midst of a pack of dogs. "Fishermen's children," remarked Jacques carelessly. "There are four or five new families around the point now. Only place the population has grown, except for the mission folks. And we don't need any more fishermen." He shrugged under his heavy pack. "They just manage to live, and that's all. I guess I know. Remember how Mother used to take in washings?"

"Does she still do that?"

"No," said Jacques proudly. "I can help now. She does make some shirts for the fur company store—lots of the village women do that. They get twenty cents apiece."

Men were all around us, looking ahead to the large building with the letters on the front, AMERICAN FUR COMPANY. Their hips lost the gliding motion of long tramps in the woods and took on a swagger. Walking in their midst, I felt a surge of freedom go through me. Away from the convent where every minute had been allotted for some duty, I felt a sympathy with these men swinging along with packs on their backs. Freedom— that is what one must have. Discipline may be good for the soul, but the heart wants freedom. I felt like a deer that has been reared in a lodge, and at the first chance, driven by the voice of his ancestors telling him what is his right and natural way, springs away into the woods. Alive—how alive this island was! How much more alive even the shade of a tree than the shade of a dull stone building—the one is moving and changing as the sun moves, as the wind blows, as leaves turn on their stems. But the other moves regularly on its way only as the hours march past.

Among all the people we met, there was no familiar face. A number of Ottawa men and women slouched past, and I delighted in the sound of their feet moving softly on the path. I saw some newly bought finery on them—a white blanket, a pair of cloth trousers, a look-ing-glass dangling at a man's waist as he walked, but not as many ornaments as they would have later in the season. After payment time they would all appear in bright colors, like the gay-feathered peacock in one of my books, suddenly spreading his glory for all to see.

"Michel lives over at St. Ignace now," said Jacques. "He took up carpentering. I felt kinda bad at first, when he didn't want to come out with me. But anyway, he's too tall. No room in a canoe for his long legs."

I remembered that anyone who grew beyond five feet six was excluded from that kind of work, like one who grew too heavy. Big Charlie was the only exception I had seen, and he was said to have a genius for handling men.

"Michel's married now. Currance Ruggs, remember her?"

I thought back over the years. "Yes. I saw her once on the beach when she was a little girl."

"She's always sick, or thinks she is. Michel didn't get much."

He was silent a moment, and then looked up at me with shyness in his dark eyes. "You remember Ros-anne—"

"Of course I do. How is she?"

"Fine. And pretty as a bolt of red cloth. She and I —well—" He looked up at me again, and his dark face reddened a little. He lowered his voice, confidentially. "We're going to get married when I get a little more money."

"I'm so glad, Jacques," I said. "You're very happy, aren't you?"

"*Oui*. I have the prettiest girl in the world, and the voyageur's life was made for me. I want to be out in the woods in the winters. I don't know what I'd do if I couldn't go out. Whether I carry canoe, or canoe carry me—all the same. All I want now is the black feather of the brigade leader, and enough money to get married."

We had reached the store, but Jacques hurried on to the tall office and warehouse where a long line of men was waiting to turn in the packs of fur. At the end of the line was Charlie.

"I can't wait for all these—" Jacques began impatiently.

"What's the matter?" asked Big Charlie.

"I don't want to wait. I've got to go."

The other men broke out in a roar of laughter.

"Oho!" one of them shouted. "He's got to get to that girl he's been telling us about all winter."

"Some pretty little half-breed neighbor," said another.

"Guess I'll look her up myself," shouted one farther down the line.

Jacques's face turned dark with anger. "You hold your tongue," he began hotly, and lurched toward the speaker. Charlie moved deliberately between them.

"No fighting now," he said. "We have been here only ten minutes. I don't want any fights until ze pelts are all in. Then—you do what you like."

"We're not out in the forest," Jacques flared up. "It's every man for himself now."

"Not until ze furs are in ze company's hands," repeated Charlie patiently. "But you leave your pack with me, boy, and run along. I'll turn it in for you."

"Thanks, Charlie," muttered Jacques, half ashamed. His face cleared, and he dropped his pack.

"I'll walk with you as far as your house, and then cut across the meadow," he said to me.

We turned on to the back street, walking faster in mounting excitement. I picked up my long skirt and held it out of the dust of the footpath. It seemed queer to be going down that street in such clothes.

"Does Mrs. Ruggs still live here?" I asked as we passed the low white house.

"Still did last summer, anyway—boarding travelers, selling milk, and peddling news."

Beyond, the open stretch of grass waited for the tents of the voyageurs when the company barracks had been filled. It lay empty up to the picket fence of the big white house that seemed to confront me with mystery as it had twelve years before. Seeing the long roof with its dormer windows rising from shrubbery grown tall with the years, I wondered if it would accept me this time. I wondered what my life would be like there. Twelve years I had been gone—and the thought brought back what that meant. Twelve years of training such as I had had—given me by Pierre and Madame. At that moment I wondered how I could repay them. What could I do for anyone so self-sufficient, so capable as they were. And I had had so much. Before I gave thought to anything beyond, my debt must be paid.

As we came nearer, I saw a white-capped figure bending among the lilac bushes. Hastily I straightened my skirts, glad they showed no traces of my unusual method of arrival. Jacques stopped as I did, waiting in spite of his hurry, to see the meeting between me and Madame. Leaving him in the middle of the path, I ran up to the picket fence and along it to the front gate. I stopped there in sudden confusion, wishing that I had waited in Montreal for Pierre.

She raised her head sharply at the squeak of the gate. "Well," she said, and put down her trowel. She wiped her hands on her apron and came across the lawn. She stopped in front of me, taking in every detail of my costume. Her wrinkled face peered out of her white bonnet with the same expression of mild severity, and her black eyes were just as keen as I remembered them.

She was looking at the bonnet Pierre had selected, at my gray dress with its white frill at the neck and the

251

long skirt heavily trimmed with braid. She looked me over twice from head to foot before she spoke. Then the wrinkles softened.

"You look very nice. I hope you know how to behave as well."

I said nothing, but made a curtsey before her. I had hated it from the moment I had learned it, but I knew of all the things I might do, that unnatural bit of obeisance would please her most.

And, in the instant of seeing her again, I remembered that this frail old lady must be lived with on her terms. Thinking sadly of my feelings of freedom of a few minutes before, I curtseyed again.

"Well, come in," she said in a new tone, weighted with approval. "I'm glad you arrived safely. But where is Pierre?"

"He was delayed. I have a letter for you—"

At that moment, we heard a door slam in the house beyond Madame's, and a young girl ran down the path to the front gate, jerked it open, and came down the limestone path in a flash of color. With a shout at the sight of her, Jacques started forward, and she threw her arms around his neck.

"Oh, *mon bon ami*." She held tight to him and wept.

Jacques folded her so close in his arms that I could see only her dark, curly hair, bound with a broad red ribbon, and a tanned skin filled with roses of excitement. Her arms were bare to the elbow, above which were wide puffs of a sky-blue dress.

"It isn't—" I began.

"Yes, it is Rosanne. She works next door every morning. An invalid lady lives there."

Rosanne and Jacques were lost in each other. Curly heads together, they started to walk away in close embrace without a word to either of us. I watched them start across the meadow path, distressed that Rosanne had not even spoken to me after all those years. Madame touched my sleeve. "Never mind her—she is not very well brought up." There was something new in her tone that allied the two of us against such as Rosanne. "She has a certain charm, of course—but look, here's someone you will remember."

I turned around. A boy was standing on the steps of the house, frowning inquiringly at Madame.

"Paul!" I exclaimed, with tears flooding my eyes. I took a step toward him.

"Come here and speak to your sister," commanded Madame sharply. "This is Oneta."

Paul's expression lost its frown, and he looked me full in the face in a way that forbade my coming any closer until he had made up his mind about me.

Hurt, I stood still and looked at him. But of course, I thought, he was less than two years old when I went away. He would not remember me. He was a sturdy boy, with a face full of intelligence. His heavy black hair was combed straight back; he had black eyebrows curiously startling above eyes gray like the long twilight, and with something of sadness in them. Though he was not large for his age, he seemed much older than his thirteen years. As his calm eyes looked me over, I knew at once whom he resembled. That way of holding his head was not exactly like Pierre's stiffness. It was something else—it was the way my grandfather had held his head, with the eagle feathers proudly erect.

"Paul," I pleaded, holding out my hand.

After an instant, he came up to me. "Comment allez-vous?" he said, and gave me his hand.

"That's the little man," Madame approved. "Now you two get acquainted again, while I go in and get you something to eat. You must be hungry. Where is your baggage? I didn't even see the ship come in."

She hurried into the house without waiting for an

answer or glancing at the harbor. I was glad I didn't need to tell her I had swung down by a rope ladder into the voyageurs' canoe.

I sat on the front steps and motioned for Paul to sit beside me. "Don't you remember me at all?" I asked gently, trying to get him to talk. "Do you remember our old cabin around the point? Do you ever go to see Marthe?" I was eager to hear his voice. The brief greeting in French was all I had ever heard him say since his baby-talk days.

He looked around. A noise from the far end of the house showed that Madame was busy in the back kitchen. Suddenly Paul put a brown hand on mine, and lifted his gray eyes with a look of acceptance in them. "I've waited a long time for you to come back," he said in Ojibway.

He tightened his clasp, and we looked at each other as two people who recognize a bond between them. The years dropped away, and I felt as I had when I held him in my arms after my mother died. We were brother and sister, and we stood together against all the world. The time between had been only a time of waiting for us both. From his complete acceptance I felt he had planned on my return, hoped for something from it.

"You won't go away again?" he asked, as if he had followed my thoughts.

"I won't go away again, as long as you need me," I promised, and the Ojibway syllables were strange on my tongue. "But they've been good to you?"

"Grand'mère is all right," he said, "but if it hadn't been for Baptiste and Marthe I would have run away."

I waited, fearful of breaking this new bond if I showed surprise or questioned him. He sat silent, looking out over the village toward the beach, where the big *canots du nord* were being turned over and set in a row back from the water's edge.

"Let's go and see Marthe now," I said.

"All right. I'll tell Grand'mère." He ran into the house and I heard his serious voice explaining to Madame that we were going to take a walk.

"*C'est une bonne idée,*" I heard her say. "See that you're back before eleven. I'll have these biscuits out then, and we'll have an early dinner. Show your sister all the new buildings—"

I wondered why he hadn't told her where we were going.

Halfway across the meadow, Paul stopped. Shoulder to shoulder we stood alone on that level ground below the wooded heights, and looked across the low firm mat of new grass, over the little fishing cabins, and out on the restless blue straits pouring out of the channel between St. Ignace and the mainland.

"Oneta—"

"Yes, Paul."

"Marthe told me Tecumseh was your father."

"Yes." With a queer stirring I realized no one had mentioned that name to me since I had myself heard it from Marthe.

"Why couldn't he have been my father, too?" Paul's words were not childish curiosity; they were mature and loaded with bitter resentment. Hearing them, I wondered what problems I was going to have to face with this little brother.

Three

❧ As we stood in the path, watching the blue rushing waters of the straits, parted by the island beneath our feet, we heard a hail from the beach road, and Baptiste limped across to join us.

"How's it happen you ain't in school today?" he greeted Paul in a voice that seemed to have grown as thin as the high notes of his fiddle.

Paul shrugged. "I don't go every day."

"What does your grand'mere think of that?"

"She scolds a little." Paul smiled slowly. "I'm not going tomorrow, either. I'm going fishing with you."

Baptiste rested his hand on the boy's shoulder as we went on toward the cabins, and I noticed that Paul was only an inch or so shorter than Baptiste.

"Sure," said Baptiste. "I'm goin' to put a patch on the old boat right now, so we won't get our feet wet again."

"I'll help," said Paul.

They went down to the shore, and began examining the side of the broad mackinaw boat resting on the shallow waves.

I took only one quick glance at our old cabin. It had been enlarged by a lean-to at the back, and was surrounded by small children and dogs. The grapevine sprawling over it and the familiar worn steps tightened about me a coldness left by the death of my mother and never quite taken away by the years. Without lingering there, I went up Marthe's steps.

As I looked into the dim room, it seemed as if I had never been away. From the rafters still dangled herbs, and packages of dried fish, and pegs about the walls hung full of caps and trousers and old mackinaw coats of Baptiste, and a clutter of sacking towels, most of them soiled. The same deer antlers were there, the same muskets and hunting knives hanging from nails. On the floor was the same line between the thickness of the dust under the bed and the open space in the room where it had been tramped away. The usual fish net awaited mending in one corner, and a heap of dirty clothes lay by the door.

The air was full of drifting flakes, and through their haze I saw Marthe kneeling at the hearth, vigorously raking out ashes with a frayed duck wing. A wrinkled calico shortdress too large for her fitted her thin back as carelessly as a mat over lodge-poles. A yard of faded

256

blue list-cloth was wrapped around her as a petticoat with the white border at the bottom. Dust lay everywhere about her, and ashes were falling on the unwashed dishes that cluttered the little pine table. There was a stale odor about the place, as if something were concealed that had needed washing for many months, rivaling the odor of decaying fish heads seeping in from the beach outside. At once I realized I was noticing those things—almost drawing back from them—in a way I would not have done twelve years before.

Aware of my shadow on the threshold, Marthe turned, indifferently at first. Then, with a second glance, she stood up and looked at me.

"I thought it was one of the fort ladies," she said, looking up and down my gray dress, and I realized I should have changed to something else before coming to see her. And then I held out my hands. "We see each other," I said. She took my hands, and repeated the soft Ojibway greeting, "We see each other." Her face cleared then, and she swung a straight chair around for herself, and watched me sit in the barrel chair and arrange my full skirts about me. When I looked up, she was regarding me with an expression covering an emotion I strangely recognized as if it had once been my own. It was the way I had felt when I stood on a hillside with my grandfather and watched the Ojibways in their newly bought finery.

"You have the form and glossy hair of your mother," she said. "You have your father's eyes." It was as if she were flinging defiance at some thought.

"Tell me about yourself, Marthe," I urged.

Marthe lifted one hand, and let it fall to her knee again, as if in that slow, uninteresting, fatalistic motion she had summed up all her life into nothing worth speech.

"But tell me everything that has happened."

She lifted her hand again in that peculiar, lifeless

257

movement. "Down here, nothing. Among the lodges, some changes. Gray Wolf is chief now in your grandfather's place. The Ottawas have a new chief, too. Chief Migisan."

"I remember Gray Wolf, of course, but not the Ottawa."

"Chief Migisan is the father of Four Legs, the conceited one."

Marthe's words brought back the whole scene on the beach just before I went away. I could still see the foppishly dressed one, with raccoon tails tied at his knees.

"Is Four Legs still the same?" I asked, smiling.

"He looks the same. I cannot tell what he is. I have never seen him when his stomach was empty of firewater," said Marthe.

Her words led me to think of others I knew. "Ajawin?"

"I never see her. She has married into another tribe, one that goes to Prairie du Chien for payments."

"And Chase—did he get the girl, when you made the charm for him?" I didn't realize that my question suggested any doubt of her skill until I saw the flicker in her eyes as she lowered them to her ash-covered hands.

"Yes. He had a happy lodge-full of children."

"Had?"

"Chase is gone along the path of souls. Two moons ago."

From Marthe's dulled tone, I knew there was something behind the statement. "What happened, Marthe?"

Marthe began as if it were a tale she was too weary to tell, and would use no more words on it than it needed.

"Chase and Four Legs went to trader's camp on Little Traverse, with all the furs from their band. Trader took furs, gave them firewater. Two days after, when they could stand upright again, they asked for food and new clothing. Trader said they had drunk up all the furs in firewater. Chase and Four Legs went back to lodges. All the braves rose and went back to hold a talk with trader. Trader saw them coming, and his men got guns and fired. They killed Chase and plenty more." Marthe spread her fingers once, withholding her thumbs. "Ottawas went back to lodges, fetched guns and tomahawks. They fought until all the traders lay in their blood on the snow. The Ottawas moved farther back in the woods, where many bands were camped. By and by, some white men came, saying, 'Who did it?' No one knew."

Marthe told the story with no feeling, either in words or tone, touching no causes, placing no blame, as if it were something that must come as long as the same elements were there; one of the long series of clashes, of which only the numbers changed and the scenes moved westward with the frontier. She told it as if it made no difference which way it came out.

We fell silent then, as I regretted the passing of one I had liked, feeling the new loneliness that always comes with such news. There were no others I could ask about. I realized for the first time how few were left of the ones remembered from my childhood.

At last, hearing Paul's voice outside, I said, "Paul seems to think a great deal of you and Baptiste."

A quick flicker of light went through Marthe's eyes. "Paul is a good boy."

"He goes fishing often with Baptiste?"

"Since he could walk across the meadow by himself," said Marthe.

"Does Pierre ever come here with him?"

"Never has Pierre's foot made a print on this beach since you went away. His steps lead only from the big house to the fur company, and sometimes up to the fort."

"Does Paul go to the fort, too?"

"No. Paul cares nothing for big guns and uniforms and marching. One with Indian blood never makes a soldier to fight in a straight line. Paul will not be a soldier," Marthe ended with some satisfaction.

"Does he know what he wants to do?" I asked.

"He has said nothing. But it will come out. His own nature will tell him. And not even Madame can keep him from it."

"She has been good to Paul, I think."

"Yes, in white woman's way," Marthe admitted grudgingly. "Paul is a good boy."

Having come around in a circle, we were silent. After a moment, Marthe picked up a knife and a pan of potatoes and began peeling.

"You passed into womanhood long ago," she said, with the air of bringing out a heavy thought that had been long with her. "Did you build yourself a little shelter in the woods and fast for a guiding dream?"

"No. I wouldn't have been allowed to. We couldn't even go outside the convent fence alone."

Marthe looked her disbelief, not of my word, but of my understanding. I saw that there was no use telling her about the convent life. We sat quiet, while from outside came the sounds of lapping waves, of children playing, of happy voices in Louise's cabin, where her own sweet voice mixed with the deep tones of Armand and Jacques, and a light ripple that must have come from Rosanne.

Then Marthe spoke again. "Passing into womanhood is as the coming of dawn, of understanding, where you only dimly saw before. Your mind is opened to the teaching of the spirits."

"My mind has been opened to many things, Marthe."

Suddenly I could find no words that would reach her. All the urgent need to see her had dropped away. Something delicate that had been between us was gone, like a wild-cherry petal beaten to earth by a storm. The cabin and Marthe were just the same. It must be I who was different. I knew it when I felt again an urge to get away from the dirt and stale odors around me.

"I must go home," I said gently. "Madame is getting an early dinner for me."

Marthe got up and put down the pan of potatoes, careless how the peelings trailed across the floor. Before the bed, she suddenly dropped to her knees and thrust her long arm under the edge, pulling out a little box, its edges scraping a path through the dust and piling up a little ridge before it. She took some rags that were on top and laid them aside. From the bottom of the box she pulled out a tiny deerskin bag.

When she came back to me, I noticed how bent she was, how her hands fumbled. Her shortdress had been worn for many weeks without being washed. Its front showed traces of all her work in that time.

She thrust out the deerskin bag before her. "These are the charms I made for you before you went away. I came to Madame's door with them, but she would not let me in."

"I'm sorry, Marthe. I didn't know that." As she was still holding the little bag out to me, I took it. "Thank you, Marthe."

The abrupt withdrawing of her hand as she let it go was almost a gesture of dismissal. She said nothing more, and I knew we were at an end. I turned and went, with no word from her as to whether I was to come again. Used for so long to the voluble, polite leave-taking of the French, I felt it strange, and then I remembered Marthe had her own way of thinking about such things. I would come again, or I wouldn't, and just now she did not choose to interfere with what would be. I had a sudden impulse to go back and sit at her feet. But I only paused at the door, and then picked up my long gray skirt and went down the steps.

Paul waved at me from the water's edge. "I'll have

to stay a little longer. Baptiste can't hold this patch and nail it, too."

"I'll start back alone, then," I said.

"Come again soon," said Baptiste.

"Tell Grand'mère I'll be there in a few minutes," said Paul. "Here's a loose piece over on this side, Baptiste."

Baptiste set a nail where he was pointing, and the hammer came down on it.

I hurried back toward the village with a curious feeling of having gotten something over with. I didn't want to look too closely at what I felt about it.

Halfway across the meadow, I remembered the little bag in my hand. I opened the drawstring. Of the herbs and roots that had been in it, nothing remained but a little heap of dust and dried sticks in the bottom. It was medicine made to keep me safe on a journey and in a strange land. But I had returned unharmed. I wondered why Marthe had given it to me now. Perhaps only to show me she had not forgotten to do what she could before I went away. Slowly I turned the crumbled charms out on the new grass of the meadow.

A few steps farther on, I turned a little way off the path and dropped the medicine bag at the base of a scrub-oak. I couldn't risk losing Madame's new approval of me by carrying it home.

Among the birch canoes beyond the wharf, a white-winged schooner, its canvas no longer limp, was coming into the harbor.

Four

Waiting for time to show me something I might do for Pierre and Madame, I settled myself into the ways of their household, but I began taking one hour a day for myself, satisfying a need I could not have explained. Long before the others awoke I slipped out of the house, climbed the heights, and crossed behind the fort grounds to the eastern side of the island to bathe in the waves below the arched rock. Probably I chose that place because no one else would come—the descent to the water was too perilous for anyone with untrained foot. But there were many such places along the shore. Something else drew me there. It may have been the mystery of that great span of rock above the lake, all that was left to show where the manitou had closed beneath it the entrance to sacred burial caves the day the first white man set foot upon the island. I may have felt that a fitting place to greet the rising sun. I do remember that, alone with water, shore, and sky—where everything resisted change or eternally renewed itself, I felt that time had gone. I might have slipped into those cool waves a hundred years before or after, and even the very song-sparrow in the low bush of meadow-sweet might have chirped the same note. Long before the morning gun at the fort, the first rays of the sun started the birds singing in every tree. Pierre had told me once of a great statue in the old days that gave forth a musical sound when the rays of the morning sun first struck it, and I felt that sunrise at arched rock struck a faint natural melody in me that was silent otherwise. More, I felt that what came to me then came to every pebble, every leaf from which night's dew was departing, every pine needle against the clear sky.

That morning hour became a rite of infinite renewal that was more natural to me than going to mass with Pierre and Madame. With hair flying behind me, I ran back across the heights and was in the house before any of the rest were awake, and if Paul noticed my damp braids at breakfast time, he said nothing.

When I came to know that the young doctor had

not been on the island long before he knew every nook and corner of it, every rock formation and every known cave, I wondered that I never met him while he was out exploring. But after all, my morning walk toward the sun was long before reveille at the fort. His walks down to the village never happened to fit with mine, or I failed to pick him out in the swarming crowds on village street and warehouse yard. Nor did I meet him in the trips I made out along the shore to the cobbler's cave to have my scuffed shoes repaired. It was not long before I got out my old moccasins for my morning trips, hiding them under the bed when I got back, putting on my store shoes before Madame's day began.

Madame was the bundle of energy I remembered, and I could not see that the years had touched her at all, except to settle her more deeply into comfort and happiness. Having Pierre and Paul to take care of was a delight to her, and she industriously spun and knitted for them, and put tiny stitches for hours on end into the fine linen of their shirts—no common ones from the store for them. She liked to cook, and her table was the most varied of any on the island, unless it was the major's. In a village where potatoes and pork, bread and fish was the accepted diet, we had cheeses from a little low country across the water, odd fragrant spices with a hint of mysterious lands, and in the little cellar below the kitchen stood row after row of port and Madeira wine.

Plenty of work came to my hands in those first days, and yet I could not see that Madame took any more time for rest. I followed her through soap-making, candle dipping and molding, the making of bread and butter and cheese. We tended the garden together, and I went forward cautiously making acquaintance with her ways as on a hilly path unknown to my foot

I would gain one step and look ahead at the next to come.

"It seems as if you have been here always," she said to me about a month from the time I came, and I felt as one who has been set a task and has completed a small part of it.

That was the day Pierre came home. His unannounced arrival on a schooner that came into harbor in mid-afternoon sent Madame into a flurry of preparation of all the dishes he liked best for supper. She dispatched Paul to the store again and again, and kept me in the back kitchen stirring up a pudding to steam and a brandy sauce to put on it, while she made her little white biscuits and set potatoes to boil and pork to fry, running into her garden for greens and radishes between times.

When we were taking the kettles from the crane, and were almost ready to call Pierre from his room where he had gone to lie down. Rosanne came running up the walk and stood in the doorway, like a bright bird poised for flight.

"There is a party tonight—don't you want to go, Oneta?"

"No, I don't think I care to. Anyway, Pierre's just home—"

"I don't see how you can stay away! How can you not be excited?" Her own cheeks were flushed. "*Moi, I* go to them all. Every night I go."

"Oneta won't dance except at the company parties when Pierre and I go with her," said Madame. "Do your mother and father like you to be out every night?"

"Oh, they don't care." Her impish look implied that it made no difference whether they did or not. "Father is at most of the parties, playing fiddle, and Mother is down at the lodges all the time."

"You want to be with Jacques all you can while he is here, I suppose," I said.

"As long as he is here, I go with Jacques." Rosanne looked defiantly at us both. "But when the northern brigades have gone—I go to parties with anyone who asks me. But don't tell Jacques. He would kill—" She lifted her hands and opened her eyes wide, so we could fairly see her imagination running on. "Sometimes his jealousy is a nuisance," she ended, and turning with a flare of red skirt like the sudden opening and closing of a bright umbrella, she was gone down the board walk and out the gate.

During supper, I remember that Pierre told us one or two incidents of his trip, but he ate with such enjoyment that even Madame was content to look at him and ask no questions. I noticed Paul asked none, and it was never his way, any more than it was mine. People would tell us what they wanted us to know, and we had no right to ask more.

After the last of the bake-pans was back on the shelf beside the fireplace, Madame hung over the fire a kettle of raspberry jam that had been set off while the crane was in use for getting supper. I filled Pierre's pipe and lighted it, holding a coal in the tongs. Gratefully he settled back in his armchair, letting the smoke rise in solemn content. He could have lighted his pipe himself, but I felt that ceremony, no matter how little, belonged with smoking, and Pierre liked the little attention. I heaped some pine cones on the fire to give a pleasant scent of the woods, and sat in a low chair beside Madame, who was already in the rocker opposite Pierre, taking up the mass of brown wool her needles were turning into socks against the approaching winter. I began sorting bright embroidery yarn to make a flower border around a canvas on which Madame had cross-stitched the motto, *"Dieu nous garde."* The firelight picked up one detail after another of the room, very little different from what it was like when I had first seen it. A room once settled to Madame's liking seemed to resist change. It was restful, as if movement had come to an end there. It may have been something about the old portrait on the wall, the squares of old linen, or the precise arrangement, never changed, of the candlesticks and clock on the mantel—but I always felt that if someone were to come in at night and move them, they would somehow be back in place by morning.

Paul had seated himself behind us at the dining table, now back against the wall. With a packet of ink powder and a tin cup of water, he was making up a supply of ink.

"Push the cloth back, *petit*, so you won't get a spot on it," Madame said to him over her shoulder. "When you get through, I must finish my letter."

"All right, Grand'mère." Paul poured the dark powder slowly into the water, watching the color flow and deepen as he stirred it.

"I believe your grand'mère writes letters to everyone she knows," said Pierre, gazing lazily at the fire curling up over the logs. "It is like sowing seed in her garden. She wants a plentiful harvest of news. How many will you have ready for the next boat, *ma mère?*"

"Three are finished, and two others are done in my head, waiting only for the time and ink to set them down."

"You will keep your friends poor," said Pierre, with a slow, amused smile. "I wonder how long they have to let your letters lie before they can get the twenty-five cents to pay for their delivery?"

That made Madame indignant, as he knew it would. "None of my friends are poor!" she exclaimed.

"Perhaps they think you might prepay one or two when you send them."

"Nonsense. I wouldn't waste money that way. The

letter might never get there. No, we have an arrangement *entre nous* always to pay when we get the letter."

"That's why I had to pay for the letter I got at Montreal. Mr. Stuart thought it might miss me entirely."

Madame looked up, impatient. "Well, hurry up and tell us. Ever since Oneta came home alone and said you had gone to see Mr. Astor, I've been eaten alive with curiosity. I went in to see Mr. Stuart right away, but he didn't know a thing about it."

"No, I don't believe he would," said Pierre.

Madame's needles clicked impatiently.

"I had a very interesting talk with Mr. Astor," said Pierre. "It was an experience, of course, just to see a man I had heard so much about."

"It was that way the first time your father saw the King," said Madame. "He had heard his name on every tongue, and could hardly believe the man had much the same sort of body everyone else had. Something about such a figure should be different from the ordinary man, he thought."

"One could feel that with Mr. Astor, too," said Pierre. "Or anyone who heads such an empire of wealth. There *is* something a little different, though it isn't apparent immediately. He speaks with a heavy accent, and has a square forehead, heavy nose and full lips. But his eyes are quick, and he has a mind that passes judgment on your words even while you are uttering them."

"Well, what did he want of you?" Madame interrupted Pierre's musing.

"I didn't know myself for quite a while. When we were alone in his office, he began talking of all sorts of things, particularly of how he happened to get into the fur business through meeting a trader on the boat when he came to America. He told me how he learned to pound and salt furs for the tanners, and finally set up in business for himself, getting the Indians along the

Hudson to trade with him as a beginning. He quizzed me then as to how I came to be in this work—"

"What did you tell him?" asked Madame.

"I told him how our family fortune was lost, and that my interests were really scholarly and not naturally for trade. But I told him I was interested because it was a *vena porta*—a gate-vein—of wealth."

"A very proper speech," approved Madame.

"I thought so. But it sent him off into the queerest discussion about Indians and how to get along with them, and how to handle voyageurs, and know the value of furs. I told him I did nothing of that here—our traders handled such details, and Mr. Stuart supervised them. I told him I did nothing but the accounts."

Strangely I remembered how, years before, I had looked at Pierre's hands and wondered that there was no sign of work upon them. Striking into the flow of his voice as he went on, came the thought that keeping accounts was the only kind of work on Mackinac that he could do.

"On the wall behind Mr. Astor," said Pierre, "was a big map of North America, with pins marking trading posts—our own in black-headed pins and opposing companies in white. Mr. Astor kept looking at it, and talking about how he plans to get control of the whole fur business of the States. He wants to have someone dealing in furs for him at every favorable place in the hunting grounds, every waterfall that makes portaging necessary, along streams, everywhere canoes and pack mules pass. I tell you, Mother, when he talked, I could see boatloads and mule trains going to ships on every coast, and see those ships setting out loaded, for Paris London, China."

"But what did all that have to do with you?" asked Madame. "Why had he sent for you?"

"It may mean a great deal to me. He told me of new

269

chief agents he would need, and said he was looking over the men who work for him now for that very reason. He had just appointed a new agent at Montreal, where he bought out the Southwest Fur Company, some years ago."

"Oh, I wish he had sent you there," said Madame. "I should love Montreal!"

"The peculiar thing was that Mr. Astor strongly hinted *my* future was right here on Mackinac."

"I know!" exclaimed Madame. "I think he intends to send Mr. Stuart and Mr. Crooks west again, and make you the head here—*ma foi*, it sounds promising."

"Yes, the future looks good," said Pierre, gradually settling back into contentment. "We shall have as much money one day as you had in France."

Madame and Pierre both fell silent in long reverie, and I felt their thoughts had slipped away to the far-off place Pierre had named with affection. While I waited for them to come back, the room began filling with the pungency of boiling jam. I finished a corner of the sampler, and looked across at Paul. "What is that little book you are writing in?"

"Mr. Stuart gave me this for my birthday. It's like the one they use at the store to write down what people buy."

"The petty book, they call it," said Madame, beginning to rock contentedly.

Paul put down the quill and poured some sand over what he had done. I smiled, seeing Pierre's gesture in the little flourish he gave it. Carefully running off the sand into its box, he got up and brought the book over to me.

"This is going to be my account book," he said.

I took it from him, and Madame peered over my shoulder to see. There on the page was a row of pictures, all of fish, some long and thin, some broad—big fish and small ones, each kind grouped by itself. "What is this?" I asked.

"Each picture is ten fish," said Paul. "That's what Baptiste and I caught today."

Madame took the book and looked at the pictures. Paul leaned over the arm of her rocker. "That wasn't all we caught in the net. That's my share."

"Your share? You didn't bring that many home, thank the good saints. We never could eat them! What do you mean by your share?" exclaimed Madame.

"Baptiste says I'm to have part of the money when he sells any fish. I do a lot of the work. Those went into the barrel he sold this morning."

Then I understood a scene that had puzzled me. While we had been in the rush of getting supper, and Pierre had been resting in his bedroom, Paul had come in and taken a small handful of coins from the pocket of his gray plaid shirt. He had laid them on one side of the mantel, his fingers lingering on the silver pieces, arranging them in a little pattern, as one would stretch up a skin after a hard day's hunt.

"Why didn't you tell us sooner about earning your first money?" asked Madame playfully.

"I don't know," said Paul.

I understood better than he did why he hadn't. No hunter I had known had ever come bursting in with a story of his catch. Rather he left it outside, came in and silently took off his clothes by the fire, wrung out his soaking garments, put on a robe handed to him by his wife, and ate his dinner before he said a single word.

"Baptiste gave you some money, you say?" asked Pierre.

Paul went over to the mantel and gathered it up. "Here, Grand'mère, you may have it."

"Nonsense. You keep it for—well, the things boys always want," said Madame.

"You will give it back to Baptiste," said Pierre. "It is bad enough for you to waste your time in such things. I won't have you being a partner—"

"That's what Baptiste says I am, now. He won't let me go out any more unless I take part of the money."

"Well, it would please your grand'mère and me if you stayed away from the fishing boats," said Pierre. "I shall speak to Mr. Stuart and see if he hasn't something you can do at the fur company. You might as well get into training for your future."

"My future—"

"Yes. You will, of course, have a position with the company one day. If I am promoted, perhaps you can do the work I am doing now."

"I don't want to work for the fur company," said Paul.

Pierre raised his head sharply. "What do you mean?"

"Now, Pierre," said Madame, tapping him on the knee with her free knitting needle.

"Now, Mother!" he answered impatiently. "He's been making some queer remarks in the last few months since I first mentioned his going to work. Let's settle it right now."

"Well, Pierre," said Madame soothingly, "I know how he feels. He thinks if you are the head agent, and he is given a good position, over some of the others, it will look as if he has it just because he is your son."

Paul smiled. Madame had given him a reason as far from the true one as it could be; he had only to be silent and accept it. But his smile went, and he leaned forward with brown hands on the table before him. He didn't look at me, yet I felt he was keenly aware of me, depending on me, and in a way putting me to a test.

"There's nothing for me at the American Fur Company," he said slowly, as if months of thought had gone into every word. "I could not stay indoors over books the way you do. I could not count and hand out trashy

272

beads and shoddy blankets for rich beaver. And a voyageur's life—he is nothing unless he becomes a trader, and traders in the woods cheat and misuse the Indians in one way or another, in order to keep their jobs."

"What *do* you think you're going to do, if you're so superior to my way of life? Are you going to lie idle and let me support you?" Pierre's voice was harsh.

Paul's hands lessened their pressure on the table top. Quietly watching him, I did not believe then nor do I believe now that he knew just what he wanted to do. Something had made him resist what Pierre had begun to force on him, but he was not ready to declare himself for anything else. He seemed embarrassed at having made such a speech. Perhaps this was where he needed me.

"You plan to go to the mission school another winter, Paul?" I asked.

"Yes."

Pierre relaxed at the reminder that the matter was not one that need be hastily settled.

"Yes, you go to school and we'll see when the time comes," said Madame. "I hope you'll find something you like to do right here on Mackinac. I shouldn't want you to go away."

"I don't think I'll go away, Grand'mère."

"Well, then," said Pierre, "all this fuss is useless. There's nothing here but the fur company." In spite of Pierre's air of having settled the matter, Paul looked contented, as one who has given fair warning.

"I don't like school very well," said Paul after a while. "There doesn't seem to be much in books I need to know."

Pierre looked disgusted. Before he could say what was on his tongue, I spoke softly to Paul. "You don't want to keep your accounts in pictures all your life, do you?"

"Well, I should say not," ejaculated Madame. "You

273

got that idea from Baptiste. He never could read or count. You told me once about the books he kept when he was a trader. He had to draw a picture of every skin he took in, and pictures of the goods he gave for them, bottles, and knives—"

"Baptiste's way is all right," said Paul quickly.

"Of course it is," I said soothingly. "But it is shorter to do it with figures. I used to do all my writing in pictures, but now I don't, because I have learned a way that tells more than my pictures could, and is easier."

I saw Paul thinking this over. "Well, maybe I'll pay more attention when they teach us figures. But they don't do much of that. We get a lot of hymn-singing—"

We heard steps coming up our front walk. Looking out, I saw Mrs. Ruggs's tall horn comb bobbing at the top of her head. She came panting up the steps in her best black merino, with a string of gold beads around her broad neck.

"What you makin', raspberry jam?" she asked. Pierre rose, but she barely nodded at him and Madame. Moving with a swish of huge skirts, she waddled over to the fireplace and looked into the kettle. Madame frowned. Not that it mattered, but now everyone else on Mrs. Ruggs's round of visits would be told we were making jam, and what she thought of its color and texture.

Not until she turned back to the door did we notice that someone else had come along behind her. "Come right in, Miss Harper," said Mrs. Ruggs.

A spare woman, not exactly young, with red hair in thick braids around her head, stepped forward out of the doorway. She had on a black and white striped dress. A gold pencil hung from a chain around her neck, and a notebook peeped from a small pocket on her waist.

"Meet Miss Harper, the new teacher," said Mrs. Ruggs loudly. When she was trying to be formal, she

274

always raised her voice. "Mrs. Debans and her son, Mr. Debans, and Paul, and—what do you call yourself?" She looked at me.

"*Miss* Debans," said Madame tartly. "She isn't married yet."

"Well, I s'pose that's so." Mrs. Ruggs laughed uncertainly.

"How do you do," Miss Harper said, looking around at us from near-sighted eyes behind silver-rimmed spectacles. Pierre bowed and frowned a reminder at Paul, who got slowly to his feet.

Mrs. Ruggs settled her huge frame on one of the straight chairs, knowing from earlier trials that she couldn't get between the arms of one of the more comfortable ones. "Sit over there, dearie," she said to Miss Harper, who was still hesitating about taking the chair Pierre had offered her. Paul put another stick on the fire, and out of the shadow came the sofa, with its two brocaded cushions. Miss Harper went to it like a bird seeking cover. Her eyes followed Paul back to the table, and she spoke uncertainly. "I have seen you at school, haven't I?"

"Yes, ma'am," said Paul.

"Paul's in the next to the top class now, ain't you?" puffed Mrs. Ruggs.

"Yes, ma'am."

"Your conversation is a little monotonous, Paul," remarked Pierre. "Couldn't you elaborate a little on that 'yes, ma'am'?"

Paul stared at the floor.

"I must apologize, Miss Harper. I'm afraid my son is not very talkative." Pierre bent toward her with his most appealing smile. Miss Harper beamed, and from then on could not take her eyes off him. Seeing her looking over his clothing, his fine-shaped head, his graceful slender hands, I remembered the first time I saw him and wondered what such a man was doing on our beach.

275

It seemed almost as if Miss Harper was feeling some of that same wonder.

"Have you met the new doctor?" Mrs. Ruggs asked Pierre.

"Yes, it happens I have. Mr. Stuart brought him in the warehouse just after I got in today, and introduced him to all of us. He seems a fine, cultured young man."

"He is a little advanced in his ideas." Mrs. Ruggs's tone was tinged with disapproval.

"Then at least he isn't out of date," snapped Madame.

"I don't know what he's doin' in the army," Mrs. Ruggs went on aggressively. "He comes of a good family, and went to Harvard. There must be something behind his coming out here. They say he used to be in a big Boston hospital. What did he leave it for?" Mrs. Ruggs's irritated tone meant she hadn't been able to find out any more. She liked to keep up her position as village newspaper—a real 'speaking paper,' the Ojibways would call her. "I have asked him for supper three times, but he never could come," she sighed.

"You must bring him here one day soon, Pierre," said Madame. "What does he look like?"

"He's very handsome, in a *young* sort of way," said Miss Harper, timidly looking at Pierre as if to say that here at hand was a more nearly perfect type.

The talk turned to the last doctor, and how he had gone because of an interest in one of his patients, a voyageur named Alexis St. Martin, who had been shot in the stomach and miraculously lived. One could look through the hole in his side and see how food digested, and Dr. Beaumont had been so interested in feeding him different kinds of food and watching what happened, and thought the study so important to medicine, that he had kept St. Martin on Mackinac as long as he could. When the restive voyageur had packed up

276

and gone, Dr. Beaumont had followed, determined to finish his experiments even if he must endlessly pursue his laboratory.

"What *do* you study at school, Paul?" Mrs. Ruggs was always hard to get away from a subject once brought up.

"Everything, I guess," said Paul indifferently. Pierre frowned.

"I'm sure he does very well," said Miss Harper. She smoothed out her embroidered handkerchief precisely on her lap as if she wanted us to see the pattern, then realizing that was what it looked like, she crumpled it quickly in her hand. Her eyes veered off to Paul again, as if she suddenly remembered something.

"I believe you're the one Mr. Heydenbruk was telling me about that did such a good piece of metal working—"

"Metal?" inquired Pierre. "Really, I had no idea such things were taught in the mission school."

"Mr. Heydenbruk teaches the rougher sort of work in the shops, but he has quite a fine taste himself," said Miss Harper. "He paints pictures, and has already sent two of them back to New York—"

"Sold 'em, too," interposed Mrs. Ruggs.

"—one of your arched rock, and the other of the west blockhouse at the fort," Miss Harper went on. "He told me he didn't like just teaching the boys how to shoe a horse and construct a barrel—he wanted to give them a glimpse of the beauty they could create with their hands."

"Yes," said Pierre. "A worker in iron need not shoe a horse if he can make a wrought-iron gate or a fine balcony for a palace."

"That's very good." Miss Harper beamed at him. "I must write it down and tell Mr. Heydenbruk. Do you mind?"

Pierre made a polite motion with his hand. "By all

277

means." He looked across at me to share his amusement. Miss Harper lifted her notebook and pencil close to her eyes, and put down a few lines before she went on. "So he does some special work with a few boys after the day's work is over. He helps them make brooches, rings, tea canisters—whatever they want to," she said.

"Paul made a beautiful canister for you, didn't he, Madame?" I said.

"Yes," she answered absently, looking at me as if she had suddenly thought of something else as I spoke.

"It wasn't a tea canister Mr. Heydenbruk told me about," said Miss Harper. "Didn't you make something else?"

Paul under her direct gaze came forward stiffly, holding out his hand. He had a ring on his little finger.

Miss Harper peered at it. "I'm sorry. My eyes are not good."

"Take it off so she can see it," said Madame sharply.

"By all means," said Pierre. "You know 'truth and beauty are in this alike, that the strictest survey sets them both off to advantage.' Let us all look at it."

Paul looked at his father, strangely reluctant.

"Oh, what a fine quotation—it was a quotation, wasn't it?" Miss Harper busied herself again with pencil and notebook. When she had finished, Paul drew off the ring and handed it to her. She held it close to her eyes. "What an unusual design! What is it?"

"May I see it?" Pierre requested. He took the ring in his slender fingers and held it close to the firelight. Paul watched him uneasily.

"It's our family crest!" Pierre was pleased. He handed the ring back to Miss Harper and she passed it to Mrs. Ruggs and then to me. It was of silver, a signet bearing the design of a castle-like structure with three stars above it. I had seen it often on Madame's linens and some treasured old silver. Paul had copied the design perfectly. .

He seemed easier when it reached my hands. "I just finished it today," he said.

Pierre was still looking approvingly at him. "That's the best thing you've ever done. Where do you get the silver?"

"Mr. Heydenbruk orders it, and we pay him. I saved the pocket-money Grand'mère gave me. But I can buy my own now, since Baptiste and I—"

"It is really very good," said Pierre hastily, shaking his head at Paul.

Mrs. Ruggs's hands fumbled as if she were trying to roll them in an apron. Suddenly remembering she didn't have one on, she smoothed down the front of her dress, and her hand caught on a bulge in her pocket. "Just got me some new salve for my pleurisy," she said, bringing out a small round tin. She pried the lid off and held it up for Madame to see. "Looks powerful, don't it?"

"Looks like axle-grease to me," said Madame.

Mrs. Ruggs snapped the cover back on and slipped the tin into her pocket. "Well, we must be going on, Miss Harper. We got some other calls to make. I think that there jam is about ready to come off the fire." Madame sniffed, and made no move to follow the suggestion.

Pierre rose, and he and Madame followed the two women to the door, urging them to come again.

"Oh, I shall be glad to," fluttered Miss Harper.

"I'll be up to borrow your candle molds tomorrow," Mrs. Ruggs called back, letting her weight down carefully from one porch step to the next. "Or maybe Paul could bring 'em down when he goes to school."

Miss Harper looked back at Pierre once as they went down the walk, and then turned around in confusion at being seen. Pierre was still in the doorway, and I suppose she thought he was looking after her. I knew from the way his head was lifted, as he looked out over the straits, that he had already forgotten her and was content with his own thoughts. From the up-lift of his shoulders, I knew his mind was going over his talk with Mr. Astor, and feeling that he was on the verge of wealth—money that would give him luxury without taking thought for it, and free time to read and study. Knowing that the fairest path may end in treacherous swampland, I wondered how Pierre could bear it if he did not find his feet on the rising ground he believed he saw before him.

"Oneta," said Madame, when the women's footsteps were gone. "I have been thinking that it might per-haps be better if you called me Grand'mère as Paul does. It may seem strange to visitors to hear you call me Madame, as if you were a servant. Yes, you shall call me Grand'mère."

I thought it over for a moment. I had never called Pierre "Father," knowing that title to be forever Te-cumseh's. But I had never known my own grand-mother. I would be giving Madame no one else's right.

"I shall call you Grand'mère if you like," I said.

The next morning when I straightened Paul's room, I found that he had left the signet lying on the low dresser. I picked it up and took it to the window for a closer look, my heart filling with pride as I recognized what careful work he had done on it. As I went back to lay it down, I caught sight of something on the in-side. Taking it back to the light, I saw that on the under side of the signet, done with as much painstaking as the crest on its face, was a long-necked bird—the totem of the loon tribe of the Ojibways. My mother's tribe—and mine—and Paul's. It was something he was not giving up. Slowly I slipped the ring into a drawer of the dresser, hoping that Pierre would never see what I had seen. Then I went back to the window and stood long before it in thought.

Five

❧ The summer passed, and the shadows of wild geese began to fall on our limestone paths and travel on to the south. The wind blew from the north, raising the waves of the straits and then smoothing them with a covering of ice. Gradually life resolved itself into a pattern, but I felt as though I were still getting no hold on the threads of it. As I look back at that time, I see that I was only a background thread, not yet ready to emerge and take my part in the design.

Grand'mère began her round of teas and whist parties with the village ladies and officers' wives, coming back to tell us the news while she rocked and knitted before the fire of an evening. She was ever the center of the room, and it lay ordered and peaceful about her. Firelight danced on her shoe-buckles and touched the gilded clock, the pans of copper and tin, the silver, the brocade cushions on the sofa, and the large ring on Pierre's hand as he turned the pages of a book. It picked out their two thin faces, kind to hers with its wrinkles, and sat like peace itself on the high forehead of Pierre. Grand'mère talked of the sewing and gossip of her days, of the repairs to the west blockhouse at the fort, and how Major Pierce's house had all been done over since his daughter came home from finishing school to live with him. When she spoke of this pretty daughter of the major's first wife, she told me that Ellen was about my age, and that she had gone away to school about the time I had come to live on Mackinac. I asked about the major's second wife, Josette, and Grand'mère told me briefly that she had died while I was away, and that she and her baby lay buried beneath the altar of St. Anne's church. Pierre stirred in his chair as she told it, and I asked no more questions to bring up memories for him.

Even that winter I didn't see Ellen. I never went to the fort with Grand'mère, and seldom to the village. In my free hours I went more often across the meadow to Marthe's or Louise's. Evenings I played chess with Pierre, or worked at embroidery while he read aloud. Paul began his last year in the mission school, and Pierre let the matter of his future rest. I remember little about that winter except the work I did with Grand'mère, and the books I read with Pierre. We read together of countries far away in distance and time, of Grecian youths who with bared limbs took part in Olympic games, which I imagined to be like the foot races and ball games of the young Ojibways, remembering them stripped to their breechcloths, covered with paint and tattoo designs. We went through the length of Gibbon's *Roman Empire* and read and talked of Ossian's *Poems* and Thomson's *Seasons*.

When I saw Pierre lean forward in his chair and knock out his pipe against the fireplace, I got up and lighted a candle and put it in his room, for he liked it so, to come into a room prepared for him. His nod of appreciation made a glow come over me, and I felt as one of the good spirits must as he goes about his work at night. But sometimes afterward, discontent came upon me. I wanted to do more for Grand'mère and Pierre than these little things. Such help as I was giving from day to day I felt no more than made up for what they were doing for me at the same time. I had to do more, to pay a greater debt. Ever after such restless thoughts came a quiet patience, as if the very forests where I had learned it said "wait."

Those months in their peace now seem to be one short time, as if we had stopped the flow as a beaver dams a stream, backing up the water and making himself a pond to live in. And then the dam broke, and it was spring and maple sugar time.

The winter had been light, so that by the end of April the ice had gone out. The deep snow had gone before the sun, shrinking and tumbling down the cliffs to swell the straits. The birds were coming back, the brown moss changing to green. The winter's furs would soon be coming in to the company, and all was alive about the great buildings as they were cleaned and white-washed, and the stock of goods brought out of their boxes and arranged on the shelves. But even that activity was stopped for the sugar party, always held by Macki-nac Islanders as soon as the sap was flowing in the maple groove on Bois Blanc.

On the last day of April a light fall of snow covered the village paths, as if the old man of winter had given his white locks a last gentle shaking out before retreat-ing from the summer sun. It melted beneath our feet into the new grass, so that Paul and I left a trail of green tracks behind us, as if we were the spirits of spring. Down to the shore we carried two large lunch baskets, and a kettle and pint pot for our sugar and syrup. Paul set our canoe in the water, and held it steady for me to get in. Pierre and Grand'mère were a little behind. They had hired a canoe-boy to paddle one of the big company canoes, and had invited Mr. and Mrs. Stuart to ride with them.

Some of the villagers, led by the postmaster, had tapped the trees a week or more before, and the sap had been collected regularly and boiled down in kettles. The party was always arranged at the height of the work, so there would be all the sweetness one could eat with the pot-luck lunch, and some to bring home besides.

"Where is the other paddle?" I asked, as Paul pushed away from the shore. Looking up at him as he stood in the stern of the canoe, I realized he had grown taller in the year I had been home. In the long corduroy trousers and red mackinaw coat he looked as manly as any voyageur that had ever dipped a paddle in those waters.

"Let me do it alone today. You sit in the bottom and ride like a fine lady," said Paul.

"Grand'mère thinks I'm not dressed like one." I looked down at the plain brown merino Pierre had bought me to save the braid-trimmed gray one from Quebec for fine occasions. Grand'mère liked the dress well enough, but she had frowned over the jacket I had put on over it—one of soft deerskin, covered with quill and bead embroidery—a present from Marthe.

"You look all right," said Paul.

On the beach, Grand'mère was just settling herself in the big canoe. Over the lengthening strip of blue water between us came her voice, speaking to the canoe-boy.

"If you splash my dress a single time, I'll pin you up by the ears to my clothesline when we get back."

I smiled. Grand'mère was in her usual form.

"That Ottawa boy is as dirty as if he had been tied over the smoke-hole of a lodge," I remarked, feeling again how much I had changed in notions of cleanliness while I was away at the convent. Before that, I would have noticed only whether the boy was painted or not, thinking nothing of the greasiness of his face above the cast-off, ill-fitting blue surtout coat.

"That's Lazy Joe," said Paul. "I wonder he'd take a job of paddling. Lies around the Ottawa village at St. Ignace all the time. Never does anything as long as he can beg his meat."

"There are a few in every camp that take advantage of the sharing."

All along the beach, canoes were being set into the water. "Looks like all the fort people are turning out for the party," said Paul, nodding toward the wharf, where a cluster of blue-uniformed figures framed a little group of ladies mostly dressed in neat black.

"Oh, do they go too—?"

"Yes, everyone goes, except the few soldiers who are on sentry duty," said Paul. He looked at me, remembering. "This is your first sugar party."

"The first since I came to Mackinac," I said. "But I was born at a kind of sugar party."

"There's the new doctor, with Ellen Pierce." Paul nodded toward two that had broken away from the others, the man handing his tall, slender companion into a canoe steadied by a figure in shabby deerskins. "He's hired an Ottawa to paddle for him, too," said Paul with a touch of scorn.

"He hasn't been here long enough to get used to it himself," I said.

Martin was in uniform, looking even more straight and clean-cut than I remembered in the dark blue garb, the single breasted, tight-fitting coat with gold buttons down the front, the absence of shoulder wings and embroidery denoting that he was a medical officer. He had only one chevron on each arm, but his bell-shaped leather cap had the usual yellow pompon of an artillery company. His description still stands on the army records: Enlisted May 1, 1830, Assigned to Company G, 2nd Artillery, stationed at Michilimackinac, discharged May 1, 1833, reason, expiration of service. Twenty-six years of age when enlisted, blue eyes, brown hair, complexion fair, born Boston, January 25, 1804, a surgeon.

As the other canoe pushed away from the beach, I looked at the girl at Martin's side. Yellow hair was escaping from her blue wool scarf. She wore a long, tight-fitting coat of dark blue, with a cape of mink over it, and carried a muff of the same fur.

We were far out in the straits now, and Paul turned

the canoe eastward, paddling slowly. Realizing how closely I had been watching the other canoe, I took my eyes off it and looked back at the village, where the clean sparkling snow revealed the dullness of the houses and picket fences awaiting their spring coats of whitewash. Frost still sparkled on the trees, and in the quiet air smoke rose from chimneys in tall curls until it was lost. My eyes rested on the two spired churches and the lower mission buildings, and then moved up the line of the cliff rising behind the half-moon shaped village, to the white fort high in the air on its crest. As I looked, a smaller banner was run up the flagpole, opening its folds below the stars and stripes.

"Look, Paul, he's putting up the fair-weather flag," I said.

"Good weather for sugar making," said Paul. "Cool and frosty nights, and days warmed by the sun."

Sober black woolen surtouts mingled with bright blanket coats and supple deerskins, and women's sober bonnets and shawls moved along among beaver hats and coonskin caps, as the islanders, laughing and talking, carrying baskets and tin pails, crossed over the beach road to their canoes. As our canoe passed opposite the mission buildings I could see all of that pebble-bordered road, from where it came across the far point and began to turn inward, following the curve of the harbor. Passing the sutlers' shops, some of which were not yet opened, it reached the center of the curve within hailing distance of the fur company's warehouses. There it began to bend outward, past the mission church and school toward the eastern point called Robertson's Folly. Those who lived in the main village in the center of the curve often showed their scorn for the poverty of the fishermen by remarking that *both* ends of the road ended in folly.

Paul was letting the current carry us along, dipping his paddle only to keep us from being carried too far to the southeast. He looked back at the snow-silvered island set in the dark rushing waters.

"You know," he said, "I never got off Mackinac much until I was big enough to go hunting with Baptiste and Armand on the mainland. I thought the island was all the land there was."

I hoped he would go on. All I knew about his childhood had come in these brief glimpses he sometimes gave when we were alone.

"I had another funny notion then." He smiled soberly. "I thought the sun slept in the water, because I saw him go down in it at night. I thought he just went under the island and came up on the other side. Then he shook himself like a big dog, and started across the sky again."

I laughed with him. Low as our voices were, they were heard in a canoe drawing up between us and the shore. Martin and the major's daughter both looked across, and he took off his leather hat and waved. Paul raised the paddle in salute, and I lifted one hand. The major's daughter nodded indifferently, and spoke to Martin, pointing to something on Round Island opposite. He turned back to her, as their canoe pulled on ahead. Other canoes, full of villagers shouting back and forth, came along, and Paul, to get out in front of the crowd again, began to paddle faster, and the sleeves of his mackinaw coat rose and fell more swiftly. In his serious brown face, gray eyes like Pierre's looked over my head toward the distant shores of Bois Blanc.

"One reason I always liked to go out fishing with Baptiste," he said between dips of the paddle, "was to get off Mackinac and see some other shores. The first time he took me on one of his long trips was up to the foot of St. Mary's rapids. It was in the fall, and we caught whitefish in scoop-nets as fast as we could unload them and let the nets down again."

"I'm glad you like Baptiste so well."

"Everybody likes him," said Paul. "I wish his fishing paid a little better. Now yesterday—we.brought in three barrels, and Armand had one. He and Baptiste sold one to the fur store. I don't know what they'll do with the rest."

"Too bad anything so good should go to waste," I said. "And to think that in Quebec they don't know what whitefish taste like. At the convent we had eels from the St. Lawrence three times a week, and sometimes cod from the ocean. The girls get so tired of eels. They'd be wild about Lake Superior whitefish."

Paul narrowed his eyes in thought as his paddle dipped and rose in easy rhythm. "I never thought about it much. I guess I supposed there were whitefish everywhere."

The water around us was full of canoes, and Grand'-mère waved as she passed. Her canoe-boy was pretending to be working hard, hoping for extra payment. Unnecessarily, he attracted attention by bending over far at the side, dipping his paddle deep into the water, sending his canoe in quick sudden spurts, so that Grand'mère's white cap ribbons alternately floated out behind and settled against her dress. Paul and I smiled.

"Grand'mère looks like the pictures of angels," I said. "Notice her wings."

"Grand'mère likes to go sugaring. She likes any kind of party," said Paul, looking after her with affection.

Bois Blanc lay close before us. Low bushes crept down to the pebbled rim, except for one open stretch of beach, just below a clearing. A few scattered canoes were drawn up there, and all the craft on the straits behind us were about to turn in and fill up the vacant spaces.

When Grand'mère's canoe was about three lengths ahead, suddenly Paul looked mischievous and began to paddle faster, bent on shooting ahead and overtaking the other canoe.

Grand'mère turned and saw us. "*Qu'est-ce que c'est*

que cela? A race?" She spoke excitedly to the canoe-boy. "*Vite!* Let's beat him to shore!"

The Ottawa boy took one look around, and began to paddle faster. "Oh, more! More! Ah—*c'est joli!*" said Grand'mère.

Mrs. Stuart smiled shyly from under her paisley shawl, and Mr. Stuart grinned in amusement, watching Grand'mère lean forward, urging the canoe on, and glaring at the canoe-boy as if she would like to crack a whip over his head. He began to spurt ahead, dipping his paddle faster and faster. Due partly to Grand'mère's excited leaning to one side and the other, the canoe rocked crazily.

"Mother, please!" said Pierre, annoyed.

Grand'mère ignored him. "Get on with you! *Vite! Plus vite!*" she shouted almost in the Ottawa's ear.

He tried, but once overtaken, he was no match for Paul. Our canoe drew up on the beach more than a length ahead.

"Such laziness!" Grand'mère scolded. "Can't you beat a boy fourteen years old?—Oh!"

The last exclamation was jarred out of her. The Ottawa had taken the shortest route, trying to slip the big canoe outside the first one in line. Watching us, he had failed to see a rock at the edge of the water, and jammed the canoe head-on into it. Grand'mère fell forward against Mrs. Stuart, and Pierre would have tumbled into the water if Mr. Stuart had not seized his shoulder with a capable hand, throwing his own weight to one side of the canoe at the same time, so that it did not go over.

The canoe-boy looked sullen. "*T'ya!*" he ejaculated, as water began to run into the canoe through the crushed-in bow.

"Steady, everybody," said Mr. Stuart.

"The careless fool—!" exclaimed Pierre.

"Never mind," said Mr. Stuart. "We're all right, and

the canoe can be fixed. I've had far worse than this happen to me in a canoe. Here, ladies, better get out before you get your feet wet—" He jumped out on shore, with agile movements for so stout a figure, and beckoned to Grand'mère and his plump little wife to come forward in the canoe as he held it.

Paul ran to help Grand'mère. Taking his hand, she hopped to the shore as lightly as a bird. "You rascal—!" she gasped, her wrinkles crinkling with laughter.

"Beat you, didn't I, Grand'mère?" he said in a matter-of-fact way.

"Ought to be ashamed," she scolded, and gave him an affectionate box on the head. He laughed, and tweaked her cap ribbons. "Oneta said you had wings—"

"If I had, you'd never have beaten us," she assured him.

Pierre stepped out of the canoe. "Don't you think such showing off is in rather poor taste?" he said coldly. The smile left Paul's face. He stepped back. Without another word, Pierre marched up the bank.

"*Mon Dieu*, Pierre!" Grand'mère called after him. "The boy was only having fun with his grand'mère." She joined Mrs. Stuart and the two of them moved up the bank to mingle with the villagers warmly dressed in coats and mittens, milling about in the clearing above.

Paul looked after his father in bewilderment. "Nothing I do is right," he murmured, as if something often close to the surface had at last broken through.

"He's very proud, you know," I began.

"Anything he doesn't do is wrong," said Paul.

"He likes dignity about things," I said, understanding Pierre's annoyance at their unceremonious arrival. He liked to step from a boat like the priest did, or like an emissary from the king in the earlier days.

"A sugar party is no place for dignity," said Paul. He turned back to Mr. Stuart, who was bending over the canoe, examining the damage. "I'll repair it for you," he offered.

"No, no. It's nothing much," said Mr. Stuart cheerfully. "A little bark will make it as good as new. It'll give this fellow something to do while he waits for us. Damned careless of him, not to look where he was going. Not your fault, Paul, my boy." He slapped Paul on the back. "You can give me a lift with these bearskins." He pulled out of the canoe a pack tied with a deerskin thong. "We'll spread 'em around for the ladies to sit on."

I went up slowly ahead of them. The sun was bright, giving light but not heat enough to melt the light fall of snow, though it was being rapidly trampled out of sight. Somewhere beyond the crowd, Baptiste's fiddle was playing, and in the center of the clearing, the most vigorous had already made up a set for dancing, stepping out the figures on the moist earth, clapping mittened hands, the shouts of the caller rising above the noisy greetings of the men gathering around the kegs that somehow appeared at every party.

Grand'mère and Mrs. Stuart chose where they wanted to sit, within view of the row of boiling kettles at the edge of the open grass-plot. Paul spread the bearskins, and all the women made that their center, drifting in until the black fur was entirely hidden by the spreading skirts, as each lady modestly covered her ankles. Children with joined hands were snake-dancing in and out among the grown-ups, and to avoid their mad rush I stepped out among the trees and came up on the other side of the steaming kettles.

Each of the heavy iron vessels was suspended from a pole supported by two forked sticks set in the earth at each side. Beside each kettle stood a woman, ladle in hand, to take off scum as it formed. At the end of the row, the largest kettle was suspended from a framework attached to a stump that had been cut off at about the height of my head. From that one, Mrs. Ruggs waved her yellow froth-covered ladle in my direction. As I started toward her, someone in the group of blue-clad officers beside her asked, "How long has this one been boiling?"

I knew the voice, even before I saw Martin with Ellen Pierce on his arm.

"This one ain't been goin' so long," said Mrs. Ruggs. "Now that'un over there"—she pointed to the middle one—"that'un's been goin' about four days. That's the one we're goin' to sugar off first."

"What are those other kettles doing on the ground? Do they have sap in them?"

"No. They've been emptied. That's just water standin' in 'em. We're soakin' 'em till we get a chance to scrub 'em out with sand."

The major's daughter was tolerantly amused at Martin's interest, and her small near-sighted eyes ignored Mrs. Ruggs completely. Her hand rested insistently on Martin's arm, and she kept making a tentative step with one foot as if to draw him away.

"Couldn't I help somewhere?" he asked. "I'd really like to."

"Martin, there comes Father with Captain Macklin." Ellen took his arm decisively. "I want to ask them about the party I'm giving next week for the men who are to be exchanged to Fort Dearborn." She pulled her mink cape up about her throat, and its taffeta lining rustled softly as she and Martin moved away. Before me, through the clouds of steam, I saw the rest of the blue-clad men cross the clearing to join Pierre and Mr. Stuart, and the jovial fur company agent raised his voice to include his larger audience.

"Was just tellin' Pierre here about a letter I got from Fat Mackenzie. He's set up a post alongside a new fort among the Nez Percés. The tradin' house is all loop-

292

holed, he says, and they have a small door for the Indians to pass their furs through and then the traders push out the goods they're entitled to. They don't dare let the Indians in the fort, and they've got a big stock of muskets, some cannons, and swivels, and a lot of bayonets, in case trouble starts."

"Oh, I say, are they really as bad as that?" inquired one of the officers.

"Well, Fat made a trip out among 'em, and sure enough he was attacked and lost two of his men. Treacherous, them Indians.—Fat ain't doin' so bad at tradin', though. He wrote about gettin' twenty beavers for one yard of white cloth—the last yard he had."

The men laughed appreciatively

"Well, the season'll soon be here," said one.

"Not long now until the first boats," agreed Pierre.

"I'm more anxious to see the first schooner up from Detroit," said the major. "I'm waiting for some official dispatches, and specie to pay the garrison."

"I'd like to get my hands on some copies of the *National Intelligencer* again," said a tall soldier. "Must be high old times there with Jackson and his backwoodsmen in the saddle."

"I'm waiting to see what he's going to do about the Indian problem." I could not see the speaker, but I knew the voice as that of Mr. Campbell, the government agent. "Indian problem." The phrase jarred on my ear. I had never heard the tribes speak of the "white man problem."

The voices grew fainter, and the little group broke up as Mrs. Ruggs called for someone to put up the pine boards on sawhorses, so the women could spread out the contents of the lunch baskets.

I saw Paul put down an armload of wood beside one kettle. He looked over the crowd for an instant, then moved purposefully through it and drew Mr. Stuart to one side. Paul seemed to be talking earnestly, and Mr. Stuart was at first amused and then interested. I must ask Paul about it later, I thought.

Grand'mère still sat with the village and fort ladies on the bearskins. Back of them was a fringe of shabby men and women from Shantytown that dared not approach the other groups. Only among the children was there no division. They were racing about the clearing together, settling here and there only to rise again like a flock of bright, chirping birds and come to rest a little farther on.

Looking about as if to find the ones I belonged with, I hesitated, in the sudden loneliness of not being attracted anywhere. Then in the woods behind me I heard a bird note, and then another. A whippoorwill—the first one, I thought, and slipped away into the sugar grove to see if I could get a glimpse of him. I wished I had worn my moccasins when I felt under my stiff-soled shoes the soft mat of rotting wood and decaying leaves. Beside each maple tree hung a little trough made of a short pine log hollowed out. Sap dripped into it from a slip of wood inserted in the tree about two feet from the ground. Half-grown boys, each with a yoke across his shoulders with a birchbark pail on each side, were making the rounds of the troughs to gather the sap.

The bird note came again from farther away, and I went on into a little grove of evergreens. I could now barely hear the voices at the camp, and the spruces and tamaracks stood serene. Patches of ice and old snow lay in the shadow of rocks and trees. At the base of a hemlock I saw the trail of a porcupine, the tracks looking as if they had been made by tiny human feet. Then, in wind-still air, I saw a hawk cross above, going toward the north. As I watched, he turned once and looked backward. Marthe had told me that when a hawk did that, he was on his way with a spirit-message to the land of souls.

What message did he carry, I wondered. Perhaps it was of the approach along the path of souls of a chief or warrior deserving a joyous welcome into the spirit-land. Or he might bear a warning that some loved one whose work was not finished on earth was in danger and might die without honor before his work was done. I followed the hawk with my eye until he was beyond the trees, leaving the island again, like the perpetual essence of life itself, coming from the unseen to the seen and passing again to the unseen. At the end of his flight was my own home-lodge, I thought. Time is no more in the land of souls, and all remain the same age they entered it. Tecumseh would be a tall, strong warrior to whom all others yielded gladly the most shining lodge of all, my mother a young woman glowing with happiness to be eternally with him, perhaps regretting that I must be alone on earth, held to it by Paul's need of me, and a web of duty, no less strong for being unseen. Little as I had seen my father, I knew he loved me, too, for children—never numerous in the lodges—were ever beloved, keeping alive the ambition of the father. I wished I might do something to make him proud of me.

A hoarse croak above me aroused me from my thoughts, and told me I had caught up with the whippoorwill. With one more trill he ceased his song and flew leisurely away, as if, having given announcement of his arrival, he had something else to do.

I do not remember how long I stayed there, delighting to see how the woods opened their secrets to one who had lived with them. I felt closer to my early days than I had for many years. The grove seemed a little outpost of the forests that had been home, that one as much as any other, for in memory rose no particular forest—only trees and running water to set a canoe in.

When at last I went back through the sugar grove to the noisy clearing, there was a flutter of preparation for lunch. The women were talking of the coming summer, the "season," as they spread the baskets of food on the long pine tables, setting out jars of pickles and preserves, stacking plates, arranging heaps of hard-boiled eggs. There was nothing new in what they said—their complaints of the crowds and the noise, the sleepless nights while reveling voyageurs made the darkness as unquiet as the day. The dancing in the clearing had broken off for a moment, as Baptiste laid his fiddle across his knees and raised a tin pot of liquor to his lips.

"Bring yer pails for sugar," called the postmaster from beside the middle kettle. He was looking down at the earth, where he had poured a little syrup on the snow. It had stiffened. The kettle was ready for the sugaring-off, and with a quick scramble everyone caught up tinware and gathered around. Laughing at smudged faces and sugary clothes, they pressed close to the two men tilting the kettle. I saw that someone had already picked up our small kettle and pint pot. Having nothing to get syrup in, I stood back from the others. As my eyes passed over the noisy, chattering crowd, good-naturedly pushing and shoving, I saw near me a kettle that had been left untended. The fire flared up beneath it, the yellow foam had risen higher and higher, and was spilling over the top. Someone had put on too much wood, I thought as I ran forward. Tall flames were reaching up all around the kettle, licking at the crane that held it out from the stump.

I snatched up the ladle lying on a piece of birchbark, and began stirring rapidly, trying to save the syrup until I could get time to pull out some of the fire beneath. I had to stand on tiptoe to reach, and steam was rising in my face so I was almost blinded. If I had some cold water, I thought, or some fresh sap. But I didn't have time to get any.

All at once there came a tearing sound. The fire had burned through the wooden crane, and with a crash it gave way. The huge kettle tipped, and I saw a yellow flood of boiling syrup coming at me. Then suddenly someone caught me firmly by the dress from behind and snatched me away.

We lost our balance and both fell sprawling among the leaves. I had only a glimpse of him in his blue uniform as he lifted me to my feet and stepped away, but I knew it was Martin Reynolds. And then Grand'mère was upon me, tugging at my arm and exclaiming, "Are you hurt? Are you all right?" and then the whole crowd was around me. "Is she hurt? What happened?"

"I'm all right. I'm sorry the syrup is wasted," I murmured, watching it congeal on the cold earth.

The men were pulling the fire away from the charred stump, examining the broken crane, talking of how the accident had happened. I watched the syrup melting the trampled snow as it pushed its circle outward, until the others began to move away in little groups. Even more than anyone else, I knew what I had been saved from. Feeling again the breath of the hot fire, the scalding of the steam, I remembered how anxious my grandfather had been to keep me away from fire. I remembered Marthe's stories about a woman dying of boiling syrup the night I was born. I had been saved from the one fearful omen of my birth.

My chance to thank him did not come until the lunch was over, and the women were putting dishes and leftover food back in the baskets, gathering up their tins of sugar and syrup, and calling the sticky children and herding them back to the canoes. The major's daughter called to Martin, and he left the men and crossed the clearing toward her. I was putting Grand'mère's silver into her basket, and Martin swerved to speak to me in passing.

"All right now?" he asked.

"Yes. I want to thank you—" I began.

"Please don't. Glad I happened to be there."

"It was *wabeno*," I said.

"Wa-beno?"

"Yes. Mystery."

"Oh, no," he said with a puzzled look in his eyes. "I was just turning to speak to you when I saw what was coming." His voice was one that could be heard in quiet forests and not obtrude itself as something alien. A smile spread over the firm lips under his mustache. It was a quick flash, not a slow-coming smile like Pierre's, and the glow lasted longer in his eyes than in the curve of his lips. I wondered if he had seen how I wandered about alone, as one not belonging.

"I wanted to tell you about meeting a friend of yours, down in the fishing village," he said. "Marthe, they call her. She told me a good story—I guess being here in this grove reminded me of it. It was about trees. I suppose it was a legend."

I listened in surprise. I had never known Marthe to relate one of her legends to a white man.

"Perhaps you know it," he went on. "It seems a traveler came to a grove of trees, and stopped and asked them of what use they were. They answered by praising themselves—'We make good wood for fires, and houses, for boats and rafts and swift canoes.' Well, he thanked them and went on to another grove. He asked the same question there, and the trees told him how good they were for building and for fuel. Just beyond, a small tree stood alone. The traveler drew near it and asked, 'Of what use are you?'

" 'I'm sorry,' the little tree said. 'I'm afraid I am of no use at all. I am not big enough for anyone to want me.'

" 'Good,' said the traveler, and lay down beneath it to rest himself." Martin laughed when he finished. "I wrote it down when I got home. I liked it the best of anything I've heard for a long time."

"She told it to me when I was a child," I murmured, remembering it had been Marthe's favorite story for teaching the value of being just what one is meant to be.

"Martin!" the major's daughter called impatiently at the edge of the clearing nearest the canoes.

"Yes, Ellen," Martin called back. He took up my basket, and put his hand under my elbow, gently taking me along with him to join her.

"Miss Pierce, do you know Miss Debans? She and I came up on the same boat a year ago."

"How do you do," I said.

"How do you do," she answered curtly, and then turned her small, cool eyes up to Martin's face. "Well, the plans are all made for my party."

"Is that so?" asked Martin. I tried to draw away, but he still held on to my basket. "Is it going to be something special?" he asked.

"We're planning an evening of theatricals. Won't you consent to take part?"

"*Those* again?" Martin pretended to groan. "You know what a dub I am."

She put up her hand and tucked the escaping locks of yellow hair back under her blue scarf. "I have it all planned. You are to play Essex to my Elizabeth." She held her muff up against her chin and looked at him provokingly over the top of it. She had all the coaxing graces of one who knows she is pretty and better dressed than others.

"Oh, I won't be any good at that—" said Martin.

"Oh, but I insist. I have most of the lines written, and the costumes planned."

Her little eyes were hard, I thought, and I noticed that her jaw line was more than usually prominent, which lowered her beauty to a determined prettiness.

"Well, I mustn't disappoint, then," he sighed, and turned to include me. "What about you, Miss Debans? Do you ever take part in these things?"

"I'm afraid—" began the major's daughter.

"We ought to have you come and tell us stories about the island," he went on with enthusiasm. "I'll bet you know hundreds of them."

"Martin, we must go!" said Ellen. Her voice was as cold as the wind of the freezing moon across the heights of Mackinac. "I want to have a rehearsal this evening." She took his arm, and pulled him toward the canoe.

But he smiled at me and called back. "I'll see you again. You and I must pay a visit to Marthe together sometime."

Ellen raised her voice a little as Martin helped her into the canoe and the Ottawa stood ready to push off. "That girl took it calmly—your saving her from being burned."

"She thanked me well enough," said Martin.

"But without a bit of feeling," insisted Ellen. "If it had been I, I should have been hysterical. The Indians are a sullen lot."

"Isn't it part of their training not to show their feelings?"

Ellen thrust her arm out in an impatient gesture. The canoe was out on the straits, and her voice came back faintly. "Oh, that— They're just dull and ignorant."

I could not hear Martin's answer.

Going back in the canoe with Paul, over the clear, transparent water, our smooth progress seemed more like flying than riding on the surface of waves. Something inside me grew warm and comfortable, and yet stirred with queer excitement. I felt the day had been one I should never forget. Without any reason for its being so, it seemed like the one when the boy first goes on the hunt, or when the little beaver first takes his share of the work at the building of the dam.

Paul dipped the paddle silently. Spread over the straits around us were other canoes pushing on toward Mackinac beach. I could hear Grand'mère's shrill tones, and Mr. Stuart's voice with the Scotch burr upon it as he answered her.

"Paul, what were you talking to Mr. Stuart about?"

"Fishing."

I looked at his impassive face, puzzled. "Mr. Stuart isn't very much interested in fishing, is he?"

"I hope he'll be—in shipping fish."

"Shipping—?"

"To places where they don't have trout and whitefish. Like you said."

"But that's been tried, and I've heard that the fishermen didn't make very much money."

Paul looked out over my head at the path the sun laid on the water. "It hasn't been done right before. If they could be sent in a boat that had to go anyway, like the *Ramsey Crooks*—" He named a fur company schooner.

We were almost at the beach before, by questioning and guessing at what lay between his answers, I found that Mr. Stuart had agreed to let Paul and Baptiste send out a few barrels of fish with every schooner-load of furs, and in return for a share of the profits, help them find the best markets in the east.

Paul and I drew the canoe up on the shore and turned it over. What would Pierre think about it, I wondered. But I must leave that question alone until Paul himself was ready to meet it. I wondered how clear he was about his plans.

"But, Paul, will it be worth the bother for a few barrels? The schooner won't have much space for your fish, will it?"

"If furs don't come in better than they have in the last two years," said Paul slowly, "there'll be plenty of room. I've seen the regular schooners with such a light cargo they've had to take in sand for ballast in the space where they used to carry furs."

A long silence fell between us. That was the first time

I had heard that the fur company's business had fallen off. As we walked slowly up the street, I looked ahead at the great warehouse thoughtfully, just in time to see Pierre walk in its office door behind Mr. Stuart.

Six

❧ One evening, late in the moon of flowers, Paul and I sat on the front steps after supper. Into the twilight the black puff of smoke from the sunset gun floated out to be thinned to gray and lost above the straits. The deep boom echoed from island to island. Above the meeting of water and sky lingered rosy clouds, red paint for the use of the star-spirits.

"Paul, is it anything you can tell me about?"

He did not waste words asking what I meant.

"I guess I'm tired." He stirred, and stretched his moccasined feet out before him. "Been putting in long hours. Baptiste and I have had every net out. Takes us all day to go from one to the others."

I knew they had been trying to get enough different kinds—whitefish, trout, siscowet—to see what people in the east would buy.

"And then you spend half the night getting the catch salted and packed in barrels," I said.

Paul tried to smile. "I guess I just need some sleep."

"Lack of sleep would not put those lines between your eyes," I said. "Is it because Grand'mère scolded about the way you smell of fish all the time? It was just that she wanted you to stop fishing and whitewash the house and fence and clean the attic."

Paul half grinned, as if hearing it put into words took off the sting. "I'll get that done for her when our first shipment has gone out.—No, it's about taking the job at the warehouse. Father is set on having me take

302

the place of the clerk that died last week. You remember the funeral Grand'mère got so stirred up about."

We smiled. When the funeral passed, Grand'mère, never one to peer out from behind curtains, had gone out on the steps to look. The little procession had happened to pause before our house. *"Mon Dieu!* Such carelessness!" she had fumed, coming inside and slamming the door. "A sure sign of death or misfortune within a year!" After a day or two of unusual moping, and telling over the beads of her rosary, she had regained her spirits. We could hear her singing in the back kitchen.

"We'll take whatever weather
Le bon Dieu *can scrape together—"*

Paul's face grew serious again. "The worst of it is, I know Father's right." He jumped up. Thrusting his hands deep in the pockets of his dark brown jacket, raising his chin stubbornly, he walked up and down, turning at the same spot on the path each time, like a caged polar bear I had seen at Montreal. "I can't even answer him. It *would* be better for me to have a regular job. Baptiste and I are taking chances. Michel is making barrels for us, and if these first fifty or so don't sell, we can't even pay him, or Mr. Stuart either. And we don't know when we'll get the money. What do you think I should do?" He looked as if my answer meant much to him.

I knew what was behind this worry. If Paul failed, Pierre would insist on paying the debts he had made. And Paul could not bear that. After opposing his father, he could not take money from him for the needs of the very thing that stood between them.

It would be as humiliating as for Pierre to have to take money Paul's fishing had earned.

"I'll help you," I said after a little. "If I go to teach at the mission—"

"No," said Paul. "I couldn't use your money."

303

In the silence that followed, I sat thinking of the offer Mr. Fisher had made to me a few days before. With many preliminary questions about my convent training, satisfying himself that I would not spread Catholic influence, he had asked me if I would teach sewing and weaving in his school. Pierre and Grand'mère had thought it might be interesting work for me, but both had been indignant when I suggested I might use the money to pay my share of the household expenses. I was beginning to think I could never do anything for them. But here was a chance to help Paul, if he would let me.

"But, Paul," I said, "I have nothing else to do with the money. Pierre buys me everything I need."

Paul walked up and down, shaking his head, as I went on softly urging. At last he stopped beside me and stood in silence, looking out over the water, in the position that reminded me so much of my grandfather. And yet Paul's reluctance to take my money was not the Indian way.

"Please, Paul—" He did not answer.

"I shall take Mr. Fisher's offer anyway," I said at last, "and I'll save all the money he pays me. If you ever need it, it will be ready for you. You could pay it back to me sometime."

He laid his hand on my hair in a brief, unusual gesture of affection. "It would be better than taking help from Father," he said. "I won't need help unless I fail."

But, watching his face clear from its worry, I was contented. This struggle between Paul and his father was nothing I could settle. I could not change Pierre, or keep Paul from going his own way. All I could do was to make some little part of the path easier.

"There's something queer about these arguments with Father." Paul spoke as if he were taking up my thought. "Everything he says is true. And yet I can't give in."

☙ ☙ ☙

Paul went on a long fishing trip with Baptiste, and the clerkship was given to someone else. When he came back, he and Pierre quarreled bitterly, and then there was silence between them. They scarcely spoke to each other for days at a time, but beneath Pierre's silence could be seen a determined waiting. I knew he was thinking that when the fur company hired another clerk, it would be Paul.

The story of my teaching at the mission, and of the sincere but misguided efforts of that mission and many another among the Indians, would make a long tale in itself. But I remember a sentence Pierre read to me once from Voltaire, that I asked him to repeat so I could write it down. *"L'histoire d'un prince n'est pas l'histoire de tout ce qu'il a fait, mais de tout ce qu'il a fait de digne d'être rapporté."*

One late afternoon I left the school and turned toward the fur company to wait for Pierre, as I often did in that time. The summer had begun, and I remember that the island lay warm and sunny on quiet blue water. Under the eaves of the warehouse pigeons circled and murmured, and on the shore gulls were flying into the sun. Up at the fort a squad was drilling and the commands of the officer rang sharply above the village noise. Ojibway and Ottawa women with babies on their backs were out in front of the nearest lodges, lighting supper fires, and cleaning their kettles with a wisp of grass or handful of moss, or wiping them on the back of the nearest dog.

The boats had come in, and Charlie and Jacques and the others were back. Mingled with the usual stories of their winter, they had brought tales of the flight of game from steel in the heart of the forest. They told of gleaming axes, the camps of a hundred men, and of rivers of logs on their way to the sawmill. New eyes were looking at the land of the Ojibway and Ottawa. A tree that a brave would never think of cutting unless he needed it for his canoe, for poles for a wigwam, or branches for his bed, was now being seen only as standing in the way of a plow, or as so many feet of lumber. A coldness had come over me as I heard, and I had wondered about the future of the red man. He, too, was part of the forest.

Yet there seemed to be as many traders as ever, I thought, seeing them everywhere I looked on the village streets. The fur yard was full of men sorting packs at little tables, their heads bare to the slanting sun. The day had been warm, and their striped shirts were open at the throat. "Fifty beavers, twenty-seven muskrats, eight deer, third quality—" a voice droned on as I went up the office steps.

Mr. Stuart was behind his long desk, bending over a rust-brown leather journal, heavily important with the weight of its own length and thickness, and the large sums running down the margins of its pages. A door stood open into the warehouse, and the air was pungent with the odor of furs.

"Is it time for you already?" He looked up cheerfully. "Drat it, had to send my watch back east for repairs. Won't get it till spring now, likely."

"How are you today?" I asked.

"Well enough. I'll be better when I get through with the forty thousand raccoons I'm sortin'," he growled, handing me a stick of striped candy from a glass jar he kept in his desk. "How are you gettin' on at school?" He drew out another stick for himself and bit off the end.

"All right."

"That Mr. Fisher is a sober-lookin', religious rascal, ain't he? I always distrust them kind. Sometimes a fellow looks like that, and yet would cheat his own father—"

"Oh, he means well," I said, getting up on a stool by the window. "Tell me, do you give everyone candy?"

"Well, no. I am too close with my money for that. Scotch, you know." He said it proudly, as if it were a totem on his chest. "Remember our agreement. If anyone asks you, you bought it in the store." His plump figure shook with mirth. "Whist! Hold your tongue and so will I!"

Not wishing to disturb him if he wanted to work, I sat looking out over the fur yard.

"Just heard from that shipment of your brother's."

I swung around quickly. Mr. Stuart was holding up a letter.

"You tell Paul to pack up all the fish he can yank out of the straits."

"You mean—"

"Sold every barrel, and at a good price, too. Even before it got to Buffalo. All sold in Detroit and Ohio towns. That gives me an idea. I'll fix up a dicker to trade whitefish for the cheese and flour we buy in Ohio —yes, and the corn and lard, too. Hell, yes—excuse me. But we're sending schooners half full of furs these days. Might as well fill them up with fish."

"If it's as easy as that, why hasn't someone done it before?"

"Ain't nobody tried it that had our connections. Do you realize we've got the smartest men in all these towns in our employ already? If I say to them 'sell fish,' they'll sell fish. Paul was a smart boy to get the American Fur Company into it," said Mr. Stuart gleefully.

"But Paul ought to use some system about it," he went on seriously. "Tell him to map out the fishing grounds around here—at Detour, and the Sault, and Lake Superior—get someone workin' for him on each one. Get some Indians and half-breeds to fish 'em for him, say on five per cent commission. I'll get an order out for new nets right away." Mr. Stuart spoke with the enthusiasm that had laid out the fur company enterprises, locating posts all through the country where they could suck in the furs like great whirlpools. "But you tell him to come in and see me. I'll go over it all with him."

With a gesture he dismissed the subject, and his face took on an annoyed look as he rummaged in the drawer of his desk. "Now here's another letter—this one beats the Dutch! An epistle from Mr. Astor. Complainin' about the number of pelts. Wants to know if we're dwindlin' off to shippin' 'em one at a time. We've just had a couple of bad huntin' years, that's all. The trade'll perk up again, but the old coot can't wait."

"Did you write Mr. Astor that?"

He looked at me severely over his glasses. "I can see you don't know old Mr. Astor. He's boss. And he'll keep us all on the jump until he begins his last sleep." Mr. Stuart jerked open a drawer of his desk. "That reminds me, here's another pile of sheets for you to practice figurin' on. I began a lot of letters lately by expressin' my mind too freely."

I took the sheets with a smile.

"All kinds of trouble in a job like this," he grumbled. "That reminds me—I've got to do something about them pelts." His eyes went to a small bundle on the floor in the corner. He sighed, and turned back to the leather-bound journal.

Looking out at the activity in the fur yard, I saw that with the lowering of the sun the shadow of the great warehouse had stretched out as if trying to cover the whole village, like the greater shadow—unseen but just as surely there—reaching west and south, pushing farther and farther until all the distant hunting lands had felt it over them, making an empire known as far away as London and Paris, where the courts reveled in its furs.

"Ze very good silver fox, that pelt. Count him as thirty beavers, no?" A familiar voice came from one of the sorting tables. It was Big Charlie, still heavier, his

308

bronzed face still broader than when I rode in with his brigade. *"Mais regardez—!"*

The bright wool sashes of the men made a rainbow of color as they drew close around Charlie's table. "What you got there that's worth looking at?" one of them asked.

"Must be something of his own. Whatever Charlie brings in is the best," asserted another in a teasing voice.

"Oui," said another solemnly. "Thees Charlie, he catch always the animal in the trap by the tip of the left hind foot, so they are no marks on him, no broken skin. *Il est merveilleux,* thees Charlie."

A loud laugh broke out. Charlie smiled good-naturedly, waiting for the joking to die away. He never minded being laughed at. *"Attendez, messieurs. Venez donc."* He waited until there was an expectant circle around him. Then he pulled a bearskin cover from a small pack, and slowly pulled out a black velvety fur.

"Black weasel! Miniver!" the men exclaimed and admired.

"Attendez donc," repeated Charlie. And with a gesture he held up in one hand, dangling by their tails from his large fingers, a dozen small pelts, white except for a black spot on the tip of the tail. The pure white and the extreme fineness of the fur stood out among the wolf and deer pelts scattered on tables and ground as silk among homespun.

"White weasel—ermine! And so many of them!" The circle narrowed as the men tried to get closer to examine the furs, putting their arms about one another's shoulders.

"They came from ze far north," said Charlie slowly. "I met an Indian that had traveled three hundred miles to one of our posts. He claimed a Hudson's Bay man had cheated him, and he wouldn't trade with them any more."

I had never seen ermine before, and I thought how strange it was to see a fur that instantly reminded me, not of my early life, but of pictures in a schoolroom, and the words of one of the nuns who had lived in England. I could almost hear her voice bringing to my mind pictures of lords and ladies in purple or crimson velvet, of gold and silver fabrics for performances at the opera, of girls fluttering in exquisite materials made up by famous modistes, almost covered by fur-trimmed robes. State occasions she told us of, when a glittering coach with wheels of gold, drawn by sleek cream-colored horses, made slow progress down famous streets lined with the curious and adoring people. High Gothic arches, of an ancient building, a jeweled crown—God Save the King! Jewels, robes, cloaks, and dresses, and in the midst, everywhere, in two rows on the train of a baroness, three on that of a countess, and four on the long train a duchess may wear—the ermine. Coronets of velvet with gold tassels, a band of gold, and below that—a band of ermine! A Mackinac weasel goes to court!

My thoughts were drawn back from the word-pictures the nun had drawn in that Quebec schoolroom, as I saw someone pushing his way through the crowd surrounding Charlie. It was Jacques, his buckskin shirt open at the neck, a scarlet sash around it. He was pushing insistently against men much larger than he, forcing them to give way. Just as he reached Charlie, I saw that his face was dark with anger.

"So," he raged, "*you* have stolen my weasels. From my pack they are gone. I come here, I find you bragging of them. Give them to me!"

"Why, you—I have myself traded for these, *tous*." Charlie was amazed. "May I have to eat my moccasins, may I perish in deep snow and the wolves feed on my carcass, if I did not."

"You thief—you call yourself a brigade leader—"
And Jacques began swearing in a rapid *patois*.

"You're drunk, Jacques," said someone in the crowd.

Jacques answered with renewed shouting and cursing.
I watched uncomfortably, certain that Jacques was
wrong. The man of fewest words in a dispute is usually
the one who is right. Marthe had told me that years before. And Charlie's reputation for honesty was known
through every brigade.

"I didn't take your pelts," said Charlie, puzzled, when
Jacques paused.

But Jacques was beyond listening. He struck Charlie
full in the face, as if a blow could prove the falseness of
a statement. The men looked amazed, for no one tried to
fight Charlie. His black feather was assumed to be his
as long as he could carry a voyageur's pack. But they
recovered quickly, and spread a circle to give them
room.

The fight was on. Jacques, quick and lithe as a
panther, got in the first blows, on chin, nose, stomach.
Charlie, tall and strong as an oak, began slowly, trying
more to push Jacques away than to return his blows.
But whenever Charlie's big hand lashed out, Jacques
staggered back against the circle of men. Tossed to his
feet again, he would start forward slowly, crouching
low, while Charlie waited for him. Such solidity was
impressive. Jacques had no lack of courage, but he could
not contend with the strength of Charlie, as, impassive,
his breathing not even quickened, he stood ready to floor
Jacques as fast as he could rise and come back for it.
Jacques kept coming back, rushing Charlie with sudden
blows or kicks in the stomach. There were no more rules
for a voyageurs' fight than for a dogfight. The crowd
grew about them until I could see nothing but their
heads, Charlie's hardly moving, Jacques's curly one
ever falling out of sight and coming up as he fought

311

with every ounce of his small body. But there was no man in the world who could stay long in a fight with Charlie. It was like trying to attack a tree with one's bare hands.

I had seen the beginning of many a fight in the season, for summer meant fights as surely as the bringing in of furs. I had never watched one to a finish before. But somehow with this one I had no choice. I stood on tiptoe trying to see, and discovered that Mr. Stuart had come up behind me and was looking on with an expression of complete enjoyment. "Get up and hit him again," he exclaimed softly. But Jacques was through. The crowd parted a little and I could see him lying where he had last fallen, his gay scarlet sash trailing in the dust, his black curls shaken down over a bloody face.

One of the men, running around to find a better place to see, happened to look up at the window. The moment he knew he was seen, Mr. Stuart's expression changed to sternness.

"Hold!" he cried, and rushed out through the office door. "What in blazes!"

The circle opened to let him through.

"Don't you know fightin's forbidden in the yard?"

At the sound of his thundering voice Charlie stood back, sheepish. Jacques picked himself up, wiping his face on his sleeve, ashamed and obsequious before the sturdy figure that dominated the whole yard.

"We must have discipline. Now, who started it?"

"I, Monsieur, I started it," admitted Jacques weakly. "He has taken my weasels."

"I have them not. These are mine." Charlie glared at him.

"Mine are gone," insisted Jacques stubbornly, striking clouds of dust from his trousers.

"So ye had some weasel, and it's gone! Ye fule, why didn't ye report it to me?" roared Mr. Stuart. When excited, he spoke with a pronounced brogue. "I hae some weasels in the office this minute that I'm tryin' to find the owner of. If ye would come in and see me instead of lashin' out with yer fists the minute ye get into trouble!"

"You, M'sieu, have my weasels?"

"They may be one and the same. Old Chief Migisan's son had 'em. That worthless son-of-a-gun they call Four Legs. I was suspicious when he brought in some weasel, he acted so sneakin'. His tribe don't ever hunt in weasel territory. And he never did a day of huntin' in all his life. Sponges on all the rest of his tribe." Mr. Stuart snorted. "When that Mr. Heydenbruk at the mission painted his picture last week, Four Legs spent half a day gettin' himself decorated and painted up for it, and that's the most work he's ever done.

"So," he went on, "I took him in the office and got a confession out of him. He's coolin' hisself off in the garrison jail right now. He didn't know whose pack he got 'em out of, so I been waitin' for someone to report 'em. Come on in and get your skins."

Jacques, mopping the blood from his face with a blue bandanna, looked up at Charlie and offered his hand. Charlie shook it cordially.

"Back to your places, all of you!" shouted Mr. Stuart, and the men drifted back to the tables. Mr. Stuart came toward the office door, muttering something about "discipline in the yard." "I'll lay a barrel-stave against the head of the next one that starts something," he promised darkly. The men grinned at one another. Jacques followed Mr. Stuart.

"And you, Jacques—any more fights like this and I'll put you in the Lake of the Woods outfit."

"Oh, *non*, M'sieu." Jacques almost cringed. "I will give no more trouble." The leaders in the Lake of the Woods brigade had a well-deserved reputation for extreme severity with their men. Troublesome voyageurs were always put in it for punishment.

313

Feeling that Jacques would not want me to see him just then, I slipped through into the warehouse, and looked around for Pierre.

He stood behind a high desk at the far end, a long sheet of foolscap in his hand, checking the rows of figures on it against some columns in an open ledger. Men in calico shirts wet through with perspiration were coming and going from the yard, carrying armloads of pelts and stacking them on warehouse shelves and floor. Pierre, cool and crisp-looking as usual, shrank back against his desk as they passed. He didn't need to; his presence made a little circle into which they would not have thought of stepping.

"Oh, there you are. It is so late?" He pulled his large gold watch out of his black satin waistcoat pocket. "So it is. I'll finish here in a minute. Do you mind waiting?"

"Of course not." I stepped to a narrow window between shelves of furs reaching to the ceiling. The men outside were back at work, cutting the buckskin thongs and sorting the furs, while a member of the fur company staff counted the kinds and made a note of the grades, setting down the value as fast as a man could lay a skin before him. A brigade leader stood by in each case to represent the men of his brigade and check the accuracy of the clerk's judgment. The fight was gone from their minds, and between packs they had begun the usual voyageur talk about dogs, canoes, unusual men, and all women, boasting of their love affairs and their winter adventures, expanding all the stories to the farthest point of belief, reminding me of the common island saying, "Voyageurs never see little wolves." At a word from Charlie, a new note spread through their talk, a rejoicing that the next spring they could eat beavers' tails—their favorite delicacy—even in Lent, for hadn't the priest written to the Sorbonne to get a ruling on it for them, and hadn't the letter come back saying that they might, for a beaver being so near like a fish, it was all right, they were not sinning?

Jacques was back in his place, his face as serene as Charlie's. As he cut the thong of another pack, a shrill whistle from above made his hand stop in mid-air. Rosanne stood on a little rise beyond the fence, vivid in a dress of bright orange calico. She had a kitten in her arms. With a feeling of annoyance I knew she was carrying it only for the contrast of its black fur against her dress.

She was looking at Jacques, but taking all the other men in with little side glances. "And what will you give me for this?" She held the kitten out by the scruff of its neck. It drew itself up into the elongated ball of an animal carried in its mother's mouth. A dog from the beach lodges stopped and sat back on its haunches to await developments.

"Don't drop it!" said Jacques, pointing to the dog.

The other men were all looking at Rosanne, hoping for some amusing interruption to their work. Rosanne glanced at the office window, and saw that no one was looking. She began boldly flirting with a voyageur near her, just because he was the nearest. But when she caught Charlie's attention she turned all her wiles on him. At once I knew she had been there all the time, and had watched the fight, not drawing attention to herself until she was sure Mr. Stuart was out of sight, knowing how gruff he was with village girls that lingered around the fur yard.

She smiled at Charlie, half closing her eyes, and shaking her black curls in a provoking way. She was really striking in looks, and she knew all the tricks. I realized as I watched her acting, how much more French she was than Indian. Leaning over the railing of the yard, she said something to Charlie. Delighted, he moved his broad, calm face closer to hers and they whispered together.

315

At last she nodded, and he turned around with a beaming face. With a light laugh, she ran toward the ascent to the fort, without a glance backward. She didn't need to look around to know that every eye was following her slender figure and flying curls. I wondered as I had so many times, whether she ever walked—always running or dancing, she seemed to take life on the tip of her toes.

I turned to look at Jacques. His face darkened with anger, he went back to the pack he had started to open, slashing at it viciously with his knife. Too viciously— the knife slipped, and blood spurted from a gash above his wrist.

Charlie was the first to reach him. "Quick! A doctor!" He began to tie a great checkered handkerchief above the cut, working swiftly.

"Just a scratch," protested Jacques, glaring at Charlie. But the sleeve of his shirt had reddened with blood in a large circle.

"Let me look at it." The voice came from beside the warehouse, just out of my range of vision. As a blue-uniformed figure moved swiftly to Jacques's side, I saw that it was Martin.

The men stood back in respect as he took hold of Jacques's arm. "Good tourniquet, Charlie! Now, we'll be all right in a minute." He turned up Jacques's sleeve, and as someone brought water in a tin cup, he washed out the wound, and finished by bandaging it deftly with his own cambric handkerchief.

"Thank you, M'sieu," said Jacques, embarrassed at the attention he was getting, knowing the men were laughing under their sympathy. They knew what had made him so angry that the knife slipped.

"The cut isn't bad," said Martin. "You'll have forgotten it by your wedding day."

This was a favorite saying among voyageurs, and they laughed in appreciation.

Martin started back across the yard to the fort hill,

316

but one man after another stopped him with a greeting. I caught fragments of his talk as he went on. "Getting on all right without that tooth, Jean? André, if you don't stop taking Marie out, Josie'll sink a knife in your ribs, and I'll have a real case on my hands." Traces of his passing could be seen not so much in the men's laughter, for there had been laughter before he came, but in the special quality of the smiles they turned upon their work when he had gone.

At the edge of the yard, he laid his hands on the railing and jumped lightly over. Still they would not let him go. A lithe, black-eyed young voyageur called after him, and he had to turn once more. "There you are, Louis. Leg as good as ever? Next time you start a fight, don't let anybody drop a table on you!" With a wave of his hand, he ran up the incline to the fort.

"I'm ready now—shall we go?" asked Pierre behind me. I joined him by the desk. At the top of the page he had written in tall slanting letters "Michilimackinac, 10th July, 1831." Below the entries for that date he drew a line, halfway across the page, inserted "11th" and continued the line to the margin. He was ready for the coming day. I said nothing to Pierre about Paul's first barrels of fish being sold. I thought of it again, of those barrels going out in the empty spaces in schooners that had once carried nothing but fur. It was as if they were taking the place of something. I looked at Pierre, neat, straight, fastidious. I sighed. Paul's success would not be pleasant news to Pierre.

"Best day of the season so far," Pierre was saying, looking down at the rows of figures with satisfaction. In his eyes was a flicker of the same light I had seen in Mr. Stuart's, and in the eyes of the men as they gloated at the sight of Charlie's fine pelts. Fur had been so long sought out beyond reason, so recklessly, so passionately, that it had become something more than its value in gold, I thought.

Thrusting his quill back in its glass dish of shot, Pierre closed the ledger. The black designs in its brown leather cover shone in the last slanting beams from the western window. Just then came the boom of the sunset gun, releasing all the men from the day's work. The smoke from it hovered over the village as Pierre and I stepped out into a street filled with sinewy, weather-browned men hastening to tents and barracks, and soldiers on the way to the fort incline.

The heat of the day had lingered into the supper hour. As we turned toward home, Pierre drew out his fine linen handkerchief and dried the perspiration on his forehead. A row of braves on the way to their lodges passed us so closely that their blankets almost brushed against us. Pierre stepped aside absently, and somehow as he replaced his handkerchief he missed his coat pocket and it fell to the ground.

The last brave in line, a Pottawatomie in a dirty white blanket, two ragged feathers stuck in a green yarn sash about his head, saw it and bent and picked it up with a grimy hand. With an unsteady motion accounted for by the strong smell of rum upon him, he offered it to Pierre.

Pierre looked at the handkerchief with distaste. "Do me a favor, if you will. Drop it on the nearest campfire, please."

The Pottawatomie hesitated, holding out the handkerchief, puzzled that Pierre made no move to take it.

"Can you make him understand what I said, Oneta?"

I repeated his words briefly in Ojibway, since most of the tribes understood it.

"*T'ya!*" exclaimed the Pottawatomie in surprise. Then, realizing that Pierre did not want the white cloth, he spread it on the ground and bent over it, exclaiming in delight and wonder that a man would throw away so fine a thing just for a whim, never dreaming his own touch had spoiled it for Pierre.

318

Seven

✤ The coming of August has always meant two things to me. It was the canoe-building moon, when the sap of the birch has started moving from the branches downward and the bark is loosened so it can be easily taken off. And August meant the departure of the first brigades to winter quarters.

Every summer evening on Mackinac brought the sounds of fiddle music from houses where there was dancing, but no party was quite as fine as the one given by the fur company itself on the night before the first brigades—Lake Superior, Upper and Lower Mississippi, and Lake of the Woods—left for the winter. It was one of the few that Pierre and Grand'mère attended, for they, like the government and fur company officials that were their friends, found no pleasure in the rough and riotous gatherings in which some voyageur spent all his winter earnings in one glorious, generous fling. Only the balls given by the fur company brought together the broadcloth and deerskin circles of the island.

Pierre was immaculate as always when he came out of his room ready for the last ball of 1831. His gray hair lay in smooth waves, his blue broadcloth coat hung open to show starched ruffles in his bosom. A heavy gold watch chain crossed his blue satin waistcoat, and a small diamond pin sparkled in the center of his black cravat.

He stood with his back to the living-room fire, watching me in silence as I sat in the low rocker with my hands folded in my lap. Behind the closed door of Grand'mère's room we heard muffled tones of singing, broken by impatient exclamations marking her progress in making herself pretty. It had not taken me long to dress in my long, full-skirted yellow muslin with sprigs of blue flowers in it. I had smoothed my hair with sweet oil fragrant with the crushed leaves of rose geranium, binding the braids around my head, and fastening at one side a tiny comb with brilliants in the shape of a star—a Noël gift from Pierre that had ever touched me with a reminder of the part played by the stars at my birth and naming.

There was approval in Pierre's eyes. "That's a new dress, isn't it?" he asked at last. He was in a special good humor party clothes always gave him, and the warmth of the fire put a lazy content into his voice.

"Yes, Grand'mère made it for me," I said.

"Someone talking about me?" Grand'mère opened the door and, moving in a cloud of soft perfume, came rustling out in a new black taffeta dress with a wide lace collar falling over her shoulders. A white lace cap sat on top of her white curls. The bodice of her dress was tight and I suddenly noticed how frail she was, for all her liveliness.

"You look very fine tonight, too," Pierre teased. "Are you out for some conquest?"

"No, why?" Grand'mère asked quickly. "Are you— or is Oneta—out for a conquest?" She turned her snapping gaze on the two of us, and then bustled over to the table and emptied the contents of her reticule on it, sorting the objects and putting some of them back in with quick movements. She had forgotten what she had said, and didn't even listen to our answers. "Paul in there?" She looked at the door of the room beyond Pierre.

"No," I said. "He hasn't come home yet."

"Not home?" asked Pierre. "Isn't he going to the party?"

"Yes. He said he would—"

"Maybe that's the boy coming now," Grand'mère interrupted me. She turned to face the door, the half-filled reticule in her hands.

I knew those were not Paul's footsteps. Even before we could hear the little heels clicking on the boards of the walk, I knew the tripping feet of one who had put off moccasins almost as soon as she could talk enough to coax her father for shoes like those she had seen in the village. And then into our doorway she came, her dark eyes excited, her cheeks dimpled, her lips moist and round.

"How do I look?" Rosanne asked, pirouetting. Below a blue waist swirled a bright red skirt. Her dark curls were subdued to a mass on the top of her head, from which they bobbed in all directions as she moved. She ended her pirouette in a low curtsey facing the door, to include Jacques coming in softly behind her on new moccasins.

"Beautiful!" he said. His bright shirt and orange sash made his bronzed skin and unruly curls seem all the darker. A proud light was in his eyes as he looked down at Rosanne, and taking her hand he pulled her up to the curve of his arm.

"*Bon soir*, Jacques," said Grand'mère. "Rosanne, come here and turn around. There is a hook loose on your waist. Oneta, my sewing basket."

Grand'mère found a needle and a reel of thread, and plunged her finger into her silver thimble. Rosanne knelt, and her skirt settled in a circle about her like the great ruffled edge of a scarlet flower. Grand'mère sewed with long, firm pulls on the thread. "There." She gave the girl a little push as she finished. "You can dance all the night, and *je veux dire que* that hook, it won't come loose."

"*Merci*, Madame." Rosanne arranged her skirts carefully as she rose, and smoothed the wrinkles from her tight waist. She stood looking at Jacques, including Pierre in a sudden sidewise smile. She never neglected any man, no matter what his age.

321

"Come, I want to go," she said impatiently.

"I thought we might go along with Paul and Oneta," said Jacques.

"Paul isn't home yet," said Grand'mère.

Pierre frowned, opened his gold watch and snapped it shut. "It's a little late for him to start dressing now."

"The fiddlers have gone," said Rosanne. "Father and Armand were just ahead of us. I don't want to wait. I must be there from the very first."

Jacques hesitated, and Rosanne tugged at his orange-colored sash. "If you do not hurry I shall go with Louis Lefevre. He is just going past—"

"No, you don't." Jacques scowled. "I heard you went dancing with that *mangeur du lard* before I got in this summer."

Rosanne stamped her foot, and ran with quick steps to the door. "He is not a lard-eater. He has been in the woods two, three years. I like him. And I am going now."

"Promise you won't dance with him, or I won't take you," shouted Jacques.

"All the men will dance with me," said Rosanne. "Even M'sieu Debans, won't you, M'sieu?" She danced up to Pierre and curtseyed, bringing up her hand to sweep his cheek as she rose.

"You were not at home when Shyness called, were you, Rosanne?" commented Grand'mère drily.

Jacques strode to the girl's side and took hold of her arm. "Come on with me, you little fool! Why do you act so? M'sieu Debans will think you a wild one." He dragged her toward the door. "Come on!"

"*Mon ami*, you are hurting my arm!" Rosanne burst into tears. Jacques let go, and she threw her arms around his neck, sobbing.

"My heart, my sweet one," murmured Jacques. They clung together, the bright colors of their garments like a rainbow in the twilight-grayed doorway.

On the limestone path coming up from the meadow, I heard footsteps I knew to be Paul's, yet they stopped before they reached the gate. I had a puzzled feeling that he had heard Rosanne and Jacques and was waiting for them to go.

Presently Rosanne's head jerked up. "The party! It will begin without me!" She wiped her eyes, shook her curls, and took Jacques's arm. They paraded out, Rosanne's face tilted back, one hand holding a fold of her skirt out at the side. "We shall see the rest of you later, *non?*" called Jacques, and then they were gone down the board walk. "Hello, is it you, Paul? Better hurry." We heard Rosanne laugh carelessly, and then there were sounds of running feet as she and Jacques raced down the path to the village.

"Such a temper those two have," said Grand'mère. "That Jacques, now. Jealous as he is, he'd be a hard one to live with, but you can leave him to Rosanne. They're a natural pair. They'll fight and tear each other's hair out, and then they'll both weep and be sweet again until something else crosses one of them. *Je me pense*, it's the best thing that could happen, that the two of them fell in love. It would be tragic if either of them had picked out an ordinary person." Grand'mère snapped her reticule shut and picked up her flowered shawl. "But I don't see why they don't get married. They've been old enough for years."

"Rosanne won't set the date until he has a post of his own, even if it's just a jackknife post," I said. "And she wants him to have a black feather."

"Well, *ma foi*," exclaimed Grand'mère. "Why doesn't he get one?" Her gesture indicated that they were to be picked up anywhere.

"Because he must win the right to wear it," I said. "And he's in Charlie's brigade. No one is likely to take it away from Charlie."

323

"A lot of to-do over a feather!" sniffed Grand'mère. "Well, who's coming now? We'll never get to the party—"

Paul was approaching our door, and I heard a reluctance in the coming of his feet. With her bright shawl over her arm, Grand'mère went to the doorway, peering out into the dusk. "Is it you, Paul? Why are you dawdling so?—Merciful Heaven, what have you been doing?"

She backed into the room as Paul came to the threshold, his clothing torn and mud-spattered, his face bruised and streaked with blood, his hair rumpled in spite of his efforts to smooth it back with his hand.

"You've been in a brawl," said Pierre, and disgust rode heavily on the words.

"Are you hurt?" exclaimed Grand'mère. "Speak up! What's wrong?"

"Nothing, Grand'mère," said Paul. "I just had to—"

"Who were you fighting with?—Come here, *vite*." She took him by the sleeve and started pulling him toward the back kitchen. "A washcloth, Oneta, quick. Let's see how bad it is."

"It's nothing, Grand'mère," said Paul, gently loosening his sleeve from her grip. "I'll be all right."

"I think an explanation is due," said Pierre coldly. "And an apology for coming in looking like that." He was still motionless with his smooth-coated back to the fire, his hands clasped behind him.

Paul faced his father. "Baptiste and I hire some Ottawas to help us fish," he began quietly, "and a crowd from Shantytown has been raiding their barrels at night. Tonight I caught one of them beginning early. I had to give him something he wouldn't forget."

"There's no 'have to' about fighting," interrupted Pierre. "Such a thing should be reported to the authorities."

"They were only robbing Indians," said Paul, patient

324

with an effort. "Indians have no protection under American laws."

"Well, it wouldn't concern you," said Pierre, irritated, "if you hadn't got yourself mixed up in such a business, and with the lowest class of people—"

He was interrupted by a sound at the back of the house. With raised heads we all listened. Footsteps were mixed with guttural exclamations, and then came a thumping as someone lurched against the back door.

"Nuisances!" shouted Grand'mère. A breath of dainty perfume crossed my nostrils as she dashed across the room, seized her broom from the corner and whisked out through the kitchen. Close upon the last sight of her flying skirts we heard heavy blows followed by groans. "Get off my flower beds, you varmints!" she shouted. More groans, and the soft quick pat of running moccasins. Grand'mère came back, waving her broom aggressively. She set it down and smoothed her lace cap and adjusted her collar.

"Who was it?" asked Pierre.

"That silly Indian with the raccoon tails tied to his knees. I don't know who the others were." Grand'mère was breathless. "Too much rum in their stomachs now," she fumed, "and I suppose they're on their way to get more."

"Disgusting," said Pierre, still with his back to the fire. "No self-control."

"Too bad there hasn't been some control over the men that sell the stuff," said Paul quietly.

"It isn't necessary to make a pig of oneself because there is liquor to be had," said Pierre.

As Paul lifted his head sharply, I could almost see erect upon it the eagle feathers of my grandfather. So had he once looked at a trader he had thought unfair to us.

Grand'mère had stepped into the kitchen, and came back in the midst of the silence. "Keep quiet!" she said sharply, as if the air were full of clashing sounds. "Any more argument and I'll take my broom to your backs, too. Paul, get on in the kitchen and clean yourself up. Pierre, come on—the party will be starting without us, as Rosanne says. Oneta—"

"I'll wait for Paul."

Grand'mère took up her shawl and reticule, and her black taffeta skirts slipped over the threshold no less gaily than had Rosanne's bright one. Following her with beaver hat in hand, Pierre turned at the door. "Try to keep out of brawls after this if you can. A Debans should be a little above getting into fights over something of no importance."

Paul did not answer. He looked thoughtfully for a full minute at the ancestral portrait before him, and the old-fashioned dueling swords crossed below it. Then he turned and went into his bedroom and closed the door.

Pierre's voice came back faintly as the front gate creaked. "That settles it. If Mr. Stuart will make a place for him at the office, he shall begin there tomorrow. We'll put an end to this nonsense once and for all."

"All right, all right," said Grand'mère. "But now let's go to the party."

When Paul reappeared, his face was cleared of traces of his fight. His hair was smooth and he was dressed in his best gray broadcloth trousers, with a blue coat. He wore a soft black cravat at his throat, and a red sash about his waist.

"You look nice," he said, his eyes resting on my yellow sprigged dress. "Am I all right?"

"Very handsome," I said, smiling, thinking that in his own way, he made as fine a figure as Pierre.

"Aw, I mean—is everything all right—nothing looks funny about me?"

"Not the least bit funny," I said, as we went out the door.

326

Twilight had passed, and as we walked down the street toward the warehouse, I looked up at the trees on the heights, thinking how it always seemed that darkness came up from the island, not down upon it. The evergreens with their constant murmur of secrets created their own darkness, which then spread out and up, finally forcing the stars themselves into existence. I realized there was a threat in the air that winter was approaching. Birds had been gathering for weeks on the shore, sanding their crops for the long flight to the south.

The dancing had begun at the warehouse, but at least half of the men were still outside, talking loudly.

"That's two fights in one day. Louis will be sent out of the Illinois brigade."

"What did you say? Them Indians on the shore make such a racket—"

"They're having a medicine dance to cure a sick chief —I said Louis will be put in the northern—" His voice was drowned out by one nearer.

"Aha! You are wrong. I did not lose my shirt. I won two otter skins from that Indian before I got through with him. I know that bone game—"

"Two hundred bales today, the best furs I ever—"

"We packed more than that."

"How do you know? You can't count." There was a scuffling near the door.

"Beavers is pretty cute all right. They're smart enough to fell a tree just where they want it. They're learnin'. They're cute enough to spring a trap and go free—"

"M'sieu Beaver, he aims to go on wearin' his pelt even if some nobleman in France would like to have it."

"Us voyageurs opened up this country. Why, we went clear across, back and forth, before anybody else even got over them mountains way back there along the seacoast."

327

"You're right—with a canoe on our backs we widened the Indian trails until they're drivin' oxen and wagons along 'em now."

"I've seen things I didn't like. Things that weren't pretty—"

As though struggling in a tangled thicket, Paul and I worked our way from one open space to another in the crowd outside the wide-hinged door. Just inside, we passed a bench piled high with red peaked caps, with a few black straw hats among them. On another table was a neat row of beaver hats. The warehouse floor was crowded. At first sight, voyageurs dressed in their most showy outfits seemed to fill the room. Everywhere were the familiar short muscular bodies, the swarthy faces, and flashing eyes. The room seemed awhirl with their striped and checked cotton shirts, flannel and deerskin trousers or leggings, red, orange, and green sashes and kerchiefs. This was what they looked forward to when portages were hard. The floor was smooth, with a good surface for dancing. Candles in wall sconces threw shadows on the timbers above, and made spots of dim light that brightened the clothing of the dancers as they whirled into its glow and out again to the darker parts of the room. All tables and desks were gone, except those left to hold the hats, and a long one in the end of the room for the food that would be brought in later on. The walls were lined with chairs, all filled, and every available space on the dance floor was taken by sets of couples advancing and retreating. The skirt hems of the ladies spread wide as they circled and whirled in the lancers, to the strains of fiddlers hidden from us across the room.

After a minute I saw that three groups of people more restrained in dress were clustered about the walls of the room, looking like the tiny green St. Martin's islands in the ferment and convulsion of the straits. The major in full uniform and decorations was surrounded by ladies in long lace and satin dresses. Delicate fans waved, as jeweled and beribboned curls and puffs gracefully bowed toward him with now and then a nod to other uniformed figures.

Not far from them, in the center of another island of calm, I saw Pierre talking to Mr. Stuart and Mr. Campbell, the government Indian agent. Mr. Fisher, solemn in shiny black, was just joining them. Near-by, Grand'mère sat with their wives, very precise ladies in dark silks, looking on at the dance with patronizing airs. With them sat Miss Harper, her near-sighted eyes following Pierre.

Paul and I stood where we were until the music stopped. The couples applauded and shouted compliments at the fiddlers, and the crowd began surging toward walls and doors. Michel, in a new broadcloth suit, passed us with Currance on his arm, in a figured white muslin dress with a black petticoat beneath to show off the pattern.

"There's Paul and Oneta," said Michel. "We got these clothes with the pay for them first barrels," he whispered happily. "All fixed up for once in our lives." Someone called to them, and they were swept away from us by the noisy crowd. As the center of the floor cleared a little, I could see the fiddlers on a low platform against the opposite wall.

Baptiste and Armand might be fishermen by day, but at night they were transformed, as a weasel changes his coat to white against the winter's snow. It would be hard to recognize the Baptiste that had sold fish at back doors or hauled wood by dog team, in the proud leader who sat on the straight-runged chair dominant as a chief on his bearskin robe in council. His fiddle had dropped its sheath of aged gray wool beside the platform, and nestled between his chin and a bright red kerchief on his shoulder. He was directing the tuning before the next number, and memories of my days in the cabin

329

flowed back as he drew his bow repeatedly over the A-string until the other three fiddlers returned the same tone, and then rested his instrument on his knee while each man brought the other strings, quivering, mellow, or deeply vibrating, into harmony. Baptiste's face was animated, and he was made a different person by the certainty that if he were not here, the party would be less fine, as the knowledge of being needed ever gives one serenity. Trying a few bars of an old melody as a test, he nodded his head in satisfaction. He settled forward in the rush-bottomed chair, and his foot began to beat out the time. Then with another nod and a sudden emphatic downbeat he swung into the fast movement of "Money Musk." This was their hour, these fiddlers.

The postmaster arose and began calling the dance, and all over the room couples moved into their places. Skirts of bright yellows and blues and reds swirled indiscriminately back and forth around uniformed legs, around the deerskins of the traders, or the best village broadcloth. The blacksmith led on to the floor an Ottawa girl with a flush on her dusky cheeks. Near her moccasined feet the high heels of officers' wives in elaborate evening gowns clicked on the bare boards.

Some sets had no women at all, and men danced with one another as there were not enough women to go around. Those finding no room on the floor clustered around the walls to talk. Their voices came up between the shouts of the caller, mingling with the tap of hard leather and the soft shushing of moccasined feet. One trapper near us was telling the story of the dreaded Loup Garou, another of the phantom bateau that always goes to the east on the *jour de l'an,* high above the trees, carrying the spirits of voyageurs back to their home firesides. Old men were telling what they had done, their voices drowned out by young men telling what they were going to do, and all watched the women in the dance, selecting partners for the next one. Several had looked at me when I came in, but I had shaken my head and stayed close to Paul.

We were still watching, near the door, when that dance ended. Near us, Ellen's pink net gown billowed wide as she curtseyed. Its soft color was set off by the blue of Martin's uniform. He bowed to her, and turned to offer her his arm, laughing at something she said. They passed in front of us, Ellen carrying her long silk-lined train over her arm, revealing a glimpse of embroidered white stockings and white satin shoes. The brilliants on her shoe-buckles glittered as they came into the circle of light near the door. Martin waved his hand to us, and Ellen stared. "Quaint, isn't she, in that muslin? The boy is handsome enough. Looks a little like his father, I think." Her brittle laugh crossed our ears, as she drew Martin over to the gay crowd about her father.

"Come on, make up a set with us," said Michel at my side. Louise was on his arm, looking as gay and lively as her tall son.

"Devil's Dream!" called out the postmaster, and sets of six couples formed all over the room, each in two lines with women facing men. When the scrambling for places was over, Paul and I found ourselves at the head of one set, with Michel and Louise next. As the lively music started, we had to begin the dance, as the others beat time. Down the outside of the set, joining hands, up the center and back, right and left with Michel and Louise. I followed the caller's directions without taking thought of them.

As we reached the foot of the set, Michel and Louise in their turn began to lead, while Paul and I rested as the foremost gander in a flight drops to the rear after his time is up, to rest from breasting the wind ahead.

331

Seeing Paul dancing, I realized for the first time that to the bodily strength and endurance of my grandfather was added the easy grace of Pierre.

At the end of the dance, one of the soldiers, an Irish private, approached me, and while I took my place with him for the next quadrille, Paul went over to the group around Mr. Stuart. Pierre had moved over to the major's circle, still followed by the wistful eyes of Miss Harper.

"First couple lead up to the right,
Make a star with a right-hand cross,
Ladies bow, gents know how,
Hold your holds and get there now;
Circle four,
Right and left through and lead to the next."

Weaving in and out of the easy steps opposite the soldier, I found time to watch Rosanne in the nearest set. Her full lips parted as she danced and chatted. Jacques, too, was dancing hilariously with sinuous and graceful movements. Rosanne's hair curled around her face in moist tendrils, and her long dark lashes swept her cheek.

As the fiddlers brought the dance to a triumphal finish with a long upstroke of the bow, then a dramatic sweep down and away from the strings, Rosanne finished in an elaborate pirouette, not part of the dance, but showing her grace to advantage. She fell back at the end of it into the arms of two buckskinned figures who brought her up laughing, and she was immediately surrounded by a circle of men begging for the next dance.

"Excuse me, I cannot dance no more," she protested breathlessly, at the same time looking them over to pick out her next partner.

The Irish boy took me to Grand'mère's side. Paul, sitting close to Mr. Stuart, looked a question at me

332

when the next dance began. "I'll rest this time," I said.
Paul nodded, and turned back to Mr. Stuart.

"Take your lady by the wrist," shouted the caller,
"Around next lady with a grapevine twist,
Back to the center with a whoa-haw-gee,
And around the gent whom you did not see—"

"When will the new nets be here?" I heard Paul ask.
"I don't just know," said Mr. Stuart. "Hope they'll
be in time for the fall season. We got a batch of orders
in today. Brewster at Detroit wants a hundred barrels
of siscowet." Mr. Stuart chuckled. "Brewster bet me a
barrel of onions that first shipment of fish was too big
to sell. This letter says he's sendin' me enough onions
on the *Fur Trader* to spoil my kissin' for the whole
winter. He wants to know if he hadn't better put up
a new warehouse at Detroit to handle fish alone.—And
say, Buffalo wants whitefish, and New York will take
six hundred barrels if we can get 'em. But you drop
in tomorrow and gather up the orders. I'm goin' over
there for a minute."

Mr. Stuart jerked his head toward Pierre and the
major, who were talking with a man in a green suit
with a narrow red stripe in it. The stranger's face had
a shadow upon it.

"Who is that man, Paul?" I asked, as he slid over
to the vacant seat beside me.

"I don't know his name. He's been around town
two or three days. A land agent of some kind."

I watched the man in the green suit, as Paul and I
took our places for the next dance.

"It sounds like a good investment," I heard the major say above the music and the sound of feet. "Of
course I shall have a large grant of land from the government when I retire, but I am going into this Wis-
consin deal to turn over my money. If it can be bought

333

up at the price you mention, a tidy sum can be made by selling at regular prices. I've heard it's no trouble at all to get three dollars an acre from settlers now."

"That's right," said the man in green. "If I can just get enough capital to take up the option I have on those lands along the Fox River, there's fortunes to be made in it."

Mr. Stuart's voice came in. "I think I'll put in what I can spare when our inventory is taken and profits figured up. Mr. Astor has it arranged now so I get a percentage and I don't know how much I'm going to have until the last raccoon is counted, shipped, and sold. Now you, Pierre, you get your salary regularly—there's no need for you to delay."

Pierre agreed. "I could use some extra money. There are some rare volumes I should like to own, and Mother would like to make a trip to France before she dies."

"I'm leaving in the morning on the *Henry Clay*," said the man in green. "Any time before sailing you can find me at Mrs. Ruggs's and we'll sign the papers."

As I think now of the scraps of talk I heard that night, remembering that roomful of people and the shouting and pounding of feet that shook the warehouse, I think it a picture of how life pressed us on every side in Mackinac's summers. Hundreds of people in such a small space between cliff and water, we were continually being shaken against one another by ceaseless motion. Wind and the sound of moving water always in our ears added to the effect of movement from which we could not escape.

> *"All join hands and forward and back,*
> *Swing on the corner,*
> *Swing partners all,*
> *Swing corner lady and promenade the hall,"*

334

ended the postmaster, and Paul and I went back to Grand'mère.

A few feet away from us a voyageur in a red flannel shirt and green woolen sash snatched his red cap from his head and waved it at Baptiste. "You play that fiddle so, we jump around until we go crazy. How long can your arm keep it up tonight?"

"As long as you can stay on your feet," Baptiste called back.

Suddenly I saw Big Charlie crossing the floor, moving through the surging crowd like a heavy mackinaw boat through light foam. He pushed aside the voyageur that had shouted at Baptiste. "Excuse me."

"*Prenez garde* behin'," shouted the voyageur, bringing up his fists. "Oh—" He lowered them. "Go ahead, Charlie."

I saw that Charlie was making his way toward Jacques and Rosanne, and then my view of him was cut off by Pierre and Mr. Stuart strolling past. "I think five hundred dollars would be a good amount to start on," said Mr. Stuart. "That should easily return a thousand."

"I shall put in all I can get together when I am paid," said Pierre, "if you'll carry me on the books for supplies until next salary payment, or until the money comes back from the land sale."

"That's all right. Get everything you need at the store and pay me when you can. Just so it's before inventory time next year."

"How about this dance, Oneta?" Michel stood before me, and as I got up I heard one of the voyageurs say,

"This is your tune, Jacques. Take a fiddle and show these lard-eaters how you play it for us in the winter camp."

Jacques grinned and shook his head, but, urged, he at last took the fiddle from Armand's hands and tucked

335

it under his chin. He lifted the bow and began the strains of "The Girl I Left Behind Me."

"First couple lead up to the right," sang the postmaster,
"Balance there so kindly,
Pass right through and balance two,
And swing with the girl behind you.
Take that lady and balance to the next,
Balance there so kindly,
Pass right through and balance two,
And swing with the girl behind you."

Somehow as Jacques began to play, there was Charlie with Rosanne in the same set with Michel and me. I saw Jacques frowning, and when the dance ended with an "Allemande left and a grand right and left," he gave back the fiddle quickly. Making no acknowledgment of the applause, he hurried over to our set and pulled Rosanne to one side. "The next one is mine," he said.

Michel left me with Grand'mère. As the scrambling for places for the next dance began, I was thinking how different this dancing was from that I had known in the early days, remembering how Mother had tried to describe the ball when she had danced with Pierre. My thoughts were interrupted by Grand'mère.

"What's the matter with you?" she hissed, tugging at my sleeve.

I looked up. Martin stood before me, smiling.

"I believe the young lady was dreaming," he said. "Are you too tired for the next dance with me?"

"Oh, no!" I arose. He leaned over Grand'mère and whispered some compliment in her ear. Beaming, she tapped her lace fan against his cheek in mock reproof. He laughed, and tucked my hand in his arm, letting his fingers rest on mine while he searched the room with his eyes. Finding a vacant place in a set, he led me to it. Baptiste poised his bow to begin, and just beyond Martin's shoulder I saw Big Charlie stand up slowly and stride across to Rosanne. "I think this dance, she is the one you promised me."

"You make a mistake," said Jacques, with exaggerated politeness. "This one is also mine."

"The lady will have it with me," retorted Charlie, no less politely.

Jacques's compact form grew taut. "You keep away from my girl. You get a girl of your own—"

"Oh, be still, Jacques," said Rosanne. "I can dance with Charlie once, can't I?"

"You do as I tell you," said Jacques grimly, "or I'll take you home."

"*Moi*, I would not go. You cannot make me go home."

Jacques pulled up his shirt sleeves and thumped his arm. "You see that muscle? All day I carry a pack of one hundred pounds without tiring. If you do not behave I sling you like a pack on my back and carry you out the door, before all the people."

Rosanne wilted. She never minded a scene, but she could not stand being made ridiculous in one. "So sorry, M'sieu Charlie," she murmured, taking Jacques's arm. They stood waiting for a chance to get into the dance, as the caller swung into another change,

"My father and mother were Irish . . ."

Above his voice I heard Jacques complaining, "Rosanne, you have driven me crazy this whole summer, running after men. I am glad when most of the brigades go out tomorrow. Maybe in the two weeks before Tahquamenon River brigade goes out, I can have some peace." He pulled her into a set as the caller sang,

"My father and mother were Irish,
My father and mother were Irish,
My father and mother were Irish,
And I am Irish, too."

337

Charlie stood looking on, and as Jacques came near him in a "swing-your-partner," I heard him interrupt Jacques's scolding.

"Do you not know," he asked slowly, "that you too go out tomorrow?"

"What?" Jacques wheeled around. "Do we then go out early—"

Charlie shook his head. "You are no longer in my brigade. You have been put in another one."

"What is that?" asked Jacques, as one who is not sure he has heard rightly.

"You have been changed to another outfit. Me, I know no more," shrugged Charlie.

"Rosanne, you—wait here," stammered Jacques. "I must see Mr. Stuart." There was worry in every line of his body as he hurried across the floor, pushing his way between the sets. Annoyed exclamations marked his progress.

Charlie slipped into place beside Rosanne. "Now, we can have our dance."

"The next will be a polka," shouted the postmaster. "Get your partners for a polka."

Martin smiled down at me. "Shall we have this one, too?" I nodded.

Martin's lightness in dancing made the two of us seem like two bits of milkweed down that, having met, hold each other with dainty touch, and fly together wherever the wind wills to send them. I felt above the earth, no longer of it, but far afloat, tossed by the four winds, caring not whether I ever came to rest again.

Then there came a sudden jolt. Jacques, coming back, had plunged right through our set.

"I was not put in the Lake of the Woods," he was shouting, but his relief was mixed. "But I'm to be in Jean Coutreau's Lake Superior brigade. It is true, I must go out tomorrow."

338

At once he stopped, and as Martin and I finished the last quick steps of the polka, I saw what Jacques was staring at. Charlie was bending his head over Rosanne's curly one, and she suddenly kissed him on the ear. Smiling broadly, Charlie whispered to her. "As soon as Jacques's boat is gone," she said.

Jacques heard her, and his face twisted with fury. His hand went to the knife at his side. I drew in my breath, and Martin followed the direction of my eyes. He stepped quickly to Jacques's side, and as the knife flashed, upraised in the candlelight, he caught Jacques by the arm.

"No. You're not out in the wilderness, you know. Put your knife back." Martin spoke as calmly as if he were suggesting that Jacques's legging had come untied, or that his kerchief were unknotted, but his grip on Jacques's arm was firm.

Jacques wavered. "But he try to take my girl!"

"It won't help any for you to be in the garrison jail, will it?" asked Martin quietly.

Jacques looked at Charlie again, his face smoldering in hatred. But he slid his knife back in its sheath, and suddenly breaking loose from Martin, he ran out through the open door, and disappeared in the darkness.

Martin came back to me, smiling. "He'll cool off out there, and be back in a minute, gay as ever." I knew he was right.

Martin and I danced once more that evening. It was the lancers after supper. "Thank you," said Martin at the end of it. "This time we weren't interrupted by melodrama." I smiled up at him, wondering if he had shared any of my feeling of two bits of down riding the wind. He tucked my fingers over his arm, as he took me back to Paul. He went to join Ellen, and Paul drew me into a set forming for the last dance.

Muted fiddles began the jig of the hanged, and I must have gone through the proper steps, but I remember nothing about it, except that at last, with the lilting *"Bon soir, mes amis, et au revoir,"* Baptiste made known that the ball was over.

Eight

❧ On the way home from the dance, Paul told me that he and Baptiste were going to take out the mackinaw boat the next day, starting north, to be gone for perhaps a month, charting the fishing grounds and employing all the idle men they could find in near-by settlements to work for them in the fall fishing season. The next morning when I arose for my early walk to bathe and greet the sun at the arched rock, Paul was already gone.

Knowing that at breakfast Pierre would be angry, finding himself balked in his resolution to put Paul into the fur warehouse that very day, I loitered on the way home, putting as far off as I could the scene that would destroy the peace and renewal I had found in the quiet waters below the great stone arch. Instead of descending the cliff near Grand'mère's house, I went through the grounds of the fort just as reveille was sounded, and walked down the incline and through the awakening village to the beach.

Two brigades lay there in readiness to leave, the *canots du nord* waiting so close together that there were little jars and grindings as they touched. These were northern brigades, with routes of long portages, beginning with the long one around the half-mile long, swirling rapids of the St. Mary's, wild-flowing, though named for Mother Mary, the mild one.

Seeing by a wooden clock in the window of a sutler's shop that I might still linger for a few moments, I sat down on an overturned canoe to await the departure of the boats, the event that always brought closer to us than even the flight of the birds, the real sadness of autumn. A foretaste of loneliness came then, as, seeing the voyageurs go, we wondered how many of the ones who had been so merry would come back alive after the winter dangers.

One brigade had finished loading, and the boats waited, twelve in that brigade, the men hurrying back on late-thought-of errands. The second brigade was just beginning to load. Each voyageur had slipped into the chapel with his little offering to St. Anne before carrying his pack down to the beach, where he worked rapidly, eagerly, but without the shouts and laughter that went with the unloading of furs in the spring. Long months of work were ahead now, a serious matter.

At once I saw Jacques among the others. Lowering his pack to the ground, he stopped to speak to a voyageur leaning against a pile of wood stacked on the beach for the use of steamers.

"There you are, Jean," he said. "I was told to ask you whether you could play with Armand at a little dance at the postmaster's tonight. Baptiste is gone on a fishing trip, and I am going out—" His voice trailed off as he looked at the first brigade, awaiting the command of the leader to push off.

Jacques's shoulders gradually straightened, as if drawn backward by arms flexing themselves to the dip of a paddle. He swayed slightly, as if already caught in the rhythm of life on lake and river, that was not the rhythm of Mackinac dance-halls. His careless air left him, and he turned slightly so I could see his eyes, could watch them fill with a far-away look as he saw the packages being loaded. His experienced eyes took in the packing away of every man's baggage in the bottom, and the boxes of goods for the trading. Critically he observed the arrrangement of the tarpaulin, as large as a house, meant to cover the goods in case of a storm, so that good bearskins need not be used for that.

Jacques had forgotten the dance, forgotten all ties with Mackinac. His eyes looked to distant woods, as all along the shore, the first brigade pushed off, and the boats of the second, Jacques's own, moved restlessly on the lapping waves, seeming to tug at their moorings to follow the others. He smiled a little, as if he were thinking of the race that would take place at St. Mary's portage, each brigade trying for the honor of being first across and in the water again.

As the first canoes took the lead toward the east, soon to swing around the point of Robertson's Folly to the north, the boat song began, and the voices were joined by a hundred voices from the shores of Mackinac, spreading back from the men on the shore to others who joined in where they stood on the streets and in the doors of shops. The tones swelled until the echoes of "Nous Hivernons" sounded from the mainland, Round Island, and far Bois Blanc.

So occupied was Jacques that he didn't even see Rosanne coming along the beach road with a basket on her arm, her dress of black and white check with red collar and cuffs reflecting the change in Baptiste's earnings, being a finer one than she had ever worn before. She smiled at Jean, and spoke softly to Jacques, holding out the basket. She had brought something for him. He, lifting up his voice in song, did not hear her. She stood smiling and dimpling, waiting for him to turn. Then, ignored, she grew serious, and suddenly piqued, stamped her foot and took a few steps away. She turned then and waited, but when the departing brigade was out of sight, Jacques rushed down the beach and began stowing away his own pack, talking to the other men.

Not understanding that something else was so strong in his eyes he did not see her, Rosanne was thoroughly angry. She whirled about and started on a brisk run to the village. As she passed a crowd of voyageurs idly watching the loading, I saw Big Charlie separate himself from them and join her. He took her basket, and they walked on toward the company store, with his tall form bent over hers.

Nine

✤ While Paul and Baptiste were away, the last of the canoe-building moon passed, and half of the moon of fading leaves. When I left the mission one late afternoon, I knew the first of the autumn storms was almost upon us. The air was quiet in the calm of preparation, as if the four winds had withdrawn for a council in the nest of the thunderbird. Every leaf on the bushes growing rank and tall in the dooryards lay inert. No speck of dust was being raised on the path, and washings hung limp and tired on backyard lines. With easel before him, Mr. Heydenbruk was sitting on the beach, painting and looking toward the western point, behind which the sun was setting in thick murky light. The island rested in the silence that came down upon it when the last of the boats had gone, and on the beach only refuse and charred remains of burnt-out fires were reminders of the departed row of lodges. The echoes from island to island were no longer awakened by ax strokes of choppers getting wood on Bois Blanc to prepare the lyed corn and tallow for winter rations. No shouts were borne on the air, no sounds of drum or fiddle, no scraps of song. Those who had made Mackinac lively were now singing on distant waters or beside far-scattered campfires.

The street was empty. The feet that had hurried over it during the day were at that moment under supper tables all over the village. Sharply on the quiet air came from the open doors an occasional voice and the clink of knives and forks on earthenware. There was a tired listlessness about the street before the American Fur Company, as if peace were now its due, and it resented even my hurrying feet. The porch of the company store was deserted, and inside, one Dutch clerk was reading on a high stool.

"Grand'mère wants a pound of bacon and four yards of brown cambric," I told him. He turned his book over on the counter and dropped slowly to his feet. I waited near the shelves of trading goods—clothing, blankets, knives, tobacco, firearms, powder and shot, all marked as to how many beavers they cost. The store was full of odors—tobacco, rum, chocolate, spices, and cheese, the smell of new blankets, of coffee packed around loaf sugar in a freshly opened barrel. And sometimes all these odors were gone and there was only one, a tart whiff from a vinegar barrel in the corner.

The clerk wrapped up the bacon and cambric, and entered the amount in the petty book. "You're late tonight," he drawled. "I saw Mr. Debans go home already."

I took the packages. "Thank you."

Out on the street again, I looked back toward the east and saw a small cloud, often the first sign of a sudden blow. Then a cool breeze struck my face and hurried on to stir the quiet trees behind me into excited rustling. The wind came, and stones and gravel arose from the path. The sky grew dark as if the thunderbird spread his wings before the face of the sun. In a few minutes the wind was howling through the picket fences and a gale was blowing off the straits, almost hiding the village in dust stirred up from the paths. The wind tossed

344

it about and raced up the cliff to assault the very block-houses. Eyes half-closed, I began to run, putting the package of bacon under my jacket to keep out the dirt.

At home, I found it took all my strength to close the door. Then the rain began to fall. And this was no gentle spring rain, settling in the hearts of blossoms like tears of delight in the eyes of a child. This rain was fierce and resentful, as if it were tormented itself and wanted to hurt someone.

Pierre, reading in a purple silk lounging coat, shivered in the gust of wind that blew through the room. He removed his pipe from his mouth. "Blowing a little, is it?"

"Yes." I straightened my braids. "The one who takes off tree-tops is riding the wind tonight."

"You were so late I didn't wait for you," remarked Pierre.

"That's all right." I paused to look at the book he was reading.

He held it up. "This came in the last shipment. One of the chronicles of Froissart. I'll read you some of it after supper." Pierre fondled the soft leather cover, and rubbed a slender finger over the design pressed in it. "Nicely bound—the cover worthy of the contents."

"That you, child?" called Grand'mère from the back kitchen.

"Yes, at last." I put down the brown cambric on her sewing basket. The door to Paul's room was open, show-ing the dresser in the smooth order it had been in so long, empty except for the two silver-backed brushes that had been a gift from Pierre and Grand'mère on the previous Noël.

"Paul didn't get back today?" I asked, realizing that I had said the same thing every day for the past week.

"No," said Grand'mère fretfully. "I wish he'd come home."

Pierre's face took on an irritated frown. "He's got to give it up," he said crossly. "Worrying his grandmother like this—"

I said nothing, for I knew that his remark concealed his real feeling. The frown on his face was there because Paul was refusing to obey him, was engaging in a kind of work revolting to his every instinct—and was making money by it.

I went out in the kitchen, and laid down the bacon on the little table where Grand'mère was scraping plump red carrots with her favorite paring knife, an old one worn almost through to the back. The kitchen was full of the smell of gingerbread. Grand'mère wiped her hands on her big apron, and handed me a well-buttered slice. "I'd give a lot to know Paul is in out of this storm somewhere," she said.

Uneasiness grew in me, as I listened to the wind and beating rain.

"What made you so late?" asked Grand'mère, taking up her knife again.

"One of the children was ill, and Mrs. Fisher asked me to stop and see her after classes were over. She is a grandchild of Ajawin—a woman I used to know—"

"The way they pile work on you in that place!" Grand'mère's hands flew among the carrots, working with the quick grace of little wrens.

An iron skillet was ready for the fire, filled with trout dipped in cornmeal. I took it up and went out to the big fire in the living room. Grand'mère came bustling after me with a kettle of vegetables. She put it on a crane and swung it over the fire. Then she stopped and listened to the storm.

"*Ma foi*," she sighed, and Pierre stirred restlessly.

Another gust of wind tore around the house, and there was a renewed attack of rain on the streaming panes.

"The devil is making his grand tour," said Grand'mère.

346

It was the sudden storm dreaded by fishermen, for it destroyed their nets and overturned their boats.

We were silent at table, while the storm beat at the house without mercy. When supper was over, Pierre took up his book and began to read aloud,

"Thus they set forth as they were ordained, and they that went by sea took all the ships that they found in their ways: and so long they went forth . . . that they came to a good port and to a good town called Barfleur, the which incontinent was won, for they within gave up for fear of death. Howbeit for all that the town was robbed . . . there were found so much riches that the boys and villains of the host set nothing by good furred gowns—"

The storm lessened, and then came back more fierce than ever. Hanging up the last copper pan by the fireplace, I felt an urgent thought come over me, and I accepted it as I accepted the lightning flashing through the sky, both being beyond my understanding. At once I turned to the others. "I must go down to Marthe's," I said.

"In this storm?" exclaimed Grand'mère. "You can't go out in this."

"Surely not now—" began Pierre.

But I was already in Paul's room, pulling his old oilskin coat from the nail in the corner. "I won't get very wet in this. I must see if there is any word from Paul."

Outside, the streets and houses looked as if they cowered under the lash of the storm, and the waves on the straits foamed high and broke far up the shore, lapping at overturned canoes. Rain came down so hard that it rebounded from the earth, while the thunder shouted at the forest, and the lightning spread sheets of flame again and again across the sky. A blinding flash came

347

once, as the manitou with flaming arm splintered another branch from the pine on the heights.

The wind fairly drove me around the corner of Marthe's cabin, and someone appeared out of the storm and stood beside me. "Baptiste! You are back?" I gasped to the rain-drenched figure.

Without speaking, he took me by the arm and pulled me through the door, where we both stood dripping pools of water on the bare floor. Marthe arose from bending over someone on the bed, someone lying very still. "Paul!" I sobbed.

Baptiste held me back from the bed. "*Eh bien.* Don't get him all wet again from your oilskins. I just brought him in and Marthe's got him all dry and warm."

I slipped out of the oilskin coat, and knelt beside the figure covered with a heap of blankets. "Paul! What is it?"

"He can't hear you just now—but don't you get excited," soothed Baptiste. "He's just had a little accident, and right now, he's fainted from the pain. Marthe'll fix him up."

"We must get a doctor," I said, careless of the hurt look that went over Marthe's face. "What happened?"

"It was on the way home," began Baptiste in a low, embarrassed tone. "We got all through with our business—got somebody all signed up to fish for us in every likely spot, and then set out for home. Stopped over on the north mainland for the night, and this mornin' as we was gettin' ready to come home, we sighted a beetree. Well, we started to cut it down. I don't know just what happened, it was all over so quick." Baptiste took off his sodden cap, wrung it out over the washbasin, and hung it on the antlers. "Somehow just as the tree was about to fall, stupid-like I caught my moccasin in a root, and bein' awkward anyway—my lame foot, it was—I didn't get away. Paul made a dive for the root with the ax, and cut me loose. But he didn't get out

348

from under the tree in time. It caught him right across the leg. Pretty smashed, I'm afraid."

"Oh!" I put my arms around Paul. He was limp, and his face was as white and cold as beach pebbles in the freezing moon.

"I got him back to the boat, and started home," Baptiste went on. "*Tu vois*, it was about three miles by land to a settlement. I thought I might as well bring him home. If I'd been a little farther from shore when the storm come up, I'd never have made it." Still the true voyageur, he would rather risk his life in any fashion on the water than make a trip by land.

"We must send for the doctor," I said, this time gently, and Marthe stood silent, as if admitting that her powers of healing did not reach so far as crushed and broken limbs. She took up Paul's moccasins from the floor at the foot of the bed, and set them to dry near the hearth.

"The bone-setter at the fort is a good fellow," said Baptiste. "I'll go right along and get him."

"Don't tell Grand'mère or Pierre yet," I said, "until we know how bad it is."

Paul was so still and white I was afraid his heart might give up and accept the rest that is death. I knelt still holding him, dreading to feel stiffness, for that would mean life's warmth had gone back to the sun. While I waited, the storm quieted to a gentle rain. The winds from Lake Superior had blown themselves out, and now Lake Huron was sending them back tamed and subdued to mere breezes.

Baptiste came, bringing Martin. Slipping out of his oilskins, Martin talked cheerfully, saying that he had just gotten back to his room when Baptiste came, that he had been caught in the storm himself, on the highest point of the island, among the ruins of the old British fort. "I got three new plants today for my collection.

I'll soon have a specimen of everything that grows on the island."

He stepped to Paul's side, and gently loosened my arms from around him, leading me over to a chair by the hearth. "You just sit here a minute, and we'll see about this brother of yours."

He hung his blue uniform coat on a chair, rolled his white shirt sleeves to the elbows, and folded back the blanket from the motionless figure. He looked down at Paul's leg in silence for a moment before his hands began to work, and I knew the injury was no ordinary one. I could see a leg twisted out of its own shape, with blood upon it, and a splinter of bone coming through the skin. Baptiste's voice came over to me. "Marthe and me tried to be careful takin' off his clothes. But the trip home didn't help him none, I guess. The old straits acted like a bear rockin' a baby's cradle, and he got thrown around some."

"I'll work on his leg while he's still unconscious," said Martin quietly. He worked quickly, every movement of his hands carrying a task forward with no indecision or pauses. His eyes were fixed on his work, his lips quiet as if the quick smile had been turned inward and made to help him there. As I watched him, the coldness that had seized me went away, and warmth filled the room again, though the fire burned no more brightly. I realized after a time that Martin had led me to the same barrel chair in which I had waited for Paul to be born. Once again I sat looking into the fire, waiting, but now Marthe was opposite me, her knitting in her lap. The ball fell and rolled along the hearth close to the fire, but she paid no attention. Baptiste, calm beside Martin, responded to his murmurs by handing him what he asked for from the kit on the pine table. Martin seemed at home in Marthe's cabin, as much as among his own kind, as a stream fits its bed and yet when a little of it is lifted, fits a birchbark cup as well.

350

My eyes wandered from Paul's white face and began to notice signs of Baptiste's new prosperity—a black japanned pitcher and bowl on the wash-bench, with orange poppies on their fat sides, the five-point instead of three-point blankets on the bed, the new calico of Marthe's dress, a gilt-bordered mirror hanging from a nail near the row of Rosanne's dresses, even the number of those gay frocks being greater than in the old days.

At such moments time has little meaning. As I look back I have no idea whether it was ten minutes or an hour later that the leg was set and lay in a cocoon of bandages. Then Martin began to rub Paul's other limbs. Minutes passed, and the young doctor kept steadily at it as if he had no doubt of success. When I was almost despairing, the color came back into Paul's cheeks, and his eyes opened.

Marthe rose and dipped a cup of pungent brew from a steaming kettle and went to stand beside the bed with it, waiting passive beside Martin until he saw it, in her gesture a challenge, a test of her own for the young man.

Taking in the earthy fragrance of the steaming cup, Martin turned his head and saw her. Without comment, he put his arms beneath Paul's shoulders, lifting him and helping Marthe guide the liquid to his lips. When Paul had taken half of it, Marthe herself withdrew the cup, setting it on the crowded mantel. Sitting again by the fire, her plain face relaxed into contentment.

Paul's eyes searched the room, resting on Baptiste, Marthe, and me. He tried to move, but a look of pain crossed his face, and his eyes closed again.

Martin pulled up the blankets over him, and came over to the fireside, near me. I sat forward in my chair, waiting.

"Not a whimper from him," said Martin, and pride rose in me. "It was a bad break," he went on. "But there's no reason he won't get over it in time. He'll just have to stay in bed for a long while."

The smile was back in Martin's lips and in his eyes, and I felt it a part of the healing he gave Paul, as a song goes with distilled herbs in Marthe's healing. We all felt the relief in the air. I became less rigid, as if some of the healing had spread out to me. Baptiste, tired, leaned against the chimney. Marthe's face was peaceful, and somehow we all felt drawn together.

"Can we take him home?" I asked.

"Paul should stay here," said Marthe. "I will take care of him."

Without appearing to, Martin had been looking around at the crowded disorder of the room. "I don't know what Madame Debans will say if we don't bring her boy home so she can take care of him," he smiled. "It might be better if we made a stretcher and took him."

"We'll be glad to keep him here," said Baptiste, "but I'll get the postmaster's cart if you think you want to move him."

Martin looked at me, and I nodded. He drew on his coat, and began folding up his kit. "Yes, we'll take him home. I can make his leg comfortable enough so no harm will be done. He'll lie relaxed."

The rain had stopped, and a few stars were in the sky by the time Baptiste brought the little handcart to the door. "The postmaster reminded me this was the property of the United States Government when he let me take it," he grinned. "I promised to treat it with respect —for its age."

Marthe put new moccasins on Paul's feet, and Martin took a new blanket from her hands and wrapped it about Paul and lifted him up, his straight uniformed back bending but little under the weight. Strangely to my mind came the memory of Marthe lifting the slight body of my mother from above the steaming kettle.

And to take Paul home, Martin was using the cart that already held so many memories for me. On that cart Pierre's goods had come to our cabin when he and Mother were married, and it had brought Grand'mère's bags and boxes when she had come to join Pierre. It had carried my mother's body up to the graveyard on the heights.

Grand'mère was in the door, peering out into the darkness, Pierre looking over her shoulder, as we came up.

"*Mon Dieu,* is he dead?" she shrieked.

Martin smiled at her. "He needs a warm bed and something hot to drink," he said.

Able to take hold of something to be done, Grand'-mère's threatened hysterics were gone. By the time I was in the house she had dragged the blankets from Paul's bed and was warming them by the fire. At sight of me, she started giving orders. "Get some more hot water in the kettle. What happened to him? Put some fresh cases on those pillows if they're warmed enough, will you?"

Martin carried Paul into the house and laid him on the bed. Paul opened his eyes and looked around the room. "You're all right, fellow. You're home," said Martin.

Paul's eyes went from one to another, until they rested on me. With a look of content, twisted by a moment of pain, he closed them again.

"What happened?" asked Pierre.

Baptiste told him the story of the tree falling. "And now, if you don't need me," he said at the end of it, "I'll be gettin' along. The postmaster's probably already frettin' about his cart."

I followed him to the door. "Thank you, Baptiste."

"I didn't do anything. If it hadn't been for my clumsiness, the whole thing wouldn't have happened."

He started down the path, and then came back. "Now, don't let Paul fret none. Armand and me'll look after the nets." He scratched his head. "Seems funny to be so danged busy. *Eh bien*, I was goin' to tell you—the morning Paul and me left on this trip, Marthe looked up at me as we was eatin' our pork and potatoes and asked me suddenly if I still wanted to know where that copper was found. I told her, hell no! I ain't got time now to go huntin' it up."

Standing in the doorway after he had gone, I saw that the pines were holding themselves in quiet triumph against the stars.

The first week after that was an anxious one. Besides his broken leg, Paul came down with the ague, and I stayed away from the mission school to take care of him. At times he opened his eyes and smiled, relapsing again into a restless sleep. He often whispered as if he had something on his mind, but we could make out no words.

Grand'mère kept a pan of sliced onions on the sick-room floor to take up the disease out of the air so none of the rest of us would get it. Once a day she purified the house by sprinkling finely ground coffee on a hot shovel and carrying it through the rooms. Martin came in every day to renew our supply of ague bitters, and dress Paul's leg, for there were cuts as well as broken bones. Paul seemed more content under Martin's hands, and I found myself moving often close to the young doctor as if I would keep him there.

"How long will it be before Paul can get out?" I asked Martin once as he finished an early morning visit. Grand'mère and Pierre were still at breakfast in the next room, and I heard a pause in the sounds of their eating as they listened to Martin's answer.

"It's hard to tell right now," he began.

354

Paul turned his head weakly. "Tell us, I want to know exactly."

Martin looked at him searchingly. "It will be a good three months before you can stand much on that leg," he said quietly. "How long after that before you can get around actively, is something I can't tell you right now."

Paul's face did not change expression. "Thanks," he said, and turned his face to the wall.

"Oneta!" called Grand'mère. I stepped to the doorway. "This is Monday morning. Don't you think you ought to go back to the mission? I can manage now."

I turned back to the bed. "Would you rather have me stay with you, Paul?"

He turned his eyes to me, and smiled faintly. "No. You've been kept in long enough. You go back—"

"Yes," said Martin cheerfully. "I think you're right. You won't need much attention during the day, and your sister can sit with you evenings. You can sleep— get caught up on some rest."

Paul smiled again, and turned his face away. Martin followed me into the living room, where Pierre was just drawing on his coat.

"Well," said Martin, "your son is coming along nicely. It's just a matter of time, now."

"Entirely unnecessary, all of this," said Pierre. "It's his own fault."

Martin was startled by the bitterness in Pierre's tone. "Oh, I wouldn't say that, sir. Accidents happen, you know."

"Paul's wouldn't have happened if he had been where he was supposed to be. I had forbidden him to go on with this fishing business, and he went out once more to defy me. If he hadn't, all this sickness with its hard work for his sister and grandmother wouldn't have happened."

"Oh, hush, Pierre," said Grand'mère.

Pierre went on over her words. "But perhaps it's a good thing. This will put an end to his fishing, and it may be, lying here in bed for a little while, he'll come to his senses."

"Here," said Grand'mère, handing him his beaver hat. "Take this and go on to work."

Pierre looked at her for a moment, as if he would say something more. But the expression on her face stopped him. He took his hat and turned to Martin. "Going my way, Doctor?"

"No," said Martin. "I'm going on down to the fishing village. I'm taking some lessons down there."

"Lessons?" I asked.

"Yes, from your friend Marthe. She's teaching me something about herbs."

"Well, good-by then," said Pierre, as he went out the door.

As soon as his footsteps had died away, and Martin was gathering up the rolls of bandage and putting them back in his bag, Paul's voice came weakly out of the sickroom. "Dr. Reynolds."

"Yes?" said Martin, stepping to the doorway.

"Tell Baptiste I want to see him, will you?"

"Of course."

"He's been asking about you every day," I said. "But Dr. Reynolds thought you shouldn't have company."

"It's all right now, though, boy," said Martin. "You just keep that leg as quiet as you can. I'll tell Baptiste."

"Now, don't you fret, Paul." Baptiste's voice came out where I sat alone by the fire darning socks, and feeling the relief of being within reach of Paul again, after my first day away from him at the mission school. Pierre and Grand'mère had been invited for supper at the Stuarts', and Paul and I had had our soup and bread at his bedside. Then Baptiste had come, and I had gone out

356

by the fire, putting my feet up to it, grateful for its warmth in the chill fall air.

"But all our plans," said Paul wearily. "Just when we got everything ready to give fishing and shipping a real trial."

"Well," drawled Baptiste, "no reason why we shouldn't go right on with it, is there?"

I could hear Paul turn over quickly, and then groan. "You see, I can't even move. How can I do anything to help?"

"Well, now, Armand and me can look after the fishing end, but we ain't neither of us good with figures." Baptiste hitched his chair closer to the bed. "You do the book-work and keep track of the sailing times of the schooners. Armand and me'll have to be away lookin' after the nets. Your sister can carry messages for you, and help keep everything goin'. Marthe'll hire some Indians to help with the saltin' and packin', and see that they load the barrels on the schooners."

Their voices went on, Paul's objections growing weaker and his enthusiasm rising as the plans grew complete. ". . . stations at Grand Portage, Grand Marais, L'Anse, Whitefish Point . . . the north shore . . . give each man nine men under him and two coopers . . . let him furnish Indians with salt, nets, and barrels, and pay them three dollars a barrel . . . in the winter let them cut wood for barrels and hook poles . . . Indian women to dress and pack fish. . . ." The words fitted in smoothly like touches on a fine beaded pattern. Life came back in Paul's voice for the first time, and at the end he laughed with Baptiste over one of the stories of his trapping days.

But as Baptiste got up to leave, Paul's tone grew serious again, and doubt crept into it. "It sounds good. The fall fishing plans, I mean. But I'm really not doing anything to help. You'd better just leave me out and go on with it."

357

"*Sacré bleu*, no," said Baptiste mildly, drawing on his dark blanket coat. "You started all this in the first place. And the book-work ain't to be sneezed at, you'll find. You mustn't think just because you ain't got your hands right on the nets that you ain't important." He took up a red knitted cap. "You can't always tell by the looks of things," he went on. "You watch a crowd of beavers sometime, and you'll see one of 'em lyin' on a log stickin' out of the water, seemin' to be sunning hisself and doin' nothin' while the rest are all workin'. But you make a little noise, and that beaver's tail will come down on the water with a loud slap and every beaver there'll take a dive in the water. And they won't come back to work until he sticks his head out, sees if the danger is gone, and gits up on his log again and slaps the water twice with his tail."

Baptiste paused at the door, his hand on the knob. "You can kinda be our look-out beaver."

Ten

Early in the moon of falling leaves, winter began to threaten the island in earnest. The morning hoar-frost silvered the bright colors of the leaves until the sun melted it away. Daily biting winds chilled us, summoning their best show of strength to blow weaklings from the very face of the rocky island.

Boats no longer set out from the shore, for ice was forming. Baptiste and Armand carried Paul's canoe up from the beach and laid it against the back of the house, covering it with a piece of canvas. Down came the snow upon it, lightly at first. But as soon as it had fallen, the wind shifted to Lake Superior, and came whistling through ice-covered pines in higher tones. The loose snow was gathered up and driven again into a hurricane of white particles, drifting and piling up until the canoe was a long white mound. It was like the burial of summer itself.

Dog teams appeared in the streets, their bells ringing as they dashed through a village sparkling white in the sun. Faint threads of smoke rose from roofs heavily piled with white. In the center of the straits a thin strip of black water rolled and tumbled in defiance of the ice. And then even that break was closed, and the whiteness stretched unbroken to the horizon.

The trout had moved into their spawning grounds near shore late in August, and we saw little of Baptiste in the two moons before the end of the whitefish season in November. When he did come, the talk that drifted out of Paul's room was of orders for gilling, holland, and sturgeon twines for nets, of headlines, wooden floats and lead sinkers, of getting enough salt and barrels, of complaints about a shipment of nets with mesh so large the trout and siscowet could escape, of other seines so weak they broke with the weight of the fish. Mr. Stuart came in once a week and I knew from his words and from papers I carried back and forth between him and Paul at other times that money was coming in from the sales in distant places. Until Paul could be about, Mr. Stuart was keeping it all in the big iron safe at his office, giving enough out to Baptiste and Armand for their shares and to pay their helpers. Already a great number of these men, far scattered through the Superior country, were sending barrels of fish to the Sault, where the *Ramsey Crooks* loaded them and took them to Detroit and the lower lakes, bringing back salt, goods, and provisions for both fishing and fur posts. Mr. Stuart was delighted with such an efficient use of the schooner.

Holding letter paper against a small board in front of him, Paul wrote letters and orders, and his bed was covered with account books until Grand'mère and I could scarcely straighten the blankets. He told me one day

359

after the last of the fish had been shipped that over a thousand barrels had gone out, and that the next year all their men and supplies were in readiness to net and ship from June to the close of November, and that two thousand barrels should go out in that time. Paul himself did not get out of doors until February, when the fishing had stopped except for a few nets strung under the ice, the fish being hauled from them by dog teams. Michel took on an apprentice to help him make barrels, half-barrels, and quarter-barrels for the next season. Paul, having yet to be careful of his leg, spent most of his days in Marthe's cabin, helping to clean the fish that were brought in.

About the time Paul first got out, epidemics of eye disease and cholera struck the mission school together. One child died and another went blind, and the villagers kept their children at home. No one was allowed to go in and out but Martin.

"You'd better go home, too," he said to me on the first day. I was silent for a moment. I saw the worried looks on the faces of the missionaries, and thought of all the sick Indian children. And Paul was well enough to be out again, no longer needing me.

"I'll stay," I said.

"Have you thought of your own safety?" asked Martin. "I can't let you take risks for yourself."

I raised my eyes to his. "I shall not take the disease. I am not afraid." And under his searching glance, I remembered saying that to another doctor long years before.

All lessons were given up, for even the care of the sick was more than we had strength for. Each sunrise found us with more to be done, until we never got rid of aching muscles. The first time Paul limped up to the mission to make sure I was all right, as he did every day through that long winter, I had him bring my moccasins from home. I put them on again for their silence in the sickrooms and for their comfort in the constant going up and down stairs and through the draughty halls. I had never known so much fatigue before. I saw myself at last only as feet to go, and hands to carry heavy trays of food from the kitchen to the sleeping-rooms, and as a voice to coax half-delirious children to take spoonfuls of the broth. The women had the burden of caring for the sick, for Mr. Heydenbruk spent his time bringing in wood and food. Mr. Fisher helped him a little, but most of his time was given to holding funerals that came so often the carpenter's supply of coffins was used up, and he was hard put to it to get lumber to make new ones as they were needed. Daily I heard Mr. Fisher giving numbers. "Thirty-eight males and eighteen females left," his dry voice would say, and a week later it might be "Thirty males, ten females." As I came and went I could hear his voice through the thin walls, sounding like a warning to the living, "Then shall the dust return to the earth as it was and the spirit unto God who gave it."

So tired I was that I often came with a strange surprise upon work I had done, as a traveler lost in the woods makes a circle and coming on his own track again wonders who has passed that way, not knowing the print of his own moccasin. Martin was in the midst of the work, helping everywhere from kitchen to the long rows of beds in the sickrooms. He seemed to be ever appearing beside me, taking a tray from my hands, forcing me to sit down for a moment, while he finished whatever I had started to do.

Whenever I did get a little time to sleep, I always awoke to the realities of a cold room and sick children crying in the next one. Leaping out of bed and into a robe and moccasins, I would take up the burden again.

The winter wore on until April, when the diseases seemed to leave as suddenly as they came. There were no more new cases, the few children left in the school were getting well, and at last came a day that Martin told me to go home for a week or two of rest.

When the breeze came from the mainland below, touching our cheeks with a warmth not even chilled by the ice between, we knew spring was about to come to Mackinac. Leaving the mission on that last day of April, the snowshoe-breaking moon, I felt that soft touch on my cheek, and my step lightened on the path. I took long breaths of the first out-of-door air in weeks, and my mind began taking stock of the time of the year. The first of the birds had come back, their song telling the ice in the straits that it was time for it to go out. Already in the village there must be the usual talk of when it might be expected to go, the oldest inhabitants being asked for the earliest remembered date of breaking up. People were talking of something at that very moment, coming out of shops and houses, seeming a part of an agreed-upon movement, but in my eagerness to get home I took no thought of its meaning until, coming out of the company store, I met Paul. He was wearing a brown leather coat and leggings, a fur cap jauntily on the side of his head.

He waited for me to come up, a quiet pleasure in his face. "Want to come down to the wharf?" he asked.

I turned and followed the direction of his glance. The people leaving the shops and homes were gathering near the log and stone dock. In the far distance a group of dark spots was bobbing up and down on the ice, a man and a dog team. "Oh, the mail!" I said, and turned to walk with Paul. The only signs of illness were a little paleness in his face, a thinner look to his body. I noticed that he had no limp, and, reading my thoughts, he said, "My leg hardly bothers any more. I'll be in fine shape by the spring season."

Clustered around the shore line by the time we reached it were uneven rows of soldiers, shop-keepers, and housewives with shawls about them. Even Pierre was there, standing at one side with Mr. Stuart and the postmaster, while the major was near-by, spyglass in hand. "Yes, it must be the mail," he was saying, and then, with new anxiety, "I wonder if he'll make it."

Mr. Stuart narrowed his eyes to look across the white sheet, and shook his head. "He may have to go back."

A sigh went through the crowd. For the mail not to come would be a great blow. They had looked forward to it since the last, more than a month before. Those with families back east awaited reassurance that all was well with them, and the mail would bring fresh news, so they could leave off going over and over the last, which by that time had been ground fine under the talk.

"He must get across," someone said, and it was as if he had spoken what all had in their hearts.

The major put up his spyglass again. "The ice looks bad. It has been getting honeycombed these last days."

"It goes to pieces quick when the wind changes," said the postmaster.

Far out on the snow and ice, the black dots grew slowly larger. Paul and I walked down to the edge of the wharf, where Baptiste was standing near a group of children sliding on the ice.

"Can't tell nothin' about it," he said. "I remember last spring I went over to Bois Blanc in the morning after wood, with the ice as firm as ever, and by night I couldn't get back with my dogs."

Soft airs were coming over the ice, and it seemed as if the water were stirring beneath. The sled could be seen now, bobbing up and down behind the dogs on the uneven footing, the mail carrier himself running alongside to relieve the tired animals from his weight. Constantly he could be seen putting one hand on the sledge to keep it right side up.

At once there came a low rumble, and then a roaring

as of distant cannon. A gasp went over the crowd, as it turned toward the point of the island where the first crack always came, between Mackinac and Bois Blanc. There it was, the dark stirring water growing wider as we looked. Then there was another roar, and a great grinding sound, and a crashing and breaking, and a rush of water, as the Huron came through like a furious chief laying about him with tomahawk and ax, his great blows striking the ice into crumbling, tossing cakes. The wind, ineffective on the hard cakes, pounced on the water between and lifted it into white-topped waves.

The sledge was only a few hundred feet from the shore when it lurched sidewise, tumbling from a tilting ice block into the dark, widening cracks. We saw the man's arms threshing the air, and then he fell into the ice water between the tossing white blocks. The water was a confused mass of dogs and man and sledge, and the ice blocks were drifting so fast by that time that it seemed anything living would be crushed between them.

The tired dogs, entangled in their harness, barked and yelped shrilly. Then nothing of the man could be seen, and we all crowded close to the wharf, silent with anxiety. Ice blocks crashed and ground against one another as they moved past the island. Then, one large block caught against the wharf, catching and holding others, so that for a few moments there was a piling up of a sharp-edged mass far out into the straits.

Suddenly Paul left my side, and ran out on the dock. Warnings were shouted as the crowd saw his intention. But Paul was already out on the drifting ice, jumping from one surface to another on sure-footed moccasins. I felt stiff and numb as again and again I saw the block he had just left tip upright and crash down again. On and on he went, now stopping for a few seconds, then leaping quickly, just in time to avoid being swept out of his way by another floating mass.

At last he was close to the struggling dogs. He made

one more jump to a cake of ice approaching them, squatted on it and waited until it turned and twisted, bringing him within reach of the animals. Then he lurched forward, seized the lead dog by the scruff of the neck and hauled him out with a great heaving to the cake on which he himself was standing. Paul shouted a command. The dog responded. He gave a quick shake and began to pull. Whining and yelping, one after another the other dogs gained their footing and dragged out the sledge, to which the man, seemingly dazed by his fall, was still clinging.

I saw Paul lift him and lay him on the sledge, and run with a shout to the head of the dogs, urging them on. The hole into which they had fallen closed with a roar of tilting blocks. If the ice jam would only hold! Broken edges were jammed together almost like a row of knives. On, over the uneven, restless pathway they came, while I held my breath, wondering if the ice would loosen. It would sweep with fury when it went, crushing anything caught with it. With unbelievable sureness, Paul ran as if something within him were directing him, something that knew the vagaries of the ice, the exact second to leap, and where next to set his foot. Behind him came the lead dog, jumping when Paul jumped, pausing when he stopped.

The ice held. The dogs pulled the sledge up on the shore, their whines of joy at being on solid ground drowned out in the loud crashing of ice. Their weight on the last cake next the wharf had loosened it, and the whole jam was moving, grinding and merciless, down toward the lakes.

"Fine work, my boy!" The major rushed to Paul, thumping him on the back. The excited crowd closed in about him, and everyone had a word of praise, loud and hearty or quiet and tearful, according to the nature of the one who spoke.

"Here, some of ye," shouted Mr. Stuart. "Come along and take this poor half-drowned fellow to my house."

Dripping icy water in little pools about him, the carrier was stiff with a chill only a little less than death's. He could not stand. Someone came running with a buffalo robe. It was put about him, and he was lifted from the sledge. Part of the crowd broke away to follow as he was carried up the street.

"Get off them wet things and give him a shot of whiskey," shouted Mr. Stuart after them. "I'll be along as soon as the mail is opened."

So many villagers still surrounded Paul that I could see only the top of his fur cap. I moved around the crowd and patted the dogs on their dripping heads. I put my face down on the neck of the lead dog to hide my feelings. When I could look up with an expressionless face again, the postmaster was untying an oilskin parcel from the bottom of the birch sledge.

"I'll be goin' along to the office with this," he said.

"Open it right here, can't you?" shouted someone back in the crowd.

There were other shouts, urging, insisting. The postmaster shrugged and opened the parcel, glancing over the crowd as he did so. "Guess I might as well. Seems to be someone here from every house in the village. Here are your letters, then. Come and git 'em. Have your change ready for them as ain't been paid for."

The postmaster began to call out names, and the crowd drifted away from Paul, and then I saw that Pierre was beside him. They stood there, each straight, each proud in his own way. Paul's fur cap was pushed back on his head, and suddenly I noticed something I had not seen before. Around his temple was a faint curl, where new hair had come in after his long fever. It was exactly like the curl showing at the edges of Pierre's beaver hat.

"It is always good to save a life," said Pierre at last,

letting his hand rest on his son's shoulder. "That took courage."

Their eyes met, Pierre's softened with approval, and Paul's filled with a new light I had never seen in them. He was unable to say a word, but I knew this was a high moment for him.

"Saved a life, and just by chance, some mighty important mail." Mr. Stuart came over cheerfully. "Fine work, Paul. Ought to have a reward of some kind. What'd you like?"

Paul shook his head. He had already had enough.

"Here's a letter for you, Pierre," said Mr. Stuart. "From Mr. Astor—I know that writin'. Fact is, I've got one here myself." He ripped open a square envelope in his hand, while Pierre drew out his pocketknife and neatly slit the end of one just like it.

Mr. Stuart ran his eyes down the page. "Well, this *is* something. Mr. Astor wants me to come to New York as soon as I can get a boat out. Hints that new plans are on foot for the company. And he says—does your letter say the same as mine, Pierre?"

Pierre was holding the sheet in his hand, and it trembled slightly.

"Yes," he said quietly, "I am to be in charge of the headquarters here while you are gone."

Sharp edges of stones gnashed under Pierre's shoes as he turned and went up the slope of the beach. Unlike moccasins that would have let him feel the little ridges and hollows, his stout leather shoes leveled the path and kept him from knowing it was rough. As I watched him go, the same thought came that I had had the first time I ever saw him—what was he doing here? He looked more than ever like one just alighted from a boat for a brief look at the island. He was a different kind, just as his white shirt ruffles were different from striped shirting and red flannel. And yet in his own way he had followed the sheen of the beaver.

Mr. Stuart walked silently in moccasins over heavy wool socks. As he caught up with Pierre, I heard the short little man say, "Better let Paul go on with his fishin' this summer, without sayin' anything about his coming into the fur office. Might not look right, you puttin' your son right in."

"Yes, you are right," said Pierre, and Mr. Stuart turned and winked at me.

Paul drew a deep breath, as if something new-born that he valued had been given a chance for its life. There would be no renewal of the struggle between him and Pierre for that summer, at least.

A few people were still around us, reading letters and looking over the pages of newspapers as they slowly began to withdraw from the beach.

"The last one's for you, Doc," said the postmaster, turning the oilskin wrong side out as he handed the envelope to Martin. "From Boston, I see."

Martin ripped off the end of it, and pulled out the single sheet inside. A soldier beside him began humming. "The Girl I Left Behind Me."

"Not at all," Martin laughed shortly. "It's from the hospital." He glanced up from his reading and I saw he was looking sharply at Paul as though he were seeing him for the first time. "Paul," he called, "you haven't moved since you stepped on shore. What's the matter? Hurt your leg?"

"Just a little, I guess," Paul admitted.

Martin called to one of the soldiers. "Here, Bill, we'll make a chair with our arms." Clasping each other at the elbows, they made a support of four strong arms, which they lowered so Paul could sit on them. They started off up the slope, and I walked behind them, feeling guilty that in all the other emotions that had swept over me, I had not noticed that Paul was hurt again.

Fragments came to my ears from other letters being read aloud. The clear voice of the government agent

368

came out above all the rest. "Hell and damnation! Wonder what those fools down in Washington will think of next? I never know what's going to pop out of that mail-bag at me. Listen to this—they're planning to move all the Ojibways out of this territory and move this agency farther west, probably to Fond du Lac. And they say the payments this summer will be mostly in goods." He broke off, and swore at length. "They can sit on their plush chairs and think up things like this, but I'm the one that has to tell the tribes their Great White Father is renigging on another treaty. I don't look forward to no pleasant summer, no sirree!"

Strangely breaking into his talk, I remembered a bird-call I had heard a few moments before, and knew it must have been the notes of the first robin. I searched him out in the tree, the too-early one, and as he called again, I noted that his voice was harsh, and I remembered words of Marthe's taken up by the four winds of Mackinac and accepted as their own,

"When the robin's note is harsh . . . it means war and trouble. The robin was a young girl of our tribe, who made a promise that she would ever come and tell us."

Eleven

⁋ Martin found that Paul had strained some ligaments and must stay off his leg again for a few weeks. Under Martin's cheerful words about its being only a precaution, Grand'mère gradually became calm, and when he and the soldier had gone, she drew up a little chair at Paul's bedside and began to play at piquet with him, smoothing a place on the bedspread to hold the cards.

Moving in a serenity made up of the peace of being

at home again, and the new light in Paul's eyes since he had heard Pierre's brief words of approval, I took my place in Grand'mère's house. I changed into a calico dress and combed my hair into braids and put them up around my head. As I went out in the little kitchen, hearing the quiet murmur from Paul's room, I felt a warm glow over us all, and knew it had been left there by Martin. How much we owed him for Paul's sake, I thought, as I filled a kettle with water and brought it out to hang on the crane where a kettle of soup was already filling the room with an odor of savory richness. All through Paul's illness Martin had relieved our minds of worry. Such a one must have been sent by the manitou for a special work, I thought, and I whispered a little wish that he might find it, and happiness in doing it, the wish spreading a soft haze over the familiar work of my hands as I shook tea leaves from the tin canister into the earthen pot and set it close by the hearth in readiness for the hot water, and moved to the cupboard to set the table with the red and white soup-plates. I could see Paul and Grand'mère over their game, his dark head close to her white curls as she bent over the bed, trying to see the cards in the gathering dimness.

"Ah, *voilà!* I win again." Grand'mère threw up her hands in excitement. Paul smiled out through the door at me, as Grand'mère picked up the cards and put them into their red box. It was more fun for him to play so that she won without her suspecting him than it was to win for himself.

"That you, Pierre?" Grand'mère called out, as a step was heard on the porch.

"Yes." Pierre came in and went directly to the door of Paul's room. "I heard you had to be carried home. Is it anything serious?" he asked, with a new edge of kindness on his tone.

"No. I just have to keep off my leg for a little," said Paul.

"He is a hero, they tell me," said Grand'mère, letting her wrinkled hand rest on Paul's forehead. "I don't see how he did it."

Paul shook his head restlessly.

Pierre, in the doorway, had a faint smile on his narrow lips, and his shoulders were straight, as if something were keeping them from slipping to the little droop they had had of late. Remembering, I said, "We didn't tell Grand'mère about your letter, Pierre."

"Letter? What letter?" asked Grand'mère.

"Mr. Stuart has been called east for a conference with Mr. Astor," said Pierre. "He will go on the first schooner."

"*Eh bien*," exclaimed Grand'mère. "That's a queer thing right at the beginning of the season. Mr. Crooks will be here this summer?"

"No," said Pierre. "He isn't expected."

"Who then will be in charge?"

"I shall." Pierre's shoulders straightened.

Grand'mère clapped her hands like a child. "But that is wonderful! What do you think it means?"

"I don't know exactly. Mr. Stuart's letter hinted of new plans for the company, and he has had such hints before. Mr. Astor has been displeased that we aren't doing as well as we did in the early '20's."

"He wouldn't call Mr. Stuart all that way just for a scolding, would he?" asked Grand'mère.

Pierre smiled. "He might. But Mr. Stuart thinks Mr. Astor has some plan he wants to talk over with him."

"*Moi*, I know what it is," cried Grand'mère. "Mr. Crooks and Mr. Stuart are to make another try at getting company posts into the far west—and then you will be in charge here!"

"I am in charge here for the summer, at least." Pierre could not keep the satisfaction out of his voice, calm as it was.

"*Voilà*, we must celebrate!" Grand'mère's excite-

371

ment was growing. "Oneta, get some of the best wine!"

Paul had been staring at his father. "You—you are to deal with the traders and Indians—yourself, as Mr. Stuart does?" he asked, suddenly.

"Yes. What of it?"

"*Il est merveilleux, cela*—the confidence Mr. Astor shows in you, is it not so?" exclaimed Grand'mère.

"I think it is," said Pierre simply.

"Oneta, go fetch the wine, *toute de suite!*"

As I went through the door to the kitchen, my last glimpse of Paul showed him staring at the ceiling, all expression gone from his face. Though Grand'mère and Pierre were still in the room, Paul seemed to have withdrawn from them, as a chief, having had his say, goes alone into his lodge.

In the three weeks Paul had to stay in bed, Pierre spent long hours at the fur company, working with Mr. Stuart as goods were unpacked and preparations made for the season. Mr. Stuart gave him constant instructions about parts of the business Pierre had never paid any attention to before. "I'd put Charlie in charge of the yard as soon as he gets here," said Mr. Stuart one night as I was waiting for Pierre. "Let him handle the men. You stick pretty close to the office and take care of things here."

As the first soft airs of spring floating into his cave make the bear come out from his long winter, so the arrival of the first bateaux awakened the village from its long sleep. On one of the first days of the moon of flowers, we heard shooting around the point, and knew it was Baptiste joyously welcoming the boats again. The boat song came faintly up to the windows of our house. Grand'mère stood in the doorway. "Here they come again. Hearts of devils with voices like angels," and her tone made it a compliment.

It was Saturday, a half-holiday at the mission, and I had been reading to Paul most of the afternoon. I got up and went to the window to watch the crowd gather at the shore.

"Is it the Illinois?" Paul asked, naming the southern brigade, usually first in.

"No. It's the Tahquamenon River, early again this year," I said, thinking Pierre would be glad to have Charlie on hand so soon.

Suddenly from around the point I saw a flash of color, as Rosanne ran down the beach toward the line of boats coming to the shore.

A little later, as I got up to put the kettle on for supper, I heard voices passing the house. I looked out and saw Charlie himself swaggering past, his black feather prominent above his reddened face, his deerskins and moccasins shining with newness, his big face glowing as he looked down at Rosanne as she danced along, clinging to his arm. Thoughtfully I watched them out of sight.

And that night when Pierre came home, he told us that he had had a talk with Charlie about taking charge of the fur yard, and Charlie had invited him to his wedding. He and Rosanne were going to be married as soon as the priest came back from his winter rounds to take up his residence at Mackinac for the summer. Later, Rosanne herself came in to ask me to be a bridesmaid, and Grand'mère scolded her roundly for such treatment of Jacques.

"Marrying another man even before he comes back from the winter—even before you know he will come back alive," she said. Rosanne answered angrily, and flounced out of the house without even waiting for my reply. We didn't see her again, but we heard the day had been set for the wedding, the next Saturday, one week from the time Charlie's brigade came in.

✤ ✤ ✤

So quickly did the first voyageurs take the village life into their hands that when I left the mission the next Saturday noon, the season was as busy as I had ever seen it as its height. The long sorting tables in the fur yard were surrounded by swarthy men. The bell of the door of the retail store had been taken off the nob, for no longer was there only an occasional customer to call the clerk from the back room. He had two helpers now, and they all had to jump in lively fashion to keep up with the needs of men with money restless in their pockets. Everywhere appeared the color of the new buckskins, and shocks of dark hair hung down over the red and green of new kerchiefs.

Though only two more brigades had come in besides Charlie's, the tents had already been put up in grass-plots, and the noise of shouts and laughter, back-slapping and scuffling filled every street. From all the houses where voyageurs stayed I could hear the singing of men as they washed for dinner.

The steamboat *Henry Clay* was unloading the first summer visitors. Shopkeepers came out of their sagging doorframes and scurried like mice toward the wharf, and a breeze skipped off the little green waves and raised a cloud of dust along the beach road behind them. At the dock an officer surrounded by privates awaited supplies for the post. Two large mail-bags were swung into the postmaster's cart.

In front of me, a few newly come Ottawas in unkempt hair and bright new calico padded along toward the beach, where stews were cooking over the outdoor fires. A pack of lean dogs, hurrying in the same direction, swerved around the men's legs in passing. A few violin notes, already a forerunner of the evening, came from one of the shops, and a voyageur in new yellow buckskins broke into a jig in the middle of the beach road.

The Ottawa lodges were not far from the wharf. On a sudden impulse I turned from the path, and instead of

374

going on to the warehouse to stop for Pierre, I went down the beach road. I passed the Ottawas, and spoke to the children. They stared at me until their mothers whispered to them, then their eyes opened wide. The women smiled in friendly fashion, and I was about to go near and speak to them, when, beyond, I saw a procession coming around the point from the fishing village.

At the head of it was Big Charlie, a broad scarlet sash separating his striped shirt and blue trousers, and a scarlet handkerchief covering his heavy neck. There was no mistaking his tall form even at that distance, if I hadn't already recognized the slender girl in white clinging to his arm. Behind them came about a dozen voyageurs, with village girls on their arms. It was Rosanne's wedding procession, but it did not go at once to St. Anne's. Noisy with songs and laughter, it turned around the corner of a narrow street opening off the beach road, and into a new eating-place whose owner had been a voyageur with Charlie before age and a hernia had made him take up easier work. I remembered talk I had heard about the plans for this wedding. One would know Rosanne would be different from anyone else, people in the village had said. It was her idea to have a big dinner before the ceremony in a tavern where the noon crowds would be gathered, and she would be the center of attention.

As the last of the party went into the tavern, my ears were caught by a boat song, and I turned around to the straits. Waves caught the sun and flung it in my eyes, but I could see that coming around the point was a brigade of a dozen canoes in a long line, paddles working in that last burst of speed, as if the men could not wait to set foot on the island. White in the sun was the sail of a schooner beyond, a joyous sail, seeming as little tied to anything as one of the gulls flying out toward the boats. Hands over their eyes, other watchers on the shore tried to name the brigade.

"Coutreau's, from Lake Superior," one of them called out. I felt a quiver of excitement run along my spine, an excitement that seemed to pass on down the line along the shore. Everyone there knew it was Jacques's brigade.

"Maybe he isn't with them," said one. "Maybe a tomahawk got him—maybe some wild beast—"

But when the first *canot* came up to the shore, one short figure stood up, shouting, "Me, I am back!"

It was Jacques. He leaped up on the beach, smiling broadly, waiting for something. The crowd moved back, like snow melting before a firebrand. Jacques, puzzled, looked around. "What is wrong? Do you not see this? Why don't you say something, tell me you are glad?"

Our eyes obeyed his pointing. Jacques was wearing a black feather!

Quickly I went toward him.

He went on boasting, uncertainly. "Before half the winter was gone, I took this away from Jean Coutreau. And I drove out an independent trader on Sturgeon River—" He saw me, and stopped. "Oneta!"

The crowd was still watching at a distance.

"Come, Jacques," I said. He should not have to learn the news before all these curious ones.

He took me by the arm, almost roughly. "Rosanne has died, and they will not tell me!"

From the tavern down the beach came a burst of laughter.

"No, Jacques." I took a few steps away, and with a long look at my face, he followed. We went beyond the village, to a place where a small growth of juniper cut off the view in every direction except that out over the straits. Just beyond was an open space, hard-trodden, the council and ceremony place of the tribes for many years. "Come, sit here, Jacques."

Jacques threw himself on the ground. "Now, quick,

376

the bad news, and then I must find Rosanne and she will weep with me. Together we will do everything. At last, I have the black feather and a little home. You should see the nice cabin—"

I lifted my hand to interrupt him. "Jacques, you cannot marry Rosanne."

In the sky beyond him, seeming smaller than Jacques's head, a black cloud moved along as if bent on collision with a dark mass just above the horizon.

"Not marry—but that is just it—now I can marry her. I have everything she always wanted, the things she made me wait for all these years."

It was hard for me to have to crush that eager look on his face. "Jacques, she is marrying Charlie—today."

Stunned, Jacques was motionless for a second. Then he dully turned his cap in his hands, straightening the feather in it. "The long months in the silences of the woods have made my ears hear things that are not said—" He peered up into my face, and saw that the words were true.

"Where are they?" He jumped to his feet. "Where is this damned rogue—" He looked wildly in all directions. "Have they gone to the priest?"

"They are now on the way," I said.

Jacques started off on a run.

"Jacques!" I called suddenly, and at the urgency in my tone, he stopped.

"You know you cannot beat Charlie in a fight. It will only please Rosanne."

He came back slowly, and threw himself again on the beach beside me, letting his hat with its gay black feather trail in the sand. He ran his fingers through the tangle of his curls, as if that would clear his thought. "Where are they now?"

I told him.

He lay motionless in thought for a moment. Then he

377

rose, and brushed off the leaves and sticks clinging to his buckskins, removing every trace with a slow progression from one to the other that was almost unbearable to watch. He straightened his jacket, adjusted his knife at his side, and put on his cap, careful to get it on with the black feather exactly in front. He stood motionless for a moment, but as a rock protruding from a cliff is motionless, yet ready to leap from its fastness and crush whatever lies in its path below. Then he turned away as if I were no longer there, a haziness in his eyes, as if they were fixed on something else.

"What are you going to do?" I asked.

"At least with a knife I am quicker than Charlie."

"Jacques, won't you listen?"

He turned away as if he hadn't heard, and I had to let him go. Stalking down the beach road, he was a pathetic figure, brightly garbed as he was for summer joys.

He passed one of the picket-enclosed lawns, and to my surprise Martin came out of the gate. Jacques spoke to him curtly, and rushed on past. But Martin called to him, and I saw that he was asking questions, and getting answers that were angry at first and then defiant. Walking thoughtfully beside Jacques a little way, Martin at last took him by the arm and drew him to one side of the crowded beach road. Near the doorway of one of the shops they stood for long minutes, talking earnestly, paying no attention to the noise and stir around them, the groups of voyageurs sauntering past, or the children and dogs that chased one another along the hard-packed road. As I came along at a distance, I saw that Jacques was listening now with eager interest. He leaned forward, his eyes on Martin's face, taking in every word. At last he nodded several times, and then they turned and started on again. Seeing the alertness in his step, I knew he had changed his mind, and that he had a new plan.

At the corner near the tavern, Jacques paused and

leaned unconcernedly against a wooden building. Martin went on across the street.

A few voyageurs stopped to speak to Jacques. Others called to him to join their noisy groups. He answered them all shortly, and did not move. As the minutes passed, he grew restless, but still he stood there with his eyes on the tavern door. At last the voices of the wedding party grew louder, and then the door opened, spilling the gay voyageurs and their girls out on the street again. Rosanne was tossing her curls and laughing. About to take Charlie's arm again, she caught sight of Jacques.

"Oh!" Her hand flew to her mouth, eyes wide in excited anticipation of a quarrel. She would have liked nothing better than a fight with herself as the prize. Then her eyes grew puzzled, as Jacques stood still, smiling at her. Six or eight men of Jacques's brigade came up behind him, ready for anything. Charlie stood in the middle of the street, with impassive face, waiting for a rush. But none came. Jacques looked up at him with a childlike smile.

"Ah, just in time to wish my old friends luck," he said.

Charlie's face was comical to watch, as he heard that.

"You are to congratulate me, too," said Jacques smoothly. "I have a black feather—" Rosanne's eyes opened still wider as he pointed to his cap. "I have a post of my own, and I have a nice little woman waiting there for me when I go back."

He flung a glance over his shoulder at his own brigade, who had by then gathered behind him in full force, ready to back him in a fight. "A beauty, isn't she, men?"

They had been open-mouthed at his words, but they recovered quickly. "Yes, a beauty—the whitest skin— gold hair—black hair—red hair—" The shouts arose behind Jacques, as each man hurriedly made up for himself a picture of Jacques's woman.

Jacques went on smiling, while Charlie stared at him, uncertain, and Rosanne's face flushed with red from her white dress to her tossing curls.

"Let me wish you luck," bowed Jacques, with a composure I had never known he had. It was as if strength had come to him from some mysterious place where strength for such times is kept and released to mortals in need of it.

"Jean!" Jacques called over his shoulder, without looking back. There was sure to be a Jean within hearing. A short, stout man separated himself from the crowd. "Yes, Jacques?"

Jacques still kept his eyes on Rosanne. "Bring me a fiddle, Jean. I will play the processional music as my friends go to the church."

An amazed murmur of delight went through the crowd. Jean hopped into a near-by shop and came back at once, thrusting a fiddle into Jacques's hands.

Jacques tucked it under his chin and sauntered toward the beach. "Now, let the procession form," he said. "I will play you to the church."

Rosanne tossed her head, but it was a sobered girl that took Charlie somewhat uncertainly by the arm again. In perfect silence the watching voyageurs fell in behind, as the little group started hesitatingly toward the little church of St. Anne's, where the priest was on the steps, wondering at the delay.

On the beach, Jacques sat down on an overturned canoe. Soft notes came to my ears as he bent over, tuning. At once he raised his head, lifted the fiddle in his hand, and brought the bow down upon it.

Against the sound of waves swishing over pebbles, he sat there and played. But it was no wedding march that came from that fiddle. Strains that were as wild as a storm at sea or in men's hearts, took a sudden turn into rollicking measures of light indifference. Then the music moved into smooth cadences that spoke of a sunny country-side, of a little stream that might flow beside a log cabin with smoke rising in the air. Scraps of tunes from the dances he and Rosanne did so well broke off into a gay song we had sung as children when we skated on the straits, and then to another we had shouted as the four of us dragged our sled back up the fort hill after a long, thrilling slide down and far out on the ice. And then, smoothly, came harmony in a soft mood like the warm hazy days of Indian summer, with the sun red through the misty air, reminding me as I knew it must be reminding Rosanne, of the little dark-haired boy sitting on the beach before the fishing cabins, playing his first notes on his father's fiddle.

The procession neared the foot of the church steps, where the priest was waiting with impassive face. I saw Jacques look up, and then he began a loud crescendo, a hollow menacing sound as if a whirlwind swept across the lake and into the woods, and a staccato like huge branches torn from pines or trees falling in the forest, like the storms that had always sent Rosanne to cower in Jacques's arms when they came up as we played on the heights.

And then he stopped. There was no sound but the wash of the waves on the shore. I looked at the church, and saw Rosanne about to set her foot on the first step. She hesitated, and stepped back. Then she tore her hand from Charlie's arm, and with a quick swirl of white skirts, she began to run. Back down the little street she flew and out on the beach, where Jacques rested his fiddle on his knees and looked out over the straits washing up near his feet. "Oh, Jacques! Jacques!" sobbed Rosanne, and as he rose and turned around, she threw herself into his arms. "I love nobody but you, *mon bon ami!* Tell me there is no other woman at your post!"

With a look of unutterable peace, Jacques gathered her close to him, looking on beyond triumphantly at Charlie. As if on signal, all Jacques's brigade turned toward the big voyageur, and laughter rose and grew as other brigades joined in, until the whole village of Mackinac seemed filled with the roar of merriment.

A slow grin spread over Charlie's face, and he lifted his shoulders in an enormous shrug, as if he would say there were as good does in the wood as any that had come out of it.

"The drinks are on me," he shouted over the heads of the crowd. The laughter changed to roars of approval as the men fought their way into the nearest saloon, Charlie among them unconcerned about the sudden change as one who could set sail when the wind blew or take to the oars when it failed.

On the beach pebbles, the fiddle lay forgotten with only the companionship of the murmuring waves, and the waves reached for it, as if asserting once again the part the two of them played in the life of the voyageur.

On the steps of the church, the priest stood with contentment in his face, watching the two figures on the beach as they broke from their embrace, and hand in hand went toward him.

I turned to look for Martin, but he was gone, and there seemed a peculiar emptiness about the street, crowded as it was with men jostling one another to get to the saloons. I walked slowly westward down the beach, marveling, for directly came upon me the thought that while I had tried to help Jacques endure what must be, Martin had helped him get what he wanted. I wondered if I had not stumbled on a wider thought, that behind it was one difference between my race and his. Indians were ever better at renunciation than the white man. I wondered, too, as I walked, how he had come to know the heart of Rosanne better than Jacques and I, who had seen her grow up.

Twelve

❧ The summer went on much as the others had gone, except that in all the noise and excitement, we missed Mr. Stuart and the feeling of balance and solidity he had given. But Charlie, ignoring the daily jokes about his marriage, took hold of the affairs of the fur yard, firmly settling disputes and stopping fights, leaving Pierre utterly happy in the management of the office and warehouse.

By midsummer, Paul was able to go out of doors and walk with care. Martin forbade him for some weeks after to go fishing, or even out in a boat, lest some sudden twist put too much strain on his leg. Paul obeyed, unhappily at first, but he found content before long in looking after the Mackinac end of his growing business. Keeping an eye on the packing and loading, checking the accounts and keeping the credits in order took all the daylight hours, so that he would have had little time to go out to the nets.

It seemed a peaceful time, though if I had not been so occupied with my own work at the mission, with Paul's work, with pleasure at Pierre's new happiness, there were signs that I should not have missed. There was a rising discontent among the tribes as they came to the beach and heard, one after another, that the agency was to be moved, and that the government was planning to move the tribes out of Michigan Territory, beyond the great father of waters. Even then, they did not know about the change in payments, but awaited the gold they expected to pay off debts and buy what they had set their hearts on.

They brought word of troubles down below that I heard sometimes from Marthe, stories of attacks on

383

settlers' villages that had been set up on lands belonging to some tribe, even on the graveyards. There was rumor of trouble in Illinois, and I heard more of that on the day Martin dropped in to see how Paul's leg had stood moderate exercise.

It was about an hour before supper, and Grand'mère had not yet come home from a whist party at Mrs. Stuart's. Pierre was still at the warehouse, and I sat with Paul before the fire, waiting to take the supper loaves of white bread from the oven. I had taken up a pan of raspberries that needed washing, and my fingertips grew stained with their juices. Paul got up when we heard the familiar light step on the porch, and stood with welcome on his face. The late slanting light sparkled on Martin's gold buttons and turned his brown hair to red as he pulled off his leather cap in the doorway. I spoke some word of welcome, and he came gaily in.

"How's the schoolmistress?" He bowed over my berry-stained hand.

Paul was already stripping off his moccasin and rolling up his trousers leg, his face raised to Martin with hope in it.

"Felt any pain?" asked Martin. Paul shook his head, and Martin knelt beside him at the hearth, and the firelight took up the lighting of his hair, doing it no less well than the sun. His fingers ran up and down Paul's leg, pressing here and there, while his low voice questioned. At last he stood up. Paul looked at him mutely.

"No reason you can't do anything you want to now," said Martin.

The light in Paul's eyes spoke his thanks better than his words. He offered his hand to Martin, and then, like a strong bird that has been fettered, he ran out of the door and down the path, with the joy of release upon his flying feet.

Paul had gone, free now, in body and even in mind, for Pierre would let him alone in his fishing at least until

384

Mr. Stuart came back. There was nothing more I could wish for him, and tears rose to my eyes.

Martin was gazing out of the door. "You think a great deal of your brother, don't you?" he asked softly, half turning his head.

Breaking into his words came quick footsteps across the porch. Grand'mère was in the doorway. "*Mon Dieu,* I thought those old women would never be willing to quit." The old women were at least twenty years younger than she. "*Moi,* if I ever take whist as seriously as that, may I—oh, it's Dr. Reynolds."

Martin sprang to take the shawl she was trailing over one arm. As he came near her, she suddenly seized him by the shoulders. "You're a nice boy, and I like you." He kissed her on the cheek.

"Well," said Grand'mère with approval, standing off and looking at him. "And did you fix up our boy?"

"Paul's all right. No reason he should ever have any more trouble with that leg."

Grand'mère's eyes were wet. "But that is wonderful to my ears. He has been so patient—" She drew Martin to sit down beside her, as she talked of Paul and how good he had been through all his suffering. Martin's back was toward me, and he was held firm by Grand'-mère's chatter.

The fire being out on the hearth I knelt and kindled it, taking dry moss and rotten wood from the tinder-box, laying the flint upon it, striking it with the steel ring. As the sparks from the flint caught and grew in the long-dead wood, strangely to me as I worked came some words of Grand'mère's—a woman that can build a fire will never get herself a husband. But in watching the dried moss flare up and catch the wood above, I tossed away her words, letting them be consumed in the bright flame.

Remembering my baking, I opened the small door of the brick oven, and the odor of fresh bread filled the

385

room. When the door was closed again the fragrance lingered. Martin's eyes sparkled as he sniffed the air.

Grand'mère laughed. "Won't you stay to supper with us?"

"Sorry," said Martin, "but I am invited to the major's tonight. We all are—I mean everybody at the fort. It'll be a small party, at that."

"What is all this about the soldiers leaving? We were talking about it at Mrs. Stuart's. I never heard of such a thing before."

"No one else has, I guess," said Martin. "The orders that came said that replacements would be here in a few days and then this whole company was to start for Fort Dearborn at Chicago. From what he's heard, the major thought the company should go at once. He sent the men on, and he and a few of his staff are staying until the replacements come."

"*Mon Dieu*, what has happened?"

"Trouble along the frontier in Illinois. There have been skirmishes, and a big general uprising is expected. Some leader of the Sauk and Fox tribes is gathering his forces for an attack."

"Such a nuisance!" ejaculated Grand'mère. "Taking our army away like that! How many of you are there left?"

"Less than a dozen. It will be the first time the major could have his whole company about his supper table."

"You aren't going to leave us, are you?" asked Grand'mère.

"Not right away," answered Martin slowly. "Maybe later—I have had a letter I'm still thinking about—" He broke off, and took up his leather hat. "Well, I must go." Taking Grand'mère's hand he squeezed it gently. "I'll accept that invitation for supper some other time, if I may."

"Of course. As soon as you can."

As he started toward the door, Grand'mère went on into her room. Martin looked at me, but I was staring out of the doorway. "What—what is the name of the leader of the Sauks and Foxes?" I asked.

"Black Hawk, I believe," said Martin.

Black Hawk! Grand'mère's house seemed to dissolve in air, the day being gone into another, and I was a little girl, peering from a lodge door, seeing a group of men around an open fire, my grandfather among them, and by his side a stranger with head shaved to his scalp-lock, his full lips slightly open as he looked around the council. I could hear my mother's words to Marthe, words full of tearing sorrow, "A warrior named Black Hawk . . . was with Tecumseh when he fell. . . ." And I saw the Sauk again at the council-fire as he stood and raised his hand, saying, "Sometime the Long Knives shall pay. . . ."

I was entranced, as if my spirit had left my body and gone on an errand of its own, from which I could not summon it. As though through a haze I knew that Martin said something in farewell and went out the door.

Grand'mère came bustling out of her room, a plain cambric dress on instead of her party dress, tying a great white apron about her waist. "Well, has Dr. Reynolds gone?—What's the matter with you, child? You look as if you were moonstruck—come on, we must hurry. Pierre will be home any minute."

If I had not been so full of my own thoughts, I would have noticed at supper that Pierre was unusually silent, that there was no talking at all except Grand'mère's chattering about her whist party, and that it was only Paul who gave her a word now and then to keep her going.

I don't believe Pierre spoke at all until we went out on the back porch, where we often sat for the last minutes of daylight. That night Grand'mère rocked placidly, her shawl about her, humming to herself. Pierre walked restlessly up and down behind her, while I sat on the top step, looking out over the garden. Paul's striped shirt was open at the neck, and a battered tin pail swung against his brown ribbed trousers as he went up and down the rows, watering flowers and vegetables. Along the fence stretched delicate orange clusters of bittersweet, still unripe, each little globe awaiting the moon of falling leaves to open the covering in golden points and reveal the scarlet berry inside. I looked at the snapdragons, those flowers that one could squeeze so they opened their mouths to bite; the white bloom of the hydrangea that would later shade to red and purple; the rosemary with its long whorls, the love-apples among the shy mignonette, for in those days we grew love-apples among the flowers and never thought of eating the plump red globes. The sun sent his last rays through a juniper tree at the corner of the garden, and went below the hill, leaving behind a golden sky. "Don't forget the vines along the fence," I said to Paul.

"I noticed Mrs. Stuart's mallow isn't in bloom yet." Grand'mère stopped her humming and pulled her shawl closer against the coming of the night air. "Poor woman, she's getting impatient for her husband to get back. First time she's ever stayed alone so long."

"When is he expected?" I asked.

"No one knows, I guess. Of course she woudn't be so nervous if Mrs. Campbell didn't keep running in every day and filling her ears with the agency worries. It seems the payments haven't come, and some of the redskins are getting impatient about it. Want to be off for some harvest or other."

"Wild rice," I murmured.

"Mr. Campbell is furious about the garrison leaving as it did, too. He seems to expect some kind of trouble, though why, I don't know. Things have been peaceful enough here, no matter what stories people bring in from uncivilized places."

Paul stood up, pail in hand, and looked off toward the north, where a low cloud seemed about to settle on the heights.

"No use watering any more," he said. "Thunderstorm coming."

"Yes, I feel it," I said. "A tightness in the air."

Grand'mère fastened her shawl with a great pin, and rolled her hands in her apron as she rocked. She stretched lazily, and looked around. Pierre was stepping over her rockers in his constant pacing of the little porch.

"Pierre, stop it! You've been as nervous as a fish ever since you got home!"

Pierre stepped in front of her. "You would be, too, trying to deal with these worthless Indians—"

Paul, about to set the watering-can down beside the steps, stopped with it in mid-air.

"Not I!" said Grand'mère, resuming her rocking. "*Moi*, with my broom I can settle any redskin. I don't get nervous about it—I just hit them."

"I did hit one," said Pierre slowly, "but I'm not so sure it settled him."

We all turned to him in astonishment. Pierre the restrained, the fastidious—

"You—hit—one?" Grand'mère's voice was shrill.

Pierre resumed his pacing. "That lazy rascal that has made trouble of some kind around here every summer for years—Four Legs. No more worthless human being ever drifted to this shore. He's thieving, low, dirty—"

"*Ma foi*, yes. He is one who knows the feel of my broom," said Grand'mère with grim satisfaction. "Now, Pierre, calm yourself and tell us what happened. What did this Four Legs do?"

"He came in the office today and demanded credit. He said the payments were late, and he wanted some new clothes right away. The artist man wanted to paint his picture again, was his excuse. I looked in the books, and he owes us for last year's hunt—he brought in just two packs of wormy stuff this spring."

"And Mr. Astor has said you must be strict about credit," approved Grand'mère.

"Yes," sighed Pierre. "But I wouldn't have been inclined to be lenient with such a worthless fellow, anyway. He sat there and kept saying, 'Trust me thirty skins' worth until the payments come.'

" 'Nobody but good hunters get credit here,' I told him."

"What did he say about that?" asked Grand'mère.

"Just sat there and kept mumbling 'Thirty skins' worth.' After a while I got tired of it, and ordered him out of the office. He got up then, but he started toward me. His dirty hands even reached out toward my clothes." Pierre shuddered. Though the night was cool, he stopped and wiped a linen handkerchief over his forehead. Then he resumed pacing, and the rest of the story came out, one word treading fast on the heels of another. "Four Legs kept coming, and I backed up until my foot struck a box that had been brought in from the warehouse. I glanced down at it, as I stepped aside. It was a box of dog-team whips. Somehow I found one in my hand, and cracked it above the Indian's head. The filthy fellow took another step toward me, and I lifted my arm again, and saw him cringe as the whip wrapped around him. . . . I don't know how many times I struck him," Pierre said. I knew it was true, remembering another time I had seen him in a rage, remembering the white-hot anger as he had pulled Paul from his cradleboard, smashing the frame to bits of wood, tearing the beaded wrappings.

"Were you alone in the office?" asked Grand'mère, her voice shaken a little.

"Yes . . . he began to back up then. When I let

the whip fly the last time, he fell out the screen door onto the porch, and got up and slunk away."

Pierre's steps on the board floor were the only sounds in the silence that followed, while each of us searched out the meaning of this strange happening, knowing it was not fear that had made Pierre seize that whip. In it were repulsion and disgust. The blows were a lashing out at a sight, a smell, a way of life irritating to his fastidiousness. He had in these last years moved toward that blow, in growth like that of some plants that take food from air and earth and turn it into poison in their leaves. Even now I can feel how heavily that knowledge pressed upon me.

"Well," said Grand'mère at last. "I wouldn't worry about it. He's just a drunken coward."

Paul came slowly up to the porch. "He is a coward, but his memory may be long. Was he drunk when you hit him?"

"No," admitted Pierre. "But what difference—"

"If he had been drunk, he wouldn't hold a grudge, any more than he did when Grand'mère got after him. He'd come around and apologize and blame it on the drink. But now he won't forget it," said Paul slowly. "And Four Legs is the son of Chief Migisan."

"Why do you say that?" Pierre looked at his son, appealingly, as I had never seen him look before. Not one word of approval of his action had come from any of us. He wanted approval, and most of all from Paul.

Paul looked up at the cloud growing larger along the horizon. "Chief Migisan controls most of th Ottawas."

Pierre waited, but Paul said no more.

"Was Four Legs hurt much?" asked Grand'mère.

"I don't know." Pierre passed his thin hand wearily over his forehead. "I didn't see him again. But I think about every other Indian on the island came up and looked through the door at me after that."

We were silent for a moment.

"I wish Mr. Stuart was back," said Paul.

Pierre looked angry, then hurt. He started to speak, and then with worry deep on his face, he began his pacing again.

The clouds hung lower, and the sun was gradually slipping beneath the waves of the lake of the Illinois. Its brief splendor was no sooner gone than we heard a distant rumbling.

"Thunder," said Grand'mère in surprise.

The sound rolled up more distinctly.

"No," said Paul.

We listened, silent and motionless.

"Drums," said Grand'mère. "I never heard them like that before."

I shivered. I had.

We sat quiet, listening. Then a cold wind came around the corner of the house. At once a storm was upon us. Sheets of rain beat on the porch, and we hurried inside. The wind was growing, and like the trees on the heights, the house seemed fairly to bend under the strain. Paul stirred the fire, and brought more sticks to pile on the andirons in front of the long backlog. They caught and blazed up, a promise of warm comfort. We huddled close as if seeking more from it than warmth. Out of the window nothing could be seen but rain, wind-twisted in its fall.

"At least the rain has stopped the drum-beating." Pierre was thinking aloud.

"Yes," said Paul.

The next day when I left the mission school, I walked down the village street, and for a little way along the beach road in front of the lodges. Going home, I was troubled. Outwardly the life there was just the same. The kettles were still boiling, the children playing, the women quiet over mats or beadwork. I had heard no unusual word spoken, but every man was busy at his lodge-door. His usual apathy gone, he rubbed a tomahawk to brightness, oiled a musket, or took stock of his powder and shot. Knives that had been used for rough work around the lodges were being sharpened to the keenness of scalping knives again, and even the little boys were feathering arrows. At the door of the blacksmith shop waited not one or two but at least a dozen braves, with muskets in their hands and a few skins to pay for repairing them. One chief, bent over a small looking-glass on the sand, was painting his face with vermilion, spreading it in a pattern on his hands and pressing them to his face and naked shoulders. Not an unusual sight, but it was the design that caught my eye. There was no peace in the lines of it.

My first look at Paul when he came in told me he had seen what I had. At supper, Grand'mère was the only one with a mind to talk. Lightly she plunged into what was troubling us all.

"Did you see Four Legs again today?"

"No," said Pierre. He looked at Paul and me as if he would question us, then lowered his eyes to his plate, and said, "No Indians came in at all."

Paul and I looked at each other, adding this to the signs we had seen.

"Well, that must have been a relief," said Grand'mère, spreading butter thickly on a hot biscuit.

Pierre smiled faintly. "I dropped in for a talk with Mr. Campbell after work."

"And what did the government agent have to say?" asked Grand'mère gaily. "Did he tell you how his wife took all my money away at whist this afternoon?"

Pierre went on with an effort, as if it was due us to know what he had done. "I told him about yesterday's encounter."

"What did he think?" asked Paul quietly.

Pierre sighed, and crumbled a bit of bread beside his plate. "He was annoyed with me. I must say for a gentleman to use such language—however, what he said was that he had enough troubles as it was. The tribes were angry about the agency being moved, and every day the payments are delayed he can see more ominous signs of their impatience."

"They won't like the payments when they do get them," said Paul.

"He's afraid not. And the replacements at the fort haven't come. There's only a handful there, if any trouble starts."

As if in answer to his words, the drums began to beat on the shore. Long after Pierre and Grand'mère had gone to their rooms, Paul and I sat beside the fire. We winced at the sound of the drums, as if unseen flames flicked our skins. I wondered how much Paul knew about that sound that seemed to fill all space, even above the rioting of the few voyageurs that had not gone, above the thin strains of dance music coming from one of the shacks near the beach. Listening, I heard the rolling of the drums taken up at last by the encampment on Round Island, and a deeper, farther throbbing that might come from Bois Blanc, and no mere echo was it of the drums on Mackinac. It was heavy, insistent, a response to a signal, the signal I had heard in the forest only when the tribes had begun to work themselves up into a frenzy for the warpath.

By the next noon, Pierre's face had grown wan, his eyes sunken. He ate his dinner in silence and went back to the fur company. In the hour before I had to go back to the mission, I set about making the barm for bread-baking, feeling how strange it was that such familiar things must go forward, no matter what the trouble in our minds.

The bench where I was working stood in front of an

394

open window. A heavy fragrance came toward me from the honeysuckle vine clutching one post of the back porch, as it stretched upward to get a firmer hold on rough shingles above. As the breeze changed, the odor was gone. I picked up a double handful of delicate green blossoms newly gathered from the hop vine and enjoyed their pungent odor for a moment before letting them fall one by one into a kettle. I measured a gallon of water and poured it over them. Carrying the kettle to the living room fire, I stepped softly. Grand'mère was taking a nap. She lay on the sofa, a frail sleeping figure wrapped in a huge brown shawl whose fringed ends trailed off on the floor. Even when she was asleep, there was energy in her pose. Her knees were slightly drawn up, and one foot dangled off the edge as if she might get up at any moment.

I returned to the kitchen, putting flour and water into a bowl to mix for batter. It was quiet, and I heard the gentle buzzing of the wasps that had a nest along the eaves. After a while, Paul came in the back door, and listened to the sounds from the living room. Grand'-mère was still asleep, giving forth the softest of murmurings. Paul nodded in satisfaction, and stood close to the bench where I was smoothing out lumps with a wooden spoon, letting it make no sound against the dish. I looked a silent question at him, for I knew he had made a quick trip to the village after he got up from the dinner-table.

"I saw Mr. Campbell," he said softly. "He's talked to Chief Migisan, but it's no use. They think Father's whipping of Four Legs is an insult by the fur company to all the Ottawas."

I waited, while he paused long enough to be sure we hadn't wakened Grand'mère.

"And it's worse than that," he went on. "Mr. Campbell called in one of the Ojibway chiefs to see if he would try to calm them down." Paul and I looked at each other thoughtfully, knowing such an action would be interpreted to mean the agent was trying to set one tribe against another.

"The payments have just come. The boxes of goods are being unloaded from the schooner right now," said Paul. "Mr. Campbell hopes the tribes will just take them and go away. But he's far from being easy about it." He was silent for a moment, while the buzzing of the wasps mingled with the sounds of Grand'mère's breathing.

"I suppose he's worried about the soldiers being gone," I said. "Any uprising now—"

"Yes," said Paul. "News came by the schooner that replacements were on the way. They'll be up from Detroit perhaps tomorrow—"

We looked at each other. Would tomorrow be in time, our thoughts were asking.

Thirteen

When the afternoon was nearly gone, Mrs. Fisher came to the door of the girls' workroom and beckoned me away from my class in weaving.

"The doctor is here to look at Eliza Bird's rash," she whispered. "But even he can't do a thing with the child. She seems afraid to let anyone touch her. Will you—"

The dozen girls in the room had raised their heads when Mrs. Fisher appeared and then turned back to the designs growing before them on the looms. "Keep your mind on your pattern," I remember telling them, knowing as I used Marthe's words that she had ever meant the gentle warning to reach far out beyond the weaving of mats.

Martin looked up at me with a quick smile as I went

in the dormitory. "It was good of you to come," he said.

Drawing near to him was to me like approaching a hearth when one is cold. Happiness flowed like warmth over me from his tones, and I held his words close.

I picked up the unhappy, frightened child, and she put her brown arms around my neck. In a few minutes her sobs had died away to whimpering, and she lay quiet. Martin bent over the four-year-old and looked at the spots on her arms. As he talked to the sick child, his quiet voice seemed to enclose a space in which we were all alone, and the other children in near-by beds, and those passing the open door, were but dim shadows beyond. I could smell the cleanness of him, and a fresh odor in the folds of his blue uniform as if he had but lately come through a grove of balsam. I could have laid my fingers in the shining lights of his brown hair.

"You're going to be a good girl now and take this medicine when Mrs. Fisher gives it to you, aren't you?" he asked at last.

Eliza looked at him doubtfully.

"You want to get well," I said to her. "The medicine will drive out the evil spirit that is keeping you away from our weaving class. The others are getting ahead of you."

Eliza considered this, and nodded her head at Martin.

He smiled. "You're going to have a room by yourself for a while, young lady. I'll come back to see you tomorrow." Eliza's black eyes looked at him solemnly.

"You won't cry next time, will you?"

Eliza thought a minute, and nodded vigorously. Martin and I laughed together.

"She's honest about it," he said. "Cute little mite. There's something about these children—I feel so much more important when I do something for them than when I patch up a fighting voyageur, or fuss over some old woman that's eaten too much and will do it again.

These children are growing up in a world different from anything their parents knew—" He broke off, and began to pack the little bottles and boxes in his brown bag again. "I wish I could handle them the way you do," he went on after a little. "There's something about you— a stream of health flows from you that quiets the sick."

I stroke Eliza's head, lying against my white ruffled waist. I could not answer.

Mrs. Fisher was hovering outside, waiting. I tucked Eliza back in bed, and Martin waited for me to go out ahead of him.

"That's a pretty necklace you're wearing," he said.

"Paul ordered it from New York for my birthday."

"Amber, isn't it?"

I nodded.

"It's just the color of wet sand on the beach, or the lights in rich maple sugar."

When Martin stopped to talk to Mrs. Fisher about Eliza, I went back to my class, walking slowly, as if not to lose the soft warm cloud that enfolded me.

Going down the path to the village, after the day's work was over, I remember that the inner glow I felt seemed a part of the late summer sunshine. The trees were rustling, and birds flashed their bright plumage among the leaves and sang as if they wanted to give the island something to remember them by when they were gone. Three soldiers—all there were now except for Martin and the major and one lieutenant—were digging in the fort garden at the foot of the hill, handling their shovels more slowly than they had in the spring, as if their eagerness for gardening had passed, leaving them only with potatoes that had to be dug. They stopped often to look toward the east, watching for the ship that would bring the new company to the fort

Along the half-moon beach, the water was full of

canoes. The last brigade was testing its boats and loading, ready for a start in the morning. Each canoe was set in the water with a shout or a bit of song, as if with this testing of the canoes, voices were being tried for their readiness for the boat songs.

It was early enough so that Pierre would be still at the warehouse, and I turned that way, intending to wait for him. Groups of women were coming from Mrs. Stuart's white house where the sewing circle had been meeting, and scattering toward their homes behind white pickets the whole length of the village. A little way ahead of me, in front of the company store, I saw Ellen in pale pink. Her arms were carefully shielded from the sun by long white gloves, and a calash of green silk and rattan was drawn over her yellow hair to shade her face. She was talking with Currance.

As I drew near along the path, Currance, in plain blue gingham, was admiring the fine lawn of Ellen's dress, the wide green satin ribbon marking the high waistline, the ruffles edging the long full skirt, and other ruffles of lace that circled Ellen's ankles below the skirt.

"What do you call those?" I heard Currance ask, pointing to these lowest ruffles.

"Haven't you seen pantalettes before?" Ellen laughed in her high, light voice. "It's the very newest fashion in the east."

"They're rather odd-looking. How do you keep them up?"

"These are tied on just below the knee," said Ellen. "They only look odd because you aren't used to them yet."

"You always have the latest styles, don't you?" sighed Currance enviously.

"Oh, yes. One must try to keep in the fashion. It's the only way to endure life here in the west. I am so glad I shall live in Boston when I am married."

"Boston?"

"Yes. That's where Martin was, you know, and he has been offered the directorship of the hospital if he will go back. We can have such a nice life there—"

"Oh!" said Currance excitedly. "You and Martin—"

"Oh, well, you mustn't say anything about it, yet," said Ellen, with an attempt at coyness. "But you'll hear an announcement before long. Probably at the party we shall have when the new officers come."

The light of the day had suddenly gone, as much as if the sun had ended it hours earlier than he should. Martin was going to marry Ellen! There was no room for any thought but that, and it grew until I felt the whole village was shouting it in my ears.

Dully, I knew Ellen and Currance were still talking, and the words struck at me like little darts of lightning still playing upon a shattered pine.

"You are very lucky," Currance was saying, earnestly. "He is such a fine man."

"You mustn't say that." Ellen slapped her playfully on the arm with her white fan. "You must say that he is the lucky one."

"Well, of course. We had him come over to St. Ignace when Michel fell from a roof, and he was so nice to us. He wouldn't take any pay, either. I suppose he could see by our house that we needed money for so many things. He's such a nice man." Currance sighed.

"Of course," said Ellen impatiently, as if Currance had missed the most important thing. "He comes from one of the best families in Boston, you know. They're all brilliant—doctors and writers, and people like that. It is natural he should have turned to me. There is really no one else on the island of his kind."

With no other thought than to get away I turned around and walked rapidly toward the beach. It was the only direction I could go without being seen by the two girls or risk encountering Martin leaving the mission school.

So the things he had said to me were only in friendliness. He had liked me as he liked an unknown island plant, as he liked to watch the traders grading pelts, as he liked all the color and movement of the life here.

My cheeks burned, remembering the thoughts that had made my step lighter on the island paths. Shame sent a dull red fire along my veins, and I hardly knew where I went. I knew that I was passing among the lodges, that I saw braves lounging about the blanket doors, so immovable that their buckskin fringes never stirred, and that I avoided three young ones on the beach, playing a silent game of cards with twists of tobacco as stakes. I remember circling an open fire where two small children, driven by some trace of fire worship in their blood, were leaping back and forth across its edges.

I came alongside a pile of steamer wood near the water. I stopped and leaned against it, my head on one arm, and gazed out over the straits, as if there might be some solace in those regular, breaking waves. My grandfather used to stand that way, summoning an answer from distant stretches of water. But the waves gave me no ease. Ever coming toward me and falling back, they could not wash away Ellen's words. No one else on the island was of his kind.

I tried to watch the people coming and going on the beach, but they were blurs of movement and color. Into my misery came sounds that told me a brigade was loading, and I was dimly conscious that near me stood a group of Ottawa girls, sending admiring glances at the gaudily dressed voyageurs, and giggling among themselves when one turned from his work to throw them a coarse remark. I watched them as they stood there in their calico dresses with trimmings of buckskin fringes and beads. Their long braids were fastened with beaded strips, and beads shone from their moccasins. Each one of them was actually putting her best foot forward, to show she could work moccasins better than the rest.

I looked down at my broadcloth skirt and white linen shirtwaist and saw them as symbols of the difference between my own life and theirs. A good manito had watched over me. I thought of the fine gray dress I had worn home from Quebec, the many others of soft dainty materials that hung in my room at Grand'mère's. I thought of my years of study with the good Ursuline nuns. No other girl on Mackinac had as good training in books, in music, in the ways of French ladies. I let my mind rest upon that thought: I might not be Martin's kind, but I was not like these girls.

I felt a new surge of gratitude toward Pierre. His picture came up in my thoughts—as he walked, as he stood with other men, his very way of standing making him different. I remembered how he always spoke, slowly, fastidious of his words as of his person. His voice was ever low and courteous, so different from the rough, coarsely jovial tones of the men of the loading brigade. I heard one of them talking to the Ottawa girls at that moment.

"Ah, ze pretty maidens," he was saying in a mocking voice. I turned away in disgust to look out over the straits. One of the new fleet of Paul's fishing boats was lowering its sail as it slid toward the beach around the point.

Behind me, the voyageur was still talking. "They have told me when I came from Montreal yesterday to join up with the fur company that I would find ze beautiful Indian girls here—all ze girls you want, they tell me. Just go down to the beach and pick one out. A different one every night, they told me. I tell them, I pick the prettiest one." He laughed loudly. I could hear his feet

402

crunching on the pebbles as he walked around the giggling cluster of girls. Then he seemed to have centered his attention on some one of them. "Aha! I choose you. Yours is the lodge I will bring my presents to when it is dark. Only tell me, my little chicken, under which tent flap must I crawl to find your soft arms, my pretty one?"

Grand'mère would wipe her broom on such a one, I thought, turning to go home.

As I did so I saw that the narrow eyes below the low forehead and bushy eyebrows were looking directly at me! I was the one he had been talking to all the time! For a moment I couldn't take my eyes off that repulsive face. I could see only those curling lips, stained with tobacco. He was talking to me, Oneta Debans, as he would to any loose, ignorant girl who lived in a tent and let men crawl under its flat at night!

After that first look of shame and horror I let no further sign show of the feelings tossing and tumbling within me. I did not speak, but walked deliberately away from the beach, back toward the village and up to the fort. Once through its gate with its friendly sentry, and past the quarters, I began to run, out across the parade-ground and past the rifle range and down the trail called Alexander Henry's.

I followed the trail, at first parallel with the cliff, and then plunging down into evergreen glooms and up again. Over mossy logs I leaped and my feet sped over roots and grass, and the dead leaves of many summers. The deep-worn path became less distinct, and at last I came where bushes and trees were closely interlaced above it. In one of those dark hollows, the trail broke into a group of raveled ends. Blindly I followed one of those traces, heedless of the evergreen branches against my face and arms. Back into the forest I ran, out of the sight of the sun, deep in the shade where others seldom went, following the trace until it was lost in leaves and moss. There I threw myself down on a grassy spot near the upturned roots of a wind-fallen tree, careless of the damage to my dress from sodden leaves and mossy rocks. I was ashamed of my clothes. Couldn't that voyageur see that I was different? No one would ever say a thing like that to Currance, or the major's daughter, or even to Rosanne, for all her free ways with the men. And I, Oneta, had for years belonged to a family as good as any in the village. I am not like those others, I thought, and the trees waved above and let the lament pass through, as if they had heard it many times rise from the hearts of women.

Why I hadn't gone home, I didn't know. I knew only that I had to run back here, where there was no one—no one at all. I lay prone on the earth, my flushed cheek pressed into the welcoming cool moss. I shook with sobs, turning my burning face from one side to the other. A chipmunk paused on a log to gaze at me curiously, then went on about his own affairs, under the curling tips of a cluster of ferns. I lay there for a long time. Between my sobs it was so quiet I could hear in the trees the sound of wings and of little beaks exploring loosened bark.

Ellen's words had hurt, but that feeling had been nothing to this greater humiliation. To the careless eyes of a new voyageur, I was only an Indian girl. Lying there, I realized how far I had gone in building on the knowledge I had gained from books, on the fine clothing I had, on the feeling that I was as good as anyone on the island. Abjectly I faced for the first time the meaning of this truth. I was one of my tribe. All the years at the convent and in Grand'mère's home were as nothing.

At last the stillness of the woods and the odor of the spruces began to quiet me. My sobs died away, and something like a quiet patience came to me, as if from the ground below, where there was no grieving, no regret.

I felt myself absorbed by the earth as if I had ceased to be, and the very wanting to be had been stilled. The woods calmed me with the soft green mystery they had carried, endlessly, since the beginning of time.

I didn't even hear the approach of Marthe, when she came, quiet as an animal, with no cracking of twigs underfoot or swishing of disturbed branches. She had come from the eastern shore and was returning home, her root-digging stick in one hand, her faded calico apron full of roots and herbs gathered up and held in the other.

"Oneta!" she said, peering around the fallen tree. "I saw something red, and knew no flowers grew in here. It was the ribbon on your hair." She came toward me, feeling her way into the dark grove. No, there were no flowers there, where the thick overhanging foliage almost shut out the daylight. Nothing grew there but moss and thin grass about the base of the trees.

Marthe sank to her knees beside me, on one of those grassy spots, and I could feel her looking down at me for a long moment. I did not turn my head.

"Why are the eyes wet, the face red when it should be brown and cool, so close to your mother, the earth?"

I lifted my head only to let it fall on my outstretched arms. "I am all right."

Marthe loosened the strings of her apron and laid it with its burden of herbs to one side. Then she lifted my head, and laid it in her lap as she braced her back against a tree trunk. "It is no evil spirit in the body that puts such pain in your voice?"

I clutched Marthe's hand. Her hand was the first one that had touched me when I was born. She had been a part of my life from the beginning. And she was with me now. Briefly, and as clearly as I could I told her what had happened on the beach.

When I was at an end, Marthe sat as though waiting for me to continue. At last she said, "There is more.

There is more than a stupid voyageur who could not recognize Tecumseh's daughter."

Somehow her mistaking the feelings I had had for pride in my birth was more than I could bear. All within me broke, and with the words tumbling over one another, I told her everything.

She was silent a long time when I had finished. When she spoke, she began slowly and talked in fragments, as she had so often done when she told me stories long ago. "White people have given you strange ideas. You think to be good, to have their respect, you must be like them.

"The young doctor has sought me out two, maybe three times and asked me for my secrets of healing. He has spoken with me as he would with any white woman.

"He likes our people. He has had one of the boys from the mission teach him the language. Several times each moon the boy goes up to the fort and teaches the Ojibway words to the young doctor.

"You must wait. It may be cold at the base of a pine, while its top is still catching the sun."

A pine—it was a pine that had been my mother's manito. The huge pine in an open spot on the island that had been struck again and again by lightning until its top was gone and the trunk split into long dangling strips. And still it lived. Marthe and my mother were like that. Twice a blow had fallen on Marthe, once when my father had chosen someone else, and again when his death had fallen on all of us, and especially on her.

Pines and cedars held their foliage close over us, forming a natural lodge. The cool damp moss was fragrant. There was something about it of earth and growing things, of life working out its own way here in a darkly overhung place, without sky and sun to help. It was like being hidden from the world, and it was pleasant. I lay for long moments, unmoving. I felt a part of this place, akin to the earth and plants, and for the first time in years, to Marthe. We were silent so long I forgot there was anything to life but regular breathing and woodland odors and Marthe's nearness.

I must not be afraid. The thought struck me as suddenly as if a ray of sunlight had penetrated the grove. But our shade was undisturbed. A new surge of warmth began to work through me, giving me strength. Yes, I must wait. Time would direct my destiny. I let go of Marthe's hand, and began to smooth the twigs and leaves from my hair. Marthe got up, took up her apron and root-stick, and moved toward the edge of the grove. "Are you going now?"

"No, Marthe," I answered. "I want to be here alone for a little while. I am not yet ready."

Marthe's footsteps passed out of the cedar grove and became silent. I do not know how long I stayed there, close to the earth, drained of thought and lulled almost to dreams by its cool comfort. Twilight came, when the border between the real and shadow world grows vague, and the rocks and trees put on strange garments. Faintly through the woods sounded the evening gun of the fort, booming the separation of day and night. The trees became indistinct, only the birches showing white against the purple shadow.

I felt as quiet as if I had gone back under Marthe's hands to the moment of my birth. Life seemed to be renewed, my senses resharpened to aromas and faint sounds. The day's noises grew hushed, as all wild things settled to rest. The odors from small flowers hidden in the lush grass came to me on soft night breezes. They seemed not to have the essence of that summer night, but of last summer, or many summers ago. A sweetness filled the place, but as of flowers just dead whose fragrance lingered in undisturbed hollows. It was as though they refused to crumble and pass into scentless dust.

The feeling came over me that I was where one time overlapped another, being all the same in eternity. As if

407

sweet tones of music could stay in the air and moons later come to the ears of one who made himself quiet enough to hear, something arising out of that ground floated me back into things that were past, and told me they were not gone.

Memory and this new harmony with the earth where I lay recalled to me then that those were not ordinary cliffs above a lake. Down in the caves far below me lay many a warrior with his belt of wampum, his knives and paint and feathers, his bow and arrows beside him. These were the aged ones, and only those who had been in the front of battle. I was above the bones of my ancestors, like a flower that had grown there. As if wafted up through rock and moss I felt stir in me a reminder of the wisdom and courage that had inspired a Philip, a Pontiac, a Tecumseh, to feel that he must not be less than those who had gone before him.

Tecumseh! Like a clear tone that drove out all other sounds, I seemed to hear again the words of Marthe, ". . . a stupid voyageur who could not recognize Tecumseh's daughter."

And then I saw how I had let the new ways put aside the value of what I was. I knew the blood that ran through my outstretched arms and pulsed in the cheek against the cool earth. I had heard it in the talk around the lodge-fire, and Marthe had tried to keep it before me through the years, but I had not listened or heeded what she said. Stronger than all the legends, the lore of the greatness that was Tecumseh's was built up in the minds of all Indians, pieced together from the stories they had heard into a whole of such grandeur that only the name was enough to bring respect to their eyes. Anyone who had known him was thereby become a greater one in his tribe, and it was his greatest pride, more than the number of his wives or children, his bear claws, his wounds, or the scalps he had taken.

I felt a new stir of life along my veins, as words of

Marthe's, said in my childhood, sounded clear in my thoughts. "You are all there is of Tecumseh remaining on this earth." I sat up, a new excitement running through me, a quiver of pride such as I had not felt for many years. I was Tecumseh's daughter! All things that had troubled me had come because I had forgotten who I was. Whenever Tecumseh appeared, all others gave way and waited for him to speak, their faces turned to him. They never questioned that he was better than their common selves. To my shame I saw that if I had borne myself with Tecumseh's pride and dignity, no voyageur would have taken me for a common girl.

I rose, and moved erectly out of the grove and turned my face toward the village. Up the green tangled height I climbed, as alive as the twigs of the close-set bushes, to the mystery of the autumn night. Over the heights hung a covering of fog, but I moved with confidence up the almost hidden trail, walking over long pine cones that lay strewn on the ground like discarded spirit sheaths. At the top, I came out on the cliff overlooking the beach. I stepped from the yielding leaves of the path to the firm granite of the rock that ran like a backbone through all the island. Still in the exultation of my new feeling I moved to its jutting edge and looked over. Again I felt I might be in the past, for the pale gray fog unfolded itself upward and back against the cliff, hiding the village from sight. One could not tell what period of its history lay beneath. Gone were the stores and warehouses and the dormered homes. Gone were the flag of thirteen stripes and the scarlet coats that had come before it. Gone were the black robes and their crosses and their lilies of France. The beach lay clean and pure, a strip of pebbles below the bluff, the fog revealing only the first rows of the lodges.

The moon appeared from the heavy gray clouds and gave shifting lights to the mist. Silence gave way then and the beating of my heart was caught up into a rhythm. I heard again the great echo that swings from island to island, aware of its deep music before I heard what had started it. It seemed right and natural, as if the stirring within me had grown until silence could no longer be. The throbbing seemed to come from all directions at once, distant but clear. Even when it grew closer, more insistent, and I recognized the thumping of hands on drumheads from the beach below, it was still a part of what I had been feeling. Through the grayness of the fog, as through a curtain of the past, I saw figures emerge from the lodges. On the beach, kettles were empty beside deserted fires sending up their last threads of smoke, throwing a flickering light upon the ceremony beginning in the large open space beyond the lodges. It was the corn dance, the ceremony of thanksgiving that had come after the harvest since the early days. The aged ones could have arisen from their burial caves and taken their places in it without fault.

The two drummers sat at the edge of the open space, but the flute player could not be seen, for by custom he was at a distance, away from the light of the fires. But his notes came shrill, in a rhythm of their own.

Slowly a circle of men began to move around and around to the beating of the drums. As they moved into the firelight and out of it again, I saw some fully dressed in shirt, breechcloth and leggings, with blankets across their shoulders. Others had only a breechcloth and feather adornment, with painted bodies. On the outside, the women and children began to make another, larger circle. With feet scarcely lifted from the ground, they danced in a slow, sidewise gliding.

Satisfaction glowed deep within me. It was almost as if I had commanded that it be done, and watched from my place of honor. I nodded in approval as one brave left his place, beginning a faster dance as he wove in and out of the two slow-moving circles, swaying and twisting as he stepped. The music of the flute was for him, and he followed it in fantastic movements while the circles kept on in their monotonous step to the regular thumping of the drums.

In and out went the lone dancer, sinuous and graceful, accompanied by the steady pulse of feet, and back of that the whisper of water breaking on pebbles. Finally his dance reached its height, and standing in the center, he lifted his arms. I knew he was speaking to the great spirit, making an offering of whatever he had in his hands, in thanks for good things received. High above him, I lifted my own arm in approval, as he stood there repeating words I had no need to hear. The same ones had been used by the tribes since the beginning of life.

Under cover of the fog, away to the right, I heard the soft footfalls of moccasins coming up the trail from the village. The bushes stirred at the top, and someone in a brown jacket, hatless, pulled himself up by them and came into view. It was Paul.

"Oneta!" he called, with urgency in his voice.

"Yes, I am here."

Paul peered at me, coming closer. "Marthe said she saw you up here. I've been looking for you."

"Have you?" I asked, and I remember that at the time my own voice seemed to be coming from a great distance.

Puzzled, Paul stopped just back of the rock ledge. "Don't you see what's going on down there?" His voice was full of excitement.

"I have been watching. It is the corn dance."

I could see a perplexed look spread over Paul's face.

"They don't do the corn dance these days, you know, until the payments have been made. The agent gave out the goods tonight. The tribes are ugly. They didn't get much gold. The war-dance will be next—" He broke off, and came to stand on the ledge beside me, raising

411

one arm and pointing toward the beach. "See that pile of stuff down there?"

I looked, and saw a great mound, higher than the heads of the squatting drummers. It looked dark until the flare of a near-by fire gleamed upon it. It shone white then, a-sparkle almost as if it were snow.

"The agent gave them salt!" said Paul. "They don't use salt. They emptied it in that pile."

The fog shifted a little, and against the white picket fences below, a breeze from the straits sighed a warning, as if an unfriendly spirit rode upon it.

Paul went on, his usually slow voice quickened with alarm. "Nothing can stop them. They hate Father—our house will be the first. I've been looking for you. We must do what we can."

I lifted one hand to stop him. "I shall do what is to be done."

"*You* will—?"

"Yes. I shall go home," I said, but I looked not toward the house of Grand'mère and Pierre as I said it.

"Half the young men are painted now. It won't be long—"

"I shall take care of it," I said. "I shall tell them what they are to do."

I remember how sharply Paul raised his head at the authority in my voice. The confusion I saw in his face would have been ludicrous at any other time.

I walked back to the ledge of rock and faced him directly. "I am the daughter of Tecumseh," I said. Paul stared at me as I went on speaking.

"When Tecumseh summoned, no man would fail to answer. His call would go from campfire to campfire through the forest until it was heard by thousands and every brave would rise and go."

I turned toward the beach again. "I am of his blood; I have his eyes as a sign that I am worthy." At that moment I knew how true it was, and everything else I had been dropped from me. The way opened clear and fresh. The high demand had come, and strength had risen in me to meet it.

I remember watching Paul's face in the moonlight, seeing how over the worried look slowly the light of belief came to his eyes. I remember that he stepped back a little, as if something new in my presence made a charmed circle about me in which he had no right to be.

He made no answer, and in the silence a new clamor arose from the beach. A little procession of drunken Ottawas had come from one of the saloons and plunged into the middle of the corn dance.

"Look, Oneta," said Paul. "All the old men—"

I looked toward the lodge at one side, from which came an old man, and then another, and a third. Even then the blanket flap did not close, for they kept coming out, all older men. The first one stood at the side, a large council pipe in his hand. Old Chief Migisan, his red robe trailing behind him scarlet in the firelight, stepped to the center of the rioting braves. He shouted in anger, and all but a few stopped and shrank back from his wrath. Two of them he seized by the scalp-lock and shook until they cowered at his feet.

Into the space before him stepped a medicine man, a shaman. I could see his rattles, his white elkskin jacket, his cape of feathers. He began addressing the chief, and their gestures became eloquent.

"I must go," I said. "The old men have sat in council, and they have not agreed. They will hold another, before all the tribes, and the medicine man will try his powers. By the signs in his hand, I know he is going to try the most powerful of all medicine. He is going to call on the spirits of the dead."

Paul drew a long breath. "It's war, for sure."

413

I nodded, knowing that I must act quickly, to keep smoke and flames from the village, and blood from the limestone paths.

"They seem to be putting up a new lodge," said Paul, looking down at the women putting up lodge-poles, near the clump of junipers that closed the west end of the clearing.

"Yes. The medicine man uses it for the secret parts of his ceremony."

I saw that clump of junipers, and I knew what I must do.

"Come," I said. "I may want you."

He stepped aside and waited silently for me to go before him down the cliff.

Fourteen

✖ Grand'mère was dozing on the sofa, her white hair gleaming against the brocade of the cushions. Pierre, reading before the fire, scarcely looked up as I slipped into my room and reappeared with my moccasins on and my deerskin dress under my arm.

"Going out again?" he asked kindly.

"Yes, for a little while." I stood for a moment behind his chair, looking at the brown wavy hair I had admired from my first sight of him. I could see it dangling at the belt of some triumphant warrior, and the thought gave a new urgency to my steps. I hurried on into the kitchen where Paul was waiting.

Whispering for him to light a candle and follow me, I went softly up the attic stairs. There in the dark I changed into the deerskins and took the pins out of my hair so it fell in two braids once more. By the time Paul had come with the candle, I had already felt my way along in the dark and moved the boxes piled on top of the little one marked INDIAN GOODS. I opened the box and laid aside the dresses, the silver armlets, the blue blanket of my mother. I drew out the hunting coat of Tecumseh, and shook out its crushed fringes. Laying it to one side by itself, I took out the things Black Hawk had brought with the news of my father's death. First, the headdress of bright red feathers with the two eagle quills extending straight back from its center, the very war-bonnet Tecumseh had worn in his last battle. I laid this with the hunting coat, and reached into the bottom of the box. Out came a necklace of grizzly claws, and entangled among them was a silver chain. I separated them, and laid the grizzly claws with the coat and war-bonnet. The chain I slipped over my head, letting the medal hang on the bosom of my deerskin dress. Another groping in the box brought out the little medicine bag of charms that had been with my father in all his dangers, and a stone, with little chipped places all over it. The arrowhead. I held it in my hand, remembering. Tecumseh thought there might be a young warrior in his lodge, to grow up to be as brave in battle, as eloquent as himself. A queer stirring went over me, and I slipped the arrowhead in among the charms and tied the little skin bag to my beaded belt. Better medicine I did not ask for. The glow of the candle was steady, and it is only my memory of that which tells me Paul was there. At that moment I was alone in a world that had flowed out of the box and filled the attic to its very beams. In a trance I took up the armful of Tecumseh's garments, and went down the stairs. The candlelight followed me to the kitchen, and as I went out in the darkness, behind me came the soft sound of Paul's feet, keeping close upon my heels.

Darkness and mist made dim blue shadows of the outlines of the island, as we silently crossed the gardens that lay between us and the beach, passing houses where tallow dips gave faint light through small-paned windows. I drew near the council ground, and slipped in among the shadows of the juniper thicket. Paul followed, and we stood close and motionless, knowing I must wait for a favorable time.

In the firelit space before us, eight poles had been set firmly in the ground, and bound at the top with withes to form a lodge which the women were covering with mats. Like the day itself, its door of entrance was at the east, of departure at the west. One side of it was almost within reach of my arm.

As the women finished, they took their places back of the young men, so far from the council-fire that only now and then as it flared high could I see a bent form, a bit of printed calico, or a patient, mild face.

We were just at the edge of the shadow. With the fire for the center, a hard-trodden circle about fifteen feet across had been left clear before the medicine lodge. Around this sat a circle of chiefs and head men. One had a robe of wolf, another sat hunched under worn-out lodge skins, the poorest garment a man could have, but each wore a silver medal on his chest. Close together sat four hard-featured Ottawas with red stripes of paint around their arms. At the end, staring thoughtfully into the fire, tired-looking, but as one gathering strength for something he had to do, sat a stranger. He was too young to be a chief, yet he sat in an honored place. From his dress, his paint, and his half-shaved head with its tuft of short feathers, I knew him to be a Fox.

Back of the chiefs, in little gatherings by tribes and ages, sat the young men and boys, looking impatient as if needlessly kept back from the excitement of the warpath. Their faces were made ugly by their thoughts. Sullen and purposeful rows of men, cross-legged, with arms folded or resting on their knees, reached so far back from the firelight that I could not tell how many hundreds there might be.

The medicine man was squatting before the lodge, silent. The fire cast red lights on the folds of his white elkskins, brightening their Midé symbols. Wound in a broad strip on his wrist was his medicine necklace, its parts taken from everything known to run or fly in northern forests—claws, toes, tails, especially of deformed animals, for they were greater medicine, having received some special attention from the manito. The medicine man stirred the blaze before him, and the firelight spread its reflections in quick darts that lighted up the beach, the water, and reddened the mound of salt. Though the circles of men sat motionless, shadows flickered among them, and as one after another was lighted and then left in darkness, it seemed as if their bodies were moving, that they were already swaying in the first slow measures of the war dance.

In the leader's place, Chief Migisan was waiting, but several others would be asked to speak, the minor chiefs first. Calmly I stood among the junipers, like one of them, waiting. I would let others prepare the way and make the time right for me.

When the silence had been unbroken for several minutes, Chief Migisan arose, his rusty green frock coat with brass buttons nearly covered by the red blanket drawn across his shoulders, under his right arm, and held together with his left hand, leaving his right arm free. The medicine man lifted a red stone pipe, handling with respect the long stem with its dangling strips of beaded cloth and bright feathers. He drew a brand from the fire and lighted it. Chief Migisan took it then, and presented its stem to the north and south, the east and west, then upward to the great spirit, and downward to the earth. After taking one puff himself, he handed it gravely to the leading Ojibway chieftain, occupying the next place of honor. After a puff, the long-stemmed pipe passed on to the next chief, and after

I could no longer see it, I could follow its progress by the clouds of smoke arising and mingling to show the great spirit that harmony was in the council.

In the silence I heard the slightest of noises, the crackling of a stick on the fire, the heavy breathing of the old Ojibway chief, the soft flapping as a sudden breeze caught the blanket door of a lodge and whirled it briefly upward against the mat covering.

When the pipe had made the rounds, Chief Migisan lifted his hand. "Greetings, my friends of many tribes. I see before me Hurons, Pottawatomies, Menominees the rice-eaters, our relatives the Ojibways, and my own Ottawas."

A few murmured responses followed his words. He stood still, dramatic, an experienced orator, until all was quiet. The medicine man put another stick on the fire, so that he would not have to disturb the coming speech, and settled back on his haunches. The flames leaped, their glare thrown on the lodge-flap, the serious faces, the old chief in the center.

The young men watched sullenly.

"The dark bird of trouble has alighted among us. We who once ruled here have been treated like dogs begging before the doors of the white men."

A growl arose from those in war-paint, but Chief Migisan went on firmly. "In council here, my brothers, your chiefs shall speak, and the spirits of the dead shall listen, and send us good medicine. Then we shall lift our axes and knives, our guns and torches, and begin to take back our own." He nodded to the first chief in the line, and sat down again in his place.

With a tinkling of the rattles on his elkskin robe, the medicine man bent low. His face close to the ground, he began to beat his little drum, softly through the talks that followed.

Little Bear of the Menominees arose. "We are from Sandy Lake. The spring flood destroyed our gardens and

418

the wild rice. We were depending on the payments of the Great White Father. In former days when there was no rice we could live by hunting. But now there are no tracks of animals. The trees are falling in the forests; the naked land will flow to meet the sky. Every year the game is driven away and goes beyond the sound of axes."

The next chief arose and spoke briefly. "A drought cut short our crop of corn, and game was scarce. We need the gold promised for the land we have given up." He wrapped the worn lodge-skins about him and sat down. The next one in line shook his head, and did not rise. The lesser chiefs had finished. Besides Chief Migisan, there were only two others of importance. Now was their turn to speak, and they would be the last before the medicine man began his ceremony, unless the stranger, the Fox, had come with a message.

The chief in the wolf robe arose, and stood tall in the center of the circle. "I am Gray Wolf of the Ojibways."

I looked more closely at the wrinkled face of this friend of my grandfather, aged, but erect as ever.

"In the old days," he was saying, "there was no sickness. Our numbers grew, and countless braves could we raise in a moment, trained for war. Once we were happy. Whatever was in the land was ours—ours the game to eat, ours the fur of otter and beaver to wrap ourselves in, of bear and wolf to lie upon, deerskins to keep the cold wind from our lodges. Men died on the warpath or of old age, honorably.

"Now the white men have come to sit down among us. They come first with smooth words, but when they have power over us their words grow rough. They bring diseases our lodges never knew before; our medicine men know nothing of them. They take our children into the teaching wigwam, and when we come for them, they tell us the child we gave them from our arms is in a box in the ground. Where is your child, and yours, and yours?" He swung about the circle, pointing to figures

419

that responded with groans. With stern, bitter face he waited until they were silent. "I have come to the island of the turtle for the first time in many summers, and I find my people in great unhappiness. I say let one life pay for another. Let the white men die to pay for our children."

A murmur of approval that turned into an angry roar followed as he took his place in the circle. Chief Migisan raised his hand for silence, a reminder that one more chief must still be heard.

In the pause between, the medicine man laid down his drum and his drumstick carved like the head of a loon. He spread out some bones and a tuft of hair before him on the beach. He threw sweet-smelling grease upon the embers, and purified the bones in the smoke. Settling back on his haunches, he stared at the sacred stone heating in the center of the fire.

The oldest man, Chief Old Wing of the Ottawas, arose with the dignity of one who is to say the final word. His gray head was decorated with eagle feathers and tufts of colored hair. A blanket covered with scalp-locks hung from his shoulder, and his free arm gestured as he talked.

"They have made treaties, and have broken every one. They say 'as long as the sun shall shine and the rivers flow with water,' and after one winter's snow they hold out a new treaty with gun and knife in hand.

"To pay for our land they have sent us salt instead of gold. We have piled their salt on the beach for the waves to come and take.

"Chief Migisan's own son has been whipped like a dog from the door of the big fur wigwam that has grown fat from our winter's hunt."

A snarl came from someone back in the council. "The paleface who whipped! He will not see the sun again!"

A murmur of approval came from the young men, impatient with the talk. Listening, I wondered whether

420

the council would break up at that moment, whether the old men could hold the young ones back any longer. But Old Wing was still on his feet. "They tell us now that we must go far to the west to live, away from these lakes our canoes have known so long. It is time now to say we will not go. We cannot go west into the land of the Sioux. We have ever been at war with the Sioux."

A growl of confirmation went back over the throng, and unrest began among the young men, started by two or three with rum bottles in their hands. One young brave arose, and his face, streaked with red paint and charcoal, showed hideous in the firelight. Suddenly raising his voice to highest pitch, he uttered a loud war-whoop. Around him others leaped to their feet, and with a yell of rage, they rushed to the lodges for knives and guns. I held myself ready. My time might be here now.

The young men came out of the lodges with empty hands, shouting and cursing, running toward the women, who had hidden the weapons as they ever did when firewater entered a dance. The nearest one crouched with arm over her head, ready for a blow. I waited, ready to step forward.

But the pause before the women were attacked was enough for Chief Migisan to make himself heard. "Get back in your places," he shouted in anger. "We will not raise the war-whoop until the spirits have given us good medicine for the warpath." He strode over to the one who had uttered the forbidden cry. "So you take authority upon yourself in the presence of older men." Chief Migisan looked at him sternly, and then jerked the three feathers from the young brave's head.

"It is the firewater," he said, "that makes our young men act like fools. We were better when men drank only pure water from spring or cool-flowing stream."

The murmur of approval came from the row of chiefs.

The medicine man still gazed into the fire, relaxed. It must be then that one more was to speak before the ceremony.

When quiet came again, Chief Migisan beckoned to the one with the Fox war-paint. He rose and stood in the center of the circle, arranged his blanket over his arm, and was still.

Chief Migisan spoke. "A voice brings us news of great trouble among another nation of red men. Our brother from the tribe of the Foxes has come a long way to speak to us. He brings a wampum belt, asking us to join with his tribe in war."

The Fox was a little less than the common size of men, and some looked at him doubtfully. Chief Little Bear stirred and spoke to him. "What have you done in war? How many scalps? It is not our custom to follow a leader who has not told us of his deeds."

The Fox warrior slowly spoke. "Brothers, you see me thin and sore of foot; my paddling arm is weary. Many moons have I journeyed from one tribe to another. I shall not now stand here before you and extend my arm to the east and west and boast of the battles I have been in. I shall not tell you what I have done, for I come to speak no words out of my own mouth, but the words of another, of Black Hawk."

A stir of excitement went around the circle, and Little Bear raised his hand as a sign that he was satisfied. No one there needed to be told of the exploits of Black Hawk. If this stranger spoke as with his mouth, that was enough.

"All these things you have named in council have been suffered by Black Hawk. He has been whipped, he has been driven out of his home grounds, and now he has resolved to take them again. He holds a treaty in his hands that once promised the land was to be his tribe's forever. He calls on you to join him to hold his hills and plains, so the tribes of the great lakes may live there together, on this side of the land of the Sioux.

"Black Hawk says, I put my ear to the ground and I hear the coming of more people, a multitude that will want our land. They reach back to the great water of the rising sun.

"Black Hawk says, Where shall we go? Must we go to sit on the very edge of the ocean? Must we climb to a high place, driving the eagle from her nest? Is there no place in all the earth where we can live?

"Tecumseh was the last who tried to lead you against them. Like the fall of a mighty oak in the silence of the woods came the word that he was dead. With Tecumseh gone, our spirit was broken, and in the time since then we have again been pushed to the westward. But Black Hawk has not forgotten. He calls the white men thieves; he names them murderers, liars, dogs. He has been getting ready, and now he asks you to help him. The Sauks and Foxes are united with him, the Winnebagoes have promised me to join him."

Chief Old Wing lifted his hand and spoke. Only he of all those in council was old enough to presume to interrupt a speaker. "Where is Black Hawk now? Where does he want us to go?"

"Black Hawk has been driven beyond the father of waters. But he is ready to move into his own land again, when he hears that you will fight beside him."

The Fox warrior was silent, and waited with expressionless, tired face for his answer. In the shadows I took up his words, turning and fitting them into my own purpose.

A stirring was heard again among the men. "Our tomahawks are asking blood to drink," shouted one. "We will kill the white men here, and go to Black Hawk."

The Fox messenger lifted his hand for attention.

"Brothers, Black Hawk pleads that you fight only when the tribes are united, as one greater than he told you long ago. Let the white men have this island, but we will keep our hunting grounds. If you go on the warpath here, some of you will be killed by cannons from the high-fenced-house-of-thunder. Dead warriors on the isle of the turtle cannot fight beside Black Hawk."

But the young men rose in an angry roar, shouting. Young and old seldom agreed in council, but I knew the chiefs would be able now to keep the more fiery ones under control until the medicine man gave the word to act.

I watched the medicine man, for it was his time. As I watched, he arose to assert the authority of his stick. "We must seek the approval of the spirits. Only the spirits can give approval to the warpath."

Agreement came from the circle of chiefs, and the young men quieted, holding themselves poised for the moment the shaman should give the word.

The Fox warrior seated himself, his shoulders bent in a knowledge that he had failed.

When all was still, the shaman came forward, and threw his head back and howled like a coyote under the moon. "I call upon good spirits to come and drive away the evil ones." He waved his arms as if he would speed their coming. He bent and with a long forked stick removed the sacred stone from the heart of the flames. Taking up a bowl, he let water fall from it upon the stone. As the steam rose, he began a chant of pleading to the spirits, continuing until the stone had cooled and steam would rise no more.

This was the time I had been waiting for. In a moment he would begin his incantations in the lodge, beating his drum, shaking the walls, and making strange voices appear in the air. If the listening tribes were once under the spell of his conjurations, I would lose them.

I started forward from the junipers, and just as the

medicine man, with drum in one hand, the sacred bones in the other, backed into the lodge, I moved forward into the circle of the firelight, and laid before me on the ground the garments of Tecumseh.

A ripple went back across the multitude, as if the earth had moved beneath their feet.

"You wait for the spirits of the dead," I began in clear Ojibway, raising my voice so I could be heard at the farthest edge of the council. "I speak for the dead. Listen to my words."

An angry roar arose, and the young men started up. "A squaw in council! A squaw!"

I lifted my arm, imperiously. They waited, puzzled. Silently all eyes moved over me from head to foot, and were held by the bright garments spread there.

"The Fox has spoken to you with the tongue of Black Hawk. I speak with the voice of one long gone. But he comes alive on my lips—Tecumseh!"

A movement went over the circle again, and at the edge of it Chief Old Wing stirred, as from something in his memory. He rose and took a step toward me. "My eyes are nearly gone," he mumbled. "Who is this that names Tecumseh?" His face was creased in a heavy frown as he came so near I could have touched the eagle feathers on his head. But he did not look at me then. Stiffly, he knelt and looked at the deerskin coat at my feet, and laid his hand reverently upon it and upon the feathers of the headdress.

"Yes, I have been in the front of battle beside this very war-bonnet," he murmured. With his eyes lingering upon the garments he slowly rose to his feet. As he raised his glance to my face, I looked straight at him. For a moment he frowned, straining to see, and then suddenly a glow came into his face, and a look of awe.

"The same high forehead," he murmured, "and the same dark brows—and those eyes! Those are Tecumseh's eyes! Our shaman has done well."

425

Respectfully he backed to his place in the nearest row of chiefs. All sat tense, as I began to speak, without art, without rule, and in the shortest way to their hearts.

"I am the daughter of Tecumseh," I said, "and I speak with his words."

"A squaw in our council!" came again a voice thick with rum. A young man stood up far back in the circle, and through the air came a flash of metal. I stood motionless while a hatchet grazed the edge of my head, lifting a strand of my hair, and buried itself in a tree beyond. There was a little murmur of admiration, the first approval of me they had shown. But the young Ottawa ran forward around the edge of the circle and raised a tomahawk above my head. I stood quiet, exulting, unafraid, as a warrior feels when he has danced his war-dance and sung his song of death or victory. Before he could lower the tomahawk, a firm hand gripped his arm, and Gray Wolf tore the weapon from his grasp and threw him to the ground. It was then I noticed the raccoon tails tied to his knees.

"Tecumseh's blood still flows in her veins," said Gray Wolf sternly.

Chief Migisan was on his feet. He glared down at his son, and raised his hand in an imperious motion. "Go. My only son piles disgrace on me. Never have you done anything honorable in war."

"Speak, daughter of Tecumseh," said Gray Wolf, and sat in his place again. Four Legs, holding his twisted arm, crept away into the darkness.

In tense silence the tribes sat before me, and in all the circle no movement stirred fringe or feather. The fire had burned to a heap of coals, and sent out only a soft glow, and even the shadows were motionless. The quiet seemed to spread over the village, the island, and the rolling straits.

"Tecumseh's heart would be sore for you in your

426

trouble, as mine is," I began. "Backward have you been driven from the sea to the setting sun, *nekatacushe katopolinto*, like a galloping horse."

Chief Old Wing nodded. "The very words of Tecumseh."

"They come as the fire in the forest, and you have seen the trees die and the game run before them. No one of you, no tribe or nation can hold out against them, but if all would stand together you could hold your land. You older men have heard these words from the lips of one who never lied to you. They speak a truth that is unwavering like the north star, the star-that-never-moves.

"If you fight in one band at a time, killing the innocent who have never broken a treaty, you disobey Tecumseh, the wisest one who ever spoke to you.

"If you fight here, you can take a few scalps, but the cannons will speak, and you are helping the great wave of white men by destroying some of yourselves to no use. Only when you have made a union of your fires can you drive the white men back to the last treaty line, and hold your land for your own. It is your only hope.

"To unite, you must have a leader. Tecumseh's daughter names that leader. Black Hawk is fighting an honorable war, for his home, for the children of all of you. You shall follow Black Hawk, friend of Tecumseh."

A silence followed, into which came only the endless breaking of the waves on the shore of Mackinac. I waited, while the rows of men sat unmoving before me.

The gray mist was still rising from the straits like a curtain to separate us from the rest of the world, its white folds reminding me that many times the sun had broken the mist over Mackinac at dawn to light strange events that had lived their day and gone. The early day when there was no life but the birds whispering in close-huddling trees and soaring over its white cliffs

427

and rocky heights, swinging down again to bathe in a quiet bay, shaking the drops from their wings like dissolved sunshine, was only slightly disturbed by the red men coming to draw up their canoes under the lee of a headland and carry their offerings to leave at the manitou's rock, or the bodies of their dead to leave in the underground caves. The early French explorers had touched the shores and gone on to the west. Other Frenchmen had come and taken over the life of the island, until the waves of the British rolled over them. They had been great in their time; their soldiers roamed the sweet-flowered paths, but their cannons spoke in vain from the heights when the Americans came. Was time about to come around in a circle, and restore the island to the red men and the birds? Or did men think so only because they wanted to? And could I change what was to be?

At last, Chief Old Wing was the first to stir, and his voice came from the distant spaces of memory. Low, and with feeling, he said, "She speaks good words."

Like a deep sigh, agreement spread through the assembled tribes.

Chief Migisan rose and stood before them. "The voice of Tecumseh has spoken well," he said. "Tonight our tomahawks and guns shall sleep, and tomorrow's sun will find us on the way to join Black Hawk."

The Fox leaped up, his tired face suffused with joy. Eagerly he named routes, places, and times, holding out the wampum belt. One after another the men arose and followed Old Wing as he came forward to lay his hand upon it.

I stood at one side, watching the procession come from the darkness into the firelight, and out of it again. Suddenly I knew Gray Wolf stood beside me.

"Tecumseh's life was spent trying to help us," he said. "Does Tecumseh's daughter come to us with empty hands?"

Silence fell, and I saw that he was right. Having taken the authority, I must take up the duties that went with it.

"Tecumseh's daughter is ready," I said. "What would you have her do?"

"We who have seen many winters will soon be on the path to the land of souls. It is no use to teach our children our ways. We shall go with Black Hawk, but this is not the end. Let Tecumseh's daughter think of it as we go." He drew his wolf robe close about him, and stepped forward to touch the belt of wampum.

I took up the coat and war-bonnet, and slipped quietly away beyond the medicine lodge. Once away from that firelit circle, I felt as if I moved out of a shining cloud of light that had been like the past itself enfolding me. I was emerging from a strangeness, and yet like an aura it still went with me, and I knew I should never again be as I had been before.

Paul and I walked slowly down the beach in the moonlight. Eternal, the straits rolled past the island, while darkened Mackinac houses rested for a new day. I thought of Pierre and Grand'mère, with my mind at ease in the warm glow of knowing my debt had been paid.

As I looked along the shore at the roundness of the white pebbles at the water's edge, I saw among them a different shape, an unsoiled black and white feather, newly fallen from a passing loon-bird. I caught it up in joy, remembering that, as a token, the loon always dropped a wing feather when he was pleased. I held it in my hand, caressing it, and then tucked it in the band about my hair.

"You have won your 'black feather,'" said Paul.

As we turned from the beach at last, we heard someone following. It was Martin. He was in fatigue-dress, with a musket under his arm.

Coming up to us, he set the musket-butt on the ground. I remember how strangely he looked at me, and I remember holding my head high, still with the calm upon me of something greater than myself. For a slow moment he looked down at me, as if he were seeing me clearly for the first time. In memory that look of his seems longer than whole years of unimportant time.

"You have saved a great many lives tonight," he said.

"For my people, too," I said calmly, "this way is best."

He looked at the garments in my hands. "Your father must have been a great man." He paused, and looked off into the distance. "He was one who had courage to leave the easy path and take the one to the heights."

I remember he seemed only to be speaking his thoughts aloud, and I made no answer. I waited, looking at the musket.

"I came," he said, "but you didn't need me."

I knew from his words that at last he saw me as I was, and I was content to have it so. My roots had reached into firm earth, and I could stand tall and straight.

"In the morning the tribes will go," I said. "I want no one in the village to know my part in it."

"I shall tell no one what I have seen," said Martin. "And I have seen tonight far more than you know. More than even I know myself."

Looking once more into my face, as if he felt an emanation from it he could not understand, he took one step backward, and brought his hand to his cap in salute. Then he turned and was gone in the darkness.

Fifteen

❧ The next morning when I came back from my early dip in the water below the arched rock, I stopped on the back porch to hang up my towel. As I spread it neatly

430

on the line across the corner of the porch, my familiar movements seemed a quiet restraint I was putting on the contentment that was running over me in smooth waves as if I were still in the cool waters of the straits. It was no ordinary return from a swim. After what had happened at the arched rock that morning nothing would ever be as it had been before. The mystery of it all seemed to flow into all the objects on the porch, letting them keep their shape but making them more comely, with richer colors, like wooden bowls turning to silver, or earthen kettles turning to wampum. I knew I would say nothing of what lay behind this new radiance of the day, until I had held the wonder of it close to me for a little while, but I felt something of it might show in spite of me. The glow upon my face was more than that of health and rousing exercise.

The back door stood open. I knew someone must be up, early as it was. I went in through the little kitchen and paused in the doorway of the living room. Pierre was looking out one of the front windows, and I noticed the old erectness had come back. The sunlight touched smoothly waving hair on a head held with pride and confidence. Behind his back, the fingers of one hand tapped the other with satisfaction. He looked around briefly, speaking my name as he saw me, and his smile was the old slow-coming one. But over it lay a secret triumph.

Grand'mère was not yet up, and no breakfast was started. The table was spread instead with opened account books, and Paul, after a quick curious glance at me, bent over them again with forced patience. I remembered how often that summer he had gotten up at daylight to work on the columns of figures so he could be free to go out to the nets with Baptiste later on. Paul's very back seemed a curve of protest against an occupation with quill and paper instead of boats and nets and barrels.

In a few minutes, he laid down his pen with a little sigh. "I knew you'd gone swimming," he said with a glance at my wet braids. "I'll help you get breakfast now if you like. Haven't heard Grand'mère stirring yet."

"We'll fry some bacon," I said, smiling. "That'll bring her out from under her blankets like a kitten from its nest."

Paul laughed, with something of relief, and yet I remember noticing he was puzzled at the quiet gaiety that made my manner not quite like the old one, and yet not the one he had seen the night before.

I turned to the hearth where a small fire had already been laid. But Pierre coughed gently, and when I looked up, he moved over a little and made a sign for me to join him at the window. When I first looked out of the narrow panes, and let my glance pass over the village, I felt a new glow, seeing it whitewashed and secure, with peaceful smoke of the new day arising from chimneys instead of from flattened, charred remains. Beyond, a steamer was unloading at the wharf, and I remember thinking Pierre's elation might be from seeing the soldiers come in, for at that moment the files of blue-clad figures were leaving the dock and straggling toward the incline to the fort. A few ladies in black traveling capes were watching the unloading of boxes and trunks.

But from Pierre's manner I knew if he had seen the soldiers he had dismissed them from his mind. He was not looking that far to the east, but straight ahead toward the clusters of brown cone- and egg-shaped lodges.

"I see they're leaving this morning," he said, gesturing toward the activity on the shore, where canoes that had been turned up against the lodges were being put into the water again after their long rest.

Such content and satisfaction filled his tones that I

turned and looked at Paul. He shook his head, as puzzled as I. Pierre had not been told. I could only wait to see how he had explained it to himself.

"They are cowards, after all," he went on with easy contempt. "They beat their drums and make a big noise, but when they are spoken to with authority, they get up and go. Pity it couldn't have been done sooner—but of course it couldn't be before the payments came."

I looked up at him, startled, but he only gazed toward the shore, his lips curved in a smile of elation. That was the way I might expect him to take it. It was almost as if he were giving himself credit for the peaceful departure of the lodges. But how could he know what had happened?

He turned away from the window and glanced at the clock with the gilded pine cones. "Will it be long before breakfast is on? I'm a little anxious to get down to the warehouse. I'm sure I saw Mr. Stuart getting off among the first soldiers that landed from the steamer. I'd like to hear what Mr. Astor wanted to see him about."

"I'll hurry," I murmured, and as I took the frying pan from the shelf and went out in the kitchen, I noticed that Pierre, drawing his coat-tails carefully around him so they wouldn't wrinkle, sat down in his easy chair. His eyes wandered up to the picture of the man with the sword. Again I wondered, for he never looked at it except when he was feeling pleased with himself, feeling that he could look into those piercing eyes as an equal. The picture was something to measure himself by.

While I sliced the bacon, Paul came out and began to put some coffee beans through the little mill on the kitchen wall. At last he said quietly, "The soldiers will find things different from what—" What might

433

have been, he was going to say, but Pierre's voice came from the other room, taking part in our conversation in unusual good nature.

"Oh, yes, different from what they're used to. Every post is a new experience, I expect. Mother has been hoping their ladies will be good whist players."

"Good morning." The voice was Mr. Stuart's, and it came from our front porch. Glancing through the kitchen door, I saw Pierre get up quickly and extend his hand as the short Scotchman came through the door.

"Well, sir, this is a pleasure," he said with real warmth in his smooth tones. "I saw you come in. I hope you had a pleasant journey—but won't you have some breakfast with us? Oneta and Paul will have something ready in a moment."

As our names were spoken, we came out.

"Hello, there," Mr. Stuart greeted us with a broad smile. "Well, you look unusually sparkling this morning," he said, pinching my cheek. "Did your friend Marthe give you a dose of one of her potions? Seems like you've taken on quite a glow." He looked intently into my eyes for a moment, and then turned to Paul. "How's the fishing magnate?"

"Fine, sir," answered Paul.

Mr. Stuart continued to beam at Paul and me so long I began to feel he was putting off the moment he must turn back to Pierre. I was sure of it when I saw how slowly he went to take the chair Pierre had drawn up beside his own at the fire.

"No, I won't have any breakfast, thank ye. My woman had the coffee pot on at home, and she rustled up some potatoes and fried pork." He chuckled briefly. "Seems good for a man to get his legs under his own table again, after a whole summer of journeying about and staying in strange taverns and such." His face grew serious again.

Paul began to clear his books and papers from the table, and I took down the breakfast china from the shelf, hearing the next words over the soft noises we made.

Mr. Stuart sat upright in his chair as if he were behind a desk. "There's something I want to talk over with you here, Pierre, where we won't be interrupted by the flocks of people that'll be droppin' in at the office this morning." He paused. Pierre nodded and watched the plump little man closely.

"Do you want Oneta and me to go somewhere else?" asked Paul.

"No. You stay. What I've got to say affects all of you."

Pierre took up his pipe and raised the lid of his tobacco canister, still covered with the birchbark sheath I had made for it so many years before. He offered it first to Mr. Stuart.

"No. No, thanks."

Pierre laid his own pipe aside again, and waited.

Mr. Stuart gazed steadily into the fire. "I understand from what my wife tells me that the little dust-up you had with the Indians is all over now."

"Yes." Pierre smiled, and again looked satisfied with himself.

"But in the name of all the saints, why didn't you fix it up the minute it started, instead of letting it go as you did? At least, you could have smoothed things over as far as the company was concerned. I know you wasn't to blame for the other injustices they got riled up about."

Pierre winced at that description of his act.

"For all we know," grumbled Mr. Stuart, "they may never do a lick of business with us again."

"How would you have smoothed it over?" Pierre murmured after a little silence.

"Why," said Mr. Stuart impatiently, "a gift of some

435

kind to this Four Legs and some rum all around might have smoothed it over."

Pierre looked shocked. "Rum! Give rum to Indians?"

Mr. Stuart looked at him, started to speak, and then waited.

"And gifts—you know Mr. Astor's letters about giving our goods without any return," said Pierre.

Mr. Stuart shrugged. "A man's got to use his judgment when something like that comes up. Them orders of Mr. Astor were general-like, and to be taken with a grain of salt. He'd be the first to tell you that gettin' the good-will of the redskins means more to us than a few blankets."

Pierre sat up straight. "I would not have considered giving them anything, as a matter of principle. I was in the right—at least I struck the Indian only when he wouldn't get out of the office when I told him to go. Offering gifts would have been an admission that I was wrong."

"No harm admittin' that once in a while, even if you ain't," said Mr. Stuart. "This country is no place to stand on your dignity." He looked at Pierre, and turned away uneasily, as if something had come to mind he wished he could get away from. For a little he watched the sun creep in the front windows at a sharp angle, touching the side of Grand'mère's copper kettle and the edges of Pierre's books.

"But, as a matter of fact, I am the one who saw to it that the Indians are leaving. There might have been mischief if they'd stayed around much longer."

At these words from Pierre, Paul and I looked up, startled. Mr. Stuart glanced at him sidewise, and then lowered his eyes. "How did you do it?" he asked in a manner that said he already doubted what he was going to hear.

"I sent a letter last night as soon as the payments had been made to the first group," said Pierre.

"A letter, eh? What did you say in it?" asked Mr. Stuart in even tones.

"I reminded them that several bands were camped on company property, and ordered them to get off not later than this morning—"

Mr. Stuart looked at him incredulously. "From what I know of Indians that would make them rip-snortin' mad."

"But they are leaving, meek as lambs," said Pierre in a triumphant voice.

So that was what Pierre had been feeling compla-cent about all morning.

Mr. Stuart drew a long breath. "I hear they had a big council down there last night."

"Probably reading my letter to all the tribes," said Pierre comfortably.

Mr. Stuart went on as if he hadn't heard. ". . . and it was one of the queerest councils they ever had. They won't tell exactly what happened, but my wife's hired girl was down there with a sister of hers. I pried enough out of her while I was eatin' so I can pretty well guess what happened. But I ain't sayin' nothin' about it—" He shot a quick glance at me. I shook my head.

"No, I won't say nothin' about it. But it must have been a wonderful thing. I'd like to have been there." He beamed at me, unseen by Pierre, who was staring into the fire with a polite, uncomprehending smile on his face.

"Now that this is all taken care of," Pierre said at last, "what about your talk with Mr. Astor?"

A cloud went over Mr. Stuart's face again. "Well, Pierre," he said slowly, "I'm a straight-spoken man. I might as well out with what I've got to say. Mr. Astor is goin' out of the fur business."

Pierre's eyebrows twitched, and he stared at Mr. Stuart. Paul and I looked at each other, not taking in at once what this latest news meant. Mr. Astor out of the fur business! From our earliest days that name had come to our ears almost daily as a symbol of the life of the island, and of the whole Northwest. In the name of Astor our friends, the voyageurs, had paddled every stream of this vast country, through all the lands of the Ojibways, the Ottawas, the Sioux, and even to the tribes I knew little of. That a man was dealing for Mr. Astor had meaning in distant villages that had no knowledge of the leaders of government or generals of the army. But they knew Mr. Astor and the empire of furs he had carved out for himself. He had crushed the little men who stood in opposition as the great kings in Pierre's books had crushed the little dukes who stood in their way. Astor —the name had stood for many things in this land. I had heard it spoken in admiration, in fear, in dread, in anger and hate, yet always with respect, as something to be reckoned with. John Jacob Astor out of the fur business!

"Does that mean the end of the company?" asked Pierre quietly.

"No. No, it doesn't," said Mr. Stuart. "That's what I came to tell you. Mr. Astor is getting old. You know he has spent a lot of time these last years in Europe, taking those baths and tryin' to keep his health up. But all the time he has had the worry of the business on his mind. I guess his family talked him into givin' it up."

"It hasn't made it easier for him that the company has been doing so poorly, I suppose," said Pierre.

"Well," began Mr. Stuart aggressively. "I think with the right management there is still a lot of money to be made in furs. We may have to go farther west with our posts."

Paul looked up. "The men tell me the Northwest

Fur Company has a pretty good hold out there. Even Astoria is theirs."

Mr. Stuart moved uneasily. "Yes, yes, I know. But the American Fur Company has made fortunes in this country. It will do it again." He was ever a stubbornly hopeful man, and would not see the coming end until it was upon him.

"You said *we*—" Pierre was looking closely at Mr. Stuart.

"Yes, that is—well, Mr. Astor plans to turn the company over to those of us who have been most active in it. A new partnership will be formed with Mr. Crooks at the head, and myself next. Men like Rolette and Mackenzie are to come in, because they've done such good work at their posts. Crooks and I are to pick the others. I have a list of them here—"

"Is the name of Debans on it?" Pierre leaned forward.

Mr. Stuart shifted in his chair. "Well, yes. Yes, it is. But—"

"Ah." Pierre settled back in his chair.

Mr. Stuart looked uncomfortable.

"What are the terms?" asked Paul suddenly.

Mr. Stuart cleared his throat. "Terms, yes—the terms. The old—Mr. Astor, I mean, is looking after his own dear interests, naturally. He's pretty fair, at that. He's worked out a way for us to buy him out, and take over without much hardship for anybody."

"That was very generous of him," said Pierre.

Mr. Stuart carefully interlaced his stubby fingers on his lap. "I guess I'll just have to spread all the cards out and let you look at 'em." He sighed, as one who takes up a heavy task. "In the first place, I had no idea but that you would be included, Pierre. But Crooks made the trip back with me to start the re-organizin', and he was worried all the way here. You

439

see, he's had some word of possible trouble here this summer, by knowin' what the government was planning about payments and moving the agency. And when we got here, and my wife told us the whole story of what's happened around here lately, Crooks was put out that you seemed to have got the company involved in the Indian troubles."

Mr. Stuart flicked a piece of lint from his dark blue trousers.

"Well, after a chunk of language I won't repeat, Crooks said that anybody that hadn't learned to get along with Indians in the time you'd been here wouldn't be much of an asset to the new company. He refused to have you in on it, and said that the best way to get the good-will of the tribes back again was to leave you out."

Pierre did not change his expression, but his pale face began to flush with red.

"I argued with him, Pierre. And I think maybe I can still talk him into lettin' you in quietly, say a one-thirtieth share—on condition that you can put up the cash for it."

"One-thirtieth!"

"Yes, I know it isn't much. Of course you'll have to raise the two thousand dollars at once."

"Two thousand dollars." There was no joy in Pierre's laugh. "That settles it then. I haven't even one thousand."

"What? Haven't you saved more than that?"

"You forget I put my savings in Fox River land last year. And I haven't had any return—"

Mr. Stuart whistled softly. "All your savings?"

"Yes."

Mr. Stuart scratched his face thoughtfully. "I guess they're gone, then. I had no idea. The man was such a good talker that I put a little into it myself as a flier. But I thought you knew the risks. It was a long

chance that would have made us all rich if it turned
out, but there were too many people to be trusted, to
make the scheme very safe."

Pierre shrugged. "Well, that's it. I haven't any
money at all."

Paul stirred, and glanced at his account books. "I
can let you have two thousand, Father, if you like."

The look Pierre turned on his son was a mixture of
unbelief, gratitude, and resentment.

Mr. Stuart gave him no chance to answer. "Another
thing I'd better say before you make up your mind.
About your job with the company."

Pierre looked up at Mr. Stuart a little dazed, and
took hold of himself with an effort. "My job—oh,
yes. I shall try to do my work just as well for the
new partners as for Mr. Astor."

Mr. Stuart looked more uncomfortable than ever.
"Well, Pierre, I can't offer you just the same job you
have had, not exactly. Crooks has a nephew he wants
to bring out and break into the works, and wants
you to turn over all the bookkeeping to him. You can
have a job as clerk, though."

Pierre's face was a study in confusion. "Clerk—do
you mean to go out with the brigades in the winter?"

"Yes. We'll send you with Charlie or someone that
gets along easily with the tribes."

I felt so sorry for Pierre that I could hardly bear
sitting quietly, offering no word of help. His slender
fingers were clasping the arm of his chair so hard
that the blood had gone and left them white. His eyes
were on me, and the puzzled pleading in them made
them just like Paul's when he was a baby. It was as
if they had changed places, and Paul was the older one
in that moment.

"The new work won't be so bad," said Mr. Stuart
consolingly. "All you'll have to do will be to sort and
count the furs taken in, and pay out the goods—"

"Never mind." Pierre waved the rest of the speech away. He got up and walked over to the mantel and leaned on it a moment.

"I doubt if it would be worth Father's while to go into it," said Paul quietly.

"What are you gettin' at?" inquired Mr. Stuart half irritably.

Paul looked out of the windows toward the east where the long shadow of the warehouse reached toward us across Mrs. Ruggs's Tavern and the grass plot.

"The best years of the American Fur Company are gone," he said slowly, as if he were watching the shrinking of that great shadow.

Mr. Stuart looked unbelieving, but puzzled. He turned from Paul to his father, and under his glance Pierre stiffened. He was erect, his expression fastidious, reminding me how he had kept himself untouched by all the rougher side of the island life. As he had avoided all its offensive sights and smells, he was now holding himself aloof from the touch of the unclean spirit of adversity. He was still Pierre Debans, with all that meant to him. He spoke in a voice carefully controlled.

"You may present my compliments to Mr. Crooks, and tell him I shall resign my position at the same time Mr. Astor withdraws from the company." He paused a moment, and then went on calmly, "There's just one thing. When you mentioned the list of new partners you said my name was on it—"

"I said the name of Debans was on it. But it isn't you. It's Paul."

Pierre's face reddened, and he looked at Paul, who had been balancing himself on a chair tipped back against the wall. Paul was motionless for a moment, and then brought the front legs of the chair to the floor

442

again, and raised his head, gazing at Mr. Stuart in the way I had often seen Marthe force another to speak his whole thought.

"Yes," said Mr. Stuart. "We'd like to make fishin' one of our branches, you might say. And we'd like to have you come in as head of it, Paul. Mr. Crooks was mighty pleased when I told him how profitable our little arrangement with you has been. He said to tell you it was his particular wish you'd join up with us, regular."

Paul did not answer for a moment, and then he shook his head. "I don't want so many partners. I cannot work tied down with buckskin thongs."

Mr. Stuart looked disappointed, but nodded. "I know. I expected you to say that. And I know you too well to waste time arguin'. Well, we can let you be free enough. We can fix up some kind of loose arrangement so you can use our boats, and maybe you can take on some of our extra men. Crooks says we've got to let about sixty voyageurs go next spring—just until things pick up," he added. "They know so much about the American Fur Company we don't want 'em hirin' out to some other company. It'd be a good thing all around if they'd join up with you instead."

Paul nodded. "I think we can fix that. I'd like to have Baptiste with us before we talk about it any more."

"All right, then, we'll see about the fine points later," said Mr. Stuart cheerfully.

As an accompaniment to their talk, I had heard Grand'mère moving about in her room, and now she opened her door and came out, her white curls smooth, her little cap set jauntily upon them.

"*Ma foi,* I'm glad to see you back," she said, and her shoebuckles twinkled as she crossed the room to offer Mr. Stuart her hand.

"Thank you, Madame." Mr. Stuart rose.

"What's this dreadful thing you are telling us about not wanting Pierre any more?" she demanded.

"Grand'mère," said Paul quietly. "Would you mind very much if we left Mackinac next spring?"

"Left—" she gasped, and turned to face him in astonishment.

"La Pointe would be a better center for fishing and shipping than Mackinac," explained Paul.

"La Pointe—?"

"On the biggest of the Apostle Islands, in Lake Superior," said Mr. Stuart. "I think Paul's right."

For a moment Grand'mère looked dazed, then she glanced about her, at the pine-cone clock, the picture on the wall, the brocade cushions, the red carpet almost as if she sought their advice. She sighed faintly, and then her face cleared and her eyes began to widen in anticipation.

"I guess I could go there," she said. "I've made two moves bigger than that one, following my men. I guess I can manage one more."

"Hm-m-m," said Mr. Stuart admiringly. "You're a wonderful woman."

"Nonsense," said Grand'mère, but she was pleased as she stood there, the center of all eyes.

"Well," said Mr. Stuart, edging toward the door. "I must git down to the office. How about tomorrow, Paul?"

"Baptiste and I'll drop in," said Paul.

"That'll be fine." Mr. Stuart paused with his hand on the doorknob, turned, and came back to offer his hand to Pierre. "No hard feelin's between you and me, anyway, are there?"

"No hard feelings." Pierre grasped his hand, but made no effort to detain him when he started for the door again as if anxious to be out in the air.

Grand'mère looked about her. "*Mon Dieu,* it's get-

444

ting late. You get breakfast on, Oneta, and I'll turn back the beds." She bustled into Pierre's room like one who would not let her housekeeping get out of order no matter what happened.

When Mr. Stuart had gone, Pierre sank into his chair. Deliberately he took up his pipe and reached for his tobacco. But his hand stopped in mid-air, and, forgetting to fill it, he held his pipe tightly in slender fingers he would not allow to tremble.

I remember how still the room was. No sound came from the kettles on the crane, and even the fire had effaced itself into low, even flames. Time seemed to have lost its value, as if years instead of moments might be passing. Pierre gazed before him, all motion suspended, but in the tension of his face I could read his struggle with defeat and shame.

I wondered about his thoughts, for I could see they were on nothing within that room. I felt that even the words of Mr. Stuart had gone, only their shock remaining. And I felt Pierre was withdrawing even from that, groping back beyond anything on Mackinac, into some source I knew nothing of. I sat like one watching a traveler on a distant mountain searching in despair for his lost path, knowing myself unable to reach across the great space between us and tell him where it was.

I do not know how long we sat waiting. But at last, in some way I cannot explain, a change spread through the room. As if his thoughts had come back, bringing what he sought, Pierre straightened with a new strength that pushed away this debasement, separating him from it, letting him say again, I am Pierre Debans. I saw his fingers relax about his pipe bowl. They would not tremble now. His face was calm and aloof as he reached again for his tobacco canister.

For the moment, victory. But my eyes sought out Paul's, and asked of the future. As if he had thought it out, Paul nodded slightly, and without looking at his father, turned back to his account books. He opened one on the edge of the table and took up his pen. Watching Pierre from half-closed lids, he appeared to be intent on the columns of figures, making little exclamations of annoyance and impatience. *"Ma foi,"* he sighed, and muttered *"sacré bleu."* Exclamations were not natural to him, and he borrowed them for the moment from Grand'mère and Baptiste.

I could see by Pierre's shoulders that he heard, but he made no other sign.

"What is it?" I asked.

Paul put despair in his voice as he answered "I wasn't made for keeping accounts. I've been chasing fifty dollars and some odd cents all through these pages. I'll never strike a balance." He bent low over his book, scowling.

Hesitantly Pierre got up and approached the table. "What date did you last have a balance?"

"July 1."

"And it's now September 15. Don't you know it isn't good to run on so long without knowing how you stand?"

"I know it. But I have too many other jobs to look after."

Pierre's fingers sought out a fresh quill, quite as if they were acting independently of the man. And then he bent his graying head over the table, and Paul moved aside to give him room.

"Let me work on it for a while," said Pierre.

While breakfast was eaten, Paul held the talk so rigidly to his problems in keeping accounts that even Grand'mère was silenced. Immediately it was over, Pierre pushed aside his plate and took up one of the books again, while Paul leaned over his shoulder, pointing, explaining.

Grand'mère and I finished the dishes, and she took

her market basket and set out for the store, her skirts briskly skipping along above the limestone of the path. I followed her out the door, and turned toward the meadow path to Marthe's cabin.

A deep serenity and feeling of release hung over me as I walked across the waving grass. It was as if the sight of those two heads above the account books had broken the last thread. I was free, but before I let myself revel in what that meant, I held close the picture of Paul and his father, just for its own sake.

That memory of Pierre bent over the accounts of Debans and Lamont refuses now to exist by itself for me, any more than stone can be dropped in calm water and produce but a single ripple. Flowing out away from it are other memories—Pierre bent over a succession of these paper-bound books, and later of brown leather-covered ones. Pierre standing on the beach near Baptiste's cabin, with pencil and pad in hand, tallying barrels, ever keeping as far from them as he could, wincing from the strong odor of the latest catch each time a boat came in. Pierre in the midst of the bustling new industry, and yet holding himself aloof, full of wonder that such things were responsible for the ever-growing sums in the account books. Pierre, explaining to the other villagers that he was in business with his son, and that he had felt free to leave the fur company when Mr. Astor, to whom he had always felt a personal loyalty, gave it up. Pierre getting his old confidence back as events in the fur company began to look toward the day when the fur yard would be deserted, and the great buildings would be made over for other purposes, and the big warehouse would be a summer inn, keeping—on its sign—the name of Astor on Mackinac.

Pierre entering our cabin on the shore again, when Paul bought it for an office, and had it cleaned inside and out, whitewashed, and put a sign across it spelling out the partners' names. Pierre still retreating from the fishy atmosphere when he could, crossing the meadow to Grand'mère's house in the months before the family moved to La Pointe, ever bearing conscientiously one of the big brown account books under his arm.

But as I stood in the center of the meadow that morning, with green waves around me moving in the same rhythm as the waves of the sky-tinted water beyond, seeing the breeze lift and stir them before it passed on to the trees on the heights, the images of Pierre and Paul began to drift out of my mind. As I went toward Marthe's cabin, white gulls hovered over it as if beckoning me on, and I wondered how much I could tell her of what had happened at the arched rock.

I have kept from setting it down here, because even after all these years, it is something I would hold close and silently cherish. But having set down all the rest, perhaps I should not withhold that which brought a part of my life to an end.

Awakening that morning in the still moment before the dawn comes, I had seen my eastern window awaiting the sun in the modesty of gray shadow, ready to burst into golden flame when he appeared. Drawing on my clothes, I put one of Grand'mère's towels in my jacket pocket and slipped quietly out of the house and up the heights beyond our garden. The mist had withdrawn, and daylight was coming gladly over the island, with no dread as to what it would reveal.

While my moccasins patted the soft earth of the trail along the ridge, I could see ahead of me the gray-wrapped white of the fort, and below, the neat white-washed fences and the low houses with their dormer windows and little gardens. The rows of boats of the last-departing brigade lay in a curved line along the half-moon bay, showing fresh repairs over the marks of their voyage of the year before. Beyond the scattered white houses clustered the brown heaps of mat-covered lodges, and I noticed the first stirrings among them. The children were already outside, their excitement betraying the breaking up of camp as much as the slow movements of the women taking down mats and rolling them on sticks. Kettles were boiling, and canoes were in the water, ready to be loaded. By another morning the beach would be again empty except for the scraps of their summer's living.

I turned away from the cliff and walked around the fort and along the eastern shore. The odor of sweet-briar was fresh and close, and just back of the cliff—Robertson's Folly—was a clearing filled with the crisp whiteness of daisies, fresh in the morning dampness as if they had saved their finest moment of bloom just for me.

The many summer visitors had made a well-marked trail for me to follow. But just at dawn, it would be safe enough to bathe in the straits just below the great arch. It was too early for any of the curious ones from Mrs. Ruggs's Tavern to be there to gaze and marvel.

As I climbed toward the sunrise I took long breaths of sweet-briar, cedar, and the freshness of growing things. Gooseberries and wild currants offered themselves to me against hedges of the wild rose, and wild flowers in the woods tried to lead me away from the path in every direction. But I hurried my steps, to be there in time to greet the sun.

Far back on the eastern shore, I went up the last steep ascent, and there was the high arch of rock towering above the lake. The sight of blue water filled the whole opening, and I felt the cool morning air rushing through the great space. When rising waters and storm had carried away the limestone beneath it in the early days, this high span had resisted and stood firm above the chasm. Around its base, birch and ash and low spreading shrubs were trying to keep their foothold in the crevices.

Down toward the shining water, there was no sign of a path for anyone but a squirrel. Half walking, half sliding, over the sheer rock, I went down the rough cliff under the arch. Taking off my clothes, I folded them and laid them near the edge of the water. Then I plunged in, just as the first rays of the sun appeared. I stood waist-deep in water, silent, until I saw the golden rim, and joy rose as if its light had struck a clear note within me. I could understand why my people said when fruits ripened, they moved-to-their-joy in the sun. *Ka-no-waw-bum-min-uk!* I gave him softly his Ojibway name, he-that-sees-us.

Near the shore, the rippled yet serene water reflected the trees and points of rock above it, but farther out where nothing else intruded, it held the sky. The calm lake seemed like a person with his own heart set in order, ready to be receptive to whatever is outside him, and it may be patches of heaven. The cool water was a challenge and at last I waded forward and then swam with all my strength until I was well out from the shore. There I turned over and floated, my face to the blue sky, and let the waves carry me where they would.

The air was so clear that every pine needle seemed to stand out against the sky beyond. As a sound belonging to no particular day I heard distantly the boom of the morning gun from the fort. As I drifted along the shore I heard twittering and chattering in the tree-tops, and little rustlings in grass and leaves that told of wild things beginning to stir. The sun began to climb through a blue sky toward motionless white clouds. I watched its rays pick out every angle of stone in the great arch, as it had done for ages before the first house in the village was built. Again time seemed to have stopped, and the hour seemed no part of either past or future. The serenity I felt was in the very touch of the water as it had been in the touch of the earth the day before, and it was a feeling of resting on strength outside myself, yet curiously belonging to me. As I rested there on the water, or turned to take a few strokes, I saw in the distance a dissolving line of smoke that meant a steamer approaching Mackinac harbor, but I paid it no heed. I felt detached and free, as if I need never go back to the village. I had done my work there. There was nothing I could do for Paul that he could not do for himself, now. And Grand'mère and Pierre had no real need of me as long as they had Paul. I felt as if one task were completed, and I were resting before I went on.

My mind was clear, for there was no room for anything but complete peace. As under the spell of a dream I felt the waves push against me, and at last I turned over to see that I had drifted a long way from the arch. For a few moments then I put all my strength into swimming until I was again below the high towering mass. I came out dripping and rubbed myself dry with the towel.

Dressed again, and tingling with warmth, I went up the steep slope and stopped at one end of the span. Usually I stood there for a long look at the rising sun before I went home, but that morning I followed a sudden impulse, and ran along the sheer irregular side and up to the center of the great arch itself, high above the lake. I took a deep breath at the beauty of the view before me, the very drawing of breath there making me feel I had everything I wanted. I saw as if it were all new, the little points and bays along the shore, the clear waters of Lake Huron reaching in every direction. The sun made wavering pink and yellow lights where his path lay on the water. The straits were so clear I could see far below me a fish, his sides brushed with silver, moving lazily below the surface. The vast reach of water was a deep blue, as if storms would never trouble its depths and turn them to dark billows streaked with yellow. The rippling blue was dotted with islands, not things of echoes then, but of green peace.

Birds sang around me, intent on their own affairs, but suddenly a string of notes different from the rest came into the midst of their calls and trills. I turned and sat down on the highest point of the arch, facing landward. Someone was whistling in the nearest grove. And then on the air came a song, and the singer seemed not like one having a message for listening ears but as one pouring out his feelings careless of effect, his voice making a rhythm of its own within the simple one of the Ojibway courting song.

> *"As the day comes forth from night,*
> *So I come forth to seek thee,*
> *Lift thine eyes and behold him,*
> *Who comes with the day to thee."*

And then Martin pushed through the nearest clump of bushes and stood below me. He glanced about the base of the arch, and looked down through it at the water below. In the early light he was like one of the young gods in Pierre's books. In puzzled disappointment he turned and took a few steps backward, looking along the various paths that left the clearing. Under my hand a pebble loosened from the arch, and rolled to the earth beside him. He whirled around, and the sun spread dancing lights in his hair as he pulled off his visored cap, amazement in his face as he saw me high upon the arch.

"Won't you fall—?" he exclaimed.

I shook my head.

He tossed his hat to the ground, and sat beside it, just at the western base of the arch, where he could lean back against it and look up at me.

"You look like a queen up there," he said.

I do not remember that I answered him, but I re-

452

member well the words he said next, because through the years I have kept living the scene again and hearing nim say them.

"You are one, you know. In you are the beauty and calm and strength of these rocks and trees, and the mystery of this island. I came here looking for you this morning."

"How did you know—?"

"Once when I was out at dawn, I saw you swimming far out in the straits, and several times I have seen you on your way here or returning."

I knew without his telling me that he had avoided this place at dawn, not to embarrass me, and that he had delayed coming on that morning until I would be out of the water.

"You were a queen last night," he went on softly. "I have something to ask you. Will you listen?"

I nodded.

"You want to go back among your people, Oneta. And you should. No one else can do as much for them as you can."

"They must be led, not driven," I agreed. "They must have leaders to help them over the bridge between the old and the new. Unless they can cross it, they will soon be gone, like last year's leaves, into the soil from which they came. My place is among them."

"Yes." Martin looked up at me briefly, and then gazed out through the arch at the blue water. "I want to ask you to do it in a special way. I sat by the fireside all night after I left you. I shall never go back to Boston. I want to set up my own hospital. I came to ask you to let me go with you, and set it up among your people."

"A hospital for Indians?" I asked.

"For anyone. I don't care what color he is. I want to help where I'm needed. Dozens of men can head that hospital in Boston as well as I could. But out there"— he waved his arm to the west—"I can perhaps do some-

thing of my own." His face had a vision upon it, as I
have seen on the faces of young Ojibways who have
fasted for a guiding dream and been rewarded. "And
maybe someone will have a better chance for life because of something I may learn." There was serenity in
his eyes, and I knew his mind was going, with youth's
long leaps, into the future.

I looked away across the island, over the tops of the
little trees. The wind was murmuring in the balsams,
and like a voice down the long waves of time I seemed to
hear the words, said long ago over a new baby girl,
"You will bring to your people a man who is greater
than a warrior." I sat motionless, letting the words
gather up meaning and richness to themselves until
their glow consumed all else. And then Martin's voice
began again, softly as if his own vision were still upon
him.

"Last night it all straightened itself out in my mind.
I've been getting ready, I think, in all the time I've been
on Mackinac. But I couldn't get just the hold I wanted
until I saw you in that council last night. Because part
of it, the most perfect of all, is my feeling for you. I
think I have loved you, without knowing it, since I first
saw you on that schooner coming up from Detroit."

I remember that he looked up then, and I knew he
saw the happiness in my eyes. Suddenly he had become
one from whom I would never hide my feelings.

"I'm coming up where you are!" he exclaimed, and
jumped to his feet.

"No, you mustn't! Your shoes will let you slip—" I
looked down at the masses of rock at the edge of the
water far below, seeing the danger for the first time.

He laughed, and pulled off his shoes. "Watch me."
And he ran up the arch, took me by the hand, and drew
me along to a wider part of the span, where we could
stand together. Somehow the morning would have been
less bright if I had had to go down to him.

He looked at me for a long minute, while neither of us spoke. He needed to have no part of what we felt put into words.

"I have something for you," he said, and while he kept one of my hands in his, he reached into the breast pocket of his uniform, and pulled out a little leather bag. I knew at once the embroidery upon it was Marthe's, and more than that, I knew I had seen it before. It was the one she had given me and I had dropped in the grass, the day I came back to the island.

"I found this on the meadow the first day I came to Mackinac. It seemed to have been thrown away, so I kept it. A few days ago, I asked Marthe what it was, and she told me it had once held charms to keep a dear one safe on a long journey, and in a strange land.

"I asked her to make such a charm to put in it again."

Gently against my cheek I felt the west wind, the father of the four winds. All around me the island was brighter with the rising sun than it had ever been before. A chipmunk at the base of the arch uttered a short chatter of joy. The trees dipped toward me, murmuring. The waves below washed softly on the pebbles, and I could hear the deep melody of the straits. It was as if all these sounds were giving him his answer, as if his words were something the island had been waiting for. Above the rustling of the leaves and the soft *sah-see* of the waters, from a passing canoe came a boat song that told only of joy of the long journey ahead. I could put down every word of the song they sang, for Martin learned it later on and often sings it when we sit in the garden on a quiet evening, because, as he says, the river that passes our flower beds has not heard the song of a voyageur for many a year, and he thinks it might like its memories stirred.

It needed to be a joyous song. As Martin has often said, humming and getting me to sing with him as we made our way on snowshoes over the trail to a distant lodge where someone needed us, it takes light-hearted folk to get work done and never break down under it. With us as with the voyageur, it would be hard to set down all the things gaiety has brought us through.

And when people have asked, Are you never lonely? Martin only smiles, and I shake my head. We could not have been lonely, no matter what our life had held. For even that last journey of all—over the deep water—would not be hard if one could have the companion he would choose. The depths would be laughing waters instead of threatening whirlpools, and the jagged rocks would be pleasant stepping-stones because there would be no fear.

And in that moment, with my hand in Martin's, I knew that what had come to me was right.

I look back at that day through the happiness of years, so I may be remembering it in greater beauty than was there, just as it is the air between and not the far-off ridge that has the delicate blue. Out of the happiness of those years has come a rich deepening of the truth I felt that day, that when there is likeness of spirit, two people are of one kind. And if there is not that likeness, the two are divided by something even greater than the accident of race.

So I feel now, as I felt that day when I raised my eyes to Martin's. I held out my palm, and he laid the deerskin bag upon it. As I closed my fingers about it, he raised them to his lips. I took his hand in mine and led him carefully, from one step to another, down the arch.